ACCLAIM FOR NOVELIST
Bob Cherry

On *West of Empty:*
"Texas is famous for promotions...Bob Cherry weaves a rousing fictional account around this little-known actual event in 1896."
Elmer Kelton, seven-time winner of
Western Writers of America's Spur Award

"A well-paced novel with plenty of tastes of the dying frontier...you'll enjoy it."
Dusty Richards, *The Natural*

❖

On *Spirit of the Raven: An Alaskan Novel*
"...characters vividly evoked, the north country beautifully described. An intricate sense of place supports a moving story..."
Larry McMurtry, Pulitzer Prize winner for *Lonesome Dove*

"...intriguing narrative and wonderful descriptions...far from the polished glitz of pop-wilderness or high-on-photos-low-on-literary-content books...an excellent choice."
ForeWord Magazine

❖

On *Inua*
"Bob Cherry has set the bar high with Spirit of the Raven *and has cleared it with* Inua*..."*
W. Michael and Kathleen O'Neal Gear, *Dark Inheritance, People of the Lakes, Bone Walker*

"Dramatic and expertly woven, Inua *will pull you in again and again..."*
Page Lambert, *Shifting Stars* and National Book Award nominee for *In Search of Kinship*

Best Wishes!

LITTLE RAINS

BOB CHERRY

Bob Cherry

Printed and bound in the United States of America.

ISBN 0-9665430-8-4

For information, contact ONE EYED PRESS™
E-mail:one_eyed_press@yahoo.com
World Wide Website:http://www.one-eyed-press.com

Cover Design: Tina Fagan
Book Design: K.T. Roes

LITTLE RAINS

BOB CHERRY

ONE EYED PRESS

Weep all ye little rains,
wail winds wail ...

from COWBOY SONG/James A. Bliss

for

Los Chavitos

Under the light of a closing moon, an old man stops and studies the river. It snakes into the night like a ribbon of hammered copper, seething and hissing at him in a foreign tongue. He listens, pausing to quiz this language, then moves with caution down the riverbank.

He carries a small willow-hewn cage, balanced atop his silver hair with one hand. Inside is an old fighting rooster. In his other hand, the old man grips a stiff ocotillo walking staff. At the edge of the water he drops to his knees on the wet sand and sets the caged bird in front of him. As an act to instill bravery, he dons his straw hat and glides the wooden bead up the string, secure against his chin. He glances behind, the final chance to measure his choice: an alien in his own land, or an alien heart where he must go. Inside the cage, the old rooster stirs and ruffles his feathers, then is still again. His message to the old man is clear.

Santos studies the opposite shore. Ripples in the river reflect the moon like a million golden coins, far too many to tally. He smiles like a child. He pushes his hat off and suspends it once more against his thin shoulder blades. Then he lifts the cage and balances it once more on top of his head. He wades into the shallow river. Cool water washes dust from his worn leather huaraches and bathes his feet, wicking itself up to the waist of his ragged trousers.

Santos takes in a quick breath of night air, steadies himself and his caged treasure. With a careful prodding of the staff, he tests the muddy bottom as he moves deliberately and with no sound except the sucking of water about his thighs. He locks his eyes on the black hulk of the far-side embankment to prevent its transformation into some nocturnal demon. He moves on. He does not look at the water. He does not look at the moon. He does not look back.

"No se puede pisar dos veces en el mismo rio," he mutters, and then he practices the words in English, "One can never step twice in the same river, one can never step twice..."

ONE

Jesse Pierce spoke in a voice blunt with sleep, *Get up JD.* Her words breached the predawn stillness as though she hovered over the cot of her nephew, Jimmie Dale Mitchell.

Words. Just three, tumbling from the wake of her milkpail as she scraped it across the Mexican tile countertop. Her voice hung resonant above the clap of the bucket's wire bail, which in turn gave way to the rush of faucet water filling her old percolator. And then more words, *She won't like waiting,* and finally the punctuating whisper of propane flame.

From his bed inside the storage shed only two screendoors away from Jesse's kitchen, JD groaned and then growled too low for her to hear, *Females never do.* He pulled the pillow over his ears and turned toward the wall, buying another five minutes. He heard nothing more from Jesse, so he drifted in halfsleep, dreaming.

When she called again, Jesse pressed her nose to her doorscreen as she listened, *I don't hear any moving around out there...* Her voice came louder and he muffled its taunting melodiousness inside the folds of his pillow. He burrowed deeper into the blanket. Even so, JD knew she was not standing right over his bunk, not like a mother might. He stirred and loosed the pillow, but in so doing, allowed into his cocoon the slow scratching of Jesse's fingernail across the inside of her screendoor, back-and-forth.

Jesse could have dropped a half dozen empty milkpails on the concrete floor beside his bed with less irritation. Had he heard giggling too, it would have been dreaming sure, that sound from Jesse's nail like a zipper gliding down the back of a Bettye Lee Collins prom dress, except that had always been faster and with just giggling, no words. Jesse was making a slow sound like tough canvas being ripped. Bettye Lee would never let JD move that slow even if he ever wanted to, which he never did.

He jerked awake. He blinked and swung bare feet onto concrete, cold, a reflex like touching white hot steel. He frowned and focused on the kitchen lightbulb, hazed and filtered through both dusty screendoors, and wondered how the hell words got through. He groped for socks and soon exploded from the storage shed, jamming his shirt into Levi tops and limping in one overrun boot not quite on. JD saw just her hand through a slit in the screendoor, the bail of the empty milkpail looped over a hooked finger. The hand disappeared like a touched turtlehead the second he lifted the pail.

"You're catching on fast JD."

He wanted to ask Jesse, just a face now, immobile and muted behind her screendoor, if she might be talking about squeezing old Millie's tits, but he knew she meant everything else.

"Yeah fast." JD yawned and stamped his foot to the bottom of the boot and moved away in the half light toward the barn.

"Ain't you gonna wear your hat JD?"

He went on, hatless.

When he sidled into the grain room for the bucket of oats he did not see the tomcat. Just inside the door he heard a scratching almost like Jesse's fingernail but then he saw the rat darting like a windblown shred of charred paper atop the dark bulwark of grain-filled gunnysacks stacked against the slats of the shed. Not until he finished milking the contentious old Jersey did the familiar yellow tom show.

JD slammed his hand against the stuck door on the milk shed, sinking a sliver of weathered wood into the fat of his palm. He cursed inside his head as he backed into the corral, the bucket of fresh milk still frothed and sloshing, the handle looped inside the crook of an elbow. He tried to suck the stinging from his palm. His fingers blocked his vision, so in the threatening light he did not see the tom as it swirled under his heel, spinning him and the bucket against the recoiling door like some choreographed harlequin. He caught the dancing tom on the point of his boot, his own pirouette done long before the trail of warm milk slapped white onto the dust of the corral. Against the gray sky, he watched the tom's body arch and writhe and then hang like a visible sob in the predawn air and finally splash into the water trough.

Goddammit, he cursed at the tomcat and the cow and the wood splinter still stinging his hand. And he cursed himself too for kicking the cat. "It ain't his fault, shit..."

He gnawed at the splinter and glanced over the splitrail toward the silhouette of horizon defining the Santiago Mountains to the east, where neither sky nor range nor windworn flagstone yet showed any color at all except random shades of gray. He thought about Tru's old horse lying up there on the rockhard ground at the crest of the rise. "That ain't my fault neither. Wasn't me made the old sonuvabitch founder," and with that JD absolved himself for old horses and yellow toms and stubborn milkcows and anything else dying on the place.

The reflex was not a true kick anyway, not like one of his opening homecoming kickoffs for the Fighting Bobcats. He simply wanted to finish his morning chores and eat breakfast and get on with whatever it was Tru had cooked up for the day. He already viewed this as he would any other instinctive reaction, like clearing morning grit from his eyes as Jesse rattled him awake with the milkpail, her personalized alarm clock and one added irritant to a lengthening list that now included the stinging splinter.

JD sucked at it. He chewed it. He watched the tom struggling inside the trough and wondered what Jesse would think of him standing passive, musing about everything and musing about nothing. Jesse might help one of her dogs or maybe do something to get old Chisos standing for one last bucketful of oats up there on the rise but she would not budge for this cat either. He wondered where this shared contempt came from. Even blood could not have carried it across those ten years since JD had last seen his aunt Jesse.

He was only eight but he remembered the entire family living together on the old farmstead in East Texas, and he remembered the burial of his grandmother and then less than a year later, his mother's corpse lying in her own casket, far more beautiful than she was.

And he remembered his mother's sister, Jesse, weeping over both graves, then Jesse fawning over JD soon after, when he and his father left. If pressured, JD might confess that these events sometimes emerged from his subconscious in a collage of half-remembered traumas, like cracked black-and-white photos from some dusty album, but JD blamed no one, connected none of it to any subsequent sour luck or to his father's drinking or even to any part of his own current disposition. He simply would not think about it, force it all back.

He squinted, tried to see the splinter in his hand but it was no good in the faint light. Again he considered irritants and how after only a short time, he was asked to moved out of the inside bedroom next to Tru and Jesse and into the dark storage shed adjacent the adobe ranch house. But that was mere annoyance and not prickly like a splinter, though JD knew it meant his honeymoon was over. A quick one too but handy for Jesse, his being in easy earshot of her morning milkpail instead of exiled across the hardpan yard to the crumbling adobe bunkhouse with Linc and old Santos and his broken-down fighting rooster. JD figured any other consideration as nephew-in-residence for the summer had probably evaporated like milked slopped in corral dust.

Jesse did it tactfully, said JD probably needed the privacy. But he knew his uncle Tru was behind it, saying something to her in private about the old days and how cowhands were never pampered in the old days and how he—Fredrick Truman Pierce—had never, *ever* slept in any goddamned main ranchhouses in any bedroom right next to any boss when he was a greenhorn. Not in the old days. Not even *kinfolk* cowhands. And especially those who had never even milked a goddamned cow much less dehorned a heifer or castrated a bullcalf. JD wondered who really did need the privacy. And why.

"Every *day...*" He watched the tom struggling and then heard it thump to the ground, escaping the wake of water sucked over the edge of the trough. He saw the loose liquid roll itself into a million mudballs, the parched powder of the corral refusing to accept anything as foreign as moisture. "Right under my goddamn feet..."

The tom favored one back leg as it rounded the corner of the milkshed, dripping a trail. In a flash of guilt, JD worried if the cat would survive or if it too would end up like the old horse Chisos lying out there in the still cool air of the Southwest Texas morning, waiting for the sun to come up and bring the heat and flies, to torment him one more day—unless he died first.

"Well." JD shook his head and turned to the other cats, one feral female, tortured also but by an assortment of nervous kittens, too many and too fast to count, each an aggregate of muted colors, each from what seemed a separate litter but all belonging to her. He was not sure the yellow tom was sire but all just as ugly. What was certain as he and the brood surveyed each other was JD's daily rededicated disdain for cats and no doubt theirs for him.

The animals hesitated just out of boot range, waiting for him to pour the morning ration of warm milk into the upturned lid of a garbage can. Jesse insisted. He had no idea why, unless to counterbalance a bias as strong as his, except Jesse's seemed to be some strange antithesis to her more compassionate feelings toward the other animals. She simply allowed the cats, mousers and ratters but only because of that.

Jesse named almost every other critter on the place, like Millie. And the dogs, strays and give-aways and curs she collected from alongside the stretch of unfenced dirt road running up from Lajitas, splitting the ranch and then on northeast, dead-ending at the reopened cinnabar mine, gouged into the foothills of Santiago Peak, the names of these canines conjuring regional Mexicana as if each were an incarnation of historic import, Villa and Zapata and Madero. Jesse had names for everything. Everything except cats. And cows. Earlier in the summer JD had teased her about naming five hundred head.

"I don't name cows," she said.

"Mavericks?"

"No."

"You feed them. With a bottle, I seen you."

"I don't name them."

"How about Millie? You named Millie didn't you? She's a cow." JD grinned.

"You don't name something you might eat some day," Jesse said with finality. "I'm not planning on eating Millie." She never said why she did not name cats. JD decided if he ever caught her in a good mood he might ask Jesse if she planned on eating all these kittens sitting silent now on their haunches, staring out of the morning shadows, waiting for the milk Jesse ordered up for them.

Pour a little extra this morning, he thought, enough to make up for what he had done to the yellow tom that was nowhere in sight, though he usually skirted the area, waiting to bully more than his share after JD left. He tipped out a portion of what remained of the milk in his pail, looked at it, hesitated, poured more. Then he straightened and regarded the cats. Despite the lure of warm milk cooling in the lid, they were too wary to come closer and instead, squirmed in a tight little group just out of reach.

JD moved away. He stood leaning against a corral post. He watched as the cats darted in and went at the milk and it made him feel better. He turned away and put the handle of the milkpail over the post and left the bucket hanging. He went to the gate and turned the bullcalf onto the cow to finish whatever milk might remain in her flaccid udder. Jesse's orders, too. The calf rammed his nose into the udder, quickly exhausting his shortshare of milk. JD wondered if this critter was destined to become unnamed hamburger in Jesse's refrigerator.

He returned to the fence and folded his forearms across the toprail, his chin on his knuckles. His palm still stung so he turned over his hand and bit hard at the spot where the splinter had entered. He was thinking about cowhands in the old days never sleeping in the ranch house. He doubted they milked Jersey cows either or poured milk into garbage can lids for a pack of wildcats or worried much about splinters. Maybe he would ask Linc about it.

Linc Marks. The grizzled tophand refused even to eat in the main house much less sleep in it. Linc stayed in the weatherworn adobe bunkhouse separated from the newer ranch house by a good hundred yards and an easy hundred years, now relegated to living quarters for him and the other transient cowhands and Santos with his one-eyed fighting cock he kept inside the handhewn willow cage. The rooster would shortly be crowing alive the morning, though he could not see the sunrise through thick adobe, even with his goodeye.

Jesse had named him too.

"Gaucheye," she said the instant she saw the bird inside the cage Linc displayed that first day atop the hot hood of his idling pickup. Santos sat stoic in the cab at first and said nothing as the dogs circled the old pickup, sniffing and growling and pissing on the tires. As soon as Linc turned to speak to Jesse the old man got out and set his hat forward on his head and squinted his eyes at the dogs until finally they lowered their tails and loped toward the barn. Then Santos lifted the cage from the hood and placed it carefully in the shade of the truck.

"He don't talk much English I guess," Linc said, as Santos squatted silent beside the cage.

"Where'd he come from?" Jesse knelt to study the rooster but she was talking about the old man. She shaded her eyes from the midday sun with her palm and glanced up at Linc who shrugged and reached in to shut off the engine. She looked at Santos hunkered beside her, his hands resting on the cage. He smiled at her.

Hablo Ingles, he said nodding. "Sometimes..."

"Across the border?" Jesse stood as she saw Tru emerge from the house, adjusting his hat on his forehead just so. She said nothing else until Tru was close enough to hear and then she gestured south and repeated, "You crossed the border?"

Santos rose and shrugged, eyed Tru.

"You're not legal then," Jesse said for Tru.

"Con su permiso, I come for work."

Tru moved in front of the old man and cleared his throat and spoke low, "Like she says..."

Santos looked straight at Tru and JD thought the old man might remove his sombrero but he did not. "I am a good worker."

"You walk all this way?" Tru inspected the cage.

"Si..."

"With that?"

"Yes..."

"Why?"

"For work," Santos shrugged again.

"No I mean why this?" Tru nudged the cage with the side of his boot and the rooster jigged and jostled and then stood with his head lowered in a combative stance, his goodeye cocked upward. "Hell, looks to me like he can't even see out of that one."

The dark skin of the old man's face furrowed but then smoothed into a smile. "He is for luck. And he sees."

"Well let's see how fast you can hike back across there with him." Tru pointed south. "I got problems enough. And luck ain't never been my strong suit." He spun on his bootheel and started away.

"We could use a hand," Linc offered to Tru's back and then quickly, "Like before?"

Tru paused, glanced at Linc and scowled, some secret exposed. He turned to Santos but he was speaking to Linc, almost apologetically, "That was different, we had branding and—"

Jesse stepped forward. "He can't just walk all the way back, Tru. Not right now with the heat and—" she moved closer to Tru and whispered, "Did you see his feet?"

Tru looked down. The old man's huaraches were caked but there was blood wicking through the woven leather and into the dust. A silence fell over the group as they stared at the bloody shoes.

Finally Santos spoke. "*Sendero de Vidrio,*" he explained. "Some of the pieces cut through the soles." He shrugged and smiled as if the words were just for explanation and everyone would surely understand, even in Spanish, and it was not an attempt at sympathy. "I am a good worker, *señor.*"

Yeah, I heard of that," Tru admitted, and he was talking about the legend of the *Sendero de Vidrio*, the Trail of Broken Glass. He continued skeptically, "But I ain't ever seen it and don't know anybody else that has either." Santos did not elaborate and neither did Tru who decided the legend might be grist for one of his evening history lessons on the front patio, but irrelevant right now. He would say nothing more than that.

He surveyed each face, Linc also knew the old story but he stood impassive, his case for the old man already presented, JD giving the brim of his hat a *who-cares* tug and Jesse's eyes flashing indignation, just as Tru had seen with each of a dozen or so stray dogs brought in from the road. Tru looked at the rooster. He looked at the old man's feet and then into his eyes.

"One night," he said, and then for anyone who might have misunderstood, turned away with a forefinger raised. "One."

Jesse smiled at him leaving. She knelt again and stared mesmerized at the rooster who seemed to be looking back at her.

"*Gaucheye,"* she repeated and raked a finger across the wooden bars. The bird did not move.

"Gallo del Cielo," Santos corrected. "He likes being called that."

"Can't say it," Jesse said and then, "Even if I could I don't know what the hell I'd be saying and I wouldn't like that."

"Means chicken in the sky," JD offered from border Spanish.

"Rooster from heaven," Linc said. "And he's Santos." The leathery face of the old man worked itself into a smile again as he confirmed both names with a nod and this time touched the brim of his hat.

JD remembered how Linc had said the two names that first day with a kind of mysterious reverence and how Tru had not since brought up the question of Santos' origin nor his legality nor even his tenure on the ranch which now stretched from the twenty-four hours Tru granted into weeks. Jesse took to the old man just as with all the other homeless critters and maybe even more than she did to JD himself. JD wondered what Santos was getting paid. Or if he was.

JD sucked away the drop of blood squeezed from his hand and spat it out and then took in the sunrise. Jesse would not approve of his watching the sun come up. She said she never paid any attention to sunrises, only sunsets. She never explained but always spoke it as though she had just made it through one more day. JD watched it anyway, each morning.

He leaned on the top rail and allowed his mind to slip out of focus, thinking about nothing and thinking about everything. This morning he would think about the old horse lying up there on the hill under the flat side of this cutoff sun, pasted on this bleeding sky. He wondered if old Chisos had died.

"Well." He turned away from the sunrise. "It ain't my faithful old cowpony out there dying." He lifted the milkpail from the post and walked out of the corral toward the house without looking back. "Or dead."

Gallo del Cielo was just beginning his morning warmup from the bunkhouse when JD went inside the kitchen. He set the halfpail of milk on the countertop. Jesse stood at the stove, stirring oatmeal in a saucepan and staring out the window at the bruised horizon.

"Thought you never watched it?" he said.

"Sometimes," she whispered, and with the crook of a little finger moved a lock of near-gray hair away from her forehead. She looked at JD and spoke harder, "Mostly I don't."

He watched her eyes change hard, then soft blue, then glaze cold. He glanced at her forehead where she had moved the lock, uncovering a patch of skin, the flesh the color of horizon she had been watching. Jesse's eyes said there would be no discussion. Not about sunrises. Not about anything else. He stood aside waiting for Tru to come into the kitchen.

JD folded his arms and studied the toe of his boot, wondering about the tom. Tru entered and sat at the head of the long table just as the wall clock chimed the sixth time. As soon as Tru sat, JD took his assigned place at the table. He toyed with the flatware. "Morning," JD said without looking up.

"Morning," Jesse echoed as though she had just noticed the two.

"Mmmm..." Tru said to neither. He twisted to the shelf behind his chair and clicked on the radio. News and static and weather and static and cattle prices then off. No music. Jesse brought over steaming bowls of oatmeal and set them in front of the two. JD watched Tru stir milk and butter and brown sugar into the mush until he could look no more, the morning ritual, almost medicinal, one glass of cold milk, half into the oatmeal, half to drink, no coffee no toast.

JD looked down into his own bowl and hesitated until he saw Jesse watching. He grinned at her, trying to recapture how he had done it when he was just eight and suddenly motherless and his hungover father had been the presence at the other end of a table that Jesse had set a thousand years ago and a million miles away, probably with this same silver plate. He picked up his spoon and surreptitiously inspected his grin, reflected first in the concave side and then on the convex side but neither seemed right so he sprinkled sugar. She turned her back and stood at the stove for no reason. He saw her correct the lock of hair. Absently he stirred his oatmeal and looked out the window at the emerging sun, realizing he hated oatmeal as much as he did Jersey cows and cats. He said nothing. Cowhands never complain. Old tophands or greenhorn drovers.

Jesse came back with a plate of toast and filled JD's coffee mug and then her own. She sat and spread butter and jam on a piece of toast. Silence and eating. When Tru finished he sipped his milk and looked out the window, sucking his teeth. JD sat waiting for him to lay out the morning.

"We'll take a load down to the old windmill," he said finally, still sipping, sipping. "Start feeding them steers there too, I guess." He sighed and sucked his teeth some more and finished his milk with one swallow. "It oughta rain," he muttered but still did not look at JD. "Goddamn, it oughta rain soon."

"How much?" JD asked, but it was not about rain.

Tru had said 'we' but JD knew Tru would not be coming.

"Eighteen," Tru shot back and he looked at him now. "Take eighteen sacks of barley cottonseed mix, ten percent salt. I want them steers drinking plenty of water in this heat."

With a practiced gesture Tru retrieved his pocketwatch and snapped it open and glanced at it as he wound it tight and JD knew he was finished. Tru said nothing about the old horse lying on the hill and JD would not bring that up either. In due time, Tru would say whatever needed said. JD drained his mug and stacked his plates.

"'scuse me," he said as he rose with the dishes and took them to the sink. Jesse smiled at his manners and wondered where he had found them.

"And take Linc with you," Tru said, stopping him at the screendoor. JD turned and frowned.

"Not Santos?"

"Got another project for him. Tell Linc I said teach you to start that jackpump down there too." JD saw the familiar halfgrin and fought off the urge to turn and leave. He knew what was coming. "It's that hunk of machinery under the old windmill. Looks like a big ole bird JD. Sounds like one too when it ain't been greased in godknows how long."

Tru paused and JD let his eyes wander over the pattern in Jesse's wallpaper. When again he started to leave, Tru went on, "You know, got that diesel engine on one end and that dipping peckerhead on the other. Squeaks just like a big ole songbird, just like them pumps you got up there in the Permian Basin. Surely you seen 'em ain't you JD?"

JD shifted, leaned stiff armed against the door jamb and lowered his eyes, studied the geometry of the floor tiles this time. Tru went on. "All them oil wells everybody's got up there? You seen them oil pumps with them fat, hand planted Herefords milling around, ain't you, so's it looks like a real working ranch?"

Tru watched for reaction but JD stood impassive, his head lowered. "Same kind of pump, JD, except we ain't got any oil here on this place, just real cattle that have to drink water, real water, especially when it's hot and the wind ain't blowed a windmill in five days."

JD waited for Tru to finish.

"You oughta be able to learn how to start one. You been talking about being all over that oilpatch. Surely you seen one of them jack-pumps?" Tru smiled, pretending he was making a joke. "Hell we might even make a cowhand out of you to boot, JD, who knows."

Tru turned to Jesse who would not look at him. She fretted with the stray lock. "That'd be something, right Jesse? Send back a real cowhand? First oilman ever got his start right here on this ranch, probably the first real cowhand ever come out of the oilpatch." Tru looked back out the window and paused, his smile worn out. "It oughta rain soon," he muttered and then again with what almost passed for humility, "God it oughta rain."

"Maybe it will," JD offered.

Jesse nodded but she had not smiled at any of this. She walked over and stood next to JD and held open the screendoor. "Don't forget your hat."

JD glanced first at Jesse's eyes and then the spot over which she had smoothed the lock of hair. He went out and disappeared into the storage shed.

"It'll be hot today JD," she whispered as he walked past again, pulling down the brim of his hat and then JD thought he heard the faint dragging of Jesse's fingernail across the closed screendoor.

He was almost off the flagstone patio when Tru barked out the window, "Eighteen sacks JD, same as your age in case you got trouble remembering." From inside the bunkhouse an urgent Gallo del Cielo answered Tru but JD did not. He wondered if their voices would sound the same to Tru anyway.

TWO

Jesse sat again, picked up her half eaten toast but then returned it to her plate. She stared at the plate and then with her finger, traced the ring of tiny flowers around its edge. Tru pushed back his chair and left. She heard him moving around in the bedroom, clearing his throat and then she heard the bunkhouse door slam and boots in the gravel by the barn. There were voices outside, Linc and then JD and after awhile Linc's old pickup starting, its unmeshed gears giving over to coughing and sputtering and then low rumbles as the two eased out of the yard with their load. Suddenly, it was silent again except for Tru clearing his throat in the backroom. When he returned to the kitchen he wore his good hat and held his leather gloves bunched in one hand. "I'll be in town."

He would be at the bank again. He would come back rejected, carrying the same bitterness which would escalate into the same Fredrick Truman Pierce answer if she dared talk about her old job at the Elbo Room. Jesse knew she could still work solid tips if she wanted to. Most of the bar patrons were far closer to her own forty-five than the sixty-two hard years Tru carried. But he had saved her from them eight years ago, rescued Jesse from the random Saturday night cowhand whose tips had never bought anything from her except a starring role in next week's lonely fantasy somewhere in the rugged Chisos Basin, mending fence and pushing cows and dreaming of owned acres.

Even so, Jesse had not minded Tru's warped sense of chivalry sprung from a mostly forgotten past when cattlemen—*real* cattlemen Tru would say—obtained both their brides and their wealth by any means they could, ignoring the origins of either. Where older cowhands like Linc had adapted and even infused their wizened western authenticity with a paradoxical contemporary ethic, Tru remained horseshoe hard and obstinate, explosive of temper and fiercely independent, suspicious of anything which smacked of progress. He would far rather the grace of god torment his ranch with barely enough water from windmills and stingy random cloudbanks than to rely on motorized jackpumps artificially sucking water from the maws of the earth. Still, Jesse loved this arrogant confidence even in the privacy of their bedroom with his own paradox of gentleness and dominance.

But Tru's sense of independence had taken a darker turn. They had not made love in almost a year. Jesse could no longer deny that to herself. Tru seemed more than ever obsessed with opposing the inevitable and when his efforts at everything he attempted had lately soured due to shrinking financial resources or falling cattle prices or even his own waning masculine prowess, Tru began to transfer this hostility in physical eruptions to Jesse herself. He had not—*could* not—apologize. He seemed to pass off this dark side of his personality as a release of stress and so had she at first. But that explanation seemed far too contemporary for a man like Tru and Jesse had come to interpret it now as some obsolescent exercise of property rights rather than any neurosis.

So on this morning she did not expect apology for the night before. But he made no attempt at explanation either. Tru turned and left the kitchen. She stacked his dishes on top of hers and went to the sink and ran warm water over them. As she did this she touched the tender spot on her forehead and absently tried to press down the lock of hair again without success. Then she put her fingers under the tap and wet the lock and with more force than she needed, pushed down the hair, her eyes finally welling from the sharp pain as she watched him disappear into the old adobe bunkhouse.

When he came out, Santos followed close behind, nodding as Tru spoke. Tru stomped across the yard, gesturing with his gloves first toward the lean-to and then the barn and then back again toward the rusted pile of old barbed wire, full of kinks and splices, and then once more to the splintered fence posts under the lean-to. Santos followed Tru to his pickup. Still nodding, the old man watched him roar off and then stood in the billow of dust with his hat in his hand for a long while, as if weighing again the choices he had considered in the darkness at the big river. Finally he raised his eyes and presented an upturned palm to a cloudless morning sky. Jesse saw him shake his head and then wedge his hat back on and move listlessly toward the tangle of fencing materials.

"Me too, Santos," she whispered. "Me too."

She went back and made the bed. In a rare surge of domesticity, she rolled up the threadbare Mexican rug to hang on the clothesline and began sweeping the tiled floors, working the broom with anger into the cracking grout and the corners where the dust collected against the plastered adobe wall. Then she knelt and pushed the broom under the bed, touching the flat wicker basket stored there. Jesse lowered herself further and tried to reach it, finally pushing it out the other side with the broom. She went around and sat on the bed and lifted the basket onto her lap. She leaned over and blew away the dust.

Jesse could name every item without looking inside. She removed each in turn. She could not remember the last time she had done this, perhaps four, five years now. It always amused her the things she saved, the basket itself worthless yet priceless, one her mother had given her just before she died of cancer at sixty-four.

She began to spread the treasures on the bed, tracing each with a finger as if to stroke memories into sounds and sights and smells. There was the crushed teacup, China white and delicate, its pieces wrapped in a shimmering silk handkerchief her older sister Clair had brought back from Asia and a tour of military duty with her husband Reid Mitchell. Clair cried when she took it from her suitcase, discovering it broken but then both erupted in giggles as the two tried to fit the jigsaw back together.

A freak aneurysm took Clair the very next spring on Easter Sunday, only six months after their mother. Jesse was left in the big crumbling East Texas farmhouse with their father, RJ, who insisted that he and Reid Mitchell share not only their martyred grief over mutual loss of wives, but also RJ's favorite brand of cheap bourbon, while Jesse tried to explain the overwhelming confusion of a dead grandmother, a drunk grandfather and drunk father and now, an absent mother to Clair and Reid's son and Jesse's only nephew, Jimmie Dale Mitchell. JD was only eight at the time and as the only remaining male heir, a daily reminder to Jesse that her own biological clock was ticking away at thirty-five.

Nightmares for the boy became unbearable and so Jesse finally took him into her own bed and curled against him each night as he whimpered. The only source of peace for the boy seemed to be the musicbox her mother had given her and so Jesse wound it tight and placed it nightly next to his head on his pillow and let the music play over and over until he slept and then she would replace its lid and rewind it, ready in case the boy awoke. And then one night Reid came into the bedroom.

Jesse smells the whiskey in the darkness before she blinks awake. She squints at Reid's figure standing silhouetted and rigid, as if burned into the pale light spilling down the hallway from the kitchen. The house lies silent and even the wind holds its breath in the eerie absence of familiar muted sounds from the highway in the distance, as if all time and motion has ceased, awaiting Jesse's voice.

"Reid?" she whispers and places a hand on JD's chest. The boy stirs but then is still again. There is no answer but now Jesse hears the rasping of Reid's breath as he comes close and stands over the bed. She raises herself on her elbow and panics at the image of a dead father, slumped over a spilled waterglass of whiskey at the kitchen table, the only reason Jesse can think of for Reid standing there silent.

"What is it? He's not..." Jesse drops the sheet she holds clutched to her breasts and instead, touches her throat with the tips of her fingers and for a long moment, she is not aware that Reid's own hand is where her's has just been and suddenly she knows why he is here. "Reid... no," she whispers and pushes his hand away but with an angry move, he forces it back. Jesse sits up. She clutches Reid's wrist with both her hands and tries to clear her mind and then speaks, in a harder whisper this time, "Come on Reid, you'll wake him. Just go on, go on to bed, Reid." The boy moves again and mutters something and Jesse knows she will

have to choose: she can touch the boy's chest again and try to still him, or she can hold onto Reid's wrist and try to remove his hand which he now slips inside her nightshirt, his fingers hard on a bare breast.

"Reid...I don't want this." She says it through her teeth this time and attempts to rise from the bed but he holds her back with one hand and begins fumbling off his trousers with the other.

And so Jesse had chosen. It was as if Reid were suddenly the entire weight of Clair and their mother and their father, and even Jesse's own death, pressing her back onto the bed and then later, thrusting himself into her body and all Jesse could do was lie there, her hand stretched across the darkness, lifting the lid on the musicbox next to JD's pillow as the boy lay there in his own death-like stillness.

Jesse could only hope she had ceased resistance soon enough so that JD had slept through it. But she had never been certain of this. When Reid finished and passed out, still lying atop her, Jesse slithered from under him and picked up the musicbox and placed it on the boy's chest and carried him into his bedroom, the music slowly winding down. In his own bed, JD whimpered as if in a bad dream, as if the imminent end of the music would be painful. In a panic, Jesse quickly rewound the dying music and placed the box on his nightstand. When she saw that he lay motionless and silent, she slipped down the hall and stripped off her nightgown and cleaned herself in the darkness of the bathroom and then dried with a clean towel and donned a clean T-shirt. She returned and lay under the quilt in the single creaking cot with JD who was again whimpering. Though it was not finished, she rewound the musicbox as tight as the spring would allow, trying to free the music forever so that it might never cease, and then she pressed the boy to her body, his cheek against her aching breasts, his hair wet with her hot tears by the time she finally slept.

Jesse did not call it rape at first. She had since learned that the word did not matter, only the act itself, to which she had given no permission and only acquiesced for reasons she could not fully explain to herself, even now.

Reid and the boy left one tense week later and soon disappeared into the booming oilfields of West Texas. And in a year, following the death of her father, Jesse too began to drift. One barroom followed the next in a seamless succession of waitress jobs and tentative liaisons with men from whom she asked—and to whom she gave—nothing. Jesse heard from neither of the two until JD called the bluff she had scratched inside the card she sent for his high school graduation, half joking that he should now come to the ranch for a true education, spelling the word *true* with the capital letters *TRU.*

She thought occasionally of Reid and somehow had forgiven him. And even if she had not completely forgiven herself, she came to view the incident in a perverse twist of denial as something she had done for Clair, as well as for the boy, and therefore Jesse refused to think of herself entirely as victim.

RJ, the patriarch and husband and father and grandfather, withered and wasted, sank into a morass of despair and cheap bourbon and finally died in his own vomit. At times as she had nursed her father's health, Jesse resorted to self-pity, wallowing in feelings of abandonment and envy because both Clair and her mother were finally relieved from the hell all three women endured for so many years. And though she tried, Jesse never allowed herself the grace of selective forgetting.

As far as she knew, Reid never remarried and JD grew up motherless. Until she met Tru, Jesse remained unattached but still childless herself. She read the women's magazines and thought often about the psychology of it all, how circumstance molds our personalities and maps our destinies and shapes our choices. She thought she might still have the article ripped out and folded in the bottom of the basket, the piece about how we sometimes marry into the traumas of our past and how the cycles are often repeated and rewound—like the sad musicbox—and we never learn why. But she never read one about growing up motherless and what it does to a child, or what being barren does to a woman, for that matter. She wondered if the two conditions might be connected in some cosmic way. As a young man, JD now seemed callused, with the kind of latent hostility one might find still locked inside the anger of an eight year old who felt betrayed and deserted by the death of a mother. But if he remembered anything at all about that one night ten years ago, JD had given no indication of it and surely a groggy headed boy of eight would have been unaware.

Jesse would certainly not bring it up.

She reached into the basket again without looking and smiled as her fingers touched the cool porcelained metal of the musicbox, resting on top of the frayed journal at the bottom. She brought out the musicbox and held it in the tips of her fingers, turning it slowly as she followed the patterned scroll of tiny yellow rosebuds and darkgreen leaves, seamlessly encircling the cylinder. She tipped it upside down in her palm, careful to keep the lid in place and began to turn the little brass key on the bottom until its spring was taut, its orchestra tuned and tensed.

"What will it play this time?" she teased but there was no way to surprise herself with the familiar music held captive all these years. She set the box on the bed and closed her eyes and lifted the lid. Instantly, the strains of the hymnal AMAZING GRACE came tinkling into her head, fused with the final words her mother had spoken, "I always kept it there, Jesse, inside the basket, the grace of music to lift me when grace was needed." Her mother paused then and raised a pallid and veined hand, fingering loose the purple velvet lining from the bottom of the musicbox, thus exposing the gold double-eagle coin her own mother had passed down and already a collector's item, far beyond face value. "And *this* to save me if the music ever failed," she whispered and smiled weakly at Jesse and in a short while she was gone.

Jesse opened her eyes and put the lid back on the box, shutting off the music mid-chorus. For a moment she considered taking out her mother's old journal and reading the things she had written inside, but she stopped. She wondered why their mother had given these things to her instead of Clair. It was as if their mother knew Clair too would soon be gone and Jesse would need the grace of music someday.

Jesse returned the other items and replaced the top of the basket, remembering that neither she nor Clair nor their mother had ever been saved by the grace of music, nor any other kind of grace, from a father who would have made shortwork of the gold coin had he ever discovered it. She thought about Tru. "No use telling him I don't need saving. Not again anyway."

She slipped the basket back under the bed and picked up the rolled Mexican rug and took it outside to the clothesline. Santos was attempting to uncoil the kinks from the rusted remnants of barbed wire which now stretched across the outer edges of the open yard like the parameter of some military bivouac. Jesse shook her head and removed the clothes pins from her mouth and clamped them onto the rug. "But Tru might think about saving himself someday."

THREE

With bare hands Santos tugged free the largest piece of barbed wire, coaxed from the stack of shortends. He studied the kinks and snarls in this three-foot loop, shook his head and sighed. Tru had only said to get the old wire ready; he did not say how.

Santos shrugged. He grasped the free end of the wire and walked across the yard with it from the bunkhouse to the barn, shaking the coils loose. It lay behind him like some giant spring across the hardpan earth. When the wire gave out, he knelt and jerked on the end but it would not lie flat, the kinks and snarls still there. Immediately when he released the tension, the wire drew back into its former looping shape.

"You want to stay the way you are," Santos mused. He sat back on his haunches, lifted his hat and pulled his shirtsleeve across his forehead and replaced the hat. "Because you are old and tired and like myself you are comfortable the way you are." He tugged harder on the wire, avoiding the barbs. He lifted it and whipped it against the earth in an attempt to force it flat but when he slacked his grip, the wire slowly reformed itself into coils and kinks.

"He will defeat you, old wire." Santos chuckled. "This man Truman who is hard as wire himself will tame you and so you may as well get ready," he said and then, "Maybe I can encourage you a little..."

He rose and went into the cool of the barn and stood for a moment, his eyes growing accustomed to the shadows. Soon he could distinguish objects and shelves and stacks of derelict harnesses and tack, strewn about in the inertia of complete neglect. He began to ferret around and soon found the other things he needed: a single, complex tool that combined a staple hammer on one side and on the opposite, a curved point for removing them while in the middle, forming a set of pliers with a wirecutter. This tool was tucked inside a tin of rusted staples. Outside, Santos rattled the can of staples to forewarn his opponent. Then he clamped the stubborn wire in the pliers and twisted a small loop in the end and with a staple, secured this to the side of the barn. "There. Now you will have some roots when I pull your other end," he muttered and smiled. "See. We can be *amigos.* You can keep some of your memory but only if you are willing to give a little in return."

Santos glanced up the road and saw nothing coming. He looked at the wire, looping in defiance across the compound and he looked at the bunkhouse.

"We all have memory," the old man mused. "Not only here but everywhere, we all have memory. Trapped inside, like your coils *señor* wire, until we become that memory and that is the way it is. But sometimes we must let go of just a little so that we can keep the other. Do you understand, *señor* wire? I will let you think on this for awhile, my friend, while I have a cool drink of water. And then I will pull some memory out of you."

He smiled and turned and walked toward the bunkhouse. Halfway across the yard he looked back to see if the wire stood its ground. It did.

"And *buenos diaz* to you, Cielo," he said inside. When the rooster heard the voice, he spun around and around inside his cage and stopped in his combative crouch, his head cocked as he looked at the old man from his goodeye. "And you too have memory, do you not my old friend, uh? Of the sweetness of cracked corn and the freshness of spring water? Well, I am sorry, old rooster, but you will have to settle for barley again and water from a horse trough, though your cousins in La Perla would no doubt envy even this."

He lifted the cage and walked back across the yard and into the barn again. He set Cielo down in the shade just inside the barn and opened the cage. When he reached in for the empty halftins which served as waterer and feeder, the bird rushed for the opening. Santos spread his elbows across the door of the cage and said, "No, no, this is not La Perla, my friend. I am afraid you would not last long here. Even with a braveheart and one goodeye, there are too many here, dogs and cats and others who would have you for a meal. Ah yes, a tough meal and a small one but nonetheless they would have you, my friend."

The bird clucked and spun in protest and then sat sulking inside the cage. Santos went to the grain room where he filled one halftin with barley and then into the corral where he dipped water from the horse trough with the other. He drank the water, refilled the halftin, drank again and then filled it once more. Then he returned and placed the filled halftins on the floor of the barn, cautiously cracked open the door to the cage and then set each inside but Cielo attempted no escape this time.

"There. Now you can pretend they are filled with the same as before," but the bird made no effort to eat or drink. Santos looked at him and then squatted and sat in the shade, staring out the barn door at the wire loops and then back at Cielo and said, "Well, you will just have to use your memory," and he cocked his own head to the left and then to the right in imitation of Cielo's and then looked at the rooster's badeye, opaline and useless.

"We all have memory, Cielo, and some of it is bad and some of it is useful," and Santos removed his hat and with a palm, smoothed back the sweat from his forehead into his silver hair and shut his eyes. He leaned against the jamb of the door and remembered Cielo when he had cracked corn from Santo's own fields and spring water and both goodeyes and the same braveheart, beating inside his pure white feathered chest and he saw the bird as younger. But he could not remember the exact year or his own age or even if his wife Paloma were young or old because in his mind he could only see both of them as aged even then, despite Cielo's youth.

"Were we always so?" he whispered and furrowed his brow and shook his head but then smiled at the memory of Paloma, even during those days of desperation. He forced his eyes even tighter as if to clear them better for the remembering...remembering.

"He says there is nothing he can do," Paloma is speaking low, try-

ing not to allow despair into her voice.

"Why did you not come for me?"

"You were in the field, Santos. He said it all to me anyway. It does not matter."

Santos rises from the wooden bench beside the cookfire where Paloma kneels, working the tortillas. He toes off each ragged huarache and steps out of them onto the cool earthen floor and then goes to the small window in the thick adobe wall and peers through the vertical willow branches, long ago rammed into the ancient adobe when there was bark on them and the mud was wet but now only fingers of smooth wooden bars, intended to prevent the uninvited from entering. He thinks of Cielo, fed and watered and content inside his own barred cage in the cool corner of the room and wonders which of them truly has freedom.

"It does matter." He squints into the midday sun and then turns back and for a moment, is flooded with fear because he can only hear hands patting the dough but he cannot see his wife in the darkness of the room. She says nothing.

"Paloma?"

"Si," she answers harshly and she knows it is not at all the way a wife responds to a husband speaking her name with a question, even in times of crisis.

"It does matter," Santos repeats. "I could have shown him the paper and—" He hears her snort softly but she says nothing so he goes on, "The paper that proves it. Did you not show it to him?"

"The paper? Ah yes, the one Zapata himself gave to you? Or was it to your father or to your grandfather. The paper which…"

"Yes, the paper," he says and anger flares now in his voice. He walks the familiar eight paces across the room to the small carved wooden chest on the floor below the handmade altar, countersunk in the adobe. He opens the chest and reaches inside and holds the rolled parchment above his head in a practiced and triumphant grip, as though it were the waist of a rifle and also to prove to Paloma and the entire world that it is still there. But she knows it is there. How can she forget something which for as long as she can remember has been the daily topic of conversation during at least one meal and sometimes both.

"Ah yes, the paper," she repeats. "Which says the King of Spain him-

self…or was it the Queen…grants these Yaqui Indians and their Mestizo heirs forever and ever the right to plant this soil and use this water from this sacred spring here in this sacred valley, scorched by this sacred sun, nearby this sacred village of La Perla where—it is possible, just possible—Zapata, or was it Villa himself—"

"Do not mock it, Paloma," Santos cautions, cutting her off. "It is bad luck to mock the struggle which gave us—"

"Luck?" she says, her voice rising. "And what luck we've had!" She rises and crosses to him, her hands on her hips, straightening to her full five feet. "The luck of three children, Santos? Not one to reach the age of four? Not one ever becoming old enough even to sell chicle in the streets? The luck of this casa, crumbling on every corner so that even the sky itself shows its face through? The luck of this bird you so carefully groom inside this cage, the one who will save us from all of this, no doubt? The one who eats our cracked corn and drinks our sweet water and rests in the cool but who can lay not one egg for us to eat or to hatch, Santos? Not one."

Paloma turns away from him and kneels on the floor and pushes the heels of her hands against the dough as if to punish it and this time her voice is a whisper, "Do not speak to me of luck, Santos."

He stands silent for a long while and then shuffles and squats in front of the cookfire beside her. "I will talk to him," he says softly. "What did he say?"

"That it is not ours."

"That is all?"

"Yes."

"We will have to leave?"

"He did not say that…"

"But he meant it?"

For a long while Paloma says nothing and then repeats, "He did not say that…"

Santos rises and stands next to the fire, staring into the flames and in the flames he sees the horsemen, the Zapatistas and the Villistas, tall and fierce and feared, their rifles and pistolas and knives everywhere on their bodies and in the leather scabbards of their saddles and he sees the sun flash from neat rows of polished brass cartridges held in wide leather belts, heavy across their chests and their huge sombreros shoved arro-

gantly back on their heads and even from inside the clouds of gunsmoke and dust, their teeth shine from dark faces unshaven and mustachioed. And Santos hears the gunfire and the screams above the chaos of hoof-beats from pounding black stallions, and above the deep throated laughter from men whose names are now revered and sanctified all across the country.

"You are certain he said nothing else?" Santos probes.

"He said we should know we do not own this land." Paloma stops the kneading and now she too stares into the fire. "And one other word," she pauses for a long while as if she does not want to speak it either but then says it in a whisper, as if to make it sound different, "Mestizos."

It does not sound different to Santos. He knows the word too well. Nothing else needs saying, only that indisputable connotation from which springs no property rights from any ancient piece of parchment whatsoever, given from whomsoever and signed by whatever king. Or queen.

After a long while, he raises the fist in which the paper is gripped and then slowly presses the knuckles of this hand against his teeth and the parchment crackles. For a moment he considers flinging it into the fire but then he hears Cielo spinning inside his cage in the corner of the room and the noise brings him back from the edge of fury. Santos clinches his teeth and says once more, "I will go see him." He tucks the rolled paper inside the neck of his shirt and bends to Paloma and in the firelight he sees the wrinkles across her forehead and tries to remember the faces of their dead children but it has been too long ago and he cannot even remember Paloma's face when it was smooth.

Santos opened his eyes and muttered, "Were we always so? Old and tired?" He rose and stood in the barn door and looked up the road and wondered how long he had been remembering. Cielo had eaten the barley and was testing the water. "I see that hunger has killed your memory of better food but nothing has killed the memory of *señor* wire and so we will have to use other persuasion on him."

Santos moved out of the shade, cocking his sombrero onto the back of his head in defiance as he stalked the far end of the coiled wire, as if astride some pounding black stallion.

FOUR

"Where we taking this load?" Linc spoke around his toothpick.

"Down to the old windmill," JD said. The only thing JD had ever seen in place of Linc's toothpick was a handrolled cigarette and even then, he tucked the pick in his hatband when he smoked. "Tru says start feeding there too."

Linc nodded. He adjusted his hat further forward and shifted the pick to the other corner of his mouth. JD wondered how Linc kept from chewing the end ragged.

"He says start that jackpump too," JD continued and then with clear disdain, "Says to show me how."

Linc glanced at him and his lips parted just enough to keep the toothpick in place but he said nothing. Linc slumped against the passenger door and gazed out the side window. JD fell silent too, shifting his eyes to the rearview mirror and watching the road scroll away behind them.

The road lay unfenced from the south edge of the ranch near Lajitas all the way north to the base of the scrub covered foothills of Santiago Peak. For the past two summers, heavy dump trucks carrying cinnabar ore down from a reopened pit mine in the apron of Santiago Peak, had pounded corrugations into this road that bisected Tru's ranch—and his lifestyle—like some ragged scar. Drivers traveled at speeds closer to insane than dangerous, their trucks invisible inside a moving cocoon of dust, the economic survival of their families riding on runs to Lajitas and then down the two-lane

Camino Rio over to Presidio and the railroad.

Tru cursed the mining with growing vehemence each evening after supper as Linc and Santos joined Jesse and JD and him on the flagstone patio that skirted the front of the adobe ranchhouse. It was the best place to watch the pink of the sunset work itself into a frenzy of purple and peach and then back to bloodred as it finally exhausted itself behind the horizon of the Chinati Mountains further west. No one ever said anything until this collage of color ended and the final light cast shadows along the slope to the northeast where the mine lay concealed in the lap of piñon pocked foothills.

"Sonzabitches kill one more steer..." Tru would begin and then suck his teeth and pause, making certain everyone was listening. "...one damn steer and we'll see how fast they can run them trucks from a lawsuit. Goddamn road shouldn't been build through here in the first place."

Tru paused here and searched the shadowed faces for confirmation, which he always got in the form of silent nods all round before he continued his nightly history lesson.

"It's open range goddammit, always has been, ever since my own family homesteaded this basin in the 1800's, open all the way up from the border and past Marfa and Alpine and before that, some say, open range north, into the Panhandle and even up into Montana and not a single goddamn fence either. Hell, we got natural fences, Alamito Creek Canyon to the west there and Terlingua Creek Canyon to the east and no steer even thinks about crossing them. Nobody worried about state or territorial or even federal borders back then and none of that legal stuff. Y'all knew that, didn't you? Didn't you?"

Everybody knew. And everybody knew why the original mine and easement were there in the first place, but no one dared mention this.

But then usually Tru himself would admit in bitter confession, "The old man should'a never give no easement across here, open range or not. Or sold that side of the peak to them early shaft miners. Should'a never even thought about it." And then Tru explained again how his father had sold the original mine site, just to survive, and even allowed the road easement to those original miners for their teams of mules and ore wagons to travel into Lajitas.

"They even made papers, documents signed by god-knows-who and now these new owners wave them in the face of anybody who tries to stop them from digging out them old shafts and gouging up the land." Tru paused and then continued, "So now they roar across here, raising dust and killing my cattle. At least them old miners didn't raise dust with wagons and mules, not that much anyway. And they sure as hell didn't kill steers either. But by god, there's open range laws in Texas, even to this very day and they say you pay if you hit unfenced cattle. Problem is, you gotta first pay some damn lawyer to try and prove it. And if you're fighting big money, well...you still lose, even if you win."

Tru would drone on into the evening as candlemoths ventured forth and then one-by-one his listeners drifted off to respective beds, Linc usually the first to disappear silently and then Santos to the bunkhouse and then Jesse inside to finish up the kitchen. JD always stayed until last, piqued by curiosity about Tru's personal history lessons, the plots of which JD seemed to remember from old singing cowboy movies on television in living black and white.

JD was thinking about the dump trucks now as he listened to the gravel ping on the inside of the pickup fenders. The old windmill lay several miles toward the south end of the ranch. Its adjacent stocktank was dozed from the surrounding soil and rock and fed by runoff water from occasional cloud bursts, but after that, only by the snaggle-toothed windmill that screeched awake when the wind decided to blow. When the air was still, as it had been for the past week, the incongruous jackpump served as substitute for both rain and wind.

The awkward combination of a modern jackpump toiling under one of Tru's traditional windmills struck JD as comical. And though Tru taunted him about it, JD did know about these pumps; he had just never started one. When he got close enough to hear the squeaking of the sucker rod, he always thought about cool summer evenings parked on a gravel pad past midnight, close beside the working rhythm of this same kind of jackpump, only this one sucking oil instead of water. And then he would think about Bettye Lee

Collins. And he would think about his graduation class.

As far as JD was concerned, it had been a nowhere group all along. But then he thought about his nowhere childhood, misspent with his father in his nowhere hometown of Blink, Texas: *blink once, and you miss it,* was the story about the origin of the name. When he considered all this, JD had to confess that he fit his class just fine. Turning eighteen seemed a natural plateau in the progression from one nowhere to the next, just another silent halftime in another losing football game.

JD had come to accept reaching eighteen as a sort of impotent pause as he drifted from the rah-rah fantasies of the Fighting Blink Bobcat football squad toward the hard reality of trying to enroll in a nowhere community college. Somewhere. Anywhere. He had not decided. It would have to be a place where he could belly up to the registrar's window, unannounced, and sign up for a degree, maybe a place like the kind advertised inside a book of matches.

Long before he sauntered across the Blink High School gymnasium floor to get his diploma, a safe distance in the alphabet behind a soon to be abandoned Bettye Lee Collins, JD promised himself he would not hire out on one of the roustabout crews working for A-2-Z Oilfield Construction. No matter how much he might need the money in the fall, laying four inch pipeline across the West Texas sand in hundred degree heat was not his idea of a productive summer, especially in concert with a crew of hungover winos.

Between his junior and senior years he had already been initiated into the romance of the oilpatch, working evening towers on a drilling rig. His final lesson was taught by a weevil of a supervising driller, a long-boned Louisiana drifter who jerked a joint of well casing too fast from the catwalk on its way up into the rig, knocking JD to the ground. The driller shut down the pair of screaming diesels just in time to stop the heavy casing from slipping its wire cable. The pipe stopped and teetered just above JD's hardhat, a thin aluminum shield, useless against two thousand pounds of threaded steel. JD remained flat, hugging the ground for long seconds as he held his breath and watched white-eyed the joint of casing twist just inches above his head. Finally he shut his eyes and inside saw himself at the funeral and he wondered if they would bury him in his letter jacket because otherwise, Bettye Lee might not be able to recognize him in the coffin with his skull crushed like an eggshell.

When nothing happened JD finally opened his eyes and saw the driller standing on the deck with a shit-eating grin, his hand grasping the lever of the closed engine throttle. The whole image was not unlike the photograph JD had seen that supposedly depicted the psychopathic face of Billy the Kid, grinning and leaning on his rifle instead of a diesel engine lever. The man looked as if he were waiting for JD to correct his error, as if JD himself had been the one to slow down a multimillion dollar, tight drilling schedule. But JD could not move. He could not even speak. Finally he was able to shift his butt and then inch his shoulders from under the casing. He stood and with a quick, silent flick, sailed the company hardhat onto the grimy workdeck where it rattled to a stop right at the driller's feet, like a loose hubcap.

"What do you aim to do now, Mitchell?" the man said, still grinning. "Come up here and take a swing at me or get back to work? Or maybe you'd rather walk?"

The crew laughed at this. No one had ever seen a roughneck walk back from any shift, much less a midnight rotation. But JD had already turned away, wordless, and began the six mile hike back to Blink in the darkness, thus ending his roughneck career. The whole incident soured whatever romantic notions he had ever harbored about life in the West Texas oilpatch, at least as a blue collar worker.

The walk also gave him plenty of time to think about Bettye Lee Collins and football and how wild she would surely be during his last year as a senior member of the Fighting Bobcats. Even after he exhausted in his mind all the carnal possibilities with Bettye Lee, JD still had ample time on that nocturnal hike to think about how he would leave. That was when the idea of college hit him. The BHS counselor had mentioned to the junior class at large that such a possibility did, in fact, exist—for certain members. But the counselor never said it to JD. Now that he had shown the kind of bravado it took to walk six miles in the darkness, abandoning a good paying roughneck job, JD decided he might consider something even more adventurous.

"I might as well go all the way," he said when he saw Blink, a covey of lights that took no more than one hand to count. "Walk away from this whole fucking thing right now, just keep on walking." But that made him think about Bettye Lee again and about being a senior member of the Fighting Blink Bobcats.

Bettye Lee loved football. And she loved football players even more, especially *senior* football players with leather-sleeved letter jackets. "Maybe I oughta finish up first," he allowed. "One more year at old BHS, then maybe a college degree somewhere close, *then* I'll get the fuck outta here."

JD flushed when he thought about the way Tru made light of it all. It was not that he felt uneasy about the bullshit oilpatch myth. JD had tried and he knew no matter how grand those roughnecks might believe the oilpatch loomed, he simply could not see it from way down here this close to the Mexican border. Like most of the members of his class, it was a matter of having nothing to brag about in the first place. Some of the underclassmen sprung from oil rich ranches, but no one in his own class could lay claim to anything outside an odd rustbucket of a car or a pickup truck with twin chromed tailpipes, and certainly nothing as permanent as Permian Basin soil.

On occasion, JD shared a bootlegged sixpack with the ranch kids, hotrodded with them, listened to their drunken bragging about oil money and oil family. But as far as he knew, there was no historical lineage to brag about in his own family, no crusty old wildcatters or cattlemen ancestors or even pioneer farmers and certainly not one blood relative with the complexities of a Fredrick Truman Pierce.

One oldmaid great aunt on his father's side, had once attempted to trace the Mitchell genealogy but she stopped searching the old bibles and family records at the courthouses in east Texas when she reached the late 1800's. JD once heard his father quiz her about it in a rare sober moment of curiosity concerning his roots.

"There's more?" he said.

"There's more," she said and then dryly, "But you don't want to know about it, Reid," and then went on with a sly smile, "It might set you to drinking."

Some suspected the old woman had stumbled onto a hotbed of cattle thieves or moonshiners or something worse and so everyone dropped it. JD decided as extended Texas families went, the Mitchell's probably had come from nowhere. It was certain that none had *gone* anywhere either and that fit too.

Though he could tolerate his ridicule, and even join Tru on occasion and grudgingly admire Tru's stubborn adhesion to the way things used to be, JD could not handle the way Tru mocked his ambitions. Maybe Tru was right about the rest of the family. JD did not know what kind of drive other relatives might have possessed, but he thought of his father as different and JD figured if he ever had any kids, they could tell their friends at least the one story Reid told him again and again.

He said JD was only eight when the two made the pilgrimage from the cottonpatch to the oilpatch without a single stop except to piss side-by-side into the barrow ditch. They rode in an old rusted sedan with a cardboard box full of beer and soda pop and a sackful of cheese and peanut butter and soda crackers in the backseat and a four-by-six trailer with everything else they owned in tow. But the only memory of the journey JD would allow himself now was the leaving itself and the too long and too silent embrace of his Aunt Jesse and then mile after mile of her face fading in and out of the orange glow of the radio dial from the dashboard, Jesse's face becoming his mother's face and then back again, mesmerizing him in the darkness.

He and his father broke all bonds to the hardpan east Texas soil where first his grandmother and then his own mother had been firmly planted and so his father chose the more tentative roots in the windsifted sand of west Texas. JD confessed that it might have been less pioneering than pure survival. His father's original ties to the east Texas rural lifestyle seemed now less bond than bondage and JD was not certain exactly why, but he had long since whittled away all other memory of the leaving until what remained was only that paradox of joy and pain, etched on Jesse's silent face like some faded snapshot in black and white. And JD could not remember if Jesse had even said goodbye to his father.

JD grew up vaguely aware that deserting both the land and traditional family values had gained a certain amount of notoriety, if not grudging admiration for his father. But none of this changed the fact that no Mitchell or relative of a Mitchell had ever risen to white collar status and no one could claim anything as far fetched as a college degree, even the matchbook kind. And so his own bitter lessons from the oilpatch, along with his whole family history, were on his mind when JD got the graduation card with a twenty dollar bill paperclipped inside and the words scratched in his aunt Jesse's hand suggesting that he pack up and come down to the Big Bend country to get *"...a TRU education on the ranch."*

What happened graduation night cinched JD's decision.

With a strained sense of solemnity for the occasion, JD tried to avoid Bettye Lee at the dance but she cornered him and pulled him out onto the gym floor for a slowdance and started licking in his ear, right in front of his father and everyone else.

"Come on Bettye Lee, knock it off."

"You wanna go somewheres?" she cooed.

"I gotta do stuff," he said, forcing a stiff armed gap between them.

"What kinda stuff?" She sounded betrayed, deserted. "I thought we were gonna..."

"Family stuff Bettye Lee. Shit, you know—same as yours." He nodded toward the enclave of her brothers and sisters and assorted cousins, all sequestered in the shadows within arm length of the buffet. He looked back at her.

"Family?" she said.

"Well sure, it's just my dad but yes *family.* You too, right?"

"Course not. I can stay out as long as I want. Geezuschrist Jimmie, it's *graduation.* Nobody expects you to spend it with your goddamn family."

JD looked out over the sea of scrubbed faces, picking Reid Mitchell's from among the rows of parents and friends in folding chairs against the wall. His father's eyes locked on his in an unspoken and secret expression of male bonding. JD shrugged slightly and lifted his eyebrows and instantly Reid echoed his gesture in a kind of comic way, and not five minutes later on the parameter of the crowd his father surreptitiously dropped the keys to the old Ford right into JD's new white coatpocket and through his whiskey breath whispered something JD could not understand, and then his father left the gym and JD wondered if he had walked home or just to the bar down the street.

Two hours later, in the darkness on the same gravel pad where they had parked prom night two months earlier, the explosive popping of their favorite pumpjack engine again marking time to their rhythm, JD Mitchell and Bettye Lee Collins, recent graduates of Blink High School, whispered vows of undying love into the sweat of each other's neck, the car radio tuned and crackling out the syrupy sounds of the latest love song as they expressed in doglike frenzy their postgraduate passion.

"I'm pregnant you know," Bettye Lee said, almost casually as she later twisted in the backseat so JD could refasten her bra.

"Yeah sure." He fumbled with the hook-and-eye, already thinking about his dad and wondering if he would still be up and sober enough to talk about serious shit. Shit like college. Shit like money.

"No Jimmie, really. I am..."

"Goddammit Bettye Lee don't even joke about it." He snapped her bra and then got out of the backseat and also snapped off his condom and pulled up his new slacks and then returned to the driver's seat, drumming his fingers on the steering wheel. He pulled on the parking lights to check his watch.

"Let's go. Hurry up."

Bettye Lee did not budge. JD looked up into the rearview mirror and could see from the dashlights she was fully clothed again but she was not moving. "Awright, suit yourself."

He cranked up the engine and shoved the car into reverse and again checked the rearview mirror. Bettye Lee was crying.

"Ohshit," he said when he was certain she was serious, and he thought about the times when he was less than certain about his condom surviving intact. "Ohshit."

JD shut off the engine.

It was almost four in the morning when he coasted into the driveway next to the darkened trailer house in which Bettye Lee lived. "We'll talk some more tomorrow," he whispered and kissed her lips, cracked and salty now from all the tears. "I promise I'll call, okay?" She got out. She walked herself to the door. And JD did call the next day. But it was long distance to his Aunt Jesse.

On the phone he did not even ask what the work would be or how much it paid. She was family and he simply wanted out of the oilpatch right now, away from the temptation of A-2-Z Oilfield Constructors and Bettye Lee too. If in the process, JD could earn money for college, fine, but that was not a prime motivation at the moment.

After he hung up the phone, JD thought about Jesse and tried to remember her but the memory came blurred inside some confused haze of pain over a mother's death and a father who would never discuss any of it even now as JD explained to Reid the offer and what he was going to do. Reid simply murmured, "Mmmmm," and went right back to his newspaper and coffee laced with morning bourbon and so JD caught the next bus from Blink to Alpine and then another leg on down through Terlingua and then to Lajitas, where Jesse picked him up at the bus stop in front of the Elbo Room Bar.

"Tru's glad you came," was the only thing Jesse said all the way from Lajitas up to the ranch. But this man Fredrick Truman Pierce turned out to be something quite different from what JD expected. Tru raised the subject of bullshit college dreams enough that JD realized he still had no idea about college or even how to apply. He just knew he had to go, especially since Tru scoffed at the idea so often. He had no intention of languishing in Blink as a roustabout the remainder of his life like the rest of the Battling Bobcat squad. If he languished at all in the oilpatch, it would be in an air conditioned office with a white shirt and a tie and a company pickup truck and a sweet looking secretary. And Bettye Lee Collins would not be the one kissing him goodbye over the breakfast table, even if this kid she was carrying was his instead of one of the four or five other members of the Battling Bobcat Squad that JD suspected—no, he was almost *certain*—had been fucking her.

As JD thought about all this now inside the rattling pickup, he glanced into the rearview mirror at the plump round bulges of burlap bags in the bed and muttered, "Sorry, Bettye Lee. Don't know whose kid you got inside there but if he escaped outta one of my rubbers, we'll call him Houdini."

"Howzat?" Linc said and turned to him. JD flushed and shook his head and Linc turned back to watching the barrow ditch fly by. "Thought you was asleep," JD mumbled.

But JD did find it ironic, oilfield machinery supplying drinking water for rangy cattle. It was not a thought he dared share with his uncle. He knew the whole thing of jackpumps on waterwells was just another defeat, one more weft in the heavy blanket of acceptance being forced around the shoulders of Fredrick Truman Pierce. The pumps were a part of Tru's grudging recognition that ranching might have to enter the twentieth century—someday—and maybe even on his own ranch, a narrow stretch of yucca desert grassland which, according to Tru during his evening forums, had once been covered with tall gramma grass, this confirmed by Santos as though he had somehow witnessed it.

"Up to a horse's belly," Tru said. "All the way from here to the Rio Grande, they say, but that was before they brought the goddamned goats and sheep in." Tru always paused here to see if anyone dared defend the right of the original territorial Texans—and before that, the Mexicans—to raise whatever kind of stock it took to survive. No one ever dared, certainly not Santos.

"Goats destroyed the best of it," Tru would continue. "Filled up on grass and weeds and then wandered around shittin' all them seeds out. Eatin' and shittin', shittin' and eatin', spreading weeds all over the place. Ain't enough rain in god's kingdom to bring grass back now. Weeds suck it up first."

JD was never surprised when he saw Linc nodding agreement in the evening gloom on the porch. He had heard the same story most of his life, only from the perspective of oilpatch cattlemen as though it were some universal biblical allegory, the saga of the cowman and goatherd or sheepman conflict and all of it instilled in JD even more profoundly each Saturday morning on television. But JD found it curious that Santos always agreed, nodding the same as Linc did when Tru grumbled out the story.

"I thought all Meskins loved goats?" JD teased Santos earlier in the summer. He had wandered into the bunkhouse after lunch to get out of the midday heat and to see the rooster.

"Not Mexican, Jimmie D," Santos corrected. *"Mestizo."*

"Mestizo?"

"Si."

"What's that?"

Santos looked at him again, muscles working in his jaw. *"Mestizo,"* he repeated and that was all.

JD moved over and sat on Linc's cot, staring into Cielo's jade colored eye. "Well whatever. But you know what I mean, Santos, all that stuff about goats shittin' and eatin' and spreading weeds across this country, like Tru says," then JD attempted the teasing again, "Why do you always shake your head and agree when Tru tells about that? I thought maybe you just loved them goats?"

"Love?" Santos was stitching up a fighting gaff holder for Cielo. He held the leather across his knee, trying to fit the shiny, razor-sharp gaff into it. He did not look up. "Love is funny."

"Funny?" JD frowned.

"Well, you would say funny, Jimmie D."

"Why?"

"Because it grows only from the *corazon verdad.*"

"What?"

"The trueheart."

"Bullshit." JD saw his ruse was not working. He stood abruptly and then bent to rake his fingers across the face of the cage. "He's a pretty wore out old cock ain't he?" The rooster did not move and JD grinned at Santos. "As cocks go."

When he said this, Santos looked up and his hand slipped and the point of the gaff drove deep into the center of his palm. JD winced when he saw the instrument sticking into the old man's flesh. Reflexively, he reached over to jerk it out but Santos just looked up at him without speaking, his pupils constricting. JD paused in midreach. Santos stared down at the gaff for a long moment before he finally withdrew it slowly, allowing the wound to bleed freely.

"What's that goddamn thing for anyway?" JD said as apology and he meant both the gaff and the rooster.

"To drive into the heart," Santos whispered, but he was not talking to JD. He looked at Cielo, who turned his head to the voice of the old man. Santos went back to work on the gaff, the blood spreading a dark stain into the leather strap. "The badheart," he whispered and then repeated, "I am not Mexican. I know nothing about goats, only *gallos del combate*. And only the fighting heart."

JD turned and left without further comment. He did not know if it came from fear or respect but he had not gone back inside the bunkhouse since and Santos had not invited him.

JD glanced out the side window of the pickup now and wondered what this high desert would look like with all that grass. He tried to imagine it up to a horse's belly and thousands of goats munching away. And shitting.

Now that he was on a straight and level stretch, JD accelerated the pickup. "What do you like to drive Linc?" he said, hoping to start a conversation about something other than livestock. In his rearview mirror he watched the dust boil up and over the bed.

"Don't matter to me," Linc said. "Got my old pickup and it pulls my little old silver trailerhouse fine when I need to move on, but it don't matter. Chevy, Ford, Dodge—whatever. Hell some are using motorscooters and helicopters now to punch cattle," he snorted. "Don't matter what you drive, JD. When it all boils down at the end, all you got's your two good hands to do rangework with anyway. You can't do that from some goddamn scooter or even a pickup. That's just to get you to the work. I don't fit into that newer stuff anyway, I guess." Linc offered nothing more, his way of starting conversation that ended conversation. It occurred to JD that during the entire time he had been on the place, this was the longest unbroken string of words he had heard from Linc. He decided to press it, talking above the staccato of gravel on metal.

"Well I can tell you one thing, this rig's a piece of shit."

"Mmmmm," Linc said.

JD listened to the gravel. "Where you from anyway?"

"Denver."

"Denver?" JD had never thought of Denver as cow country.

"And Santa Fe and El Paso and Fort Worth and..." Linc said and looked straight ahead. "Any place where you can step in cowshit you might say." He was talking impassively but he was talking. JD kept silent.

Linc went on. "Or maybe any place you could get rolled hard into a pile of horseshit."

"Horseshit?"

"Yeah. I rode broncs some. When I was younger."

"Broncs?"

"Yeah. Mostly remudas on ranches, making cow horses outta pretty rank stock. But I done some arena stuff too."

"Arena?"

"Rodeo."

"Rodeo?"

"Yeah."

"Rodeo?" JD repeated, impressed.

"Yeah." Linc's voice sounded weary.

JD glanced at the back of Linc's neck. He was staring out his side window again but JD could tell he was not focused on the passing terrain. He knew Linc was not as old as Tru's sixty-two, but the wrinkles on the back of Linc's neck made him seem older. Linc would probably say saddleworn. He appeared taller than he was because he carried his thin twisting frame as though it were a taut strand of barbed wire, and he wore old fashion number five riding heels on boots that he had few reasons to slip into stirrups anymore.

But there was no doubt what Linc had done for pay his entire life. No drygoods store that JD ever entered sold the kind of outdated trousers and boots or shirts and hats that Linc wore and had repaired and wore some more. Nor could Linc acquire at any store in Lajitas or even Presidio the fragrance he left in his wake, a blend of horseshit and cowshit with a pinch of handrolled tobacco thrown in.

"Watch the road," Linc said as if he knew JD was looking at him. "One just come onto it."

"One?" JD squinted down the road to the south but he saw nothing.

"Ore truck. What'd you think I meant, buffalo?"

JD watched the road, looking for dust.

"It just dropped into the drywash ahead there." Linc pointed south now with his chin. "He'll be empty, heading back up. And in a hurry."

JD narrowed his eyes further but he could not see the truck nor even its cloud of dust yet. Linc's neck was old, not his eyes. A lifetime selecting stray steers from unbroken prairie was not the same as JD's watching Hollywood cattle stumble across a television screen.

JD finally saw the truck as it topped the crest of the road five miles south. Less than five minutes later, dual tires thwacked a fist-sized rock into the windshield right in front of JD's face, spraying a shower of glass slivers against his cheek. "Sonuva*bitch!*" JD was more surprised than angry. He forced the pickup wheels to the right, touching the looser gravel at the edge of the road. The rock did not penetrate the glass but JD's maneuver almost jerked the pickup into the ditch before he could correct it. "Sonuvabitch," he repeated as he regained the road. He slowed the pickup.

"You hurt?" Linc turned to glower through the rear window at the disappearing truck.

"Naw." JD brushed the glass from his shirt and lap with his gloved hand. He sucked in a deep breath as he accelerated again. "Just pissed. It'll give Tru one more reason to growl at me when he sees this." He touched the spot on the inside of the windshield where the impact splayed into a web of cracks.

"I think the bastard tried to run us off." Linc continued to watch the truck as though he had been thrown by a horse. "He never even slowed. It's like he never seen us."

"Maybe he didn't," JD said, a little surprised at Linc's show of indignation. "Maybe I was hogging the road. I don't know how you'd see anything inside all that dust. And I don't argue with nothing that big anyway. Forget it Linc."

"If that bastard comes on a steer at that speed— " Linc began and then caught himself. "Well. Open range just ain't meant to be drove through that fast. Not with a load of ore or a load of cattle or even empty. He'd never stop."

"It ain't open range no more, Linc, it just ain't fenced." JD managed a smile. "You're sounding like Tru."

"Well he's right." Linc looked at him as though he might have said this wrong and added, "Once in a while anyway."

"It's called progress."

"It ain't progress," Linc grumbled. "It's plain stupid. Strip mining's one thing, roaring like hell through open range is another."

"Like I said, it ain't open range," JD repeated, hoping to end it. He drove on.

When JD saw the turnoff to the old windmill, he slowed the pickup. Linc said nothing else as they snaked over two miles of rutted road west to the stocktank.

Linc noticed the cripple first. It limped and sidled at the base of the old windmill. From half a mile away, JD saw twenty or so rangy, corriente mixed steers, milling around the south end of the stocktank next to a large berm of earth dozed up for a dam. He did not notice the lone steer.

"Something's wrong," Linc observed as they approached the windmill. JD saw where Linc was looking and nodded but he said nothing.

"See him?" Linc continued. "Left leg, rear. See it?"

"Yeah."

"Flies blowing it."

JD nodded, slowing even further as he approached. He saw the swarm of flies around the bulge just above the hoof. The steer limped a short distance away, stopped and stood watching with the kind of dumb animal stare JD could never get accustomed to.

"Hoof's all mangled," Linc said. "See it?"

"Yeah." JD leaned forward with his forearms on the steering wheel. He tried to clear the dust from the windshield with his glove and then noticed Linc was already getting out of the pickup. JD joined him as they moved to the front and leaned on opposite fenders, each exchanging stares with the steer. JD listened to the ticking of the engine cooling.

"It's all the way up the leg too," he offered. "Like the hide's been scraped or something."

Linc nodded.

"What do you figure?"

Linc shrugged so JD theorized. "Maybe it stepped in a prairie dog hole or something," he said remembering the old movies.

"Wouldn't take skin off like that. Not that deep. You can see the bone."

JD could see the white flash as a swarm of blowflies raised and settled back. "Probably rocks then," he tried again. "Maybe he got it caught in a splitrock or something."

"Look around you," Linc said but he did not explain. He removed his toothpick and pointed at the rangeland. His eyes never left the steer.

JD looked. Flagstone outcroppings were much higher up and far to the west. Where they stood, JD could see ocotillo and prickly pear and an occasional pod of brown gramma grass, struggling up from soil as hard as rock, but no real rock that could house a hoof-sized fissure. "Well." He straightened, looked south. "Maybe some exposed in a drywash or something. On over."

"These steers don't graze far from water in this heat JD, even mix corrientes. You're welcome to have a look over there though." Linc lifted his shoulders and raised his chin, the toothpick in his lips indicating the top of the windmill. "Maybe you'll see something out of whack from up there." He leaned an elbow on the hood of the pickup. Between his thumb and forefinger he spun the toothpick in his mouth and regarded the steer who continued to mirror his interest.

JD pushed his hat to the back of his head and rolled his eyes up at the small wooden platform just below the circular fan of galvanized metal vanes, idle in the stillness. A narrow ladder ran up the outside of the derrick. He had already been on windmill platforms several times during the summer, greasing gearboxes and grumbling. Though he did not fear heights, it all reminded him too much of working the tower of a oilrig, and this in turn reminded him of the sweat and the oilslime stench of a roustabout crew repairing a jackpump, like the one at the base of this windmill. And all this caused him to think about other things. Things like Bettye Lee Collins.

"Go ahead," Linc said. "Just be sure and tie her down good," and JD frowned as if Linc had invaded his head. "Directional vane. Tie that out of the wind before you go up."

"There ain't no wind," JD observed. "I believe you anyway Linc. I ain't that bored. I don't need to climb all the way up there."

"Go ahead take a look around," Linc insisted. "We ain't in that big a hurry." He rolled his toothpick across his upper lip with his tongue and frowned again at the steer. JD shrugged and moved toward the windmill, deciding maybe Linc and this steer needed more time to contemplate one another as well as the whole history of the world, though the animal seemed satisfied already. It hobbled away, the raft of blowflies orbiting its leg.

At the base of the windmill, JD considered the jackpump again for a moment, remembering the reason he and Linc had come here in the first place. He tugged his gloves tighter, working his fingers to the tips of the leather like he had seen bronc riders do on television at the National Finals Rodeo. Then he pulled down the wooden axe handle, wired as a cantilever to the directional vane on the back of the fan above. The vane swung to the side, simultaneously keeping the fan out of any wind and setting its brake. With a piece of baling wire, he secured the lever against one leg of the tower then stepped away and looked up, making certain the vane was folded to the neutral position. He went back and pulled himself onto the first rung of the metal ladder and began to move up into the windmill.

At the top of the ladder he removed his hat and shoved it through the small opening and then squeezed through and scooted his butt onto the platform, testing the strength of the weathered wood. When he replaced his hat, he felt a slight breeze against its brim and wondered if it would be strong enough to swivel the windmill. He felt no wind at all at groundlevel and was glad now Linc reminded him to tie off the directional arm and set the brake. Tru had warned him too.

"Cowhands die," Tru said abruptly one evening on the porch. The sun had already set and everyone waited for someone else to be the first to leave for bed. Though Tru's sudden pronouncement about human mortality seemed amusing, no one laughed. "Just like everyone else, except harder." Linc cleared his throat but no one spoke, waiting for Tru to finish. "More cowhands die falling off windmills than off horses though. Most of them bumped right over the edge on account of being stupid and not tying off the vane and the brake. There's always a little maverick gust of wind just waiting for a stupid cowhand."

JD turned and checked the position of the directional arm now just to be certain. Then with the kind of bravado he knew would have pleased Bettye Lee, and maybe even Tru himself, he leaned against the vanes, avoiding the greasy gearbox. He relaxed a little and smiled at himself. The windmill could not face into the wind now even if a renegade gust did spike up off of the desert.

"My momma ain't raised no stupid cowpoke," he mused, and then the grin disappeared from his face. "Get right down to it my momma never got to raise nothing..." He glanced over the edge and watched Linc, who had eased away from the pickup and was stalking the steer for a closer look at what Linc must have viewed as several hundred pounds of unfinished beef, still on the hoof. "Ain't but three good hooves now Linc," he whispered, aware Linc could not hear him. "One's flyblown. You oughta be able to grab him and throw him easy and have a closer look. You got both your good working hands, right?"

JD looked around. Up here without the grease gun or wrenches or someone yelling instructions from below, he decided it was not at all like an oil derrick. No diesel engines screamed urgent choruses from below, no fifty foot joints of drill casing jerked and hammered around inside the tower like steel birds in a steel cage. This was clean and quiet and peaceful.

But this time JD had no sudden memories about laying four inch pipeline or about weevil drillers or drill casing teetering like death just above his hardhat. He had no thoughts at all about the oilpatch or Bettye Lee either. There was no sound in his head except the murmur of mild protests, which wafted on the breeze from the other steers, curious about the presence of Linc. JD allowed his mind to go out of focus as he gazed over the high desert rangeland, listening to the light rush of air in his ears and to his own breathing.

"See anything over there?" Linc returned to the base of the windmill, a five gallon can of diesel fuel in his hand. JD leaned over the edge of the platform and spoke down to him.

"I don't see nothing. Just empty rangeland that rolls right off the edge of the earth or maybe all the way south and into the Rio Grande. Old Santos came up that way, right?"

"Yeah. Picked him up right out there anyway. He wasn't there and then he was there," Linc said. He lifted his hat and scratched his head and continued, "And then he wasn't there again. Damndest thing. I never really locked in on him good till I climbed up there and looked around a little."

"You did this too?" JD was amused.

"Sure. Clears a man's head sometimes up there above it all. It's what you're doing ain't it?"

JD did not answer.

"He said he lived off there in the distance," Linc went on. "Said he crossed the river but not on that hired row-boat from Paso Lajitas on the Mexican side."

"Then how?"

"You ever hear the word *wetback?"*

"Yeah. But he ain't even Meskin," JD offered but he did not elaborate.

"Well, I never heard nothing about any other place over there very close." Linc said. "He might'a walked up from San Carlos but that's a good twenty miles south of the river. Or it could'a been La Perla, I guess..."

"How far's the river from here?"

"Maybe twenty-five mile."

"How far's La Perla south of that?"

"Probably eighty."

"Bullshit. He didn't walk no eighty miles across that desert. No way."

"Maybe."

"In them huaraches with that cage balanced on his head?"

"Maybe."

"And no water?"

"Just from the river. And maybe barrel cactus. Then he saw this windmill and headed toward it."

"Why didn't he just walk up the ranch road when he crossed over?" JD said. "Why come out through all that cactus and brush?"

"Sendero de Vidrio..." Linc explained. "Didn't you hear him tell Tru he was following that?"

"Yeah. But he never said what it meant. You know?"

"Yep."

"Well shit, what's it mean?"

"Means Trail of Glass. Broken glass."

"Broken glass?"

"Yep. That's the old story anyway. During prohibition, Mexican bootleggers came across the Rio Grande with burros loaded down with bottles of whiskey and tequila. Over the years, some slipped off as they traveled, left a trail of broken glass across the toughest part of this country."

"Yeah right," JD said, skeptical of the story. "Or maybe he just wanted to avoid the Border Patrol. Maybe it's a trail of drugs now."

"Maybe," Linc shrugged. "Seems like our neighbors across the border always know what us gringos want. And how to supply it. Can't really blame them, I suppose. No demand, no supply, right?"

"Yeah," JD said. "I guess. But my own favorite comes in a long neck bottle, made in the good old U.S.of A."

Linc grinned, "Mine too. Or maybe comes in a short skirt. And them's best found south of the Rio Grande in my opinion. I just ain't patriotic that way."

JD knew all about this too. He did not respond to Linc. He could not imagine Linc with a woman, even a Mexican whore. He thought again about Bettye Lee.

"Anyway, you seen his feet, right JD?" Linc continued. "Ain't no cactus out there could cut through leather huaraches like that."

JD made no comment. He pulled his hat further down over his eyes and squinted across the desert, searching for flashes of glass. Linc looked up and saw him scanning the landscape.

"I ain't ever found it," Linc said. "Ain't never heard of anybody else who has. You won't either."

"Why?"

Linc said nothing.

"Badheart, goodheart," JD muttered and then louder, "What do you really think of him?"

"Which one, the old man or the old cock?"

"Santos. I mean all that wild story?"

"Why shouldn't I believe it?"

"He's too old, ain't he?" JD said.

"Dunno."

"How old?"

"Shit I dunno that either, JD. *Old.*"

JD fell silent, staring into the heat that wrinkled the rangeland. After a while he said, "Them roosters fight each other till one's dead, don't they? I ain't ever seen nothing fight till it's dead." He paused, remembering the Fighting Blink Bobcats and four consecutive losing seasons. "Crazy if you ask me. Walking on glass, fighting till your dead." He paused and spat out over the edge of the platform, careful to miss Linc. "Ain't you ever seen a cockfight Linc?"

Linc moved to the jackpump under the platform out of JD's sight. "Get on down here," he said, as if he had talked too much already. "Let's get this damn thing going."

JD edged back across the platform and through the access hole and down the ladder. When he reached the ground, Linc had already emptied the can of fuel into the reservoir atop the engine and removed the plug in the fuel pump to bleed air from the line. "You ever work around one of these engines?" Linc said.

"Course I have." JD thought about the huge diesels and the Louisiana weevil with his hand on the throttle and the drill casing threating his eggshell head. "Once. Never fiddled with them though, just worked around them on oilrigs. Bigger ones."

"Well this ain't no oilrig," Linc said and blinked. "But it's the same idea. Difference is, this one pumps water. Only oil around here's on this dipstick or better be if Tru drops by and lifts it out."

"Where'd you learn diesels?" JD said.

"Permian Basin."

"You? Not an oilpatch ranch?" JD grinned.

"Yep, riding the oilpatch range. I spent more damn time starting jackpumps on oilwells than working cattle. Like I said, there ain't too many kinds of cowshit I ain't stepped in, even grainfed oil cattle."

"You never told me you worked the basin."

"I said El Paso. I meant east of there. Way east, but that's close enough."

"Hell Linc, we're practically kinfolk."

"Yeah right. Here, hold this," Linc handed JD the bleed plug from the fuel pump. He stood and put his foot on one of the spokes of the big flywheel and pushed down on it, spinning the engine just enough to work air out of the fuel line. When he saw fuel spurt out, Linc took the plug and quickly replaced it in the fuel pump.

"Always bleed off air first," he instructed. "Especially if she's run herself dry of fuel." He glanced at JD who seemed puzzled. "Tru always lets them run dry. He keeps better track of fuel that way for the IRS I guess."

Linc wiped his hands on his jeans, set the throttle and then gave another shove with his foot on the flywheel, this time a quick kick. The wheel spun the engine through a few half hearted pops and coughs and then it stopped.

"She's a little stubborn sometimes," Linc said. "Especially if she's been run dry."

"I thought she's always run dry?" JD teased.

Linc ignored him. He looked up into the tower, checking the direction of the vanes. "Always make sure the windmill's tied off out of the wind, otherwise you're working against it see. That is if a wind happens to come up and unless there's wind, it's the pump you want to do the work."

"It's tied off, Linc," JD said, wondering if Linc thought he was stupid enough to be up there without tying off the directional vane. Linc kicked the flywheel again. This time the engine sputtered and coughed out puffs of black smoke which turned to light gray when it caught and then popped to a start. Without a muffler, the sudden noise from the one lunger brought the group of steers to abrupt alert. It was almost too noisy to talk. Linc leaned over and yelled into JD's ear. "Make sure she's going good before you engage the clutch."

Linc paused a few moments, listening to the engine before he eased forward the lever on the clutch, which in turn engaged the drive belts. The belts smoked and squealed but then grabbed the drive wheel which began to move the counter-balanced weights. The head of the pump cocked back and then dipped forward like a giant bird feeding itself to the squeal of the sucker rods. Water soon spurted from a length of pipe to the small holding tank. From there the water would overflow into a rut and then into the earthen stock-tank.

To JD the sight and the rhythmic sound of the jackpump were

familiar and hypnotic. If nothing today had yet transposed him to the oilpatch, this did. In some strange and even nostalgic way, JD relived that same sound outside the open window of his dad's old sedan on that night when he and Bettye Lee parked on the isolated gravel pad next to the Dickeybird until well past midnight, that one warm spring night no more than two months ago when Bettye Lee determined by some magical feminine calculation that it was JD got her pregnant and not somebody else.

"Bullshit," he said. "It ain't even mine. It can't be...I don't think."

Linc did not hear him above the noise. "Well, that's all there is to it," Linc yelled, once more leaning over to talk above the engine. He noticed JD was not with him. "Don't worry. Nobody'll ever know."

"Know what?" JD croaked and felt his face flush.

"Know I taught you."

"*Caught* me?" JD was suddenly back with him in the noise of the engine.

"*Taught* you, goddammit," Linc was yelling now as he exposed his teeth holding the toothpick, pointing at the engine. "Taught you how to *start* it. Shit, let's just feed them and get the hell out of here." Linc pumped a thumb toward the road.

JD moved to the pickup and backed up to the feed troughs next to the windmill. He began pulling the burlap bags of mixed feed off the tailgate. Linc stood aside, studying the steers as they braved the noise and crowded around the feed troughs. The injured steer stood alone at the edge of the others, unable to nudge his way closer. Linc noted this, tugged at the brim of his hat and returned and sat in the passenger side of the pickup. JD finished dumping the feed and moved away from the trough. The cattle moved forward and went at the feed, ignoring the injured steer. It reminded JD of the kittens, made him wonder where the tom had disappeared that morning.

"Shit," he muttered again and he was feeling pretty bad when he got back inside the pickup, but he did not know if it was because of the cat or the steer or something else. He was damn certain it was not Bettye Lee. No way.

He took off his hat and allowed a sudden hot breeze from the open window to whip his hair, drying the sweat. Linc said nothing as they left the noise of the jackpump. They moved back out on the main gravel road and then north toward the ranch house and after awhile, JD looked across at Linc who was rolling his toothpick from one side to the other, agitated.

"Well?" JD said.

Linc shrugged. JD answered himself, "Probably need a stock trailer, haul him back up, put him in the barn, maybe get a vet out here to look at the leg." He glanced again at Linc to see if it all sounded enough like cowtalk. Linc kept silent but he stopped rolling the toothpick. He sat staring out the windshield, blinking. JD decided he must be thinking about Tru and how he would take all this. One injured steer out of five hundred should not cause concern but this one was not cancer eye or bloat or scours. This was a little different.

"Probably one of them damned ore trucks wasn't it?" JD offered. "Dumb bastard wandered back over here onto the road didn't he?"

Linc nodded.

"Tru'll shit won't he?"

Linc nodded again and then JD fell silent too. For a long while he shifted his attention from the rearview mirror to the road ahead and back again, but no pinpoint of dust appeared on either horizon. As he turned into the lane leading to the ranch house, JD saw Santos tugging on the barbed wire. JD allowed the pickup to roll to a stop next to the barn.

"What's all this?" JD said.

Linc shrugged, watched the old man.

"We gonna build barbed wire fences now?" JD moaned and shut off the pickup and both got out. "With that rusted shit?"

Linc stood for a moment watching Santos, then shrugged again and said nothing. He turned to walk away.

"Well?" JD said across the top of the pickup.

"Well what?" Linc snapped. "Course we will if that's what he says."

"I don't mean that, I don't mean fences."

"Then what?" Linc stopped, glared at JD.

"You never answered me before. You ever seen one?"

"Geezuschrist JD, seen what?"

"One of them fights? To the death?"

"Hell no," Linc shot back. "They ain't legal either. Not on this side."

"This side?"

"Of that big river you couldn't see down there."

FIVE

Hill Garza halfstood behind his mahogany desk. "I ever show you them old leather bags, Truman?" He reached across and opened the humidor, carved from the same wood as the desk, and then he shoved it toward Tru who shook his head. Hill fingered out a cigar, bit off the end and then pinched the sprig of tobacco from the tip of his tongue and dropped this into a silver ashtray.

Tru sat with his back stiff, his good hat on. He looked out the window and down the single empty street through Lajitas and he remembered. "Your old man showed 'em to me."

There was a time Tru would have not only taken a cigar but a half glass of good bourbon, both offered right here in the bank after a handshake loan of whatever Tru needed from T. Jefferson Garza. And he always removed his hat when he entered T. Jefferson's office. "He'd talk about them, tell the story." Tru thought about the whiskey and how the glass always seemed half full with T. Jefferson instead of half empty, as it would now seem if Hill offered whiskey. Hill never did. "Once in a while, he'd tell about it."

"Well the old man could tell it better than me anyway but you know how the story went, Truman, them never finding that silver ore, just the old man's bank bags full of nothing." Hill stood and walked toward the vault but then turned back. "You sure? Got 'em right here in the vault, sort of collector's items now I guess. Robbed this very bank, right here in Lajitas. Stomped in, stuck about twenty rifles right in the old man's face and didn't say a word. Course he knew what they wanted, so he never argued. He just set them heavy bags on the counter and the whole group left on horses and then robbed the general store on over at Glenn Springs and shot that trooper. Pissed old Major Langhorne off big time. He chased them all the way back to Boquillas Crossing."

Hill went to a large framed map on the paneled wall and stabbed a finger at it. "Right here. Right here's where they found the empties. Never found a single goddamn ounce of silver, or so the old man said. Course the government took care of the loss so our family didn't..."

"Yeah, so he said."

"Well, he tell you this? He tell you how old Langhorne didn't stop? He tell you about that ballsy old Major riding right across the damn river, right here?" Hill traced the invisible route on the old map. "People know about Pershing chasing Villa across from Columbus, New Mexico and all that, they say that's the only time U.S. troops invaded Old Mexico. But they don't know about this other invasion. Some say it was Zapata right here or maybe even Villa himself. Anyway, Langhorne followed them all the way down to..." He moved closer and squinted at the map. "Now where the hell was it?"

"Yeah, Hill, he talked about it several times. Now I wonder if maybe we could..."

"Yessir," Hill nodded. He moved to the window and looked down the street. "History's walked these old streets. Course, it's all just bullshit now." He turned back to Tru and buried one hand in a pocket and with the other rolled the cigar in his lips and spoke around it. "I mean, it did happen and all, but it's just so much bullshit today. Know what I mean, Truman?"

"About that loan, Hill..."

Hill went back behind his desk. "Well now about that, Truman." He sucked the cigar, sending curls of blue smoke coiling about his head. "I been thinking about it and talking about it. Looks like we'll need some kind of collateral. Something..."

"Collateral?"

"Well you know, something to take back to my directors over in Presidio. It ain't just us Garza's anymore, you know that Truman. Take something in to satisfy them that you'll be able to—"

"Be able to what? I ain't never needed nothing but a handshake from your father, Hill. Or even from you when you first took over. Why now?"

"Well times are different, Truman. You know how it is. New board of directors that don't even live here, don't know you and you don't know them. And they're certainly not cattlemen, they're not that—"

Hill stopped abruptly, averted his eyes. Tru finished for him, "Not that stupid? Is that what you mean, Hill?"

"I didn't mean it that way, Tru. Let's just say they got other interests that don't include cattle ranching."

"You're putting me off, Hill. Last time you said come on in, we'd talk, said you'd take it to your board first, said—"

"I know, Truman, I know. And I did. But that's how it is."

Tru narrowed his eyes at the younger man. Hill looked back at him and smiled around the cigar, but he did not blink. He removed the cigar and carefully rolled a layer of ash away into the tray. "What was it you said you were building again, Truman? A new barn or what?"

They both knew what the money was for. Truman tightened his jaw and thought about how Hill's directors would laugh at miles of fencing along a gravel road as collateral, even new barbed wire. He got up. When he reached the door Hill spoke.

"Truman..."

Tru turned and locked his eyes on Hill, searching for something to indicate Hill might be joking.

"Stop by again sometime. And say howdy to Jesse, okay?" Hill said, ending it.

"Yeah, right. Maybe you could show me them empty bags." He slapped his gloves against his thigh and went through the door, leaving it open.

Hill stared after him for a long while then got up and closed the door. He went back and stood looking at the old map showing the Big Bend country before it was a National Park, the surrounding terrain with shaded areas indicating old land grants and Texas territorial lands, but few private property boundaries. With his finger, Hill traced the parameter of the original old Pierce ranch from the south end to the north and then paused, tapped the glass where Tru's father had sold that part of his land for the original Chisos Cinnabar Company's mineshaft. Until its recent secretive reopening as an open pit venture abutting Tru's remaining property, it had lain inactive for decades.

He smiled. "Collateral's where you find it, Tru," he whispered and puffed on the cigar. "And cinnabar's working just fine for these directors," he mused. "And just maybe there's more, right over here on your side too, *Señor* Fredrick Truman Pierce?" He said cynically.

SIX

"Ask Tru." Jesse stood over the wooden ice cream churn on the countertop. She tipped the mixing bowl and dribbled the last of the fresh cream and sugar and strawberries and eggs into the mouth of the metal canister. She spoke without looking up at JD, who leaned against the kitchen door watching her. "I don't know anything about it." She fit the dasher inside the can and attached the churn handle to the top of the freezer and turned around

"I know nothing about fences." She looked straight at him without blinking. "I just cook here, right?"

"Hell nobody knows nothing about nothing around here," he said. JD rarely saw Jesse's eyes lock on him. They said Jesse knew everything there was to know about fences. And anything else happening on the ranch.

"Ice is in the fridge," she said, like a mother scolding. She turned back to the stove. "Rock salt's right here on the countertop."

JD hesitated. Jesse turned back and looked at him again until he dropped his eyes. "You act like you don't know about all this, JD." He guessed she was talking about ice cream or something else and not fences or trails of broken glass or cockfights to the death. "Have you always done that?"

"Done what?" He looked up.

"Act like you don't know...*things?"* she said and their eyes held for too long, neither blinking, until Jesse was the one who looked away this time. "Weekend's coming up or did you forget that too?" she said quickly.

He might have selective memory on some things less immediate, but JD remembered that. And he remembered there was no such thing as a weekend for a cowhand. Without asking, he would have known today was Friday. He just felt like asking.

Tru always had hand-churned ice cream on Friday, served right after supper on the covered flagstone patio. When Jesse could get them, fresh strawberry in the summer and according to Jesse, frozen strawberry in the winter, sometimes served around the hearth of the massive adobe fireplace in the living room. JD decided to add ice cream churning to the growing list of bullshit chores to which he had been assigned. He did not know who took care of it in the winter but just like Bettye Lee, he knew it would not be him this winter.

"Don't turn it so long this time JD," Jesse went on. "Maybe not so much salt on the ice. Tru doesn't like it so hard. He said the strawberries were like marbles last time."

JD knew this too. Tru was not bashful about expressing opinion, especially concerning Friday night strawberry ice cream. JD considered pressing his original question about fencing but he knew Jesse was done with it. He would have to catch Tru at the right moment, maybe while he was in a good mood, having his ice cream. One thing JD did know for certain: Tru hated fences.

He lifted the churn from the countertop and set in on the floor beside the fridge. He knelt with it between his knees and began layering the cracked ice with salt around the metal canister, amused at the irony of salt so close to sweetness.

JD looked up at the back of Jesse's head as he tamped the ice. He tried to picture her in some other pose. Aside from seeing her reaching up at the clothesline out back or in the shadows of dusk on the front porch, any image of Jesse away from her kitchen stove seemed foreign. It seemed Jesse sometimes wanted to present no face at all.

Still, he knew this face. Somehow JD had held this face engrained in his mind all these years, like some recurring dream, like his mother and yet not his mother, slightly out of focus but nonetheless there. And though she feigned it, JD knew Jesse was not a hard woman. Her face showed attempts at hardness, but as far as

JD was concerned, that only highlighted an indisputable softness. Like rock salt, packed close to such sweetness he thought. Jesse seemed that way.

JD watched her reach to the top shelf of the cupboard, her shirt pulled tight, exposing flesh at the waist, and her jeans stretched. For a moment, JD could not take his eyes off her. Then a wave of embarrassment flooded him and he flushed and turned his eyes as if Jesse had stared him down again.

He finished packing the ice and salt inside the churn. Then he stood and carried it out the kitchen door with a dish towel over his shoulder, remembering not to churn the ice cream in Jesse's kitchen sink. She complained it was too noisy there.

"And don't do it on my grass, either," Jesse called, but it was more a plea this time than an order.

"Do what on your grass Jesse?" JD teased. He moved back to the kitchen window screen. He put his nose against the screen just as Jesse did at her back door each morning.

"You know what I mean JD," Jesse spoke low. "Boy you're getting cocky for a hired hand."

"Me and old gaucheye," he said. "Both cocky, I guess."

"Just take it outside the fence, okay?" He nodded and walked away.

He had learned this lesson the hard way. The first time he made Tru's ice cream, he sat on Jesse's grass in the shade of a cottonwood tree which grew against the fence. The slow rattle of ice against the canister was hypnotic as he turned the handle, ignorant of the salt water trickling out of the hole in the side of the wooden churn and onto the grass. A month later now, the patch of grass over which he had set the churn remained a dead circle. Even though Tru said nothing about it, the absence of color at that spot in Jesse's struggling lawn was a daily reminder to JD. Tru did not make it any easier, mentioning often the time-worn term, greenhorn, as though JD had sucked up the color himself.

JD went through the gate and set the churn on the wooden bench in the shade of a cottonwood, just outside the fence where Jesse aired her flower pots each morning. No chance of killing grass here. He only had to worry about spilling saltwater into Jesse's flowers. The cottonwood got away with spilling its shade equally on Jesse's lawn and Jesse's flowers.

He threw his leg over the bench and covered the top of the churn with the towel. Then he began turning the crank slow and methodical so as not to freeze the berries inside. He watched Santos, still struggling with the stubborn coils of barbed wire that would not stay flat, and he wondered why the old man wanted it flat anyway. "Shit. He'll just have to coil it right back up. It's a cinch Tru's not putting any fence right there in the damn yard."

The ice cream was just firming when Tru drove up, not slowing until he got next to the barn. Then braked hard, gravel bunching under the tires.

By the time the dust cleared, JD saw Tru already standing inside the open door of the barn, talking to Linc, probably telling him about the ore truck and the steer. Tru's cursing spiked above the rattle of the churn. Linc held his arms folded across his chest and studied the ground. Tru gestured wildly, smacking a fist into his palm as he spoke. Finally he stalked away from the barn and stomped past without looking and JD knew he had guessed right. He did not know what else was fuming Tru. Maybe the old horse. If so, it would not be a good time to question the logic of barbed wire fences, no matter how much Tru hated them. JD turned his attention back to the churning. Not a good time to freeze strawberries either.

After supper JD took a cardboard box filled with grass clippings and a bucket of water up to Chisos. The old horse raised his head and looked up when JD got out of the pickup but then dropped it back down onto the hard ground. JD noticed the untouched clippings he had brought up last evening. He knelt and held up the old horse's head with his knee and forced his nose down into the bucket but like yesterday, Chisos refused water. He dumped the clippings out in a mound next to the horse's head and set the bucket down on the other side. JD knew he would try for neither. Flies were already settling back inside Chisos' nose when JD started the pickup and went back down the hill.

That evening on the patio, JD sat leaning against the house. Jesse sat in the porch swing. Tru dragged out his ancient oak rocker, complaining as he did this, cursing the rough flagstone. "Ain't level enough to rock good on," he said. "Probably quarried by some idiot like them up there at that damn mine."

No one reminded Tru that is was cinnabar they were digging, not flagstone. Jesse had set the ice cream freezer between her and Tru so she could serve everyone easier in her matched Mexican pottery bowls. Linc and Santos sat on the opposite side of JD in straight backed oak chairs that Jesse brought out for them. As usual, Linc never showed unless Jesse walked over to the bunkhouse and insisted. Even then, he came in a workshirt. Linc always ate a single bowl and refused refills. But Santos always wore his just-washed muslin shirt on Friday evenings and brought the sweet tooth he saved up all week. Santos needed no invitation but he waited patiently in the bunkhouse for it anyway, standing watch at the window in his fresh shirt not quite dry. When he saw Jesse coming across the yard, he whispered to Cielo who rustled with the same anticipation as though he too had been invited.

Jesse always kept Santos' bowl filled until he shook his head and said *Bastante!* at which time Tru had now begun to insist she give him one more scoop anyway. JD did not know why Tru had become suddenly generous toward the old man. But he would not ask.

JD teased the last strawberry from his bowl of ice cream and rolled it around his tongue. It was a poor substitute for a Friday night spent rolling Bettye Lee's tongue around. He reminded himself he would never see her again. Probably. He bit hard into the tartness of the berry, chewed it quickly and swallowed.

Jesse liked Friday evenings on the patio. As it darkened, Tru usually settled into his quiet monologue about the old days as though everyone gathered expressly for this. But there was rarely any dialogue and nothing broke the silences between Tru's tales except the scraping of spoons on the bottom of bowls and the uneven rocking of Tru's chair. Later as darkness settled over their faces, Millie could be heard lowing in the corral behind the barn. When sporadic conversation did come, it usually ended quickly with a nod or single syllables as everyone agreed with some observation Tru made about weather or beef prices or politics.

On this Friday evening, Tru said nothing at all. Everyone finished the ice cream without comment. Dusk became darkness and

Tru still made no attempt at either anecdotal or rangeland philosophy. Linc finally cleared his throat and muttered *Thanks* and then rose quickly and left. And then Santos whispered his *Bastante!* and Jesse stood holding his bowl, waiting for Tru to insist on one more scoop for the old man. When that did not come either, she turned away from Santos and began nesting the bowls and spoons and then carried them back into the kitchen. JD was aware that Santos too was gone, though he had not heard the old man leave. He was half standing himself when Tru finally spoke.

"How's he doing?" Tru's voice shot through the darkness like a spark across a gap and JD sat back down on the flagstone as if disciplined.

"Not too good I guess," JD offered.

"He eat anything?"

"No," JD said. "Not this evening."

"Yesterday?"

JD paused for a moment and then said no.

"Water?"

"About the same I guess."

"Which is?"

"None. I wet his muzzle though..."

Except for Tru sucking his teeth, there was a long silence and JD wondered if that meant he should leave. He sat still anyway, waiting. Candlemoths thumped on the window screen, trying to get inside to the bare lightbulb above Jesse's sink. Light spilled through the window and JD could see Jesse's silhouette occasionally flit across the distorted rectangle of orange on the flagstone.

"Ever notice how it can cloud up and rain on one little corner of this place and nowhere else?" Tru's voice was dreamlike and the tone caught JD off guard for a moment, but then he admitted he had noticed.

"Never understood it," Tru went on. "Like it picks and chooses what it wants wet. It's like a stream of sunlight too, you seen how it'll poke through that same damn cloudbank, even when it's raining, like it's just picking out what it wants lit up? You seen that ain't you, JD? How it'll pick out one lone butte and nothing else?"

"Yeah I seen that too," JD lied. He had given neither rain nor sunlight this much attention, but like Jesse's distaste for sunrises, he could see nothing wrong about all this either. JD shrugged and tried to sound serious, mature, "Little bit of rain, I guess. Little bit of light."

"This place ain't that big, JD, not for what's left of native grasses. Just ain't that big any more. If it's gonna rain it oughta rain on the whole goddamn place. All at once."

JD sat silent.

"Overgrazed, that's what's done it. Goats and sheep. They changed the weather from the old days," Tru said, ending it.

There was another long pause and JD decided that was all for the evening, though Tru usually droned on and on about overgrazed high desert. JD considered the milkcow and five a.m., having a little trouble understanding how goats could change rain and sunlight both. He yawned and stretched.

"She says you asked about the fence?" Tru said, that sudden spark across the darkness again.

JD nodded but he realized again Tru could not see him. "Just curious," he apologized. He sat waiting, listening to Tru's rocking chair across the uneven flagstones. Tru owed him no explanation.

Tru kept rocking and his voice turned bitter, "Linc's right about that steer. He probably wandered over onto the road and one of them trucks hit him sure."

"That's what I figure, too."

"Never even slowed or had the decency to stop by and tell us or nothing. That'd never happened in the old days. Somebody'd find a dead steer or one in trouble, why they'd help it or stop by for chrissake. Even if they'd caused it somehow, they'd stop by. Unless they was thieves or something."

JD nodded again and once more made a move to leave but Tru was not finished. "Hate fences, always have. Goddamn barbed wire cuts up everything, cattle, horseflesh, men. Everything." He cleared his throat and JD nodded again, though he knew Tru could not see this. "I guess a wire-cut steer's better than a dead one though," he sighed, but he said this with utter determination. "And that's why the fence."

Melting ice had run out of the hole in the side of the wooden bucket, puddled on the flagstone and seeped under JD's butt, soaking his jeans. He rose and patted his wet rearend.

"I better get this off the patio. Salt water won't do Jesse's grass no good if runs off the edge." He grabbed the handle of the freezer, sloshing some of the cold saltwater onto his pant leg. "G'night."

JD crossed through the light of the window and moved toward the kitchen door but then stopped and turned back before he rounded the corner. "Can I ask what we're fencing?"

"That road."

"The road?"

"Yeah. All of it."

"Both sides?" JD said, unable to leave it.

Tru remained silent and since JD could not see his face, he waited a few minutes longer, the handle of the ice cream freezer cutting into his palm like barbed wire.

"Every damn mile of it," Tru said evenly and then, "Both sides."

JD turned the corner of the house and paused at the back door to the kitchen. Tru cleared his throat but said nothing more.

"Bullshit," JD whispered as he entered the kitchen.

"Say what?" Jesse was drying bowls with a cup towel.

"I said where should I *sit* this?"

She looked at him and then nodded at the countertop. He set down the freezer and stood for a moment looking back at her. Through the open window he could hear Tru plainly as he cleared his throat and JD realized Jesse had heard everything.

SEVEN

The familiar scratching on a door screen awakened JD. He groaned and rolled over and then realized he had not heard Jesse rattle the milkpail on the countertop. He sat in his cot and blinked into the darkness. The sound was far too early. And it was from his own door, not Jesse's kitchen.

The noise stopped suddenly, followed by a deep throated gurgling. He held his breath for a moment, listening. When he heard nothing else, he lay back. An hour later, he slept again but woke several times during the night, not because he heard the sounds again, but because he did not.

He was up long before Jesse. He dressed in the darkness, the butt of his jeans still wet from the saltwater. When he tried his screen door, he could not open it. He shoved it hard and the door opened reluctantly. He could not see what he had swept aside, so he went back for his flashlight. At first, he feared what he might find, so he did not switch the light on. Instead, with the toe of his boot he gently nudged the object, then stepped back behind the screen door, hoping whatever was there might spring up and escape. But there was no movement, no sound. He snapped on the flashlight.

The yellow tom lay rigid, his claws locked open. The eyes were glazed, the cat's teeth glaring in the light in a grotesque death smile.

"Shit," JD whispered. He shut off the light and walked across the yard on the grass so his steps would not be heard. He eased the iron gate open and went out to the grain room then returned to the storage shed with an empty gunnysack. He clicked on the flashlight and touched the tom with the toe of his boot again, hoping the animal might move and he could reach down and pet it or take it with him as he milked Millie. Maybe even give the tom half the warm milk this morning or all of it if he wanted. But the tom did not move.

JD reached down to grasp the tail and then stopped. He shut off the flashlight and went back into the shed and put on his work gloves. When he returned to the carcass, he lifted it by the tail and quickly dropped it into the sack. Then he walked out to the old pickup and tied the top of the sack with a piece of baling wire and stuffed it in the bed of the truck behind the spare tire.

"Shit," he whispered again and then walked back toward the shed. Halfway across Jesse's lawn he stopped and hunkered down onto the grass and for a long while, he sat staring into the darkness toward the pickup. Finally, he jerked off his gloves and slapped them against his thigh. When he turned around he saw the light on in Jesse's kitchen. From the middle of her front yard he heard her rattle the milkpail against the countertop.

By the time JD finished milking and returned to the kitchen, Tru was already seated at the table.

"Linc and me'll feed this morning," Tru said before he had even started eating. "You take a look at old Chisos."

Tru hardly touched his oatmeal. JD ate only one bite from his own before he stood up and took the bowl to the sink, ignoring Jesse's glare when she saw the bowl full. He stopped at the back door. "Should I take some water?"

Tru looked up at him and blinked a few times then turned and stared out the window into the gray of the morning. "Feels like it might rain," he said and then fell silent.

JD figured that meant no, so he walked out the door and went straight to the pickup. He reached behind the spare tire and touched the gunnysack, then he got inside and cranked over the engine. Before he could leave the yard Linc walked out of the bunkhouse and waved him down. JD stopped and rolled down his window.

"Probably oughta take a shovel," Linc said as though he knew right where JD was going. "And a pickaxe."

"Why?"

"Cause if he's dead that's what you'll need."

JD jerked his head and glanced through the back window at the gunnysack, stuffed behind the spare tire. "Dead?" he said and guilt flushed his face.

"You don't think Tru would send you up there this early if he thought he was still alive."

JD shook his head.

"And if you come back down here asking Tru what you oughta do next, you don't think he's gonna say let them buzzards eat him do you?"

"You mean *bury* him?"

Linc stared at him.

"But that's goddamned hard ground up there Linc. Hell, some of it's solid rock. How do you expect me to bury a horse in solid rock?"

"That's why you'll need the pickaxe." He turned and walked away. JD sat listening to the idling of the engine. For a moment he wondered if Linc had been joking, but like Tru, Linc did not joke, especially when it came to things like livestock and barbed wire fences and horses, alive or dead.

He got out of the pickup and went into the barn for the tools. He tossed them into the bed and then chugged up the hill. At the crest, he stopped the truck and stared at the lump of sun showing in the east. He had to lean to one side to avoid looking through the web of cracked glass, segmenting the sun, and he thought about the ore truck. Surely Linc told Tru about the broken windshield but Tru did not mention it at breakfast. JD sat for a long while, postponing his approach to the humped silhouette of the horse at the top of the hill. He wanted to wait until it was full light.

"Got all day," he whispered, and then thought about digging through hardpan in the heat of the day. "But then there ain't no use killing myself. If he's dead, I oughta start digging while it's cool and if he ain't dead, I can just get the hell outta here."

He was dead.

JD knew it when he shut off the engine and coasted to a stop. He watched the old horse to see if he would raise his head or even flick an ear, but there was no movement. He did not go over to check but pulled the shovel and pickaxe from the back of the truck and walked around and started whacking at the hardpan right next to the carcass. He knew he could not roll the horse, even this close. He would have to chain one leg to the bumper of the truck and drag it over into whatever hole he could manage.

The sun was already high enough to encourage the flies when JD stopped digging and sat resting on the small mound of rocky earth. He took off his hat and wiped his hatband and flicked the sweat into the hole.

"Wonder how deep he'd want him…" he grumbled. He looked toward the pickup and thought about the gunnysack and the yellow tom. "I never promised nobody I'd dig it deep. Not in this damn heat."

He tossed the shovel into the shallow hole and stepped down into the grave to measure against his height. "Just deep enough to cover the carcass that's all. If Tru want's it deeper, he can dig it himself."

He glanced back at the pickup. "Deep enough to cover both of them, that's all." He picked up the shovel and slammed the point of the tool against the bottom of the hole and sparks shot out from the impact of steel on rock. He scratched out a half shovelful of dirt and tossed it onto the tiny pile of earth. "Shit," he said as he evaluated the size of the hole, barely large enough to cover the yellow tom, even though he had worked for two hours.

It was lunch time when he took the gunnysack from behind the spare tire and tossed it first into the dished out indentation he had managed to chip into the earth. Then he chained one stiff leg of the dead horse to the back bumper of the pickup and dragged the carcass into the hole. Next he filled the bed with flat rocks which he piled over the carcasses and then shoveled the loose dirt on top of all this. JD's shirt was soaked when he finally drove down the hill and parked the truck. Santos was again in the front driveway, sorting the old barbed wire. He struggled with another strand that he had attached to the barn.

"Time for lunch," JD said. He paused in front of Santos. "Better stop and make a burrito."

"Si," Santos said. "With Cielo." He sighed and released the

wire. It sprung back into its original coils across the hardpan. He lifted his hat and wiped his forehead on his sleeve.

"What's all this old rusted stuff for anyway?" JD said.

"For the fence," Santos explained as if JD should know.

"Tru's fence?"

"Si."

"Hell, this stuff ain't even good enough to hold them rangy steers."

"It has strong memory," Santos said, apologizing for the wire. "It has forgotten it was once a fence. It likes the way it has been for too many years, *verdad?"*

Santos walked away toward the bunkhouse for something to eat. JD took off his shirt and hung it on the fence to dry and then went in through the back door of the kitchen. He had already gulped down two glasses of cool water when he heard the music. He knew it was not Tru's radio. As he listened, he realized the sound was a musicbox, tinkling from Jesse's bedroom. JD blinked away a sudden and paradoxical sense of fear and peace, a sound both alien and familiar. The music finally wound down and he heard the clicking of tiny gears and then music again, repeated over and over until he cleared his throat and shifted his feet on the tiled floor. The music stopped and then Jesse was in the doorway. He set the glass on the countertop and took off his hat, suddenly aware he was also bare chested inside Jesse's kitchen.

"Sorry," he said and started for the door. "I'll get my shirt and wash up."

"It's okay, JD. Sit and cool off. I'll fix you a sandwich. Santos likes to have lunch with his buddy."

He nodded and stepped onto the patio and slapped the dust from his pants with his hat, then went to the clothesline and pulled off a dry shirt anyway. On his way back he ran his hands under the yard faucet and threw some water into his face and then dried his hands on his jeans before he came back in, his face still dripping. He dropped his hat on the floor by the door and noticed Jesse seemed embarrassed now also. She moved to the refrigerator, avoiding his eyes when he brushed by her and went to the table and sat. He could hear her making the sandwich but he did not watch. He sat with his hands folded on the table.

"Milk?" She held up an empty glass as she put the plate with the sandwich in front of him. "Millie's best, guaranteed grade A."

Before JD could answer, Jesse turned back to the refrigerator, already pouring the milk. He nodded as she set the milk in front of him. He began to eat. He could not see her but he knew Jesse had gone to the sink to look out the window.

"He's dead, isn't he?" she whispered.

He stopped eating. "Yes."

"You bury him?"

She turned. JD held the sandwich in mid-air. "Not very deep I guess." He did not look at her. "It's pretty hard up there, Jesse."

She came to the table and pulled a chair next to him, the closest she had ever sat and he felt a little nervous until he saw her face. He expected Jesse to go on about the horse, but she said, "How come you never say *Aunt* Jesse? We're family, remember?"

"Course I remember," he said.

"Remember what, your family? My family?"

"Some of it. But not that much, not a lot of stuff." He bit into the sandwich again and spoke around a mouthful, "It's been awhile you know." He thought about Santos and his comment on memory. Or lack of it.

"Well your grandmother, my mother, died in a treatment center," Jesse said, a small smile on her face. She inspected her fingernails. JD frowned at this sudden introduction of family history. He looked at Jesse and saw a detached contentment on her face. He sat silent, chewing.

"Oh, not insane," Jesse explained when she looked up. She smiled again. "Not that. But you know all about this, don't you JD?"

He shook his head. But he did remember the funerals.

"Cancer," she went on. "At least that's what they said." She curled her fingers and looked at her nails again. He saw they were uneven, uncared for. "It shows up in your genes, I guess. Sometimes."

She hid her hands in her lap, embarrassed at the ragged cuticles. "Anyway, they said we should put her there in Dallas and so we did.

Just your mother and me. Clair and I drove her down. But there was no cure…" She paused, looked at him and tilted her head and he saw the loose lock fall across a sad eye. "Clair cried all the way back. Why would they tell us to do that, JD?"

He shook his head and shrugged. Suddenly he wanted to answer Jesse as one human being to another and not as some dumb kid might. He wanted to move the lock out of her eye and explain it all, like Santos might have done, but instead he turned away and took an idle bite from the sandwich.

"She never got better. Your grandfather never did a thing, only went to see her once or twice, never wrote, just tried to drink it away. We got letters. She wrote everyday in her journal. It helped, I guess, the writing every day. But he never read any of it, even after she—" Jesse got up. She paused at the hallway and looked back at JD, mist in her eyes. "I still have that journal and her musicbox and…"

"That's good." JD looked at the sandwich, poised in his hand and suddenly he was not hungry any more. He put the sandwich on the plate and sipped the milk.

"Why would he do that, JD?" she said and he saw her eyes rockhard again.

"Do what?" JD stared at her. "Who?"

"Your grandfather. Completely ignore her just because she was sick and helpless? Men can be so cruel…"

She turned away and started down the hall and then he heard her in the backroom. He finished his milk and took the dishes to the sink, wondering what to do about the halfeaten sandwich. From under the sink, he took some waxed paper and wrapped it and then went out the back door. At the end of the patio, he stopped for a moment. Through the bedroom window he heard the tinkling of the musicbox again and he wondered why Jesse had not mentioned his father.

EIGHT

Even through the cracked and grimy windshield, JD saw the commotion on the road ahead. When he neared, he saw the pickup parked halfway across the gravel road, the double stock trailer backed up to the barrow ditch. Tru sat his mare, engaged in a tug-of-war with a reluctant steer at the end of a taut lariat. He was trying to maneuver the injured steer onto the loading ramp at the back of the trailer.

"Get behind him goddammit," Tru screamed but Linc could get no closer to the animal's rear since he already held its tail, twisting it. With all the jerking and screaming, Tru's mare danced around, frightened as the steer. JD did not want to spook them further so he parked his pickup some distance from the action and walked up the barrow ditch to help.

"I said *behind* him idiot," Tru yelled. "You're pulling him to the wrong side. He ain't ever going in that way."

"I'm pushing him toward the left side," Linc growled. "That's where you want him ain't it? Load the mare back in on the right?"

JD moved in to help. The animal bawled and kicked back, catching JD on the thigh just inches from his groin.

"Sonuvabitch." JD bent over double and rubbed his leg. When Tru saw this, he put his horse forward and slacked the lariat. The steer jerked free of Linc's grip and ran out the slack in the rope. He hit the end, spun around and dropped his head, satisfied to lean against the rope and bawl.

Tru swung down, leaving the mare to keep the rope taut. He

stomped over to JD, still bent over. Tru stopped and watched JD rub the spot where the steer's hoof had lashed him.

"I'm okay." JD said. He straightened as much as possible. "Damn near got me in the balls."

"What balls?" Tru said, his voice quivering. "Cowhands have balls, roustabouts don't. I said get *behind* him, didn't y'all hear?"

JD stared at him for a long moment. He wanted to ask Tru how the cowshit got on his gloves and the ache in his thigh if he had not been behind the animal. He said nothing.

Tru turned to Linc, glaring. "I ain't sure either of you's got any." He hissed through his teeth. "This is the most pitiful goddamned display of rangehand stupidity I ever seen. I said get *behind* him, not stand to the side like pussies. He ain't ever going into the damn trailer if you don't twist his tail and shove."

"That's what we were—" Linc began but Tru interrupted.

"Hell you were, neither of you was *behind* him."

JD listened as Tru continued to gnaw on Linc. But he was not hearing the words. JD focused on something else now, strange yet familiar, a sound he could not factor into the commotion of Tru's screaming and the steer bawling and the mare snorting and stomping to keep the rope taut. When JD recognized the sound, it was too late; the ore truck was hard on them.

"Geezus." JD leaped from the edge of the road, skidding on his belly down the ditch. Tru and Linc both wheeled just in time to see the truck kedging in the gravel. The hiss of locking brakes shot out across the rangeland, an alien sound which set in motion the series of instant events that JD observed lying prone at the edge of the road. His mind transformed them into slow motion, registered each frame in still life: the mare leaping forward and bucking to a halt, allowing the bolting steer enough slack to wrap the rope around the mare's rearend; the steer quickly tightening the rope again and dropping his head; the mare standing stiff legged, happy to call it a standoff, her withers quivering.

But there could be no similar standoff between an ore truck and a pickup with a stock trailer. The truck was on it too fast.

JD saw the driver lean to the right inside the cab, committed to his speed. He watched the driver's face in the freeze frame action, his mouth pantomiming a string of curses as the skidding mass of steel and ore rumbled onto the edge of the ditch behind the pickup and the trailer.

JD squinted hard. He waited for the collision. But there was none. He saw the truck emerged miraculously from behind the pickup and the stock trailer, the driver recapturing the middle of the gravel road. Then he heard the grinding of gears as the man fish-tailed the load back on track. JD shook his head and released a low whistle of relief at his stay of execution. Then JD was aware of another quick movement to this left: Tru running toward the pick-up in a frenzy, jerking open the door, groping inside for something, though JD could not tell what it was through the wall of dust. JD pushed himself up and walked outside the cloud and onto the road. Linc moved to his side, he too shaking his head in disbelief. Both stood speechless, watching the departing truck.

"Sonuvabitch!" Tru screamed and in futile pursuit, ran into the wake of dust. When he emerged from the receding cloud, he stopped, raised a lever action rifle, spread his legs and chambered a cartridge. He aimed, tracking the departing truck around the bend as he might have a fleeing antelope.

"Tru!" Linc yelled and JD sucked in a quick breath and held it, waited for the report from the rifle. But there was no gunshot. Tru stood for a moment with the firearm mounted against his cheek. The roar of the truck slowly faded until the only sound was the rasping of breath through the constricted windpipe of the injured steer, still struggling at the end of the rope drawn even tighter by the terrified mare.

Then JD watched Tru begin a slow pirouette, the rifle still raised, the left eye shut, the right eye glaring down the ironsights. At first JD was riveted by the sheer fury in that one eye but then he saw the muzzle of the rifle swing directly toward him and he changed focus.

JD's jaw went slack. Everything else disappeared, all sound, all light, all thought. For a brief moment nothing existed except the black bore of the thirty calibre, growing larger and larger in that killing end of the rifle which Tru held pointed at JD's head.

JD shut his eyes. He heard the sharp report from the rifle and his body jerked involuntarily. But the only pain he felt was the ringing in his ears. Then the ringing itself ceased and there was no sound at all except the hollow echo of the gunshot. He heard the soft blending of a musicbox, spinning around and around, and the music seemed to release all his pain, everything hidden and repressed, but he fought this freedom as if it were death itself, forced it back into the blackness, buried it again behind his eyes where there was nothing left of sight or sound or memory, only darkness.

When he opened his eyes a few seconds later, JD saw Linc blinking and releasing his own trapped breath as though he too had been spared. Almost immediately, both turned their eyes to the target of Tru's redirected muzzle. They watched dumfounded the final struggle of the bawling steer, twitching as it tried to rise from the hardpan, blood bubbling from the hole in the side of its head and staining its face.

"Sonuvabitch," Tru repeated in a hoarse whisper. He stared at the dead steer but there was no anger now in Tru's vacant face. JD turned to look at the animal. Then he heard the thud of the rifle hitting the ground behind him and Tru's boots in the gravel but JD did not turn around. Soon he heard the door to the other pickup slam and Tru cranking its engine until it coughed and caught and then slowly rattled away.

It was a long time before JD could steady his legs. Linc had already eased over and calmed the shifting mare, speaking low into her ear as he palmed her nose and then led her forward, releasing the rope still held taut against the carcass. He dropped her reins near the trailer and the mare stood restless but she stood. Then Linc took the rope from around the neck of the dead steer. He worked the kinks out of the lariat as JD finally approached. He stopped beside Linc and looked over at the carcass.

"We could butcher it out, I guess..." JD tried to speak as if everything were normal, just another Saturday morning on the ranch. He struggled to sequence all this in some kind of rational order, some logic that might mesh with a dead tomcat inside a gunnysack under the bloating carcass of an old horse and all this inside the ringing, which had returned to his ears and would always be there.

"Nope," Linc said. He stood staring at JD, the lariat looped over one shoulder. JD paused for more but Linc said nothing else.

"Well, we gonna bury it or what?" Burying it would not be complicated, not like Chisos or even the yellow tom, maybe just cover this critter with a little dirt or rocks or somehow keep the buzzards and coyotes from a free meal.

Linc stared at him for a few more moments, the same kind of vacant look JD had seen on Tru's face. Then Linc turned and went to the mare and led her up into the stock trailer. He secured the tailgate and retrieved the rifle, wiping the dust from it with his hand as he placed it back on the rack behind the seat of the pickup. Linc got in on the driver's side and shut the door. He leaned out the window.

"You don't bury something you ain't named. Jesse could tell you that, JD."

JD nodded. "Right. She says that." He thought again about the musicbox and the song which he could not name either but was still there behind the ringing in his ears.

Linc started the pickup. "You coming?" he said.

NINE

They began Tru's fence on Sunday. JD jolted awake and realized by the sunlight that he was already late for milking. He had not heard Cielo nor the rattle of Jesse's milkbucket. When he went inside the kitchen, Tru was standing at the sink filling a tea kettle. It surprised JD when Tru volunteered, "She ain't feeling good."

JD took the milkpail from inside the pantry and stood waiting at the door for more but Tru held his back to him. Tru set the kettle on the stove. When JD pushed open the screendoor to leave Tru said, "Happens every now and again," without looking up. "Mostly in winter. She get's over it..."

"How come?" JD paused.

"She gets over it," Tru repeated and went back into the hallway. JD left the kitchen and walked out to the corral. When he reached the grain room he stopped and stared at the door for a long while. Millie stood ready inside the milkshed, lowing.

"Hurting huh?" JD said. "Got a real load on ain't you? Maybe I oughta wait this late every morning, maybe you'd be a little easier to get along with."

He pushed the door open and stood, expecting something to rush him. But there would be no yellow tom today. He looked around and saw none of the other cats either.

"Pissed off," he muttered. "Well."

He scooped up a coffee can of oats and went back out to the milkshed. The sun had already separated from the horizon, so he quickly milked the cow and returned to the house, dispensing with sunrises and covens of kittens. Tru had cooked the oatmeal and was eating when JD entered the kitchen. JD noticed the old percolator was chugging on a backburner but still no Jesse. He went to the pantry and retrieved the crock with the flour sack stretched over its mouth for straining the milk. He set the crock on Jesse's countertop and began to pour the milk through the cloth.

"Jesse says she'll need some time," Tru announced. He still did not look up. "Says this one might take some getting over."

"She say what it was?" JD tried again.

Tru shrugged. "Don't matter. We got work. She's got lots of time. Like I say, she gets over it."

"I could make ice cream. Later." He looked around at Tru who kept shoveling in oatmeal. "After we're done, I mean. I could go back and ask Jesse how to mix it up and—"

"Dammit JD, sometimes you don't hear too good, do you?" Tru glared up at him. "I said she gets over it. Finish that and eat and get the hell out to the barn and help Santos and Linc load up."

JD flushed and clinched his teeth, but he held back his words. For a moment, he and Tru locked eyes, but in the tense silence, JD overfilled the cloth strainer and milk began to spill out across the countertop and drip off onto the floor. Tru did not look down at the milk splattering onto the tile. He continued staring coldly at JD who returned the stare, neither acknowledging the puddling milk. JD broke first. He finally blinked, bent down and began mopping up the milk with a dishtowel. Then he rose and held the towel over the sink, the soaked cloth still dribbling. He twisted the milk, hard, from the towel and turned to mop the countertop. He glanced at Tru who was eating again.

JD hung the towel over the edge of the sink then slopped one spoonful of oatmeal into a bowl and stirred in sugar and butter and some of the warm milk and then put the half empty crock into the refrigerator. JD tested the oats as he stood leaning his butt against the counter. Then he turned and reached into the cabinet and sprinkled cinnamon onto the concoction. None of it helped. Still standing, JD gulped down the remainder and swilled a cup of black coffee and left the kitchen with Tru thumbing the dial on the radio.

Outside, he sucked in a deep breath of cool morning air and

took his time getting over to the barn. Halfway across the yard, he heard Cielo.

Maybe she was waiting on the old rooster's morning call. Maybe she just got enough of waiting on me and having to be first up in the morning and all that. Maybe she just needs a Sunday off once in awhile and some time to read that journal. Or maybe she just deserves a little rest and privacy.

He spat out the taste of the oatmeal and said aloud, "She don't like sunrises anyway." He saw the flatbed haywagon was hooked up to Linc's old pickup and both were piled high and long with all the rusted remnants Santos had separated.

"Ain't enough," Linc observed when JD neared. "Hell, this won't even get halfway down one side."

"Well," JD said, and he tossed the last two remnants of wire atop the stack. He removed his gloves, satisfied he had done his part. Santos said nothing.

"Spud bars, hole diggers, stretchers, staples," Linc ticked off the list. "Pickaxes. Guess that's it."

JD scrutinized the gear on the pickup and the wagon. "What about posts?" There would be no fence building without posts. "We ain't just mending and splicing."

"Nope," Linc said. He moved around to the driver's side of the pickup. "We ain't just mending, you know that, JD. Let's go, Santos."

Linc got in and started the truck and then spoke out the window. "Guess we got an earlier start on our load than you did on yours, JD," he said and nodded toward the lean-to where Santos had earlier stacked all the old cedar posts he could find. "Shouldn't take you long to load them." Linc held a tight grin around his toothpick as he eased his pickup and trailer away. "See you on the road...when you get there. Don't take too long now, hear? We wanna finish by Christmas."

JD stood and watched them leave and wondered why he was being punished. "You assholes didn't have to milk any goddamn cow either," he said, his voice rising into the dust and noise of their exit. He slapped his gloves hard against his thigh and then tugged them on and went to the other pickup and started it. He backed it into a too-rapid, wide arch and hit the stack of posts, toppling them to the ground. "Shit," he said.

By the time JD arrived with the load of posts, Santos and Linc had already strung out half the old wire in random piles alongside the road. He watched them creeping along the next rise with the haywagon in tow, Santos on the back occasionally tossing off another loop of rusted wire. It took no tophand to see that even if they had twice this amount, there would not be enough wire for even one side of the road.

JD pulled the truck off the road and shifted to the lowest gear and moved with care through the barrow ditch. "Hope they don't expect me to stretch these posts out like that." He stopped the pickup and turned off the engine, waiting. "Not by myself anyway."

He tilted his hat forward and dropped his head back on the seat and closed his eyes and soon he was humming. When he heard Linc's truck and the rattle of the now empty haywagon on the road, he sat up, realizing he must have dozed off. He was glad it was not Tru. JD got out of the pickup just as Linc pulled to a stop. Santos emerged first and went behind and pulled off a couple of fenceposts. Linc lifted the spud bar from his pickup bed and handed it to JD.

"You get the honor," Linc said.

"Honor?"

"The first hole." He walked over and kicked a mark with his bootheel into the hardpan and looked at JD. "Right here."

JD scowled but then tugged his hat down and put on his gloves and lifted the heavy steel bar. He walked over and speared it at the spot, wishing Linc had left his foot. A thin flake of the hard dirt grudgingly broke loose. JD saw it would be easier than the hole he had dug yesterday but not much. And there would be a hell of a lot more of these.

Tru did not show until well after noon. Jesse was not with him but he did bring grub and more cool water and both were welcomed. Linc and Tru sat inside Tru's pickup talking low and eating. JD could not hear what they were saying from under the haywagon where he sat in the shade with Santos, but he guessed it would be about the need for more wire and more posts and how fences themselves were the devil incarnate. JD and the old man ate silently except for the scraping of tin spoons against tin plates full of cold beans and beef. When they were done, JD rose and held out his plate toward Santos who misunderstood the gesture. The old man reached to take care of the proffered dirty dishes. "No, keep your seat," JD said. "Just stack yours on top of mine." He gestured with his hand. The old man looked at JD, suspicious of this sudden show of generosity.

"I'll take care of them," JD said.

Santos did as he was asked. *"Gracias."*

"Keep your cup. I'll bring over the water."

When JD returned with the burlap wrapped jug, he scooted back into the shade and filled first Santos' cup and then his own and sat sipping the cool water. The old man poised his cup suspiciously but finally drank.

"How'd he lose it?" JD finally said.

"Que?"

"That eye," JD covered one eye with a palm. "How'd he lose it? Musta been one helluva fight."

Santos smiled and understood. *"Si."*

"Well?"

"Si, one *gigante* struggle."

"He won?"

"Si," Santos said with sudden pride but then his face turned dark. "But I lost."

"How could you lose if you won?"

"I did not say I won, I said *he* won. Cielo. I lost."

"How?"

"I will tell you all about it sometime Jimmie D. It is a long tale. Now we have a fence to build."

"Well." JD glanced toward the pickup where Tru and Linc remained seated. "I think this whole thing is—" He lowered his voice, "Stupid, real stupid. *Estupido, comprende?"* He looked into the old man's face. "You think so too, don't you Santos?"

"I do not know if it is stupid or not. I only wonder if *Señor* Pierce knows what he is fencing."

"Hell that's the easy part. He's fencing that goddamn road there," JD declared. "You know that."

Santos studied the bottom of his tin cup and seemed to ignore this and then whispered, "*Si.* But I wonder, does he know if he is fencing something out..." he sipped the water and then said, "...or fencing something in."

JD thought about what Santo said for a long moment. He decided that like Tru's little rains—spiked through with a single ray of sunlight—he did not understand the whole mystery of fences either. If Santos had quoted some Sunday bible talk, maybe it would keep ore trucks off the road and that might keep Tru happy, just this one day. JD might even give thanks for that himself.

The first one did not show until mid-afternoon. Tru had already left and JD watched the driver's face glower at them from inside the cab of the truck as it passed without slowing. It might have been a look of victory or mockery or contempt, or even grudging admiration for what they were doing, but Tru would have branded it a hostile challenge had he seen it. JD relished no further confrontations on the road as before. He did not even look up from the holes he was digging when other trucks rumbled passed all afternoon.

It had cooled off some when Linc dropped another armload of posts pulled from the pickup and said, "Enough." Without a word, Santos held onto the wire stretcher with a strand ratcheted taut while JD pounded the last staple for the day into the set stretch-panel. They all stood for a moment and studied the line of wire and posts they had completed.

"Not bad," Linc offered, but no one else commented so he repeated it. "Not bad at all for a bunch of old wire and splintered posts and old Mestizos and young roughnecks."

"And old bullshitters," JD filled in. "Let's get outta here."

Jesse was not at supper. And Tru's mare was not in the corral so JD waited until it was dark before he finally heated up the remainder of the beans and beef and ate alone in silence on the porch. He wondered what Linc and Santos had cooked up in the bunkhouse and maybe if Tru were over there eating, but then he said, "He wouldn't do that."

JD made as much noise as he thought he could get away with as he washed up his dishes, but when no one scolded him, he finished quickly and killed the light in the kitchen and walked out into the darkness. For a long while, he stood and stared up into the night sky, trying to remember what old man Simpson at BHS had said about stars and how they formed animals and Greek heroes and all sorts of things, and they were there all the time, even in broad daylight, and they had been there for billions of years. Then he thought about Bettye Lee and how she tried to show him where they were so he could pass the science class. He remembered lying on his back on the grass in his yard with his head in Bettye Lee's lap and it was summer and the night was cool and Bettye Lee was in short-shorts and JD was focused on anything but stars.

"Orion," she said. "It's right there, JD. See it?"

"Naw," he said.

"You're not looking in the right place," Bettye Lee said and she pressed her palms to his cheeks and repositioned his head. "And you gotta have just a little faith too, JD. Things aren't gonna just jump in place for you all your life. Sometimes you gotta focus."

But JD could not find a single group that looked vaguely like a horse or a crab or some guy with a sword. The only thing he could make out was the big dipper and a thin slice of the closing moon which appeared to him as though someone had just shoved a hole through the night sky with a shovel.

He thought about that entire episode in his life. "Well, she tried," he admitted. "I guess Bettye Lee did try. Maybe I didn't..."

He moved toward the corral to see if he had been mistaken about the mare not being there. But the only thing he could hear was Millie and the calf that he had forgotten to kick out of the corral for the night.

"No use doing it now," he said aloud. "Just won't be any milk for Jesse in the morning I guess. Grade A or otherwise..."

"Won't matter JD." Jesse's voice came as a hoarse whisper across the corral and he wondered if it might be inside his head. He blinked for a long while trying to see in the darkness.

"Jesse?" he said but nothing came back.

Finally he opened the gate and edged across the corral toward the voice. In the thin moonlight, he could see it was Jesse, sitting on the top rail. He moved over beside her and leaned his elbows on the rail and rested his chin on his knuckles. "What're you doing up there? Where you been?"

"Waiting."

"I thought you was sick? Ain't you afraid you might fall off there?" he teased, but Jesse said nothing so he said, "Waiting for what? Sunrise?"

"He went up before dark. On the mare."

"Oh."

"He thought alot of that old horse, JD. It's probably hard for you to see that but he did."

"Yeah."

"He's having a hard time..."

"Yeah."

"I mean with everything, not just that. He's angry."

"Yeah, but that don't give him no right to..."

"He doesn't mean to be. It's just that he's always been a little—*angry.*"

"Well I guess I could see why," JD lied and then, "There ain't gonna be enough wire and stuff. You know that. Even I can see it."

"I know. So does he."

"Why's he doing it then?"

"He's just driven."

"Driven?"

"Yeah."

"By what?"

"Well, don't you ever say I told you this, JD."

"What?"

"I think he just feels betrayed."

"Betrayed?"

"Yeah. By his own father," Jesse said.

JD said nothing, waited for her to go on.

"You know the story, JD. How old man Pierce sold off that piece of ground that was part of the place. Where that open pit mine is now, that transfer of land and that old road easement setting in motion this whole thing with the ore trucks on the road.

And the only thing left to do now is fence it off."

"Well."

"Tru was old enough to understand it. He knew it was just for survival. His father had his back against the wall, financially. The bank would only go so far with his dad and that helped of course. But it's Truman now who has to do something. About the other problem, I mean."

"The other problem?"

"Yeah."

"Well, maybe a fence ain't so bad."

"It's not just the fence, JD. Hell, that sounds like some melodrama right out of Hollywood. It's not just that, don't you see?"

"No."

"It's bigger than that. It's Tru thinking about his father's betrayal."

"But how could his old man know? He's long gone."

"He couldn't. But that's the way Tru sees it. He sees it as his father setting it all in motion, causing all this trouble with having to put up barbed wire fence. It could'a been *anything* but that."

"Yeah, I see," JD said, but his voice held no conviction.

"Still, forgiving your own father for something ought not be so hard." Jesse said. JD thought she was staring at him but he could not be certain in the darkness. Finally she said, "But it is for Tru."

Jesse fell silent. JD said nothing for a long while and then, "Yeah, I guess that would be hard..."

"Anyway, he's tried to get money. He just won't give it up," she said, and JD heard a weariness in her voice now. "He'd like to forget about fences entirely. Having to deal with all this is like asking him to walk around inside someone else's skin the rest of his life."

"What now?"

"Guess maybe I'll try."

"Asking Tru to give it up?"

"No. Try getting the money myself."

"Oh."

"Don't you say anything, JD."

"How?"

"Just you don't say anything, hear?" She got down from the rail and stood near him in the darkness and was quiet for a long time and finally she whispered, "JD?"

"Yeah?"

"You think maybe you could...hold me?"

He did not know how to respond, what to do or what to say to this. He stood with his hands buried in his pockets and then finally said, "What?"

"Just hold me JD. For a minute?"

"Well..."

She came closer and when she stood against him he pulled his hands from his pockets and could do nothing with his slacked arms now but bring them around Jesse's back, where he held them in an awkward position. They stood there for a long while with Jesse's head against his shoulder and he could feel her forehead on his neck and he wondered if the bruise he had seen there on Jesse two days ago would be almost gone by now.

TEN

Jesse brought lunch to the fence crew the next day. Right away JD noticed the sunshades which were not large enough to cover the new purple and yellow flesh at the edge of her eyes and across the bridge of her nose, colors he could not have seen the previous evening in the darkness.

"Sonuvabitch," he hissed as she filled his bowl with stew from the Dutch oven she set on the tailgate of the pickup.

"I hit a door," she said, then flushed at such a cliché. "Just eat, JD, and don't do something stupid."

He stared at her for a long while but could not see her eyes behind the dark glasses and finally said, "Stupid? Like build half a fence?" She did not speak. JD went on, "A fence that keeps nothing in and nothing out?"

"Where's Tru?" Linc said when JD approached him and Santos who sat in the shade of the wagon eating. "Posts'll last a couple days but we'll be out of wire by evening."

"Maybe he just give up." JD tried to sound blasé through his anger. "You know how he is."

"Yeah," Linc observed. "And he don't give up. You ain't seen him this morning?'

"Nope."

"Last night?'

"Nope." JD knelt and crowded under the wagon into what was left of the skinny shade.

"What'd she say?"

JD did not answer.

"We can still set posts," Santos interrupted. "Until we get more wire."

"You walk up the line there yet?" JD said. He pointed with his spoon. "Where nothing's growing?"

"There's nothing growing a lot of places around here," Linc said. "But you're right. It gets harder'n hell up there. Should work you out good JD."

"It ain't gonna work me out good. I sure as shit ain't digging holes in solid rock. Not even shallow ones."

"So what's your plan chief?" Linc already had one but he waited to see if JD's idea was to drag up his pay or what.

"No plan, just a sit-down if that's what it takes to come to some sense on this stupid thing. Or better yet, just catch the next bus outta Lajitas."

"Where to?" Linc seemed unimpressed.

JD took it as a challenge. He looked up and thought a moment. "Like you say, Linc," he brought the tin bowl up to his chin and poked a spoonful of stew into his mouth and muffled around it, "Anywhere a man can step in cowshit. Or better still, where he *won't* step in it. Crude oil either."

Linc grinned. "Sounds like a plan alright." JD did not respond. Linc went on, "You seen that fence over by Santiago Peak? Between this place and that open pit mine?"

JD glanced over his bowl. "I seen it."

"Well?"

"Well what?"

"Well it's a lot shorter, but it's in solid rock too. Bad as Tru hates fences, he had us do that several years back. Before that new outfit got ahold of it and started gouging out the old shafts. Me and a couple Meskins."

"Well it sure as hell didn't stop none of them trucks coming on the road. So what good did it do?"

"None. Except for Tru I guess. The fence and cattle guard kept his steers on this side and—"

"But not off the road," JD interrupted but no one needed reminding. "Well, I ain't no Meskin and I ain't seen no jackhammer in the barn so what the hell you getting at?"

"Blasting caps." Linc sprinkled tobacco into the cigarette paper he held cupped in his fingers. "That's how we done it. Chip out a small hole, put one cap in, blam. Crumbles it right up so's you can just scoop it out with a spade." He rolled the paper, wet it with his tongue and lit up.

"You gotta be kidding," JD scoffed. He watched the deftness with which Linc rolled the tobacco with one hand and he knew he was not joking. "Dynamite?" he said.

"Problem is we ain't got any." Linc flicked the matchstem onto the hardpan and sucked in a long drag and let it all out with one sigh. "Blasting caps. I didn't say dynamite. Dynamite's dangerous shit."

"So what?" JD said. "Hell, we ain't got enough wire or posts anyway, Linc. Maybe it's time for us all to let go of it, even if he won't."

Jesse moved over and stood at the end of the haywagon where she overheard all this. She surveyed the remaining materials on the wagon.

"JD, you come with me," she ordered abruptly and when there was nothing but silence from under the wagon she said, "On second thought," she bent over and looked under the wagon and pointed. "Santos you come. These two engineers seem to have all the plans so we'll let them finish using what's left."

The three scooted from under the wagon, brushing the dust from the seat of their pants. They stood stiff, as though some general had just walked onto the battlefield.

"Don't get rattled," Jesse said. She smiled at her ragged platoon. "It's just that I'll need some help in town."

"What do you aim to do, Jesse?" JD cocked his head and eyed her from under his hat. "Steal that wire?"

Linc managed a tight grin but then stuck his cigarette into his mouth opposite his toothpick, crossed his arms and leaned back against the wagon. Santos moved over next to Jesse, aligning himself with in his new *jéfe*. "Get in the pickup," she said to him and then to the other two, "If Tru comes out, you say I went to town."

She followed Santos to the truck.

"What if he asks why?" JD said.

"Well JD, don't try to squeeze him into somebody else's skin." Jesse smiled at the sudden puzzlement on Linc and JD faces. She got into the truck and started it, grinding the gears into place. "Just say blasting caps," she said. "And lots of barbed wire."

She and Santos roared away. JD and Linc turned their faces from the rocks thrown back.

"Blasting caps?" JD frowned. He watched the whirlwind of dust now on the road.

"Blasting caps," Linc said. He pulled a final drag from his cigarette, wet his fingers and pinched out the ember. "And lots of barbed wire. That's what she said."

ELEVEN

Jesse never questioned why she came to Lajitas, only why she had stayed. Inside the midday heat, the town quavered as if in its final death throes. She turned off the gravel road and aimed the old pickup down the pocked two-lane pavement that divided the small business district into what Jesse referred to as the *dead-half* on the left and the *half-dead* on the right.

The dead-half housed the drygoods store and further down, the train depot, both long since boarded up, all ore now trucked fifty miles over the *Camino Rio* to the train terminal in Presidio. On the right was the remaining life, its weak pulse beating inside Hill Garza's red brick bank building next to Odie Taylor's post office and Glenn Compton's Ranch Supply and finally, the Elbo Room where Jesse brought the old truck to a stop against a crumbled concrete curb.

She looked at the sign above the door of the bar and at the silhouette where the W had fallen off the word *Elbow* some time ago. Sonny Pun had never replaced it. "Says it the same with or without that W," he scolded when anyone asked. "Elbow Room or Elbo Room. Don't make no difference. What matters right now is what you're gonna have to drink."

Jesse glanced at her watch and knew even at one-thirty in the afternoon, Hill Garza would be inside having finished his usual bowl of Sonny Pun's grease-capped chili, stuffed with soda crackers and still sipping his third draftbeer.

"You wait here," she said to Santos, who had sat silent during the ride in and now simply nodded, lifting his hat in one hand and smoothing back his sweat soaked hair with the other. "One way or another I won't be long."

Santos watched her enter the bar and then looked first up the deserted street and then down the other way and he wondered where Jesse thought he might go except to have a cool *cerveza* inside where he had not been invited. He had no money anyway. He leaned his head on the tattered seatback and pulled his hat over his eyes.

Inside the darkness of his hat, Santos thinks about Gallo del Cielo and wonders what he is doing in such heat and if his tin of water is empty. And then he sees himself inside the willow hewn cage with Cielo and the cage is inside the adobe shack where he sees no face of Paloma and feels no heat even from the ashes of the cookfire which is neglected and dark, like the inside of his hat where there is also no face of Paloma, neither young nor old, only the thick adobe muting the echo of hoofbeats and rifle fire and deep throated laughter and even his own pale voice, it too an echo inside the cold empty room, "Were we always so, Paloma? Only echoes of ourselves?" and then the ghost glow of her wrinkled face floats in the darkness and he speaks urgently to her, "Release me from this cage, Paloma, and I will go and talk to the jéfe himself and make him see the words on the paper and he will understand that the land is ours," and Santos lifts the parchment in his fist and thrusts it through the willow bars toward his wife who turns her face and then is no longer there.

Jesse paused just inside the door of the bar, trying to adjust her eyes to the dimness before she realized she had not removed her sunshades. Even with them off, she could make out only the single blue neon sign behind the bar that read BEER. She smiled, remembering when Sonny Pun had dragged in the shaky ladder and with hammer and nails, hung the sign there. "What kind?" she quizzed as he plugged it in and then beamed with pride at his handiwork. "It doesn't say what kind, Sonny?"

"Don't matter," he said. "As long as it's cold it don't need a label. It's on tap anyway. A mug of beer don't have no label."

Jesse smiled and in the dim room, moved slowly toward the familiar blue glow with her hand held out. She shut her eyes because there was no need to see, only to count the steps.

"You remember good," Sonny said when she touched the varnished edge of the bar and then opened her eyes. "Ain't seen you in awhile, Jesse, but you remembered."

"Practice," she said. She sat on the familiar barstool under the motionless ceiling fan. "Like riding a bicycle, once you learn, you never forget how to find a bar, even in the dark. You okay Sonny?"

"Fame and fortune ain't arrived yet but I keep watching the door. Like they say, when my limo comes in, I'll probably be waiting over at that boarded up train depot. Guess I can't complain though," he shrugged and flicked on the fan and then because he knew Jesse would be expecting this, he said, "Except for my wart of course."

"Yeah." She lifted the back of her hair and held her neck upward into the rush of air and then looked at the sign again. "Same brand I see."

"Yep."

Jesse smiled again and said, "Maybe that's what caused it."

"Caused it?"

"Your wart. Same old beer, day after day'll do that. Foam on the end of your nose all the time."

"Well it ain't there no more. See?" Sonny Pun leaned over and cocked his head. Jesse inspected the tip of his nose. The wart was gone. So was a half-inch tip of Sonny Pun's swollen nose which looked as raw as a small fistful of hamburger.

"Jeezus, what the hell'd you do Sonny?"

"Cripes, you ain't been in for a long while have you?" he said. "Better have a beer and I'll tell you all about it." Sonny retrieved a frosted mug from the cooler and turned back to fill it from the tap.

"Don't really have time, Sonny." Jesse ventured a glance into the mirror and her eyes narrowed at the bright light reflected from the front window, but she could see Hill Garza silhouetted at the table. "Sorry."

"Well, you'll have to go somewhere's else for sody pop. I don't tell nobody about no wart unless they have a draft first."

She chuckled, feeling better than she had in a long while. She knew that even in the dim light, Sonny would have noticed her face by now but he said nothing about it and that gave her courage. "Well?" she said.

"Well what?"

"You gonna tell me?"

"For free?" Sonny began to wipe the bar hard, though it did not need it. "Oh what the hell," he continued. "Sheep dip."

"Sheep dip?"

"Yep, it was sheep dip. I just rubbed it with that stuff and rubbed it in again and again till one day, wart just falls off in my hand. Ain't come back neither."

"Neither has most of the skin on your nose, Sonny." She leaned over and inspected it with a frown." Damn, you better see a doctor. You might'a given yourself cancer or something."

"Ain't no doctor here. You know that Jesse. No big deal."

She straightened. Had there been a crowd of cowhands on a Saturday night, Jesse would have said, *Well ain't no skin off my nose,* and laughed with the whole lineup at the bar, but she was certain someone had already said this to Sonny, at least a dozen times by now. She continued to look into the mirror and said, "Where'd you get sheep dip?"

"Compton's."

"He's carrying that?"

"Yep."

"Damn, what's the place coming to."

"Yeah, sheep and goat and now, even ore stuff and—"

"Whatta you mean *whore* stuff?" Jesse looked at him with feigned indignation. She held back a smile.

"I said *ore,* not *whore.* Stuff for mining. Open pit stuff." Sonny paused, considered Jesse's comment. "Shit, we ain't sunk *that* low yet in Lajitas, Jesse."

"What about other stuff?" she said, loud enough for Hill to hear. "You know, barbed wire, posts, *cow* stuff?"

"Oh Glenn's still dealing that," Hill injected from across the room. "Still a little of that business going on around here too, I hear." She said nothing and Sonny said nothing and so Hill continued, "How you doing Jesse?"

"Fine."

"Join me over here, in the light. Can't say much for the chili but the beer's lukewarm."

She widened her eyes at Sonny who did not bite at Hill's usual complaint. He shrugged and leaned over and began to rummage under the bar. "I might have a pop under here somewhere." he grumbled. "And that'll goddamn sure be lukewarm."

Jesse moved over to the table. She dragged out a chair and sat. Hill remained seated, staring out the window.

"Who's the old wetback?"

"His name's Santos," she said, containing a slowly rising anger. "But I wouldn't say he's a wet—"

"Yeah, right." Hill turned back and Jesse knew he was inspecting her face. "By the way, how's Truman?" he jabbed, sipping his beer.

"The old man just showed up one day," she said, ignoring Hill's innuendo. "Linc picked him up. That old man and a rooster inside a wooden cage and they've just been around since. Helping out for awhile…"

She paused and looked at Hill who said, "Him and a rooster? Helping?"

"With a fence."

"So I hear," Hill said. He watched Santos but all he could see was hat. "What kind of rooster?"

"From heaven he says," Jesse blurted and then embarrassed by this, she corrected, "He says he fights."

"Well I'll be damned. A fighting rooster, and from god no less. Wish I had one like that." He grinned at Jesse, sipped his beer. "Mine are all from the other place."

"Let's just get to it Hill," Jesse. "You know I don't come all the way to town to drink warm pop and eat Sonny's chili or talk about rooster fights." She sucked in a deep breath. "I need your help…"

Under his hat, Santos dozes in the heat inside the pickup. "I need your help, Señor," he mutters and he sees himself unroll the parchment on the desktop of the jéfe who smiles and says, "And how is your wife,

Santos?"

Hill grinned at Jesse. "Well now, that ain't like Truman to send his wife in for business, so you must have come in for something else?"

"It's business," she said and clinched her jaw.

Santos clinches his jaw and ignores the jéfe's question about Paloma. "This will show you that it is ours," he says and he points to the document.

"Well, you must read me the part that says this, Santos," the jéfe leans back in his chair, waiting. Santos looks at the parchment, at the lines and the dots and the squiggling curves and he flushes. "But you can read it for yourself, Señor."

"Ah, but you are the one who believes this, Santos, not I. You can show me where it says this?" He furrows his brow and leans over the document. Santos drops his eyes, slowly rolls the paper again. "You know I cannot read," he whispers.

"Well there's business and then there's *business.*" Hill toyed with his mug. He ran his middle finger down the moisture collected on the outside and then traced his lips with this finger and then around the tip of his tongue. "What kind of business, Jesse?"

Jesse lowered her eyes, fought off a urge to get up and leave. "You know what I'm talking about, Hill."

"You know Jesse, I always liked you, right from the time you first come to Lajitas, working right here for old Sonny." He leaned over to her and Jesse smelled the chili and beer on his breath. "You ever think about that Jesse? Those good old days?"

His knee seemed to rest against her thigh accidentally until he began to move it up-and-down. Jesse wanted to get up cursing but she calmed herself by imaginig Hill as just another drunk patron from the good old days he was speaking about.

"Sometimes," she said. She forced a smile. "Sometimes I do."

Santos tucks the rolled parchment under his arm and turns away from the jéfe. "I will bring someone to read it," he says, hiding his anger as best he can.

"I saw your gallo de combate," the jéfe says. There is a different tone now in his voice. He rises from his desk and with his hands clasped behind his back, walks to Santos and says, "In your house, in the cage. Do you fight him?"

Santos turns. He frowns at the man but says nothing.

"Well, if he is truly a fighting rooster..."

"He is," Santos interrupts defensively but then he worries that even in a cockfight, too much bravado is not good for the betting. "Sometimes," he says and then he smiles at him. "But Cielo does not fight alone. We both fight."

"Mug's cold, sody pop ain't." Sonny Pun set the drink in front of Jesse. "How's yours Hill?"

"Beer's fine if that's what you mean," he said and then, "You ever been to one of them cockfights Sonny?"

"I wouldn't touch that question with a ten foot pole," Sonny said. He wiped the ring of moisture from under Hill's mug and set it back down and returned to the bar.

"How 'bout you Jesse?" Hill said.

"They're not legal," she said passively. "And neither is the betting or the drugs or the guys pushing both."

Hill smiled, drained the mug. He got up and went to the bar and paid Sonny and moved to the door. Jesse released her breath, deciding he was finished with her, too. And she had accomplished nothing except perhaps making Hill angry.

"That's right Jesse," Hill said, holding the door open and then, "They're not. Just the same, why don't you tell your business friend in the pickup there I got business friends too." He glanced out the open door at Santos. "Call it sporting business. Maybe you and me and what's his name could work something out?" Hill left and shut the door behind him.

Jesse watched him walk away and then suddenly he was standing in front of the truck, looking inside at Santos still under his hat. Then Hill returned and opened the door to the bar again and stood just inside, speaking to Jesse, "By the way, I'll stop in there at Compton's before I go back to the bank." He smiled at her. "You stop by there too before you go home, hear?" he said. "And then come by my office someday soon Jesse. Just for some paperwork on all this." He sucked his teeth and then nodded toward the pickup. "And be sure you bring in that old rooster out there in your truck when you come. If you can wake him up." Hill left, closing the door.

Jesse picked up her mug and moved to the bar and sat under the fan again. "Well." she said.

"Well what?"

"What do you make of all that?"

"Good bartender hears nothing, sees nothing, repeats nothing." Sonny wiped the bar. "You know that, Jesse."

She nodded.

Sonny studied her face, "What's going on?"

"You tell me."

"Sounds like you got what you wanted."

"Maybe. Problem is, Hill didn't." She flushed.

"He never did, Jesse." Sonny brought out another cold mug and twisted off the top of another warm pop. "Not from you. Even in them good old days he talked about, right?" He poured the soda for Jesse. "Maybe he just wants somebody else owing him money."

"Probably," she sipped. "But that ain't what you were really asking about, right?"

Sonny said nothing.

"Tru's been on a tear lately." Jesse picked up her sunshades from the bar and looked in the mirror at the faceless reflection of herself, dark against the front window. "No use putting these back on. You got eyes."

"Mmmm..."

"What the hell happened, Sonny?"

"To what?" He leaned an elbow on the bar and worked at a stubborn spot with the rag.

"All of it, the way things were, the way people got along and just did their own thing here and bothered nobody?"

"Dunno. Things change."

"You sound like a bartender."

"Some left, some stayed. Some died, some new ones come in. I don't think the slack left by the good ones was took up, though. Not by these new ones."

"Hill ain't new."

"Yeah he is. Might as well be anyway."

"Maybe."

"Just look at that board of directors he's got now," Sonny offered. "Ain't a single rancher on it, not a real one. Every goddamn one of them's got a piece of that reopened mine up there and doing that heavy betting on them illegal cockfights they stage ever Sunday, right there in the bottom of that damn pit, right out in open daylight and— "Sonny stopped, more secrets betrayed in a half-breath than in the past decade at the Elbo Room.

Jesse stared at him and there was a long silence and finally she said low, "Hill too?"

Sonny shrugged. "I already said too much."

She spun the barstool around twice and then leaned back against the bar and looked out at the bright sun. She shook her head and sucked in a deep breath. "I should have guessed it, Sonny. Dammit, I should have known."

"Well nobody told me for certain, you understand. But it ain't too awful hard to figure out, even if it is just bartalk."

"Well, if Hill *is* involved, you can't really fault him for trying to stay afloat," she said, knowing Sonny would never repeat these words, which would sound treasonous indeed to Tru. "Financially or otherwise, I mean," and she thought about Tru and how his efforts had become perhaps less financial and more a matter of survival, much like his own father's.

"I suppose."

"It's just nice to know who your friends are. Or maybe better, your enemies." She looked up at the hypnotic rotation of the ceiling fan. "Is it still up there, Sonny?"

Sonny glanced up at the fan and thought a moment. "Far as I know," he shrugged. "Ever since that first summer you worked here."

"Same time you put the beer sign up, right?"

"Yep. I brought that stepladder in, remember? I think it's the only time I ever had a ladder in here. A hundred each wasn't it?"

Jesse said.

"Best week of tip money I ever seen before or since," Sonny said. "Sealed up there in an envelope for emergencies. Taped good to the top of one blade too so's you can't see it from down here. I think it's that one with the chip out of the end, Jesse, wasn't it? See, that one?" Sonny pointed up and tried to follow one fan blade around and around with his finger. "Two one-hunnerd dollar bills from old T. Jefferson at the bank and I got new ones too, crisp with serial numbers together, let's see...shit, can't remember what them numbers were but you remember all that?"

Jesse remembered. It was the best summer in memory for the Elbo Room. Tourists flocked into the Big Bend Park and then instead of back north to the interstate, came through Lajitas and Presidio and on up to Marfa and then to places like El Paso or Tucson. They all stopped in Lajitas. Not necessarily by choice but because it was the only spot on the highway for a hundred miles to buy cold beer, even without labels on it.

But then the occasional marijuana bust changed to the cocaine invasion throughout the region and with it, a few killings and in addition, the collapse of the cattle market, and then like the *Rio Grande* itself during this extended drought, it all slowed to a trickle. The only thing now was the yearly invasion of rowdy chiliheads for the World Champion Chili Cookoff, but this crowd brought not only their living quarters, but their own beer and ice, leaving beer cans and motorcycle tracks across the eroded desert, but scant money.

"Emergencies," Jesse mused as she followed the fan. She thought about her mother's gold coin in the musicbox. "One for you and one for me. Salvation."

"Or both for you Jesse." Sonny said it quickly and without sentimentality, just to get it said.

"Thanks Sonny," Jesse turned around and smiled at him. "But I guess that wouldn't do much good against a godawful pile of barbed wire we're gonna need. Hill's line of credit at Compton's will have to work for now. At least till he decides to collect."

"Compton?" Sonny teased.

"Hill."

"How you gonna pay him back?" Sonny said, concerned this time.

"Compton?" she said, her turn now.

"Hill," he said and he forced a laugh. "You know what I mean Jesse. It ain't Glenn you'll be owing."

Jesse looked into the mirror once more. Outside, she saw Santos lift his hat and paste his sweaty hair down and sit forward in the pickup. He seemed to be looking through the window but she knew he could not see her in the dim light inside.

"I don't know, Sonny," she whispered and turned away from him and when she spoke again, Sonny heard none of the old fire in her voice and it worried him. "I just know things aren't exactly how they were in the good old days."

Sonny looked at her and frowned and shook his head but Jesse kept her back to him.

TWELVE

Tru sat hatless in his rocker in the shade of the porch when Jesse and Santos returned. He seemed to ignore them. The worst of the heat had subsided. Jesse backed the truck up to the empty haywagon parked next to the barn. When she got out, she heard the popping noise from a gas engine echoing inside the barn and knew that JD and Linc would be mixing barley and salt and cottonseed meal in the hopper to Tru's formula, just so. Santos shuffled out stiffly and went back to unload the forty rolls of new barbed wire stacked high in the bed of the pickup.

"Just leave it for now," Jesse said. "You've done enough lifting today Santos." She moved around the truck and stood next to the old man who seemed relieved. "You get some cold water from my refrigerator."

"I will see if Cielo needs water first," he said and turned toward the bunkhouse.

Jesse watched him cross the yard, little puffs of dust rising from his huaraches. She wondered if she should have told Santos about Hill and his sporting friends and his comment about talking to Santos. *What would I say? Some rich hombres want to get you and that old wore out rooster in some kind of battle to the death?*

She shook her head and wondered how in hell she would say that to the old man? And why? Santos and Cielo had no obligation to Hill Garza. Only Jesse herself. She would pay Hill back for all this. Somehow.

She surveyed the new fencing materials and worried if she had made a mistake taking Hill's sudden generosity. *Payback will be in hard cash, too. Not blood from Santos or Cielo. Or whatever else Hill thinks he might get from me.*

Still, Jesse had no idea when that much hard cash might become available, the way cattle prices were. And no rain.

Linc came out of the barn and stood next to the pickup. "Ain't seen any of these for a spell." He worked free a wooden box of blasting caps from inside the bed of the pickup where Santos had insisted on wedging them in front of the full load of wire. "Where the hell'd you get 'em?"

"Same place as wire and posts. If you know the right people you can get anything you want in the big city of Lajitas, Linc." Jesse joked and then, "Almost anything. I'm glad nothing shifted forward."

"Yeah," Linc looked at the box. "They ain't as unstable as dynamite or nitro but they can be tricky. Sure as hell ain't firecrackers."

Jesse heard the engine in the barn cough to a stop and immediately she was aware of bawling cattle in the corrals behind the barn. Soon JD emerged, his face pasted with sweat and a thin layer of pea-green cottonseed meal.

"Who's this?" she said.

"He's the main hopper man," Linc said. "Best meal man on the place." JD pulled out his shirt tail and with the clean end, wiped as much of the meal from his face as he could. Linc went on, "Can't dig postholes for shit though."

"Not in solid rock," JD said, a declaration of independence. "Not me anyhow. Not any more."

"Won't have to now," Linc said. He held up the box of blasting caps. JD studied the box but he said nothing.

"What's going on back there?" Jesse said. She indicated the cattle in the corral behind the barn.

"Steers, all the yearlings," Linc said. "About a hundred. When we come in, Tru had us saddle up and move them over from the road."

"Away from the trucks..." Jesse guessed, as if it were some kind of defeat.

"Maybe, but he never said that. Just said do it because of no rain and no grass over there. Said he wants to fatten them on feed and dump them on the market in the fall, no matter what price."

"Pen feed them?" Jesse was incredulous.

"That's what he says." Linc lifted his shoulders. "It's the best of the bunch, prime beef. That's why we're mixing right now. Says work fence in the mornings, mix feed in the afternoons."

"Blasting caps?" JD read the label on the box but when he reached for it Linc moved it away. "Easy. Them ain't playtoys. I'll show you all about them when the time comes."

"I ain't a damn kid, Linc." JD stiffened, sulled up.

Jesse walked away, satisfied Linc would handle it. Though it was on her mind as she crossed the yard, her main concern was not the safety of the project. She wondered not only how they would pay Hill back for the fencing, but how they would finance more high priced feed when the supply in the barn ran out. It would not last until fall.

She passed Tru but did not look at him, even from behind the sunglasses. Neither spoke. She went inside the kitchen and poured herself a glass of cold water from the pitcher in the refrigerator, gulped this down and then sat at the table with the pitcher and refilled the glass.

"Hot," she said.

"Where'd you get all that?" Tru was sitting right outside the kitchen window and did not need to speak as loud as he did. Jesse ran her hand under the back of her hair and held the cold glass to her face, but she did not remove the sunshades. She weighed the tone in Tru's voice.

"Too hot," she repeated and there was a long silence before she said, "Compton's," and then another long pause before she heard Tru's rocker creaking on the flagstones and she knew he was standing, probably looking at the pickup full of wire and posts. She thought about how she had told JD not to lie if Tru asked where she had gone with Santos. Then she heard Tru's boots on the stones and for a moment, she hoped he had left to inspect the load. Instead, he came into the kitchen.

"We got no credit there..." It was a statement of fact but Tru meant it as a question. He stood just inside the door, his voice more confused than angry. The question lingered. "Maybe for a little feed but not that kind of credit."

"We do now." Jesse did not turn around.

"What'd you do?"

"I went in, I brought it back. Can't you see that?"

"I can see that. But what'd you have to do?" He moved toward her.

"Well, it ain't paid for yet if that's what you mean."

Tru moved around to look at her. He reached for her arm but she leaned away and slowly removed the sun glasses. She stared cold and hard at him from inside the bruises. Tru cleared his throat and dropped his eyes. He shoved his hands into his back pockets and turned away.

"Well, that's progress," she observed. She turned to the window and tried to sound convincing, "Sonny's taking care of it," she lied.

"Where'd he come up with that kind of money? Only one place in town's got that much." Tru turned back and crossed his arms and rested his butt on the edge of the table. He looked hard at her.

"He didn't. Sonny just said he'd stand for us at Compton's," she said, and then to lend her lie more credence, "He'll put his place up if they want him to...he didn't think they would."

"They?"

"Glenn...I meant Glenn."

"I don't need Sonny's help. Or Glenn's either."

"Well then maybe you don't need a fence or all that extra feed," she said but instantly regretted it, so she added, "Tru, it's done. Just forget it. Let's get on with it while we still have the energy and some extra hands that aren't hollering about not getting paid yet, thank god."

"How do I forget it? I won't till it's paid back. Every goddamn dime. And that'll happen as soon as the market turns in the fall." He looked at her and for a moment Jesse saw a flash of desperation she had never seen before, but then Tru's face turned hard again and he moved into the hallway where he stopped without turning back and said, "About the other night, I'm—"

"It's okay Truman," she interrupted because she knew he would not be able to finish it. She got up and went to the back door and held it open and looked up at a clear sky. "Might rain," she mused. "A little rain wouldn't hurt a bit."

THIRTEEN

Linc bolted upright in his bunk at the first clap of thunder. It followed so close to the electric blue flash that he knew the storm was already on them. He had been dreaming of dynamite and blasting caps and he woke sweaty. He swung his legs to the floor but it was several minutes before he could shake off the bad dream and stand. Santos was already out of his cot and in the next flash of light, Linc saw the old man sitting with the caged bird on top of his lap. Inside, Cielo whirled and whirled as though anticipating the crackling which came this time first as a sharp snap like a bullwhip and then, the superheated air came back together with a vibrating thud.

Santos cooed to the rooster. "I think god is angry," he said.

Linc pulled on his jeans. "Angry or not, I guess we oughta shut this window." He moved to the window but the spray of rain had already soaked the floor. "Shit," he said as he stepped barefoot in the cold water. He shut the window and went to the kerosene lamp, swinging in the center of the room. He steadied it, struck a match on the bottom of the lantern and then touched the flame to the wick until it finally caught and sent an orange glow into the corners of the room. Then he went back to the window and tried to see out into the blackness.

"That was a good one—" he said, interrupted by the next flash which instantly flooded the yard bright blue. "They're close. Smell that electricity?"

Santos sat motionless except for his lips which moved in a silent rosary. He opened the door of the cage and held one hand on the back of the rooster who crouched inside. Linc anticipated the next flash at the little window and when it came, he pressed his forehead to the glass and said, "Somebody's out there," and then suddenly the door opened as though kicked in by the next deafening thud. Santos shut his eyes. But it was not god who entered.

"Get your boots on." Tru stood blocking the door. JD wedged passed him, both wearing yellow slickers and dripping large puddles of water on the floor. Linc said nothing. He sat on his bunk and pulled on his boots, then buttoned up his shirt and tucked in the tail. He took his hat from a nail and then the stiff yellow slicker which had not been moved in months.

"Him too?" Linc nodded at Santos, though he had no idea what Tru was planning.

"Just you," Tru said. He went back out into the rain.

"He's gonna move them, I guess," JD said. He tried to blink the rain from his eyes.

Tru was already in the horse corral with his bridle when Linc and JD splashed across the yard. The remuda they brought up yesterday had milled and stomped until the dust was a thick layer of mud in the corral. Linc took two bridles from the tack room and moved out across the mud and into the rain. In the next flash of lightning, he saw the buckskin he was looking for. The horse stood tensed with the others against the rails.

Tru had already caught his mare and was leading her toward the barn. In the darkness, Linc stalked the animals. He walked slow, trying to speak over the rain and the bawling of a hundred steers in the adjacent corral. All but one of the horses broke by him but Linc stood his ground in front of the buckskin gelding and then touched his neck and finally spoke low into his ear. He could feel the flesh quivering under the soaked hair so he put his hand on the horse's nose and slowly slipped on one of the bridles as he continued to talk and then he led the animal toward the gate where JD stood holding another bridle.

"I already got two bridles," Linc yelled. "Put that away and take this horse." He expected JD to say something about catching his own damned horse but if he did, Linc could not hear it through the rain on his hat. There were certain mounts in this corral Linc himself would not want to be on in a thunderstorm. He had fired rifles from this buckskin and knew he would be staunch, even in the chaos of a storm.

JD returned the bridle to the tack shed and came back. Linc leaned close to JD's ear and said, "Now hold him good till you get him into the barn and saddled, JD. He'll be alright."

Without words, JD took the reins from Linc who turned to the other shuffling horses. Linc waited for the next flash to pick one for himself, and though he shivered a little when he saw the wet ghost-like sheen on the back of the black gelding, he knew this too was a strong animal. The horse only appeared black-evil in the flashes of lightning; he was a good horse.

"Push them south," Tru said inside the barn. Though the rain pelted the tin roof, it was quieter in here and he did not need to say it as loud as he did. He had saddled the mare and stood waiting in the darkness for the other two. "String them out, keep them separated. These little rains pop up from the south. It'll move north real quick but I ain't gonna wait for that."

Linc nodded but he wanted to ask Tru how a quick rain could hang on even this long. It did not seem to be moving anywhere.

JD saddled the buckskin and led him to the door and stood beside Linc and Tru. Unlike Linc, he had several other unspoken questions. Tru answered only one, "One damned lightning strike inside that corral would wipe out half them steers the way they're bunched up. Don't let them do that, keep them strung out." But Tru's explanation did not answer the big question in JD's mind. Tru mounted the mare and rode out into the rain. Linc and JD did the same.

"Try to ride low." Linc said and in doing so, answered the remaining question, but even JD recognized the gallows humor.

"Ride low?" JD shouted, blowing spray from his lips and he thought about cowboys being swept off the top of windmills. Dying that way was a longshot compared to sitting high on a horse in a lightning storm. *"Geezuschrist, they're both crazy,"* he said.

Tru had already opened the corral gate and was inside, whistling and slapping his lariat against his slicker, trying to move the steers. The animals circled and bawled and bunched up against the farside of the corral.

"Get over here," Tru screamed. "Behind them."

Linc moved his horse slowly and JD followed against the rails and soon one steer darted out into the corral but then turned back to the others. Tru spurred the mare in front of the animal and then headed him for the gate, and soon the entire herd, each in turn, squeezed through the opening and darted slipping and falling out onto the rangeland. Outside the corral, Linc saw the animals bunch and circle nervously with each flash of light, then scatter left and right when the thunder clapped, only to regroup and repeat the chaos with the next bolt.

To Linc's right, Tru whistled and screamed commands but Linc could not understand what Tru wanted except to move them south. On Linc's left, JD reined the buckskin against the tight group and so Linc moved in behind. At the next bolt, the animals had nowhere left to go, so with the prodding of the three horsemen, the steers began to string out to the south. Linc was wishing for a fourth horseman but he felt better seeing them move. The trick would be to keep them from stampeding as they went downhill into the drywash which lay three miles south of the corrals. Tru had obviously decided this was where he wanted to take them. And if they were lucky, this low ground would not be flash flooding yet and the huge rock outcroppings on either side would provide protection, giving a lower profile for the cattle. And for the three horsemen. Tru and Linc knew this was the plan. But JD, riding left point, had no idea what was happening and without a fourth horseman, there was no way Linc could abandon riding drag to tell JD they must move the animals slow downhill and into the drywash when they got there. Linc wished now he had taken point.

A half hour passed and except for the sporadic circling, the steers continued to make progress south. The lightning did seem to move north but the rain did not slacken and even the more distant thunder made the black gelding tense and shift and snort objections. Linc wondered about JD's buckskin but knew he was steady.

An hour dragged by and then Linc saw the silhouette of the outcropping. The rain subsided some but the lightning which now outlined the rocks was further south again and Linc wondered if more was coming. Tru had seen the boulders and loped ahead to turn the cattle to the left and into the wash below. But JD did not move forward to keep pace with the lead steer, and instead of moving into the lower ground, the animal ran too far to the left and in front of JD. By the time JD moved forward to correct their direction, a dozen or so steers had escaped up the left side of the wash and onto the rocky plateau at the top of the ridge. When Linc saw JD and Tru finally push the remainder of the herd into the wash, he reined to the left and loped up the ridge after the loose cattle.

As soon as he was atop the ridge, Linc felt the wind pick up from the south. Sharp rain curried his face and lightning shot spectral fingers across the sky and into the blackness of more clouds. He saw one finger touch the ground further south and hang on and on, as if waiting for something to die before it let go. In that long moment of fixed electricity, Linc remembered some famous western painting he had once seen with lightning frozen in time just like that, but he could not remember everything that was in the picture, just a lone cowhand holding his back hunched into a storm, just like this one, and the rider lifting his slicker high above his head and above the long horns of a ghost steer, wild eyed and wet and washed with neon blue light, charging headlong toward a black chasm on the wet prairie, and it was obvious that if the steer did not change directions, it and the horse and the doomed rider would all plunge off that cliff and into the eternal darkness. Or maybe into the black of the sky. Linc did not know which the artist intended.

In the new flashes, much brighter and intense, Linc saw the group of maverick steers move into the piñons above the ridge but they had not yet scattered. He reined toward the spot he last saw them standing, terrified and bunched, immobilized by the lightning. He pulled the gelding up and waited as he squinted to see the animals in the next flash.

Then everything was awash with light, not electric blue, but white hot. It killed all his vision. The last thing Linc remembered was the sudden shifting of the gelding, as if the animal had been snatched off his feet like some toy. Then he felt a sledge hammer slam into the side of his head. He did not remember hitting the ground. He no longer felt the rain flog his face or run into the collar of his slicker or soak his now hatless head.

Awareness came with a strange amalgam of silence and singing in his ears and a passing of time as though he had been lying in the bottom of a canoe, watching blue sky and clouds above, and it was not an unpleasant feeling. Linc felt his toes move first inside one boot, still on his left foot, and then the other toes inside the bootless sock, soaked to the other foot. And then he felt his fingers move as though they were separate from his arm and for a long while, he lay in the darkness behind his eyes and refused to open them or move anything else. He did not know how long he lay on the hard ground but he knew the rain had stopped and when he finally opened his eyelids to a mere slit, he could see nothing and he wondered if he had been struck blind. He closed his lids again and swallowed and the taste was bronze and bitter and almost dry and he tried again but there was nothing to swallow. And so he drifted once more inside the canoe until he heard the keel scraping gravel.

Linc tried to sit but fell back on his elbows and this time when he raised his eyelids, there was a gray glow around him and the dark blur of piñon trees against that and the sound he heard as gravel became loose rocks under the hooves of Tru's mare as she shifted. Linc sucked in a deep breath and felt the cool damp air clear the electric taste from his lungs and throat and the singing in his head became a drumbeat of pain. His vision returned in waves of prefocused images: Tru, hunkered at the edge of the rimrock, silent and still as the flagstone itself, holding onto the reins of the mare who stood patient and calm behind him, and around them the scattered and stiffened carcasses of cattle.

Linc groaned when he finally sat. Tru sat mute, staring into the quickening gray to the east as though not only the steers but the entire universe around him was devoid of life.

"Tru..." Linc's voice came creaky and hollow from somewhere distant. Tru did not seem to hear. Linc feared neither of them was alive. He repeated, "Tru..." and the word was stronger this time. Tru shifted. The mare backed to the end of the reins and Tru rose and took off his hat and smoothed his hair with the palm of his leather glove. He looked around again at the carnage and then glanced toward Linc, still sitting. "Figured you was dead too," Tru said, but there was no relief or even apology in his voice, just a statement of fact. Tru made no effort to assist.

"How long I been here?" Linc said.

"Quite a while."

Linc was silent for a long moment as he looked around for his hat and then said, "How many?"

"Ten here," Tru said and lifted his chin. "Three more over the edge. Thirteen in all."

"Bad number," Linc said, though he felt lucky himself.

"Those three in the wash down there are still kicking but they won't make it." Tru seemed to see Linc now for the first time, "Not like you did." He reached out a hand.

"It's okay," Linc said. "I can make it." He rolled to the left and pushed himself onto his knees. For a long while he stayed in this crawling position until most of the dizziness passed and then he brought under himself first the foot that still wore a boot and then the other. He limped in a circle, searching for the lost boot and gaining equilibrium.

"This what you looking for?" Tru said and held out Linc's hat, soaked and mangled. Linc took it and tugged it onto his head crooked.

"Thanks. Now If I can just find the rest of my clothes." He lifted the bootless foot and Tru looked around but he made no effort to search.

"Where'd the horse go?" Linc said. "Boot's probably still in the stirrup."

Tru just shook his head.

"What about JD?"

"Down there with what's left." Tru turned and walked to the edge of the outcropping and Linc limped after. In the early gray they could see JD making a lazy circle around the remaining cattle a hundred yards below, pulling at the sparse vegetation as if nothing had happened. At the base of this rock ledge lay the last three of the struck steers, only two still kicking. Tru spat over the edge and turned away. He went to the mare and pulled his 30-30 from the scabbard and came back and stood beside Linc. He levered a cartridge into the chamber and lifted the rifle.

"You see JD down there, don't you?" Linc said. It was obvious JD was in the line of fire, just as he had been on the gravel road. Tru squeezed off one round, quickly chambered the next, sighted and fired. Now all three lay still. The sounds from the rifle echoed down the wash like a bullwhip and the remainder of the herd jerked in unison one way at first and then another with the second shot and Linc saw JD almost lose his seat as the buckskin attempted to head them. The entire herd scattered into the piñons and across the open range. JD reined his horse back from the futility of pursuit. He looked up at the two men on the ledge and then again at the running cattle and then back up. There was no instruction from above. Finally JD shook his head and leaned on his saddle horn and sat for a long while before he spurred up the embankment.

On top, he dismounted and stood stiff when he saw the dead steers there and below. "Lightning," Linc offered. "Hit right in the middle of us."

Tru said nothing. In the broadening light of sunrise, he watched the last of the steers scatter, some into the foothills to the east and the others to the west and finally he said, "They'll be right back over by the road, goddammit." Since he could not curse the rain, Tru said nothing else. He mounted the mare and put her forward in the direction of the house.

"Where's your boot?" JD said. He led the buckskin over and stood beside Linc. "Looks like somebody stole your horse too," he teased.

"Does look a little comical," Linc admitted. The cool damp air had relieved some of the pounding inside his skull. "Which way you traveling?"

"Today...or tomorrow?"

"Today."

"Dunno. How about you?"

Linc nodded toward the northwest, the adobe ranch house glowing peach in the sunrise.

"Well," JD said. "You go ahead and get on, I'll swing behind."

"You sure?"

"Hell I can't leave you out here," JD said.

Linc mounted the buckskin and pulled JD on behind and they

rode silent for a long while.

"Besides, it'd be hard to explain," JD finally said.

"What?"

"Burying your wore-out old carcass, one boot on, one boot off."

Linc did not respond. The buckskin snorted, neither in protest nor agreement, just for the sake of snorting.

FOURTEEN

Inside the bunkhouse, Santos watched the lantern expire in the neardawn. He felt his way over to it and groped for matches above the cookstove. He struck one, held it high but by the time he turned and moved across the room to touch the base of the hanging lantern, the match was out. He lifted the glass globe and cranked the wick higher. He struck another match and set fire to the wick and watched it smoke and spew but then the flame bent when the door opened and went out again.

"Sorry," Jesse said. In the dimness, she heard the rooster inside his cage. She closed the door and stood still while Santos moved again to the wood cookstove and she heard him bump into the ash bucket and topple the kindling. Finally she heard the rattling of matches and the rasping of one atop the iron stove and then she saw his face, floating in the glow.

"Tenemos luz," he said, and he was smiling behind the match-flame. He held a palm in front of the flame this time as he carefully moved toward the lantern and then touched the match to the wick again. It caught just before the flame burned his finger. He dropped the match and it spent itself on the floor. "We have light but we have no heat, and soon we will need neither."

Jesse came into the room and sat at the battered oak table under the lantern where she and Santos would wait.

"I will make coffee," the old man said, as if reminded by the ancient red and white checked oilcloth, branded with countless rings from hot coffepots. He moved back to the stove. Jesse watched him dip the camp pot into the water crock and lift a coffee can from the shelf and then toss in a handful. "They will be tired." He paused and thought about this and put in another handful. "And cold."

"Did you sleep?" Jesse looked at the old man's cot and noticed the string of rosary beads on his blanket.

"Before but not after." He reached for kindling, stuffed some into the firebox and then splashed kerosene from a tin cup onto it. He struck another match and held it to the oil and soon the firebox was ablaze.

"Me too," Jesse said.

"And it is too late now."

She took it as a question and nodded, "But the rain stopped. They'll be back soon."

"Cielo did not either." He moved over and sat at the table across from her. "But then he does not always sleep anyway, looking for the sun, always looking for the sun."

"Maybe he's smart," Jesse said. She sighed and thought about her distaste for sunrises. "Is he brave too?"

"Si."

She waited for more but there was only silence.

"I spoke with a man." Jesse said, making conversation. "An important man. Yesterday."

Santos nodded, "About the wire." Santos knew all about *jéfes.*

"Yes, but something else."

He nodded again but said nothing.

"He has friends. They also have roosters."

Santos stared at her but he understood. She went on with this but she did not know why except that Hill Garza did mention it, and it was something to talk about as minutes dragged. "They know it is not legal over here but they do it anyway."

He glanced at the door and then at the cage in the corner. "Mine has a handicap," he said and then smiled at her. "Some would say two, including me."

"Ummm... Does he still fight? I mean with just one eye?"

"*We* fight," Santos corrected. "Together we have three."

"I should have said you *two,*" Jesse lowered her eyes and smiled. "I don't know anything about it, Santos."

"Do you want to know a thing about it, *Señora?"* he said and when Jesse feigned indifference, Santos went on because he knew she did. "There is no mystery, unless one wishes to call death a mystery."

"Death?"

"It is about courage and it is about truth. But it is also about death. It is not always about the money."

"The winner lives," she said. "The loser doesn't. I know that."

"There can be much won and much lost depending on the betting," he said. "But there can only be one true loser. It is always so."

"Or one true winner?" she observed, and now she meant death itself and Santos understood this and nodded.

"Si." He got up and went to the stove. The coffee was beginning to boil. He lifted the lid and watched the roiling black liquid inside and then replaced it and the steam curled outward and the heat from the spout felt good against his belly.

And in the spiral of rising steam, Santos sees the face of Paloma and she is wrinkled and angry and again he whispers the question, "Was it always so, my Paloma? These wrinkles?" And then Santos is inside the fighting pit, ringed with hundreds of ocotillo shafts, driven into the sand to form a low walled arena, and the noise of the crowd pressing against the outside is deafening. Cielo is puffed and ready and the three inch razor gaffs strapped to the stubs of his heels reflect the light like tiny scythes. Santos cradles his bird under his arm, careful to avoid the gaffs. Across the ring eight feet away and under the arm of the jéfe's handler, the black jerks his head left and right and puffs his breast feathers which shine in the sunlight like a raven's. But battles have left no feathers on his opponent's head for Cielo to grasp with his beak and like Cielo's, the bloodrich wattle and comb have been surgically trimmed away to provide the lowest profile for the opposing gaffs. Bottles of tequila pass through the crowd and the early bets are called out in the cacophony and even before the fight, the jéfe's bird is pitted now at twenty pesos to one against Cielo.

"And what will you place on your bird?" The jéfe is suddenly behind Santos, smiling under his broad mustache with a cheroot in his teeth. Santos turns and for a moment he wishes Paloma were here to take care

of this important matter. But she has refused to come, chiding him not to bring back even the carcass because it would be too tough to eat. And the ten peso coin in his pocket seems paltry among the bets he is hearing.

"Well?" the jéfe says and there is a hush over the crowd now and all eyes are on Santos.

"I will begin with ten pesos," he says boldly, as if Cielo will fight many others this dusty afternoon, and the betters around him set up a low laugh and Santos averts his eyes, remembering the bad luck of excessive bravado.

"Ten?" the jéfe says and grins broadly and then he studies the bird under Santos' arm and the grin disappears. "Well, because you are a sport, you are covered my friend. But let us make it interesting," He looks around at the faces and pauses for dramatic effect and then his eyes are again on Santos and he says, "Shall we say, one-hundred-to-one odds that this chicken will lose?"

There is a sudden intake of breath which circles through the crowd and Santos is stunned. The jéfe turns away and chaos breaks loose as betters crowd him to wager against his black at these incredible odds. Santos does not get a chance to respond. But he has mentioned his ten pesos and everyone has heard it and he knows his bet is down now at one-hundred-to-one.

And now the referee calls for the birds to be beaked and Santos brings Cielo forward to meet the other handler. In the center of the arena, the beaks of the two cocks are rubbed together and the birds are allowed to peck briefly at each other to build their anger and then the referee sends them back to their opposing sides. Santos kneels on his mark and places Cielo on the sand and there he holds him until the referee gives the signal. At this, Santos releases Cielo who takes a single step and then rises high into the air to meet the black who has come in low with his gaffs slashing upward. But neither bird scores a hit. They land and circle each other in the center, their heads low, their hackles raised. The crowd has gone wild and fingers to indicate more betting are flashed into the air with each maneuver of the opponents in the pit. And then the black rises again and this time Cielo falls onto his back with his heels upward but the black avoids them and grabs a beakful of Cielo's head feathers and then slashes with his own gaffs at the white breast. Cielo rakes a gaff across a flap of black wing and suddenly his spur is imbedded into the bone of the black's wing and Cielo cannot retrieve it. Santos calls out for the referee to give the command to handle the birds so they can be separated but his request does no good. The referee glances in the direction of the jéfe who tosses back a jigger of tequila and smiles. The referee ignores Santos as if he has not heard him. Now the black is atop Cielo who can move but one heel and it jabs uselessly into the air as the two roll across the pit in a flutter of wings and beaks and flashing gaffs and dust. When they stop rolling, Cielo manages to pull his gaff from the wing but not before one sharp point of the black's gaff clips his eye. Blood flows down the side of Cielo's head and into the white of his breast and Santos knows the eye is now useless. The black moves away, one wing broken where Cielo's gaff has pierced the bone and his opponent drags it in the sand. Even now the referee does not call for a break and the crowd knows the handlers should be given a chance to nurse their birds, suck away the blood and give them a brief rest but the screaming continues and there is no pause. Santos sits back on his heels, resigned that with only one eye, Cielo is finished. But his rooster is not finished. Cielo cocks his head and continues to circle with the goodeye locked on the black who has tired quickly, his heavy wing trailing blood in the sand. Neither bird attacks or even feigns attack for a long moment. It is as if they know when they rise up again, it will be for the final time. And then there is a strange hush over the crowd and Santos has never seen this before and the birds seem aware that the noise has stopped and the tension is thick and normally there would be a call for handling. But again there is none. They continue circling. Finally, Cielo stops and crouches low and turns his head as if in defeat and the black moves in. But then Cielo springs in one final effort and the black matches his leap and both are high in the air, gaffs again whipping and when they land, there is a splatter of blood onto the ocotillo shafts and the black is on his back, a gaff sunk into the side of his neck. The crowd roars. Now the referee calls for the pause and the jéfe's handler comes in and slowly removes the gaff from the black's neck and separates the birds. He immediately puts his mouth on the neck to suck the wound. Santos lifts Cielo and holds him against his shirt to rest because he knows that such aggressive nursing as the other handler is doing can only tire a fighting rooster. He allows the blood from Cielo's dead eye to soak into his shirt. Again all is silence and waiting to see if the fight will resume.

And then there is a gurgling from the throat of the black and his head goes limp in the hand of the handler and it is over except for the paying of losses.

Outside the pit, Santos cradles Cielo and pushes through the crowd and stands on the parameter where the jéfe can find him. "You have won," the man says but Santos corrects him, "Cielo has won."

"Si," the jéfe says and looks at the bird. "He has a strong heart."

Santos nods and looks into the man's eyes and they both know what is unspoken. Finally the jéfe says, "Ten pesos, correct?" Santos nods and the man continues, "One-hundred-to-one times..." He pauses, furrows his brow.

"Times ten pesos," Santos reminds him and he thinks it will be more than enough to buy his and Paloma's small piece of disputed land and thus settle once and for all its ownership, even without the parchment.

"Si," the man repeats and then, "One thousand pesos. Well, I am sorry but I do not have that kind of money on me at the moment, my friend. Lo siento. But if you will come into my office tomorrow morning I will pay you just as I will pay the others who were lucky here today."

The jéfe shows his white teeth but Santos can only look at him grimly. What else is there to do? Take his case to the referee who is obviously in the employ of this man? Complain to the others who also have not been paid? Protest to the police who probably lost money on this match?

"I will be there," he mutters and he walks away and all the way home he feels the hot blood from the eye of Cielo, soaking against his belly, and he wonders how he will convince Paloma that they won.

Santos felt the steam from the coffee pot against his belly and he looked at Cielo in his cage and said to Jesse, "Sometimes we lose, even when we win." Absently he reached for the handle of the coffee pot and then jerked his fingers away and placed them into his mouth. "And sometimes we are burned." He smiled and grasped the coffee pot again, but this time he first pulled on a leather glove. He set two coffee mugs on the table and filled each with coffee and then placed the pot on the oilcloth and sat.

Jesse nodded, lifted one of the mugs, blew across the top of it and sipped. She would not talk to Santos again about cockfights unless Hill pressed her. She guessed Hill probably would press her, just as he had always done.

"More?" Santos lifted the pot and held it over Jesse's mug but she shook her head.

"Put it back on the stove," she said. "They'll want some when they get back."

Santos nodded, got up and returned the coffee to the stove. He opened the iron door and rattled the grate and then tossed in more wood and closed the stove. They did not hear Tru cross the yard from the corral and go into the main house. Sometime later, Jesse rose and went to the door and opened it and looked out into the morning.

"Maybe something's happened?" she said, and then as if her comment had brought them into view, she saw the lone horse moving up from the south. "There they are."

Santos came to the door to look. "But only one horse?"

"Looks like."

"And no cattle?"

She shook her head and moved aside so he could see better. "Maybe the others are with the cattle," she said. But then she could see there were two astride the buckskin and they were coming very slow. She walked out into the yard and Santos followed her across to the horse corral and they could see the black, standing behind the corrals near the water trough, his saddle twisted to one side and the reins dangling. Linc's boot hung loosely in one stirrup.

"Damn," she said and she went into the mud of the corral and over to the black who jerked his head back when she reached for the rein. She could see the horse had fallen and cut himself across the ribs. "Easy," she cooed and moved her hand slowly this time and caught the rein. "Take him in the barn and unsaddle him and brush him down," she said and Santos took the reins and led the animal away. She pulled the boot from the stirrup as he passed. "And put something on that cut."

Santos nodded. She looked around and now saw Tru's mare inside the stalls, the saddle still on her. Jesse leaned on the rails of the corral and wondered why the black and the mare had been ignored. It was not like Tru to leave animals saddled and injured and she wondered if JD had come in on the mare instead and if this was Tru on the buckskin. She looked back over the corral rail and now saw it was Linc in the saddle with JD on behind.

"Lightning," JD said when they got close, the single word enough to explain all, but Jesse wanted more.

"What happened?" she said. She held up Linc's boot.

JD swung down and held the boot while Linc pushed his still damp sock into it and then dismounted stiffly. JD looked at Jesse who stood frowning, confused. "And rain," JD continued. "One of them little ones."

FIFTEEN

"Screw it," JD said. He set the pail of warm milk on Jesse's counter and said the words again, much louder, and they echoed off the tile and bounced around the empty kitchen and then escaped, unacknowledged, through the dusty screendoor. He looked out Jesse's window toward the bunkhouse and saw nothing moving there either. "Maybe they're all dead this morning," he said.

He went to retrieve the crock and the milk strainer to cool down the milk but then changed his mind and shut the door to the pantry as loud as he could. "To hell with it," he said. On his way out, he palmed a too soft orange from a basket on the counter, bit into the peel and spat it into the yard outside, snarling at the bitter taste. "It can just stay warm. Nobody in here seems to give a shit anyway. Hell, they've slept twenty-four hours straight." He tossed the tainted orange over the fence and went into the shed. He collapsed on his cot, staring at an insect struggling inside a cobweb in the corner of the ceiling.

When JD finally realized no one on this side of the hardpan driveway seemed to miss him, he tossed everything he owned into a cardboard box and bound it with a string and walked out of his sleeping quarters, slamming the door hard. He glanced toward Jesse's kitchen door as he passed but did not pause. He stomped across the driveway and banged open the bunkhouse door with the heel of his hand. Linc was half dressed at the woodstove, frying bacon. Scrambled eggs lay warming on a thick platter at the back of the stove. Linc did not even look up.

"This is more like it," JD said, sucking in a deep breath.

Linc finally turned and glanced at JD and then back at the bacon. "What's in your box?"

"Everything." JD said. He came in and shut the door and set the stringtied cardboard box on an empty bunk and then took off his hat and put it on top of the box. "And nothing."

"You moving in?" Linc forked the bacon onto the platter with the eggs. He brought the food and the coffee pot to the table and then went to the window and pulled back the gunnysack curtain. The risen sun spilled in four angular squares onto the floor.

"Moving out," JD corrected. "Maybe you'd drive me to town, Linc?"

"Food's better over here," Linc said, ignoring this. He pointed to a chair with his fork. "Sit."

"That's okay," JD said. "I ate an orange," he lied and remained standing, surveying the room as if deciding. "I just wanna get the fuck outta here. Where's the old man?"

"Tru?" Linc scraped eggs and bacon onto one tin plate for himself and another for JD and then a third. He poured three mugs of coffee and sat. "Ain't seen him."

"I meant Santos."

"He's under there." Linc pointed to one bunk, bare except for the thin mattress. "Been there all yesterday after we come in and then all night too I guess." JD leaned over and looked. Under the bunk lay Santos. A blanket covered both his head and also the rooster cage and they were tucked as far as possible against the wall.

"Well shit," JD grinned, incredulous. "Everbody's gun shy this morning. Ain't nobody up over there either." He sat and stirred in three spoons of sugar and then lifted the mug of coffee and blew over the lip and sipped. "They're probably not under a bed though."

"Eat," Linc said. "He'll come outta there when he gets hungry."

JD tucked into the food. When he had satisfied himself that he would not starve aboard some bus to wherever, he turned sideways in the chair and leaned his elbows on his knees with the mug of coffee in his hands between them. He stared at the lump of blanket under the bunk and when Linc stopped eating and set his fork aside, JD heard whispering and a rattling like spilled beans against the plank floor. So did Linc. They looked at each other and then back to the blanket under the cot.

Linc frowned and set his mug on the oilcloth and got up. He crept to the bunk and leaned over and lifted the edge of the blanket. Cielo fluttered inside the cage but then he was still. Santos lay on one side, a string of rosary beads flowing from his hands onto the wooden floor. He held his eyes clinched and his lips moved to the whispered words and he shook his head as if to indicate he was not finished. Linc held the blanket for a few moments, looked over at JD and shrugged. He lowered the corner of the blanket back over Santos' head and crept back to his seat at the table and sat silent. JD lifted his mug to sip but then paused, regarded the blanket once more and then he too sat still.

When Santos crawled out, he seemed a man redeemed. The two at the table said nothing as he washed himself with a basin of cold water and then took the pan to the door and tossed the water into the yard.

"Gracias," Santos said at the table. He shut his eyes again, crossed himself and thanked god for the food and then began to eat but he was very somber. Linc said nothing. JD began sipping again and watched Santos over the edge of his coffee mug. When he finished eating, Santos said, "I have spoken words for you." He looked at JD and then to Linc, "And especially for you, *Señor."*

"I was lucky," Linc said and he too was grave.

"Luck is a bad mistress," Santos said. "I do not think you want to live with her."

"Maybe not live with her," Linc said. He rose and crossed to his bunk and sat on the edge. He worked the stiff leather tops of his dried boots with his hands and stared into the cracks of the floor, thinking about the painting of the lone rider in the lightning storm and the black chasm. "But it damn sure don't hurt to ride with her once in a while."

"I don't live here anymore either." JD announced. He tugged on his hat and then took the cardboard box under his arm and stood beside Linc. "Not any more anyway. Well, whatta you say, Linc?"

"I say these goddamn boots are stiff as hell."

"That ain't what I'm talking about."

Linc studied him. "You told them?"

"Told them what?"

"That you're leaving."

"Ain't nobody awake over there, I told you that and I'm telling you this."

"Still..."

"Still what? Fuck it, I'm outta here, Linc. I've had enough."

Santos looked at JD for a long moment and then at Linc but had nothing to offer. Any advice about staying or traveling or even life itself, lay safely engrained in his rosary beads.

"Fine by me." Linc strained with one boot and finally it slipped on. He sighed and then pulled on the other and sat staring at the scruffed tips of the boots. "Gets harder and harder don't it," he said quietly to no one. "Shit, maybe I'll just hook up my little old trailer house and leave with you, JD. Before my luck plum runs out."

"No sense doing that, Linc. Besides, you ain't been paid."

"Neither have you."

"They can send it. If they ever get it. I got plenty anyway," he lied.

"You oughta say bye, JD. At least to Jesse."

"It don't matter. You ain't said bye either, Linc."

"I ain't family," Linc said. "You are. And I didn't say I *was* leaving, just that I got this bad feeling maybe I *oughta* leave."

"Well." JD turned and went to the door. "I can just hoof it in."

"Watch them trucks on the road," Linc said.

JD opened the door and held it for a moment. *"Adios,"* he said.

"Hold on," Linc said. He rose and buttoned on a shirt and took his warped hat from a nail. He put on the hat and then cocked his head and stood at a piece of broken mirror propped on a shelf. Linc made a big production of trying to re-form the crown the crease in the hat. "Sonuvabitch shrunk," he said and tried to stretch it over his head but it sat awkwardly to one side. "If I ain't leaving, I guess I could use a new hat anyway. If Compton'll give me credit."

"Maybe the head got bigger," JD said. He came back into the room and offered a hand to Santos who first gave it a puzzled look and then looked into JD's face and realized the boy was serious about leaving. He held JD's hand limply and glanced over at Cielo but JD did not acknowledge the bird at all. Neither said anything, just squeezed hands and nodded, once. Then JD and Linc left.

They had rattled halfway to Lajitas in his old pickup before Linc spoke again. "Or a least a coldbeer."

"What?"

"A new hat or a few coldbeers," he said. "One of the two, that's what I need."

"Oh."

"Or maybe some beautiful Meskin border woman," Linc said. "You drink beer?"

"Only thing you'll find in Lajitas is beer. If you're lucky, it'll be cold. You better dump me off and get on back," JD said. He fingered the twine on the cardboard box in his lap, tightened the knot and looked at Linc, whom he still could not envision with any woman. "Jesse's fence and all..."

"Jesse's?"

"Well, Tru's..."

"Thought you didn't care," Linc said and then, "Well, do you?"

"Care?"

"No. Drink cold beer?"

"I ain't old enough." It was a half-lie. He and the Fighting Bobcat squad had been across the Mexican border before, where cold beer and women and everything else were legal, no matter what age. JD added quickly, "Besides, I'm catching a bus."

"That ain't what I asked. I didn't say buy it, I said drink it. I'll worry about the buying. But as far as getting a new hat or a woman, you're on your own there." Linc paused for a long moment and then said. "You're old enough to die, ain't you?"

"Whatta you mean?" JD was confused by the change in subject.

"For your country."

JD lifted his shoulders and remembered that in his haste to leave home and Betty Lee Collins, joining the military had not been an option he considered. "You was in the army?" JD said as diversion.

Linc nodded.

"Where?"

"All over."

"Combat?"

"Explosives. That was my MO.

"MO?"

"Military Occupation."

"Where?"

"All over."

"But I mean *where* all over?"

"Viet Nam and Viet Nam and Viet Nam…all over."

JD nodded. He could see Linc with horses and cattle and maybe even a woman but not with combat explosives in some jungle. "What about you? You ever think about dying?" JD said as casually as such a topic would allow.

Linc looked at him, unconvinced the remark was offhand. "You mean then, or now?" he said and then, "Lots of times. Why? You been thinking about it?"

"Well not exactly thinking about it," JD said and then reminded him, "You brought it up."

"But you have, right?" Linc guessed. "Thought about it."

"Well, that fucking storm and all…"

"That's why you're leaving?"

"No."

"Tru's fence?"

"Not really."

"Maybe them blasting caps?" Linc tried. "No need to sweat that. I told you I was an expert."

"It ain't that either."

"Well what?"

"Shit, I dunno, Linc. What difference does it make?"

"Well like I said back there, you ain't even told your own relatives *adios*, you ain't got your pay, nothing."

"I said they could send it to me."

"Where?"

"I dunno that either. Shit, I'll send you a postcard."

They rolled onto the two-lane just outside Lajitas and Linc shifted down and finally rattled to a stop at the bus sign in front of the Elbo Room. He killed the engine and both sat listening to it gurgle and snap in the rising heat. Little ever stirred on the streets of Lajitas at any time and nothing this early.

"What about your ticket?" Linc finally said. "You come on a roundtrip?"

"No," JD looked up the street one way and then back the other. Cicadas began to tune up in the Honey Mesquite along the river. "I'll just get on it and buy another oneway right there from the driver and go whichever way it's going."

"Well, it'll go that way, cut up to Alpine and then on northeast to your home stomping grounds," Linc said and took out his toothpick, pointed and then exposed a row of tobacco stained teeth, "Or west on over to Presidio and then northwest up through Marfa and on over to El Paso. Depends on which way it comes in."

JD pursed his lips and nodded and then worked his hand into his pocket and sighed. "Linc?" he said.

"Yeah."

"About that pay. Maybe you could just keep part of it." JD removed his hat, wiped the sweatband with the palm of his hand and put it back on. "I mean, when it comes, maybe you could just take some of it and loan me that much right now?"

Linc spat out the window. "Probably." He sat staring at the deserted buildings for a long while and then he leaned forward and retrieved his wallet and thumbed the bills. "Twenty-seven," he said. "And change. That's all I got JD."

"I got five."

"Shit, that's thirty-two, it'll get you home."

"I didn't say I was going home, Linc."

"Yeah. Well, it'll get you on down the road—somewhere."

"Yeah." JD inspected the twine knotted around the box again. "Anywhere I can step in cowshit, right?"

Linc watched him and after a long while said, "Or that'll get us a couple bowls of Sonny Pun's cowshit chili and at least a case of his cheapest longneck beer, but what's left won't buy any women. That is, unless we drove on down to Ojinaga."

"We just ate," JD reminded him and then pretending he did not know he said, "Where's that?"

"Right across the border from Presidio. But you gotta be real hungry," Linc joked, but when he saw JD had fallen silent again he said, "She won't like it." The comment was sudden, like the topic of dying. "Your leaving. Jesse won't."

"She won't care."

"I think she likes you, JD. I seen her looking at you like she does them strays."

"Well, like you say, she's family."

"She won't want you gone."

"I already had to leave her once before," JD said without explanation and he thought it sounded like an eight year old's pouting remark. Then he remembered Jesse with her arms around him as that same boy and again in the corral, only with his arms around her, but maybe as a man this time, and even in the heat he shivered, remembered both feelings. "I don't want to think about Jesse or Tru or Santos or any of this shit anymore. I just want to get moving, goddammit. You know how it is Linc."

"Yeah."

SIXTEEN

"What time is it?" JD said.

Linc leaned to the windshield and squinted into the front window of the Elbo Room. "Can't tell from here. Sonny's clock ain't always right anyway."

"He open yet?"

"Nope. We can open him though." Linc got out of the pickup and shut the door. He leaned back through the window, "He'll sell you a ticket. You coming?"

"I ain't old enough to go in, remember?"

"Like I said, you're old enough to die for your country."

"You're talking about dying again."

Linc stared at him and this time he was very serious. "Well, maybe I seen the other side JD." He straightened, stepped away from the truck and JD could not see his face. "And it's black over there. A man ain't got much time over here JD. Come on. We'll go around back and wake him up."

JD got out and followed Linc into the alley. Linc snaked around the garbage cans and through the broken beer bottles like a soldier in a mine field.

JD considered their conversation this morning and could not decide if Linc were a man dying or a man reborn. At the moment, Linc seemed more alive and decisive than anytime JD had known him, and he could not keep up with Linc as he disappeared around back of the Elbo Room. When he turned the corner, Linc was pounding on a weathered door, secured with a brass, disc shaped padlock as big as a cowpie.

"He does this shit," Linc said. He lifted the padlock and let it thud against the wood. "Locks himself in every night, sleeps right here in the bar. Stupid."

"Why don't he put it on the inside?"

"He's got one there too." Linc pounded on the door again. "Locks this one on the outside, goes around front, locks the front door from the inside and then puts another lock back here on the inside of this door. Stupid."

"Why?"

"Says thieves always come in the back way and this big serious bastard scares them off and if it don't, he's got a backup lock inside." He slapped the lock again and they waited. After awhile, an interior door slammed and a toilet flushed inside and then a few moments later, a voice said, "Who's there?"

"It's me, stupid."

"Who's stupid? I know lots of stupids."

Linc shook his head, leaned both hands against the door. "Come on, Sonny. We ain't got all day. It's getting hot out here." He paused and listened but there was no sound now. "We need a bus ticket."

JD heard a scratching and suddenly a large key emerged through the crack at the bottom of the door. Linc bent to pick it up. He opened the padlock and stood waiting and soon they heard the inside padlock snap open and then Sonny Pun was in the doorway with a flashlight. "Why didn't you say so?"

"What happened to your nose?" Linc said.

"Sheep dip," Sonny Pun sighed and then, "It's a long story and I ain't going into it and yeah I know, it ain't no skin off your nose."

Linc brushed past him and walked into the dark hallway. Sonny Pun blinked into the sunlight and stepped aside and jerked his head, indicating JD should follow and so he did. "You're Jesse's kin, right?"

JD nodded and felt his way through the dark passage and into the relative brightness of the bar. Sonny Pun shut the door and followed with the circle of flashlight covering just his feet. Behind the bar, Linc groped inside the cooler. He brought out two longneck beers and opened them and set one on the bar and held the other. Then he came around and sat on a barstool.

"I open at noon and I don't drink beer before that," Sonny Pun announced to no one. He rattled a percolator down from a shelf behind the bar and filled it with coffee grounds and water and set it on a hotplate.

"It's past noon." Linc pointed his longneck at Sonny's clock. "Ten minutes. Besides, this other one ain't for you anyway." Linc said. "And when did you get so damned legal? Who'd you think might drop by checking ID's? Texas Rangers got their hands full without worrying about a growed-up man and a beer. Drink up JD."

JD moved to the barstool next to Linc. He grasped the cold bottle and looked at the front door, still locked he assumed, but he did not drink.

"Go ahead," Sonny Pun said. "If you been working with this asshole you probably need it. Shit, if I'm going to jail it might as well be for a good cause." He reached over and flipped on the neon beer sign. Then he took two cans of chili and a rusted can opener from the shelf and opened the cans. He dumped the contents into a large cast iron skillet and sprinkled a half-inch layer of black pepper on the top. He tipped the concoction toward the two for inspection. "Sonny Pun's best, world class Lajitas chili," he announced and then set the skillet on the hotplate. "Secret recipe though. Don't tell any of them *serious* chiliheads, okay? I guess we're open for business now." He went to the front and unlocked the door.

JD sipped the cold beer. He spun around on the stool and looked at the barroom and then out at the bus sign. He turned back to Sonny Pun. "What time's the next bus?"

"Meskin or Texas time?" Sonny Pun said. He twisted the lid from a gallon jug of pickled eggs and reached his bare hand in and brought one out, shook off the vinegar and popped the egg into his mouth. "Breakfast," he said around the egg. He inclined the opened jug toward the two but both declined. He took out another for himself, screwed the lid back on and turned to pour a cup of coffee. JD frowned at the pungent odor from the jar, studied the clock.

"Well?" JD said.

"Ain't one today," Sonny Pun announced and he slopped large scoops of his chili into two bowls and scooted them in front of the two.

"What?" Linc said. He took a tentative taste of the concoction.

"Don't come in ever day, that's what. You oughta know that Linc. Comes in over to Presidio ever day, but that's it. Won't be through here till tomorrow." He studied his customers. "I could sell you the ticket here though."

"Presidio?" Linc said and Sonny Pun nodded. No one spoke for a long while and finally Linc said, "Guess I could run you over there, JD. Unless you want to wait and do it tomorrow."

"You'd get fired," JD said. "No sense us both being unemployed."

"I might already be fired," Linc said. "But I been worse."

"I don't think Jesse'd do that," Sonny Pun said. "Can't speak for Truman though. Eat up son." He pointed at the chili. "You may need it."

"How far is it?" JD toyed with the bottle in his hand and then stirred the bowl of chili to find the safest part to dip from. He lifted a spoonful and then stuffed it into his mouth with a few soda crackers and tried to speak around it. "Maybe I could hitchhike," he mumbled

"It's about fifty mile." Linc glanced at Sonny Pun who nodded confirmation and Linc continued, "You musta been watching all that traffic whiz by out front. Is that what you figure you'd grab a ride on?"

"What time's it come in?" JD said and then, "*Presidio* time."

Sonny Pun turned and retrieved a greasy time schedule, slid behind the mirror. In the light of the blue neon beer sign he studied it. "Looks like around two-fifteen," he said but did not sound convincing. "Course I ain't never caught one outta there myself. But then you'd already have your ticket if you get it from me."

"Could I see that?"

Sonny Pun shrugged, handed the schedule to JD who looked it over and said, "Looks like two o'clock to me."

"That's what I said," Sonny Pun seemed put out.

"You said two-fifteen."

"It's always late getting in and late getting out so I hear. Count on it," Sonny Pun assured him.

"Well?" Linc finished his beer.

JD looked at the clock. "Half past twelve here. How fast's your pickup?"

"Fast enough," Linc said.

"Gimme one of them tickets," JD said and sucked down the remainder of his beer and pushed back the chili.

"Where to?"

"Don't matter."

"Well I gotta know how much you want to spend."

JD looked at Linc and thought about gas money for the old truck over and back. "Say fifteen bucks?" he said and lifted his shoulders and studied Linc's face. Linc sat impassive and JD took it for a loan approval.

Sonny Pun ran his finger down the list of fares on the schedule. "That'll get you all the way to..." he said and he looked up at JD, his finger still on the fare, "El Paso. But it won't get you back."

"Good," JD said. "I'll figure it out from there."

Sonny Pun said, "*Good* it will get you there or *good* it won't get you back?"

"Both," JD said. He dug out his five dollar bill and gave it to Sonny Pun who looked at for a long moment.

"I said fifteen."

"Here," Linc said. He fished out a ten.

"You bank rolling this too?" Sonny Pun said. "He said he ain't coming back."

"I'll get it back," Linc said. "Give us a couple six packs of long necks and tally all this up."

Sonny Pun picked up the bills and then turned to the cooler and set two cold six packs on the bar.

"How much more, with the ticket an all?" Linc said.

Sonny picked at the scab on the end of his nose and looked at the two. Then he studied the beer on the bar and the ten and five in his hand. "Hell, keep your money." He grabbed Linc's hand and slapped the money back into it.

"Why?" Linc said, surprised at Sonny's sudden show of generosity.

"Sounds like you're a both a bit shy on cash. Besides, I'd feel real bad if you paid for a ticket and then miss that bus over there. You can pay me back some day," Sonny Pun said. He frowned and became very serious as he wrote out the bus ticket. "And even if I never see it again, just say it ain't no skin off my nose." He shoved the ticket across the bar at JD. "You better hit the road, kid. Good luck."

SEVENTEEN

West of Lajitas, the narrow two-lane cut into a barren stony embankment that rose on the right. The pavement wound above a fringe of salt cedar, paintbrushed in green along the mudbanks of the Rio Grande below on the left.

JD sat silent, watching the landscape alter itself from treeless rock slides on the right to the cool shade of beige canyon walls, cut sharply into the terrain by the river which formed the international border on the left, and then further, rolling piñon hills on both sides of the river.

He thought about those several days last spring when the senior class sidetracked their high school science teacher from more serious end-of-the-school-year matters and got him talking about Texas and the Alamo and Jim Bowie lying there dying of syphilis when those Mexicans stormed his room and how the Texas Big Bend country with all its stark changes that are evident now are more like some adolescent geologic tantrum than age-worn, because that country was actually a billion years old. He wondered about himself, if he might soon be past this fickle stage in his own life, but it was as clear as the next bend in the old two-lane that from his recent actions, he was not.

"Well," he excused himself, "At least I'm thinking about it."

"About what?" Linc said.

"About having another beer before it gets hot." Without Link asking, JD twisted the lid off one longneck and handed it across to him and then did the same for himself. He swilled the beer and studied the road ahead, ignoring the billion year old, adolescent landscape.

No interstate here, nor even near. No sign of pending cities nor major landmarks nor definitive directions for JD in whatever course he might now pursue, nothing but a single passing roadmarker which indicated something—or somewhere—named Redford was twenty-five miles ahead and then another fifteen to Presidio. Beyond that, JD knew El Paso lay somewhere first to the northwest and then on the interstate further west, but no sign confirmed that either or sought to explain why these places even existed or why a road along this desolate stretch of the Rio Grande would even connect any of them to the rest of the world. Or needed to.

No matter. JD was moving. That was the only thing important to him right now so he took a long pull, draining the bottle of beer warming in his hand. He cranked down the window and tossed out the empty and it sailed, free, end-over-end into the barrow ditch and JD felt an exhilaration watching it fly through the air, so he removed his hat and stuck his head out into the wind and screamed at the bottle, yelled nothing, just allowed his voice to escape loud and screeching, bouncing off the rock walls and back into the wind, which was hotter outside than inside the cab, so he rolled the window back up. He laughed and rattled another beer from the cardboard box and held it up. Linc glanced over and frowned but then he looked at the bottle and the beginnings of a grin wrinkled his face and he said, "Hell why not. They'll just get hot if we don't drink them." Linc finished his and tossed the empty back into the box.

"They're already hot," JD said. He twisted the lid from this one and then another for himself and both bottles fizzed over into his lap as he did this. He laughed again, feeling the beer now even more in the heat and he thought about Linc doing all this with him—and maybe even *for* him—but said nothing else.

Even Linc seemed more connected to the motion of his old pickup now than anything stable like rangeland or fences. JD saw the backs of Linc's weathered hands, stretched smooth in a determined grip around the steering wheel and began to think of Linc if not as his traveling companion, at least as his willing and silent accomplice to whatever it was JD was seeking, even if JD did not know what that was himself. But if it was important, maybe Linc knew anyway and would somehow tell JD and if it was not important, then Linc would not say a goddamned thing and that would be okay too. Linc just being there seemed to make it important.

Maybe the talk of death for some cause—or for no cause at all—spurred their moving. JD decided maybe death was important, or at least very serious. But while it sought him just like it did everyone else, he knew he was not seeking it, even though death might hover over everything, like those big black birds JD had seen as he rode back to the ranch house behind Linc on the buckskin. They were vultures or crows or ravens or whatever and like death, clung to the spot where he had buried the old horse and the tomcat.

Scavengers were everywhere, waiting, and even now as he took off his hat and leaned forward and touched his forehead to the hot windshield, he saw tiny black dots against the cobalt sky, riding thermals higher and higher in search of some hapless critter or maybe just watching the pickup move below. He leaned back quickly and put his hat back on to conceal his identity. And then JD thought about the storm and wondered if maybe the lightning had also struck that mound of rocks he had gathered, scattering them and exposing the carcasses he had buried. Exposing death. Releasing death. He was certain Linc had seen the birds too but neither talked about them on the trip into Lajitas, only about dying.

While the thought of death was alien to JD, the concept of having but one life to give for your country seemed utter bullshit. Even though there were no wars or policing action or imminent invasions to his knowledge, serving in the military seemed a hard way to evade Bettye Lee. As long as he remained on a bus going nowhere, perhaps he would never have to see Bettye Lee again. He could avoid her, even if he could not escape mortality. And if the yellow tom and the old cowpony needed covering again, maybe he could count on Linc to do that. Reburying memories which kept trying to surface through the worn layers of strata since he had last seen Jesse might be harder but damned sure easier on a bus to nowhere than in the shed right next to her kitchen.

Jesse might understand his leaving. She might even welcome the news with no goodbye, might accept that this would have been at least as difficult and complex and confusing for him as that first had been when he was just a kid. But JD could not remember why that earlier goodbye had been so hard, except that it too was fused with death. He tried to remember his mother's face but that was difficult too in the increasing fuzz of the beer and the heat. He knew she had all of Jesse's beauty but when he thought about that time in his life, instead of his mother's face, JD only saw Jesse's and his father's, inextricably bound into a single, clouded memory as if each face were an amalgam of the other, each blurring the other.

He remembered how Jesse tried to explain the story of JD's leaving once when they were alone in her kitchen, her back to him as she did the dishes. She spoke in a hushed and painful voice, as if all that death—his grandmother and then his mother, and then Reid and JD leaving and a year later, his grandfather dying in his own vomit—had all seemed to coerce her into some kind of involuntary submission from which she confessed she had never outrun. But he had yet to hear Jesse actually say his father's name, even when she spoke of the leaving. When JD thought about growing up with him, he could never remember his father speaking of the parting. And he never once heard him say Jesse's name either.

"We better get a couple bucks of gas at Redford," Linc said. He reached to the dashboard and tapped the gasoline gauge. "Should get us on into Presidio."

JD looked at the gauge, showing almost empty and he thought about gas money and time and how long it would take to stop and get fuel and get back on the road again. But he said nothing. Linc was in charge of that and he would get him to the bus station on time.

Just out of Redford, JD felt the pickup cough once and then Linc reached quickly to stroke the choke and the engine caught again, but it finally died and there was no sound except the diminishing squeal of the tires on the hot pavement and then on the gravel shoulder as Linc steered it to a halt. Both sat silent for a long while and then Linc rolled down his window and finished his beer. He reached out and tossed the empty over the cab with a hookshot.

"Damn," Linc said and then more silence except for the snapping of the hot engine and the gurgling of the radiator and a raw hot wind breathing around the cab. Linc slammed the heels of both hands into the steering wheel and then without words got out of the pickup and with a great deal of cursing and noise in the bed, dug a battered galvanized can from under a pile of fencepost stubs and rusty wire and hay. He stuck his head back into the cab but before he could speak JD said, "I'll go."

"What the hell you gonna use for money?" Linc spat a small gob of white foam onto the hot pavement and it disappeared almost instantly. "Sonny give it all back to me, remember?"

JD said nothing. He had his ticket in his shirtpocket and could no longer lay claim, even to his five, folded inside Linc's ten dollar bill tucked somewhere in his clothes. He sipped at his warm beer and felt guilty, even though the ticket had been a gift—or a loan—from Sonny and not Linc. He shrugged and looked straight ahead down the incline and into the distance where the quivering heat rose from a cluster of adobe structures. JD decided this was what the sign post had named Redford. When JD got out of the pickup, Linc was already hoofing it down the gravel alongside the pavement, the swinging fuel can squeaking in his hand.

"I'll wait," JD announced. He looked at the shade of a crumbling concrete bridge support where the old road had once spanned a drywash. "Over there," he muttered, but Linc heard neither comment.

"Save me a beer, asshole," Linc shot back without turning.

"You bet." JD tried to sound cheerful and he smiled at Linc's back. "I'll keep it cold."

He watched as Linc disappeared inside the quivering sheen of the heat, first losing both his legs and then his torso and finally just the top of his hat showed in the mirage. JD looked again at what seemed to be the inviting coolness of that patch of shade and he glanced into the bed of the pickup and saw the edge of a moth-eaten saddle blanket and said, "Why not?"

He reached in and pulled the dusty blanket from under layers of hay and horseshit and shook it as clean as it would get. Then he took one of the beers from the cardboard box on the seat and moved toward the shade. At the edge of the pavement lay a roadkilled carcass of something gray and black with its center now bloody and stringy and fresh chunks of its insides strung out red where the birds had ripped it open. He turned his head and walked around it but could not avoid the stench of death. He struggled through the rocky barrow ditch and along the embankment until he reached the concrete support. "Ain't that much," he muttered looking at the stingy sliver of shade. "But it'll do."

He set the beer on the concrete bulwark and snapped the saddle blanket flat onto the ground. When he saw how much of it was still in the sun, he nudged it closer to the concrete and said, "It'll do in a bind, I guess."

He removed his hat and swiped at the sweat with the forearm of his shirt and reached for the beer which he almost dropped because the glass bottle was so hot. He sat on the blanket and scooted his butt until his back was against the concrete, not cool, but more so than the ground on which the back of his knees and his calves lay. He tried to fold his legs into the shade but they were too long. He sipped at the beer and wondered when Linc would be back. "Maybe a half hour," he said. "Any longer and I'm screwed catching that bus, late or not." He sucked at the warm beer and frowned and felt his head beginning to float as if detached from his body, soaring on a thermal like the black birds which he refused to look up at. He could still smell the dead animal, upwind from him.

He propped the bottle of beer against the concrete and shut his eyes but it made his head spin more furiously, so he reached out with one arm and felt the blanket and lowered himself onto it. He stretched his legs back into the narrow strip of shade.

"Maybe I'll just rest my eyes a minute," he said and very soon he was out.

Behind his eyes, JD tries to soar above the black birds and not with them, but it is no good. He is forced back and in his dream, he sees it is Bettye Lee who is standing on top of him, pinning him to the hard hot ground, driving the spiked heels of her purple prom shoes into his bare chest until it is a bloody pulp. But even though the pain is unbearable, he does not struggle because he is trying to see up her billowing dress as she pirouettes atop him, around-and-around, and he does not beg her to stop because he wants to see the dark vee between her legs and he believes she wants him to see it also and that is the reason she giggles and dances on his chest with her icepick heels. And then she is gone and fear tries to force his eyes open as her dark vee is replaced inside his head by the darker and expanding vee of a huge vulture, descending in slow gliding coils from a washed blue sky. JD struggles to rise but he cannot move and very soon the weight of the giant bird is against his chest and its grotesque and scarlet head and hooked beak and yellow eyes are next to JD's face and he can smell the breath of the bird and it is like the stench of road-kill death only worse. And then it is the bird dancing atop his chest and its claws are razors, like the gaffs for Cielo's heels and they are tearing at him and digging out large chunks of bloody flesh. But the bird is not eating them. It casts the flesh aside and rips again and again and JD cries out in agony for it to stop but it does not and finally, JD brings his head up and looks in horror at the cavernous hole in his chest where a shiny object has now been exposed by the digging and he recognizes where his heart should be and then the bird lifts the lid off the musicbox with its beak and flings the lid aside as he has done with the bloody pulp of JD's chest and the music comes alive and aloud in a crescendo that pounds into JD's ears and inside his head and he gropes for the lid in the hot sand to kill the music but he cannot reach it and he struggles under the bird but its claws are holding him to the earth and shaking his entire body.

"Wake up," Linc said, and he repeated it as he shook JD's chest until his eyes snapped open, but JD was screaming when he woke up. "Geezuschrist, what the hell's going on JD? You pass out or what?"

"Yeah." JD sat up and pressed his palm to his chest which was soaked with something but seemed intact. He held his hand up and looked at it and was relieved when he saw only the glistening of sweat and no blood, so he repeated, "Yeah, passed out."

"Well let's get rolling," Linc said. "You save me a beer?"

"It's in the truck."

"Hotter'n hell probably."

"Probably." JD struggled to his feet but his head still spun so he leaned against the concrete support until he could stand.

Linc walked to the pickup without offering assistance. "Don't forget my blanket," he said. He got in and had the engine running by the time JD got to the road. When JD saw the roadkill and smelled the stench he could not hold Sonny's chili any longer. He dropped to his knees and his hat fell off and then he let everything go. Linc shut off the engine and JD heard his boots in the gravel and he knew Linc was standing over him. JD groaned and in a weak voice said, "Hell, just leave me, Linc."

"Leave you? Geezus, don't be stupid."

"I can hike into there, where you got gas. I probably missed that bus by now anyway, no use you going on…"

"You'd cook out here JD." Linc bent over and grasped his elbow and lifted but JD resisted. "Come on, get up. We're in this together now."

"Why you doing this Linc?"

"Get up," Linc repeated and tugged with both hands and JD staggered to his feet. "My beer's getting hot. Maybe you want it instead?"

JD heaved again but this time nothing came up. He shook his head. Linc reached down and picked up JD's hat and slapped it against his thigh.

"Here." He put it on JD's head and adjusted it. "Feel better?"

JD shook his head but he thought maybe he looked better with the hat on anyway. He did not resist when Linc led him to the pick-up and helped him inside. When Linc got back in, he reached over and removed JD's hat again and then lowered JD's window so he could lean his head into the wind.

"Hot air's better than no air I guess," Linc said. He cranked over the engine which spun and spun and finally caught and soon they were moving faster this time and even with his eyes shut, JD could tell Linc did not slow down, even for the 45 mile per hour speed limit through the straight, short mainstreet of Redford.

When JD woke up, the road was sloped downhill, kissing the cliffs of the mountains just east of Presidio. He could feel the late afternoon sun which had baked his forehead to a lobster red. He lifted his head and ran his tongue over his cracked lips but there was no moisture. His mouth was dry and sour and his ears hummed with the engine and the lurking headache.

"How long I been out?"

"Not that long," Linc said. "Maybe twenty minutes."

"How we doin' on time?" JD did not know if he truly gave a damn at this point but it was something to say.

"Where's your ticket?" Linc glanced at him and held back a smile. "Lose it in some barrow ditch?"

JD patted his shirtpocket where he had folded the ticket and seemed genuinely surprised when he felt it. "It's here."

Linc nodded. "We're about five mile out I'd guess." He pushed on the accelerator but nothing was left. "It'll be close..."

JD nodded this time. He reached over and put on his hat and the moisture from the cooled sweatband felt good on his head. He looked through the back window and inspected his twine-bound cardboard box holding everything he owned and he felt as ready as he could ever be for whatever lay ahead. When he looked forward again, he could see the adobe houses which lay alongside the sloping pavement leading into Presidio.

Linc slowed a little but only because they had reached the single red light in the center of town. Straight ahead was the Mexican border and Ojinaga, and two blocks to his right Linc saw the sign for the bus depot. He shifted to low and wheeled toward the sign.

As soon as they turned the corner, they saw the black diesel smoke from the tail end of a bus, spinning onto Highway 67, which ran north up to Marfa where it became Highway 90 to Interstate 10 and then on west to El Paso. And then if JD could make enough money there, on to Tucson and Phoenix, or maybe even to L.A. And JD's bright future.

"That was it, wasn't it?" JD whispered.

"Probably." Linc could not tell if JD was disappointed or relieved.

"Well."

"I couldn't see the front," Linc said. "I'll pull in and we'll just have to check and see if it was."

It was.

"Shit." JD collapsed onto a hard wooden bench next to the iron barred ticket window and set his cardboard box between his boots. He looked around the room at the wads of old newspapers and

empty pop cans and the people who were his fellow travelers but who did not seem to be going anywhere either. He smelled the stench of urine and thought he might be sick again but he held it back. *"Shit,"* he repeated.

"Yeah, well, we tried." Linc fished a toothpick out of his hatband and clamped it in his teeth. He sat beside JD and cupped his long bony fingers over his knees and looked at the floor, waiting. After awhile he said, "Should'a gassed up at the ranch...or Lajitas."

"Ain't your fault." JD tightened the twine on his box. "I'll just stretch out here, change the ticket to the first one out tomorrow." He looked at the dispatch board. "Says ten-thirty in the morning."

"Yeah," Linc said. "But it's a pretty hard bed we're sitting on."

JD nodded. "It's okay. You go on, Linc."

"Might want to sleep with one eye open." Linc lifted his chin, pointing with the toothpick at the seedy selection of loiterers, lurking in the shadows, waiting for anything but a bus.

"Well."

Neither said anything for a long while and then, "Like I say, you might as well go on, Linc," JD repeated, but Linc spoke at the same time. "Shit, I was thinking we might as well just go across the border."

"Thanks," JD said. He looked at Linc and after awhile said, "But I ain't got no money. Remember?"

"Yeah, but I do. Remember? Beer's cheaper over there and damn sure colder too. Tequila's even cheaper than that."

JD ran his tongue across the cotton of his lips. Tequila sounded terrible, but anything cold right now did not. Without further words he crossed to the ticket window to make the schedule change. Then he returned and snatched up his cardboard box and followed Linc to the revolving cracked-glass door and out into the oppressive heat of the afternoon. Tinny sounds from a trumpet, superimposed over the heartbeat from a fat-bellied *guitarron,* invaded this side of the bridge, *mariachi* music blending with Linc's complaining engine in a siren song inside JD's head. Linc parked the pickup on the Texas side. JD fished in his pocket and brought out a few of his remaining coins as they walked toward the bridge. "I'll get this," he announced and managed a little smile at Linc. He dropped the coins into the slot and watched them roll into the glass encased toll-booth. Inside, the Mexican border agent nodded impassively and they sauntered across.

EIGHTEEN

"Gone?"

"Si,"

"Where?

"No se," Santos said. He lifted his hat, shaded his eyes and looked up at Jesse and repeated in English. "I do not know."

She waited for an explanation but then decided it probably would not be coming from Santos. He sat hunkered next to the still-loaded truck in the midmorning heat, waiting patiently for someone to tell him what to do. Jesse had arisen late and found the milk-pail of unstrained milk on her countertop and assumed JD had been in a hurry to join Linc and Santos with the load of new fencing.

"Where?" she pressed and looked around, hopeful they too had overslept and that Santos was covering for them, but then she noticed Linc's pickup missing.

"No se," he repeated and stood up. "They say Lajitas. For him to ride on a bus but I do not know where."

"A bus?"

"Si."

"Linc?"

"Jimmie D."

"Damn, that's all we need." Jesse sat on the running board and soon Santos was beside her but he said nothing and finally she said, "What time?"

"Not long," Santos said brightly and then, "Not too long."

Jesse nodded and studied the scuffed toes of her boots and then abruptly stood and got into the driver's seat and started the engine. Santos joined her on the other side. "We can go ahead? You and I," he said, and smiled at her determination. "We can work the fence."

"I wish," she said. She shifted the pickup into gear. "No use trying to pound holes in that rock, Santos. We didn't have enough help as it was. Maybe I can stop him..."

She shifted and started across the yard but the over-loaded pickup jerked and stalled and coasted to a stop. Jesse pumped the choke and ground the starter and soon there was no life in the battery. She put her forehead on the steering wheel and shut her eyes, counting a full minute before trying again. When she looked up, Tru was standing rigid in front of the truck.

He stared at her through the cracked windshield and then tilted his head at Santos and spoke. "You and him working by yourselves today?"

"I'm in a hurry, Tru."

"So am I," he said grimly and then, "Fences don't get built by themselves." Tru did not budge. He looked around the yard. "Half this damned summer's nearly over. Where's our hired help?" Jesse tried the engine again and this time it cranked weakly but it caught. She shifted to neutral and gunned the accelerator but still Tru did not move.

"I'll find them," she said, trying to explain. Tru scowled and then came around to her window and reached in for the key but she grabbed his arm.

"Let go," he hissed through his teeth. "If them sonzabitches can't handle it, screw 'em. I already seen my steers scatter to god knows where. We don't need bad help to boot, goddammit. You and me can do it." He glanced over at Santos. "And maybe him."

Santos nodded, his eyes widened. *"Si."*

"They didn't scatter the cattle Tru," Jesse said over the engine.

"Well I sure as hell didn't. Wasn't me let them through. I held my side." He moved his arm again and this time Jesse grabbed it with both hands and dug her fingernails in. Tru jerked his arm free and then reached in again, only this time he gripped Jesse's hair and pulled her head back against the rear window. With a reflex, Santos reached over to help but Jesse froze.

"No," she said sharply and Santos slowly lowered his hand and then Jesse spoke in a whisper, calm and even and decisive, "Let go Tru."

Tru was breathing hard, a rattle in his throat, muscles working under the unshaven skin of his jaw.

"Let go," Jesse repeated but she did not struggle. She felt Tru loosen his grip and he took his arm out of the cab but she did not move her head. She shut her eyes. Only the clacking from the engine broke the silence which seemed to stretch on and on. Jesse finally opened her eyes and straightened and looked again through the cracked windshield.

She shifted into gear and slowly eased the truck forward, shifted once more but did not check the rearview mirror until she had crossed the yard. "Don't look back," she said as Santos tried to turn in his seat.

Tru was nowhere to be seen. And then as the small billow of dust settled behind her, Jesse saw Tru standing with his back to them, motionless and hatless in the midday heat, his hands inside in back pockets. "He'll be okay," she said but she was not speaking to Santos.

"You just missed them," Sonny said when Jesse entered the Elbo Room. "Not long ago."

"Both of them?"

"Yep."

"On the bus?"

"No bus," Sonny Pun said. He came from behind the bar and stood next to Jesse who had her hand on the doorknob. "Don't come in today, remember?"

She nodded. "Where?"

"Linc said maybe he could leave from Presidio, the kid said okay, I said where to from there? He said it don't matter. I said okay and wrote out the ticket."

"Back home?"

Sonny Pun shook his head. "El Paso."

"El Paso?"

"Yep. One way. Dead end."

Jesse turned away. "Yeah, dead end. Probably. *Damn.*"

"Linc's coming back though. They talked about it. It'll be okay Jesse."

She nodded and left. Sonny Pun shook his head and closed the door behind her. When Jesse passed the big window she finally noticed Hill was sitting inside with his noon chili and beer. He tipped his spoon at her and grinned and Jesse stopped, looked for a long moment at Santos in the truck. And then she glanced quickly at Hill and a small smile was at the corner of her mouth and she nodded acknowledgment that he was there. Hill seemed surprised. She moved away and stood at Santos' window and stared up the deserted street.

"They are gone." Santos said, a statement and not a question. Jesse said nothing. "Both of them," Santos said and Jesse continued to look up the street without responding, the narrowed determination in her eyes mellowing in the bright sun. Hill was behind her more quickly than she thought he would be.

"This your rooster man?" Hill bent over to look at Santos.

"Santos, meet Mr. Garza."

"Mucho gusto, Señor." Santos lifted his hat and held out his hand but Hill did not remove his from his pockets. Then Hill said with a cocky little smile, "How's the fencing?" He nodded at the load of materials, obviously untouched and Hill needed to remind no one it was also unpaid for. Santos held his hat in his lap and shrugged. He looked up at Jesse who admitted the fencing was going a little slow. Jesse knew Hill had heard everything inside the bar.

"Mmmmmm..." Hill rattled the change in his pockets but said nothing else for a few moments. "Maybe we need to talk? Maybe we can speed it up a little for you, Jesse?" he said to both of them this time. Jesse nodded. Hill walked away and she watched him enter the bank down the street.

"Santos, maybe you and I could talk..." Jesse began.

"You do not need to ask." He looked at her and she saw his jaw was set and that he understood far more than she imagined. "You may speak for me and you may speak for Cielo also. But you must not be tricked, *Señora.* You must make certain that it is all on paper."

"Paper?"

"Si." He said. "There are rules and there are agreements and one can be cheated."

"We'll sign something," she lied and smiled at Santos who nodded. "Don't worry," she said. "I know how to handle this man." She walked away toward the bank.

"Make certain it is all on paper," he called after her and Jesse nodded.

"Come on in Jesse," Hill said when she tapped on his office door. She opened it but then hesitated when she saw he was lowering the blinds.

"Nobody's out there to look in Hill," she said.

"Hey, relax. Cuts down the sun and the afternoon heat," he explained. "It's a business meeting. Sit."

Jesse sat in the leather armchair and tried to find something to do with her hands, but everything seemed awkward so she crossed her legs and folded her hands, covering a worn spot at the knee of her jeans.

"Lost your hands?" Hill began.

She frowned and glanced at hers but then understood. She looked back at him. "Well, one of them anyway." She shifted in the chair. "Linc's coming back."

"Yeah, right," Hill smiled and tilted his head. "I heard. You ever think about just getting out of all this yourself Jesse?"

"And doing what? Go back to the Elbo Room? I don't think Sonny's doing that kind of business any more."

"Sonny's small peanuts. You're bright Jesse. You should'a gone places by now." He moved over to the map and stabbed at it with his finger. "You see this? This whole area adjacent to your ranch and on north?"

She saw it.

"Well, all this area is where it's happening and I don't mean barbed wire and cowshit."

She continued to look at him but said nothing.

"I mean cinnabar," he said and paced across the room. "Lot's of cinnabar and it's probably right across on your land too, no real doubt about it."

"You mean Tru's land."

"It's yours too isn't it?"

Jesse knew this but she had never dwelt on community rights and boundaries or property rights, except those which might concern her relationship with Tru, and she was painfully aware of how Tru felt about that.

"I suppose," she said. "But that's not what you want to discuss is it?"

"Well, actually no. We can do that some other time. You and me and Tru. Probably need to get him involved anyway."

Jesse released a little chuckle and shook her head. "You amaze me Hill. You really think Fredrick Truman Pierce would be interested in an open pit mine, gnawing into his rangeland?"

"Well, old Truman may not always be around Jesse," he said and he moved over and stood behind her chair. "He's a lot older than you. Maybe it'll just be your decision some day."

"Maybe," she said. She shifted in her chair, trying to look up at him but he was close behind her now. "But that's still not what you wanted to talk about, is it?"

"No," he said. Jesse felt his hand on her shoulder and he continued. "Let's just take one thing at a time."

She flinched and lifted her shoulder as if there were an insect on it. Then she forced herself to relax. Hill squeezed her shoulder. "You're needing to hire more help, right?"

Jesse nodded and thought about feeding cattle all summer. "Probably."

"Well, I can take care of that too," he said in a soothing voice and he moved his hand over and she felt his thumb on her neck. "We'll just put it on account, like all that fencing out there on your truck. You can just owe me Jesse."

Jesse shut her eyes. Owing Hill Garza was almost as painful as watching Tru disintegrate. She wanted to slap away his hand and bolt from the room and buy her own bus ticket with JD to nowhere.

"Sure, Hill," she whispered. When she did not reach to stall his hand, he moved it further and caressed the soft skin under her chin. "I'll just owe you," she said.

She felt her flesh quiver and turn cold even in the heat of the room and Hill moved his hand further down and she heard his breath which carried the smell of chili and beer and her stomach churned but still she did not move. When Hill brought his other hand around, Jesse spun and stood. She forced a tight smile. "We'll settle up later, Hill. Like you say, take one thing at a time. Right now I got someone waiting."

Hill cleared his throat. "Sure." He turned away and adjusted the waistline on his trousers and sucked in a long sigh. "Later'd be fine Jesse. I've always trusted you and you know you can trust me, right?" He turned back to her and smiled and then became very serious. He leaned forward and lowered his eyelids halfway and was whispering against her face. "I've always been fond of you Jesse, you know I can't change that. But no use rushing things. Like you say, you can just owe me."

"He'll fight his rooster," Jesse said, abruptly shifting the conversation. "The old man. But he wants a clear understanding."

"Understanding?" Hill lifted his eyebrows.

"About the rules he says."

"He wants to know the rules?" Hill laughed aloud. "Oh they'll show him the rules. These guys are serious about their cockfights." He walked over and sat behind his desk and tilted his head. "What I want to know is can the goddamn bird fight, Jesse?"

"He says he can," she said and hesitated but then firmly, "And I believe him." Then she remembered Santos had said it was about death and never about the fighting alone. Or even the winning. And Santos had also said one could win the fight but still lose. Even if Jesse understood a little of this, she was certain Hill would understand none of it.

Hill nodded. "Fine. I'll tell them it won't be a cakewalk. They'll want to bet on their own rooster and they won't mind giving some odds. But even then, nobody's going to bet against them if they see some mangy old bird that can hardly stand."

"He can stand. And he'll fight. He's fought a lot. Santos says he has heart." Hill nodded but Jesse could see he was skeptical, so she added not only for Hill, but to convince herself, "His bird's still alive, right?"

"Mmmm..." Hill considered this and nodded again.

"Now—" Jesse began but Hill interrupted her.

"Let's don't even talk about that anymore Jesse. It's a done deal." He was cool and arrogant in what he knew was already a personal victory. "Compton'll get his money this afternoon and you can let me know how much more you need to pay your hands. You just make sure that old geezer and his bird show."

"Show where?"

"I'll let you know," he said. "It's better if word don't get around too much in advance about this kind of thing you understand. Don't go talking it up. We'll handle all that."

Jesse nodded.

"But that ain't all our deal's about." Hill took out a cigar to seal the agreement, if only with himself. "Is it Jesse?"

"I thought we didn't need to talk about anything else Hill." She looked at him for a long while but this time she did not smile. There was no kindness, no quarter in his eyes and as far as Jesse could see, no redeeming humanity at all, only the calculating coldness of a predator. Finally she turned away and put her hand on the doorknob. She started to leave but Hill came over and held the door shut. He leaned next to her face again and this time she became nauseous with his breath and she shut her eyes and the face of her long dead sister floated behind them and there was agony in Clair's eyes.

"Jesse," Hill said.

"What?"

"You know not to put any money on that old wetback don't you?" He opened the door and she walked out into the street and he called after her, "I mean, if you got some hid under your mattress or someplace."

She said nothing to Santos when she got back into the pickup. She started the engine but did not pull away from the front of the Elbo Room. She was thinking about the ceiling fan inside, spinning round-and-round with the hidden envelope over Sonny Pun's head, wondering if Santos would show her how to bet on a cockfight.

NINETEEN

"Dark Water," the man polishing the glasses behind the bar answered in perfect English and then in perfect Spanish, *"Agua Prieta."* He turned to the row of bottles and selected the cheap mescal and topped off JD's jigger, then refilled Linc's. "And no, I don't know how this place got its name. The only dark water around here is in the beer but that's what it means." He presented a perfect set of teeth to complement the perfect, if gratuitous, mustache and then he sliced more lime onto the saucer in front of the two. *"Salud!"* he said and gestured toward his mouth with a thumb and an opposing small finger as if joining them.

Linc followed orders, tossed back his third jiggerful and bit hard into the lime. He touched his tongue to the salt stuck to the back of his hand and then coughed and laughed and looked at JD in the mirror behind the bar. "What's the matter? All you had's one cold beer. You ain't finished even one shot of tequila yet."

"I'm letting it all settle slow," JD confessed. "Filling them cracks around what's left of Sonny's chili."

"Beer's too expensive. This is only a quarter a shot." Linc nodded at the bartender who quickly replenished his jigger. Linc spun a half dollar on top of the mahogany bar and seemed a little disappointed when the bartender swept it away before it whirled to a stop. The man slapped Linc's change onto the bar.

"Put it in the machine," Linc said expansively. The man picked up the quarter between his thumb and forefinger. He held it up, lifted his eyebrows and blinked slowly and said, "Which one, *Señor?*"

Linc shrugged, missing the sarcasm but JD did not.

"Don't matter," Linc mumbled.

"Ah but it does *Señor,"* the man said adding a feigned Spanish dialect to his English. "Thees jukebox, she is very picky with her music."

Linc flushed and then turned to the man as he rounded the end of the bar. "Something country."

"Which country?" the bartender said, and if he seemed pissed, he hid it behind the teeth. He dropped the coin into the slot and rapidly punched up a selection as if by memory. He returned behind the bar before the tune began. It was not Hank Williams.

"Who the hell's that?" Linc scowled. "Can't understand a word he's saying."

"He is singing to the soul," the bartender said and placed his hand over his heart. "About broken love which needs no translation."

"What?" Linc said.

The man turned to JD and shrugged and shook his head as if further explanation would be useless. He brought back the bottle and topped off Linc's jigger but JD placed his palm over his own glass.

"Bastante?" the man said.

"For now." JD looked around the room and the bartender moved closer as if he understood.

"You *vaqueros*, you are always looking for some...action."

It was spoken with the same dialect and the same lifted eyebrows along the Mexican border and JD was no complete stranger to it. He thought about the times he and other members of the Fighting Bobcats had crept out of Blink in the middle of a Friday night following a particularly grueling football game and pointed their headlights south. It was usually after an embarrassing defeat—and there were plenty of those—but a huge win or even a squeaker would serve. The only thing that mattered was enough gas in someone's beatup sedan and a few dollars for a case of beer for the trip down and a few more for the whores and tequila across the border, then gas money back. The only thing finally needed was the macho challenge from whomever was the horniest of the bunch. The selection of grimy little border towns within four hours of Blink did not matter. It was generally left up to the lucky driver to make that decision at the edge of town.

The women were the same. It made no difference which crossing was chosen. If the woman wanted to show that she was not just good but very good, there would be many drink tokens rattling on a bracelet around her wrist. But more than often, only a couple were kept in sight on the bracelet to provide a thin clatter as she moved about the barroom, and thus presenting the appearance of a poor night.

JD never cared if the woman had any tokens at all. In his fantasies, she was always a local beauty who just happened into the bar and fell hopelessly in love with him and he could rescue her from some cruel *patron* and sneak her back across the border and they would live happily on love and tequila and love and burritos.

But he knew all these women were professionals, licensed and presumably inspected, just like the cab drivers and everyone else who catered to the sometimes lucrative, sometimes fickle tourist trade. On one occasion in an almost deserted nightclub on the far end of Villa Acuna, while his buddies were already in back rooms with women, JD sat at a booth practicing his border Spanish and drinking mescal with one woman who finally showed him a small laminated certificate, like a driver's license, and said that if she tried working independently—or even outside her assigned brothel—she might wind up soaking some drywash with her blood. She drew a finger across her throat. If she was just trying to get another watered-down drink out of him, it worked. JD believed her. It was the kind of melodrama he understood.

"Some girls?" the bartender pressed.

"Maybe," JD said. He turned to Linc since it was he who held their entire fortune, probably stuffed into the top of one boot. JD sipped the tequila like he enjoyed it and Linc nodded briskly and looked eagerly about the barroom.

"No," the man said, reading his mind. "It's not legal in here. We are licensed only for drinking. Sorry."

"Well why'd you even ask?" Linc stumbled over the words, tossed back the liquor and stood. "We'll just move down the street.

Let's go JD."

"I thought you might want something...special, just for tonight." The barman winked at JD and began pouring Linc another. "This is on the house, *Señor,"* he said when Linc tried to wave him away.

"Special?" JD was curious but not necessarily emboldened.

"Si." The man offered JD another but again he refused the tequila. Linc looked at the glass in front of him, deciding if he could walk out into the darkening street with this one on top of the others. The bartender leaned closer and in a hoarse whisper under the blare of the music said, "It is a slow night. The clubs will not have their best girls on a weeknight but the girls cannot negotiate even so, and I do not think you want something which costs a lot of money, right? These I am speaking about are, like I say, *especial,* not licensed to work the clubs because they are much younger but not virgins either. They are of age, I would not bullshit you about that, my friends. You know, they are only trying to make a few pesos on the side and so not as expensive. They have other jobs, I will confess. It would be like a date, right?" He grinned broadly.

JD frowned and said sourly, "I was born at night but not last night," and he tried to figure out how much of the money Linc would have left after buying the can of gas and paying for their drinks and he said, "What's the catch? What's your cut?"

"Let him talk," Linc said. He leaned over to listen. "Could be interesting."

"Listen, *amigos,"* the man went on. "I can set it up, in one of the small hotels, away from the lights and the noise, you can go over there in a taxi, look over the girls, talk about the money, and then make up your minds. Okay, I get a little bit of it, I confess, just like the cab driver and the hotel owner, you know, it all flows down in Mexico, *mordida,* the bite." He rubbed his thumb across the fingers of one hand, the universal symbol. "But, if you want to stay the night, you pay the cab driver which will include a little something for me, then pay for the room and then settle with the girls in the morning. That's it. Simple. A good time with no hassle."

JD looked at Linc. Neither spoke.

"Well?" the man said. "What do you have to lose? Only the

price of the cab. These are not professionals, none of that paying for drinks and all that bullshit, probably less than ten pesos a girl. And you don't have to hide your money in your boot." He laughed loudly and then became very serious. "I guarantee you will like it." He winked again at JD.

"It ain't legal that way," JD said, as if that ended it. He glanced down at Linc's boot and tried to tally up the cost of everything in his head, and even though he lost track inside the tequila, he did not believe Linc could cover it. He hoped Linc remembered that JD had given him his last five dollars and Linc still had it—somewhere.

"Ah *Señor,* you are correct, I confess. As I said, they are not professionals. But then, not everything good in life is legal, right?" and then he continued, "At your age, you could not be drinking legal tequila in a bar five minutes across the bridge, right? I promise you, this will be fine. No problem."

The bartender was right, at least about the drinking. But as JD took in the smell of the pale yellow liquid in his glass, he questioned whether this was special at only fifty cents a shot. And he worried about the other offer even more. "Whatta you think?" JD said to Linc.

"Depends," Linc offered and now seemed a little reticent himself. JD wondered if in his current condition, Linc would be able to add up all the possible expenses of a cab and a tip for the bartender and the hotel room, no matter how sleazy, and then the girls themselves, even though they were not professionals.

"Depends?" the bartender said, as if he knew what was coming.

"On what kind of deal we can make," Linc said.

"The cab is cheap," the bartender said. He raised his arm and snapped his fingers at another man sitting next to the door and it was obvious this was the taxi driver. "Only a few dollars. And so is the room." The man came over and spoke briefly in rapid Spanish with the bartender and then nodded and stepped back and said, "This way *Señors.*"

JD looked at Linc who seemed completely in charge now as he stood and tipped the contents of his jigger into his mouth. JD did the same and he swallowed fast enough so as not to taste it and then quickly bit into a lime and sprinkled a generous layer of salt onto his tongue and immediately he felt the liquor burning its way into his stomach.

"Vamanos," Linc said. He slammed his empty glass in front of the nodding bartender and then drew a dollar bill from his pocket and laid it beside the jigger as a tip. "Let's ride." He steadied himself on the edge of the bar for a moment. When JD began to move, Linc was already to the door almost stepping on the driver's heels.

The final word in the small sputtering neon sign of the *LA PALOMITA* was unlit. Had it glowed even as faintly as the first word, JD still would not have remembered what it meant. He looked around at the darkened adobe and tin shacks aligning the empty dirt road where mysterious puddles of liquid reflected the pink neon back into the black of night. The driver killed the engine and silence closed around the battered cab. Nothing else moved along the pocked road they had traveled, far from the main tourist strip.

"Means DOVE," Linc volunteered as he leaned forward in the passenger seat to inspect the sign.

"LITTLE DOVE," the cab driver corrected, "But also something else in Spanish, you know." He laughed and puckered his lips and kissed the air, but the finer interpretation of the phrase remained consumed in darkness.

"Good enough for me," JD said. He fought an urge to lock his door and slump down in the back seat.

Linc got out and stood waiting by the front door of the hotel. The driver came around and made a great show of opening the door. He held it and flagged JD in and he knew he could not back out now. When JD entered the lobby, Linc was standing at the Dutch door to a tiny room that served as a front desk. The driver said something to the hotel clerk in Spanish and then turned to Linc and said, "Well, are you staying?"

"We haven't seen the girls," Linc complained.

"If I have to wait, my meter is running," the driver said. "It will cost you more."

Linc glanced at JD who shrugged. Linc turned back to the driver and dug out three dollars and gave it to him. "No tip?" the man said sourly.

Linc looked at him and said, "You said two-fifty for the fare. Keep the fifty cents."

The driver scowled and then said, "What about Raul?"

"Raul?"

"*Si.* The bartender."

"Right," Linc said. He swayed for a moment, his eyes glazed as he looked at the cabbie and tried to think through the whole deal. If Linc had been told the details, he remembered none of it. He dug into his pocket and brought out the remainder of the bills and peeled three more on top of the ones in the driver's palm and stuffed the remainder back into his pocket.

The driver shot a quick glance at the hotel clerk and without further words, left the lobby. JD heard him gun the engine of the cab and then the noise of rattling fenders as he drove off and he wondered if they could find their way back to the border crossing at daylight.

The clerk came out and paused at the stairs leading up into a dark hallway. "This way," he said formally, "*Arriba.*"

Linc followed first. At the top of the stairway the man stopped and reached overhead to tighten a chainswung lightbulb but it did not brighten the hallway, only exposed its grimness. Then he jingled a ring of keys and opened the first door he came to.

"Crowded tonight, huh?" Linc muttered. He entered the room and the man blinked at him but said nothing as he reached over and flicked on a shadeless table lamp in Linc's room.

"We need two," Linc reminded him but the clerk was already rattling the keys and into the hallway again. He went to the door directly across from Linc's and unlocked it. JD stepped inside and switched on the table lamp which, unlike Linc's, had the remnants of a tattered paper shade. The clerk went back into the hallway. Linc was standing leaning against his doorjamb.

"You want something to drink?" the man said and then answered himself, "*Cervezas.*" He went down the stairway.

"Yeah, beer's fine," Linc agreed as if he had a choice and then called out to JD across the hall. "You wanted beer too, right?"

"We got a choice?" JD said back and returned to the empty

hallway. He could see Linc had no choice about standing on his own; he definitely needed the doorjamb for support. "You okay, Linc?"

"No sweat."

"Yeah right," JD said. "Listen, Linc, you gonna pay us out or what? Don't forget I'm flat now. You got my last five."

"No sweat," Linc repeated. He straightened, swaying as he retrieved the remainder of the bills from his pocket.

"What's left?" JD said.

"Plenty. Here's ten, that oughta take care of you." Linc peeled off two fives. JD could see he had only a few singles left.

"Linc, you sure you got enough?" JD tried to remember the day and what had been spent. He was sure Linc could not have much more than five dollars left in his pocket. Maybe Linc had more than he claimed earlier. Maybe Linc had lots, stuffed inside the top of his boot. Or maybe Linc was planning on just drinking cheap beer in a cheap room and then sleeping it off—alone.

"Like I said, no sweat. I'll put that on what you owe me. Have fun, okay?" Linc slurred. He turned and shut his door.

JD closed his too and then took off his hat and held it. He stuffed the two fives into the top of his boot and then looked around the room. The scant amber light, spiking through holes in the lampshade, showed just enough detail for a guest to maneuver without tripping on the Spartan furnishings. Under a cracked mirror hanging crooked on one wall stood a small table. Atop this was a washbasin and a pitcher of water and a face cloth and thin towel. A single wooden straight-backed chair hugged another wall and the bed against the other. He crossed and sat on the edge of the complaining bed.

Even with the paucity of furnishings there was little room left. JD guessed if there was a bathroom it would be communal and off down the hallway somewhere. There was no inside lock on the door and the clerk had offered no guest keys, and so JD assumed it would remain unlocked. The man had not yet asked for payment for the rooms. Apparently that would be settled in the morning along with the cost of the beer and the clerk's other services, whatever those might be. The bartender had said a few dollars for the room. JD thought about it and decided that the money left in Linc's pocket might be enough for his room, but not much else. And certainly not enough to cover whatever showed up at Linc's door. With the two fives JD now had in his boot, he figured he could cover the cost of any of his own services for the night, regardless what showed up at his.

"Well, he's a grown man," JD mumbled. "Been around lot's longer than me. Guess he knows what he's doing, even tanked."

He rose and put his hat back on and went to the window, which looked out onto the dirt road in front of the hotel. The clerk had switched off the neon sign and the only light remaining outside was the single bulb over the front door. A small dog, just hair and skin stretched over a skeleton, wandered up the street, sniffing at the puddles of mud. JD saw nothing else. If there were beautiful olive skinned virgins headed their way, they were coming on the dark side of the road. He removed his hat again and put it on the small table. He looked into the mirror and smoothed back his hair with his palm and showed his teeth which he rubbed with a forefinger. Then he went and stretched out on top of the moth eaten bedspread, his boots still on. And he dozed.

JD jerked awake at the sound of tapping on his door. It was not aggressive and he closed his eyes and thought he must have been dreaming, but then it was there again. He sat upright on the edge of the bed and cleared his throat and once more smoothed back his hair. When he went to the door he heard a woman's voice across the hall and then Linc saying something low and laughter and then Linc's door closing. He stood silent at his door for a long while and was almost ready to turn away when he heard the tapping again. This time he opened the door.

The girl could not have been over fourteen. She stood stiff, her checked dress straight at her thin waist and her arms hung loosely at her sides, as if useless and too long for her body which showed only the promise of curves. Someone else had obviously applied makeup to her face and to her lips and around her dark eyes which looked at JD with a strange blend of feigned seduction and terror. Even in the dim light, her black hair shone and JD looked for the fake flower which should have been attached somewhere in her hair but was not. The hair had been brushed and brushed, straight with the tips just touching her thin shoulders. She said nothing. Nor did JD, who stepped aside. She lowered her eyes and glided into the room but he was not certain she had even moved her feet. He closed the door.

The girl crossed and turned around and stood at the foot of the bed. He cleared his throat and looked at her body and then at her passive face and the way she held herself as if she were merely merchandise in an open market. And JD thought about the other times he had stood in rooms with Mexican women but never like this. Always before, there was banter and questions teasing about the size of his dick and a kind of sauntering about the room as the talk turned to money and how much and how long the woman would stay, and then the drinking of something harsh and sour and then more talk and finally groping. There was nothing here but a tense silence. JD could not even hear the girl breathing.

And then came another tapping on the door, this time abrupt and very aggressive and when he opened it, the clerk entered with a tray and two glasses and a small galvanized pail of ice with the necks of four bottles of Mexican beer showing at the top. He set the bucket on the small table and held the tray at his side and smiled. JD hesitated, but then he turned his back and put his boot on the chair and took the money out of his boot top, exposing his cache. The man laughed as if he already knew JD had his money hidden there. He shook his head and grandly waved off any immediate payment. *"No ahorita,"* he said, and then he looked very seriously at the girl. He said nothing as he closed the door behind himself. At least he had knocked, JD thought.

JD gestured at the beer but the girl shook her head. "Well," he said. He crossed the room and stood next to her, hiding the two fives in his fist. She turned to him and he spoke again, "Well, how much?"

She did not reply, looked at him blankly. He knew then she spoke no English and he too fell silent, struggling to recall his border Spanish, but all he could think of was *"Quanto vale?"* He reddened after he said it, remembering this phrase in Spanish was used to inquire about the price of merchandise like food or clothing. But it was enough.

"Cinco," the girl said, and that was it. But she still did not smile. There was no negotiation in her voice and it was spoken as if JD should have known she had no options anyway. He nodded and gave one of the five dollar bills to her and stuffed the other back into his pocket, playing no more foolish games with the top of his boot. The girl turned abruptly away and walked to the darkest side of the room and stood next to the chair with her back to him. She toed off her shoes and slipped out of her dress and laid it on the back of the chair. There was no teasing, no fluttering of eyelids or grabbing of crotches or anything to suggest this was to be an act of passion or even raw sex. She turned and stood facing him in her underwear.

"Geezus," JD whispered. He felt the mescal rise sour in his throat. He watched her hesitate but then reach around and unhook her brassiere and allow it to drop into her hands, exposing only a small rise of breasts. She looked at her bare feet, as if they were the most naked part of her body. JD shuffled and tried to clear the mescal from his throat again. He felt a sudden urge to turn away, but then she removed her panties and he could not take his eyes from the small brush of pubic hair as she walked quickly to the bed and crawled beneath the cover. The bed made no sound under the weight of her body. She held the sheet at her throat and stared up at the ceiling.

JD stood there for long minutes and then he went to the small table and looked down at the iced beer and wondered if he should kill a couple, but the thought of more booze this day caused his stomach to spin. He glanced into the mirror. His face came back jaundiced in the light and the large crack running the length of the glass halved his features into what appeared to be both youth and age. Then he looked at the reflected image of the room with the girl's cheap clothing placed carefully across the back of the chair, but he could not look at the bed where she lay immobile. He shut his eyes and turned away from the mirror.

"Shit," he whispered. "Just do it. You paid for it."

He crossed to the bed and sat gingerly on its edge, trying to prevent the springs from announcing to the world that he was there. The girl scooted over but kept the sheet up. JD unbuttoned his shirt and pulled the tail from his waist but did not remove it. He turned his head to look at her and this time she forced a tight smile but she said nothing. A ray of light through the torn lampshade exposed the fear in one of her eyes, but the other was in the shadows; he suspected the hidden eye held no passion either.

JD sat immobile on the edge of the bed for a long while. He stared at the cold Mexican tiles on the floor, uneven and mismatched and chipped. For a moment, he thought about Bettye Lee, but then he shook her out of his head and frowned and suddenly a voice—which did not seem to be his at all—came hard and angry as it hissed, *"What the hell are you doing in my bed?"*

The girl lifted her eyebrows and pulled the sheet up even tighter and smiled nervously, showing her teeth. *"Que?"*

He spoke again, deliberately pronouncing each syllable as if this would translate it into Spanish, *"I said what the hell are you doing in my bed? What the hell are you doing here?"* He stood and began to button his shirt. When he turned again to speak to her, the girl sat up, exposing her torso, but JD knew it was fear and not an attempt at seduction.

"Get your clothes on," he said, and this time his voice was softer. The girl cocked her head and raised her shoulders and tried once more, *"Que pasa?"*

"Nothing's happening, that's what," he answered. "Not a goddamned thing. *Nada.*"

He pointed at her clothing on the chair and then back at her and then at the door and this time she understood. She got out of the bed and crossed to the chair and slowly got dressed and then came and stood in front of him. From somewhere she produced the five dollar bill he had given her and held it out and looked at him with soft eyes and he saw the fear was gone. JD stood amazed. He looked at the bill in her hand and she thrust it at him again. He grabbed her wrist, hard at first and then relaxed it and saw the startled confusion in her face.

"It's okay," he said. *"Esta bien.* You keep it."

She frowned and looked at the money and then surveyed JD's face. She shook her head and tried to move her hand with the money toward him but he held it back. With his other hand JD reached into his pocket and then opened her grip on the bill and pressed the other five atop it and closed her fist and held it tight. She looked down at his fist which completely covered her own and her lips parted and this time she looked into JD's eyes. He released her fist and she let it fall to her side.

"Adios," he whispered. He walked over and held the door. The girl paused briefly in front of him but then brushed past and disappeared. He went into the dark hallway and stood listening to her soft footsteps on the stairway and heard the front door of the hotel shut quietly and then silence.

JD turned to Linc's door and tried to hear sounds inside but there were no squeaking bedsprings nor laughter nor groaning—nothing. He went back into his room and closed the door. He snapped off his lamp and then stretched out on the bed, fully clothed. He did not close his eyes. The only sound was the melting ice settling around the unopened beer.

It was still dark outside when Linc's voice, rising in slurred anger from the hallway, awakened JD. Linc spoke in high pitched Spanish but JD understood the occasional English, like *sonuvabitch* and *fuckusover.* JD got out of bed but did not turn on the lamp. In the darkness he went to the door and opened it just enough to peek through the crack. Linc towered over a small man in a ill fitting uniform who was himself in front of the hotel clerk. The clerk cowered behind, displaying to the officer a few dollar bills as if evidence. If there was a woman present in Linc's room, JD could not see her. It was obvious to JD the dispute involved the amount of money and probably a number of other illegalities which Linc was having no success in explaining, even in pretty good Spanish. Linc finally turned his pockets out and cursed in English at both men. The officer took one step back and casually pulled out an automatic pistol and pointed it directly at Linc's head. Linc froze and lifted his palms toward the two and the officer quickly snapped handcuffs on him.

JD started to open his door and offer help, but he quickly realized he had nothing but a few coins in his pocket to offer. He thought he might at least help Linc talk his way out, but his poor Spanish would probably just make it worse. He eased his door shut and crept across the darkened room to the window. He released his grip on the windowsill and dropped to the dirt road just as he heard the door to his room pop open.

He found his way back to the tollbooth at the bridge and tossed the five cent fee into the metal chute and a sleepy Mexican guard waved him through. At the other side, the United States Border Patrol agent seemed far more suspicious at JD's predawn crossing. Twice the agent asked the usual questions about goods brought back and citizenship, but then he too nodded and allowed JD through.

A streak of gray orange showed in the eastern sky as JD walked into the parking lot on the Presidio side of the border. He retrieved the keys that Linc had hidden inside one wheel well and opened the cab and took out his box of belongings. He stood for a moment, staring back at the florescent green glow of the tollbooth.

"Guess it's your problem now, pard," he sighed. "What the hell could I do anyway..." JD felt the bus ticket, still folded inside his shirt pocket. "No money in these pockets either, Linc. You'll just have to talk your way out of it, I guess. Like you said, no sweat."

He locked the pickup and stashed the keys back under the wheel well and walked up the street toward the bus depot. "Besides, you speak the language, I don't. Sure glad it ain't me. Sorry."

One block later he stopped and leaned against a lamp post. Then he sat on the curb and looked back again at the bridge.

"Shit," he said. He watched the quickening color of the sky. He pulled out the ticket and looked at his new departure time. "Ten-thirty," he said and put the ticket away. "He'll talk his way out of there long before then. He'll probably stop by the depot and say *adios* and we'll have a cuppa coffee and a big hoot about it." He chuckled and then rose and continued up the street and entered the depot.

The clock on the wall said six forty-five. Two unkempt men slept back-to-back, sitting on the floor and leaning against the wall. JD went into the restroom and stood at the urinal where the stench steamed up into his nostrils. He held his breath long enough to piss. With an indelible marker, someone had scrawled *SHIT HAPPENS!* on the wall above the urinal. "You got that right," he said.

Back in the lobby, JD considered his choices of hard benches. He sat where he could see the glass doors at the front and watch the clock above his head on the right. At seven-thirty he rose and went to the dispatch board and checked the departure time on his bus. He looked at his ticket again. "Ten-thirty," he confirmed, and surveyed the room. The man at the ticket window did not look up from his crossword puzzle.

A dispensing machine against one wall announced it would supply hot java on a twenty-four hour basis. JD brought out the remaining change in his pocket, fingered through it and wondered what the eighty-five cents would best be spent on. It was certain booze would not be an option.

"Coffee," he said. "At least that. Can't wait any longer on you for that, Linc." He went to the machine and dropped in two quarters. The black liquid was hot but that was all. He went back to the bench and sat down, sipping. He watched the clock.

At eight forty-five, he went over to the glass doors and looked out onto the street. One Border Patrol cruiser moved slowly by and as it passed, the uniformed driver looked JD over as though he might stop, but he did not. A few people moved up and down the sidewalk and another car drove by from the border crossing, but he saw nothing of Linc's pickup. He went back to the bench and sat.

"Well," he said. "Maybe the stupid shit didn't pay her or something." He thought about Linc in some hell hole of a jail cell with rats running through an inch of sewage on the rock floor. "He oughta paid her. Shit, at least I paid mine," he said and then he thought about the cost of the beer—four in his room alone—and the price of the rooms themselves and god knows what else tagged onto the whole evening. And then the bite for the bartender and probably even the cop took a cut and also whoever owned the girls, maybe the goddamn cop himself, and he might have even been their father or something. And finally JD wondered what it would cost Linc to get free. "If he's in jail at all," he scoffed. "Which he probably ain't..."

From the passenger loading area, JD heard the gunning of a diesel engine and then a departing bus but he checked the clock again and knew it was not his.

"I mean for chrissake, you pay your *whore,*" he muttered. "At least you pay your goddamn *whore.*" He watched as a woman and a child entered from the street. "He'll stop by."

At ten-fifteen JD went back to the loading area and looked up at the bus with the destination EL PASO in its front display. He stood briefly, studying the name and then went around and stood first in line at the door, waiting for the driver to open it. He held his ticket ready. Shortly thereafter, the driver pumped the accelerator, sending out a huge cloud of diesel smoke which slowly consumed everything in the loading area.

After awhile, the blueblack smoke dissipated, exposing a somber Jimmie Dale Mitchell, standing alone in the huge empty loading arena, staring at an unused bus ticket to nowhere. After awhile, he walked over to the big opening where the bus had roared out into the bright street but he did not watch it depart. Instead, he went out onto the sidewalk and set his box down and leaned against the adobe wall. He folded his arms and from under the brim of his hat, glanced down the street toward the border crossing. In the morning sunshine, JD could see the top of the old pickup, still sitting where Linc had parked it.

TWENTY

"Hold still *gallo!*" Santos struggled with the leather lanyard, sliced from the edge of an old harness. It stretched sixteen feet in length, one end secured Cielo's leg and the other looped to Santos' wrist. Santos gathered the lanyard around his shoulder like a lariat and held the rooster in one arm as he climbed the ladder to the hayloft. At the top, he worked his way over and sat with his legs dangling. He looked down. Then he held Cielo over the edge. "See, my friend. It is not so far." The rooster struggled but Santos held firm. "Do not be afraid. It is only practice. You remember this, how it makes your good wing stronger for the combat?"

He dropped the rooster. Cielo thrust out his good wing and tried to extend the other, but the broken bone in it had never healed correctly. He flapped the one wing and glided in a tight spiral to the floor of the barn.

"Bueno!" Santos called and held the lanyard so Cielo would not escape through the barn door. *"Magnifico!"*

He tightened the slack in the lanyard and gently lifted the rooster upside-down into the loft. Cielo seemed to understand and did not struggle this time as Santos again dropped him to the floor.

When Jesse walked out with the milkpail toward the corral, she heard Santos' voice in the barn. She moved to the barn door and looked inside. Santos sat in the hayloft holding Cielo over the edge. He smiled. *"Buenos dias."*

"What in the hell…" Jesse started but Santos interrupted.

"He is training." He dropped the bird once more. Cielo glided in the spiral but this time it was controlled and smooth. "See. It is like the coils in the wire. There is memory here also. *Comprende?"*

"Yeah," Jesse said. She shook her head and smiled back at him. She wrapped her arms around the milkpail and leaned against the wall. "Santos," she began, but she saw he was not listening as he retrieved his fighter once again. "Santos," she repeated louder and he held the bird again in his arms and looked at her.

"Si?"

"Santos, I don't believe Tru would..."

He paused and looked at her for a long while and then he nodded his head, *"Si,"* he said and held Cielo out over the edge. *"Comprendo,"* he said. "I understand."

Jesse turned to leave but then looked up again. "Maybe you could just keep the shouting down a little?"

The old man nodded and dropped the rooster and this time the only sound was the whistling of air through feathers and the quiet rustle of Cielo's deft landing in the straw below.

"They didn't show did they," she said, but it was an answer and not a question.

Santos shook his head.

"Neither?" she said.

He shook his head again.

"Then you need to be ready in about an hour," she said, then left.

Santos knew what she meant. Getting ready had nothing to do with a cockfight. "I am sorry old friend but now some of us will build fences. You will get stronger."

He climbed down the ladder and took Cielo into the bunkhouse where he gave him fresh water and barley and then placed him back into his cage. "You wait," he said. "We will work again this evening when it is cooler."

He put on a pair of leather gloves and tied a bandanna around his hair with the knot at the nape of his neck and then replaced his straw hat. He turned to the bird. "Now I am a vaquero and not a cockfighter but perhaps a cockfighter builds fences too." Santos quartered and stiffened his back, then looked at his profile in the broken mirror and was pleased.

When Santos went back into the yard, Jesse was crossing with the full milkpail. She watched the hardpan in front of her boots and did not look up. She went into the kitchen and he heard her voice inside through the window screen and then Tru's, which was already hostile. Santos wondered if it was ever absent the anger. He went to the old truck, still loaded with the fencing supplies and sat waiting on the running board.

"I got plenty of wire, but we couldn't get more posts on with this load," Jesse said when she and Tru walked up. Santos thought she was talking to him so he began to look around the yard as though he might find a few somewhere. "I can get more but we'll need to offload this first," she continued and paused for Tru's reaction.

It was not as explosive as she had anticipated and she guessed the tentative truce the two entered last evening still held, Tru actually repentant. Jesse said nothing about her meetings with Hill. She knew it would simply fester to a head eventually. She chose not to think about that right now or about the other times Tru had been repentant over the years. But if all worked out with Santos and his miracle rooster, then everything might be just fine. If it did not, Jesse would face Hill Garza in whatever way it took. She thought about what she had just witnessed in the barn: a tired old man with a broken down old fighting rooster with one good wing and one good eye. She sighed, waiting for Tru's response.

"Don't need anymore posts," Tru grumbled. "Not yet. Can't use 'em unless there's holes to put them in." He tightened his leather gloves and spat and did not look at Santos who stood ready. "And we don't need any other help either." Tru got into the driver's side and cranked the engine. He looked out at Jesse standing puzzled. "You two going?"

She nodded and hustled Santos into the truck between her and Tru, who hit the accelerator hard, sending back a dustcloud. He did not slow at the main road and only let up when they approached the spot of rockhard ground where the crew had stopped working. He bounced the truck through the barrow ditch and then stopped abruptly, already pulling the box of blasting caps and a small roll of copper wire out of the back when Jesse and Santos emerged. Tru took the box and wire over to the last hole JD and Linc had picked into the ground.

"Pace it off," Tru said when Santos came up. "Six paces."

"Que?"

"Pace it off, up that way across the rock." Tru gestured impatiently and Santos nodded but he understood nothing. *"Seis*—six paces," Tru said and he began long strides following the line of the fencing. "Six between each post. See, just like before, *seis, comprende?"*

Tru stopped and turned back to the old man who was nodding. It had not been Santos' duty to measure. He smiled and stepped six times and turned around with one foot on the spot.

"Aqui," he said with authority. "Here."

Tru nodded and turned to Jesse. "Bring the spud bar and tap out a little hole." He looked at her but she was already sliding the bar from under the pile of wire. "Don't have to be too deep," he instructed when she walked by. She nodded. When she reached Santos, she lifted the bar and he quickly moved his foot. The bar struck the rock with a solid thud and a few chips of rock broke loose.

"I can do it," Santos said and grabbed the bar but Jesse looked hard at him and shook her head so he moved away.

Tru walked up and placed a blasting cap in the indentation and attached the copper wire from the roll. He backed away, spooling off the wire. "You might not want to stand there," he said and cocked his head and waited. Jesse and Santos scurried away and stood behind the pickup. She wanted to question Tru about the whole process, just to verify he knew what he was doing but she knew his eruption might be larger than any blasting cap.

Tru turned his body away and brought out a small battery. He held one end of the wire to one terminal and then poised the other over the opposite end of the battery. "What's the signal?" he muttered and then a little louder, *"Fire in the hole?"* A dull concussion filled the air and immediately shards of rock erupted from the indentation. Jesse brought her hands to her ears but it was too late. Santos stood blinking, his ears also ringing with the mini-explosion. Several seconds passed before the bits of debris stopped falling.

"Geezus," Jesse said. "Why didn't you warn us?"

"I did," Tru said. He walked over to the small area now blasted into the rock. He looked down. Santos and Jesse followed and stood behind him as he scraped away the pulverized earth.

"Ain't deep enough," he said. He repeated the process with two more caps and then stood over the hole again.

"That's better," he whispered, and Jesse could never remember Fredrick Truman Pierce ever saying the phrase. He dragged the wire ahead a few paces and turned back. "Well, pace off another one," he commanded. Santos jerked into action, counting in Spanish.

It was early afternoon before Tru stopped and even then it was only to return to the pickup for another box of caps. A dozen post-holes lined up to the top of the rocky ridge and three more lay on the opposite slope out of sight. Jesse and Santos sat in the sparse shade of the pickup, sipping from the burlap covered water jug and holding their sweat soaked hats. Jesse wet her scarf and wiped her face and then held the jug up to Tru who stood leaning on the fender but he refused.

"Maybe we oughta stop, eat something," Jesse offered. "Maybe it's not good to hurry, especially with this stuff Tru. We can't go all day long out here on water."

"Some of us can," Tru said. "I know what I'm doing." He did not look at her. He took the jug and sucked out a long drink and then capped and tossed it through the pickup window onto the seat. "Let's go."

"Tru?" Jesse said but he was not listening. He got inside the pickup and started it. Jesse and Santos stood immobile. Tru did not wait for them. He drove the truck to the top of the rise and then over the other side to the last hole he had blasted. When Jesse and Santos got to the top of the ridge, Tru held a fresh box of blasting caps and had already stepped off six paces. He stood watching them come over the slope. A hot wind picked up from the west and quickly dried their sweat but it did not cool any flesh. Jesse dragged the heavy spud bar but she refused angrily when Santos offered to take it. With each hole Tru scavenged from the hard earth, her anger increased, even as his subsided.

It was late afternoon when Tru finally said, "That'll do." He put the half box of blasting caps back in the pickup bed. "For today..."

On the road back, Santos nodded and jerked awake several times. His head finally rested on Jesse's shoulder as they swung into the yard. Jesse said nothing when they stopped next to Linc's old pickup.

She could see the tips of JD's knees showing from the truck bed where he lay sleeping, his hat over his face. Tru shut off the engine and got out. Jesse shook Santos who snorted awake and began counting again in Spanish but then stopped and put his hat on and followed her out of the pickup. Tru was halfway across the yard when he yelled back, *"Tell him he's fired."* He went through the gate and onto the patio. *"And so's his friend."*

JD bolted upright in the pickup bed. He blinked at Jesse who stood with Santos next to the truck. The old man seemed happy to see JD.

"Where's Linc?" Jesse said. JD moved to the tailgate, his legs dangling. He shrugged and looked away and she continued, "I thought you was the one leaving?"

"I was."

"Without saying bye?"

"You never say goodbye either, remember?" JD said and immediately regretted it.

"Yes I did JD," she said softly and now she turned away. "And it was you leaving that time too, remember? Not me."

"I had no selection back then," he said.

Neither spoke for a long moment and then Jesse said, "You know we can't pay you right now." She thought about Hill's offer to pay her cowhands. "But I could get it tomorrow. If that's what you came back for."

"My pay don't matter."

"Yes it does."

"I think Linc's in jail."

Jesse turned to him. "Jail?"

"Yeah," JD scooted from the tailgate and stood. "In Ojinaga. He's the one needs paid."

Santos shifted his feet at this but said nothing.

"Ojinaga?" Jesse said and JD nodded.

He adjusted his hat and looked at the horizon where just a clip of sundown remained. "Your time of day, huh Jesse?"

She sighed and glanced at the purple wash across the sky.

"I will look at Cielo," Santos announced. He walked away toward the bunkhouse, then he turned back to JD as if suddenly remembering something very important and said, "He is in training you know. Cielo…"

When Santos was gone, Jesse moved closer to JD and said, "Why didn't you just go ahead and leave, JD? Sonny said you had a ticket."

"I dunno," he said and studied the sunset. "Yeah I got a ticket. Maybe I will."

"Then what are you doing back here?"

"I thought you might have Linc's pay," he said. "That's all. Maybe I could try to bail him out or something."

"Why?"

JD shrugged. "Because you might need him."

"We need you too."

"We?"

"Me."

"Well." There was a long silence and the sun was gone and JD saw the light on in the kitchen. "Not him. He said we were fired anyway."

"Don't pay any attention to that. He needs you too. Both of you."

"That ain't what he just said."

Jesse nodded but he did not see this in the dusk. "That'd make it easier for you wouldn't it JD?"

"Make what easier?"

"Leaving. Getting run off would make it easier." She heard JD shuffling his feet. "Because if you leave first, then somebody can't leave you, right?"

"That don't make no sense," he said. He cleared his throat and kicked at the dirt. "And if you're talking about something else, remember I was just a kid. That damn sure wasn't my decision. You don't have to worry about all that shit now anyway. I'm just going, that's all. Just lay off."

They said nothing and finally JD continued, "Besides, I didn't leave Linc, did I?"

"Listen JD, I want you to go back into Lajitas," Jesse said and stood closer to him and began to speak lower. "Tell Sonny I sent you. Tell him there's a problem, a big one."

"What for?"

"Just tell him. He'll help."

"What if he don't believe me?"

"He'll believe you. Tell him it's a *ceiling fan* problem."

"A what?"

"Ceiling fan. Just say it JD. He'll understand."

"Well."

"And then you go back and you get Linc, hear?"

JD nodded. "But that don't mean I'm coming back too."

Jesse reached over and touched his face with her hand and he could feel the roughness of her palm on his unshaven cheek and he thought about last night in Mexico and he felt dirty. He turned his face away and then got into the truck and started the engine and Jesse came over. This time she kept her hands buried in her pant pockets.

"What'd that old man mean?" he said. "In training?"

"I guess you could call it that," Jesse said. She glanced toward the bunkhouse. "Maybe we all are."

"For what?"

"Life maybe," Jesse said. "Or death."

She leaned over to look inside the cab at JD. He had flicked on the headlights and in the orange glow from the dashlights, Jesse could see shadows on JD's face. He appeared much older, almost like his father. "Hurry JD," she said.

TWENTY ONE

Whatever was chasing Linc in his drunken dream was dark and ominous and astride a black horse. Then the rider became two riders, like he and JD on the buckskin, except Linc saw it was himself behind now, clinging desperately onto this grim horseman whose body was cold and clammy, pushing the horse and both riders toward the same abyss he had seen in the lightning storm. Whatever lay ahead, Linc knew it could not be good.

He forced himself awake and felt the cold steel bunk against his cheek, a small puddle of his own saliva for a pillow. He pushed up and sat on the edge and rubbed the wet side of his two day beard with his palm. He needed to piss bad. But when he touched the floor with his feet, he felt more dampness and realized his boots were missing so he held his sockfeet up, suspicious it was urine on the floor and probably not even his own. He would just hold it. He tried to moisten his lips but his tongue was dry. He sucked in a deep breath and then knew the smell was urine, at best. He felt for his hat in the dimness but could not find it and then discovered his belt was also missing. He felt naked, violated.

His thought was not about boots or hat or pissing or even how to get out. It was about JD. He squinted into the dark cell to see if he were there also, but he was not.

"Shit." He blinked his eyes and slowly adjusted to the darkness. "Always wondered what a Mexican jail cell looked like," he groaned.

Against one wall was a metal sink with no handles on the faucet. The latrine was an indentation in the floor, running along that same wall opposite the bunk, and except for a boiler plate door with no lookout in another wall, that was it.

"I was right," he muttered and looked up at a small opening high in the brick wall, exactly where he imagined it would be, except this one had a mesh grate in place of steel bars allowing even less light through. He guessed by the thin slivers of light from a sputtering streetlamp, spiking through the mesh, it was night. His huge head told him he had passed out and probably slept through the entire day following the handcuffs in the hotel, but Linc was too far beyond the mescal to remember anything else. Everything after that was a blur.

"Maybe he got away," he said. He heard the dull clang of heavy doors slamming and big keys jangling and bootheels outside in the hallway. And then a silence so oppressive it weighed him back onto the steel bunk and he knew why prisoners groaned all the time. After awhile he could no longer hold back, so he sat up again and squinted into the sheen on the floor, trying to pick out the driest spots. He tiptoed across and braced himself with both hands on the dank wall behind the latrine and was overwhelmed by the stench from below. Pissing would have to wait.

Everything rose in a coughing wretch that echoed back to him from the high walls and made him want to puke even more and when nothing remained to evict, Linc continued to heave dry. Finally he stopped and was so weak he barely made it back to the bunk. His sock feet were soaked when he collapsed. He groaned in earnest now, and slept, this time dreamless.

The man who opened his cell door later seemed suspiciously accommodating but Linc saw no food or water. He did not care about food but he would have taken water. The man blinded him with a flashlight and Linc wondered if the heavier torture started like this. Neither said anything. The jailer directed his flashlight into the hallway and Linc understood. He rose and squinted into even harsher lighting outside the cell and then walked in front of the man who had a pistol holstered at his side. At the end of the hallway a second guard, who had watched them approach through a barred window, keyed open this door and held it while they passed. The two men whispered something in Spanish but Linc did not catch it. He was wide awake now, alert to what he expected to be a flank attack, maybe with blackjacks or hoses or something worse. But then he heard voices from ahead and when he turned the next corner, he stood suddenly in the bright florescence of an outer lobby.

JD stood in front of the counter with his arms crossed. He had his hat pulled forward and an awkward but confident tilt to his chin. A uniformed man sat with his feet atop his desk behind the counter. He smiled sardonically at Linc and then spoke in Spanish to the other officer and Linc's boots and hat and belt and pocketknife appeared from under the counter and then the *jéfe* said in English, "You know sometimes it is better to pay for a good time *before* you have the good time *Señor. Entiende?"*

He looked at JD who nodded wisely but then the officer scowled and shook his head at Linc who had put his hat on and held his boots in a deathgrip, as if now ready to argue his case.

"And much cheaper if you have the good time legal," the man continued and he was very serious. He dropped his feet to the floor and leaned forward. "You are fortunate to have a young friend here with some *dinero*. We could keep you a very long time you know."

"Let's go," JD said and then repeated it through his teeth when Linc seemed to balk. He reached over the counter and grabbed Linc's elbow and led him bootless through the front door and out into the night.

"Wait a goddamned minute," Linc said and pulled free.

"Geezus, you want back in there? Both of us? Let's get the hell away from here."

"Let me get my boots on for chrissake." Linc sat on the curb and peeled off the wet socks. "What the hell did they take my boots for?" he said. "They think I was gonna club myself to death with them or what?" He tossed the socks into the gutter and tugged his boots over bare feet. "There," he said and pulled his hat tighter. He stood and a paleblue light from a beer sign spilled over his face, causing it to glow pallid and hollow. He threaded his belt back through the loops and set the buckle just so. "At least I feel dressed now."

"Well you look like a fucking corpse," JD said, but there was such morbidity in Linc's voice that JD tried again, this time for humor, "Shit they might even believe you're alive at the border if you can say *American.* Ain't no Mexican citizen would let himself get into your kind of shape. Let's go."

JD walked ahead and crossed the border, making sure several people were between him and Linc, just in case there might be a last minute connection between the two on the Mexican side. He did not want some slighted lower *Federale* to decide he needed his own share of the *mordida.* JD had negotiated—or rather pleaded down—the *bite* at the stationhouse to one-hundred and seventy-five American dollars. He held the remaining twenty-five from Jesse and Sonny's ceiling fan envelope in a tight fist, buried inside his pocket, avoiding the dubious safety of a boottop cache.

It was three a.m. when they finally got back to the parking lot. Linc went straight for his pickup and reached under the wheelwell for the keys but they were not there. He leaned against the cab and waited. JD paid the attendant for the parking and then walked over to Linc and held out the keys in one hand and the remainder of the money in the other.

"Give this back to Jesse," he said. "You'll owe her about one-eighty I guess."

Linc took the keys and the money and they both stood silent. After awhile Linc said, "Jesse?"

"Her and Sonny Pun."

"Damn," Linc said. "Where'd they come up with it?" He stood silent for a long while and JD knew at this point that an answer was not important. Finally Linc shuffled and cleared his throat and said, "You missed your bus JD."

"I can change the ticket."

"You already done that once. They'll charge you this time."

"Maybe."

"What'll you use for cash?"

JD had not considered this. "I guess I could take back ten of what I just give you or something. It ain't as if she don't owe me but then I could just owe her for it I guess," he said and then, "Along with what I owe you for the room and the booze at the hotel and the cab driver which comes to what?"

"What hotel?" Linc said. He unlocked the door to the pickup and got in. "What booze, what fucking driver?"

"Come on Linc," JD said. "I'd just as soon forget about it too." He moved to the window. "Hand me my box of stuff."

Linc paused but then reached over and grabbed the box. He pushed it through the window.

"Maybe you could just let me have five?" JD said.

"I can let you have it all JD," Linc said and he started the engine. "Here." He handed the twenty back to JD. "I'll work off the whole two-hundred or she can take it out of what's due me, but I ain't complaining you understand. I'm thinking serious about hooking up to my little trailer and leaving myself. It's just that I never leave owing nobody."

"Well it ain't as if I owe her anything either goddammit. Like I say, she owes me." JD turned and began walking toward the bus depot.

"That ain't what I mean," Linc called. "If you really need a reason to leave, just figure it your way and get the hell on the next bus." He shifted the gears and eased out onto the deserted street and idled alongside JD who refused to look at him. Linc spoke loud above the clatter of the old engine and his voice echoed into the darkness, "Tell me something JD. Why didn't you just leave me too? That would'a been simple."

"You was in trouble, asshole," JD yelled back. "That's why I come back, you goddamned idiot."

Linc stopped the truck and leaned out and the engine idled quieter. JD kept walking. "Maybe she is too," Linc said and his voice was lower.

JD took a few more steps and stopped. He dropped the box on the sidewalk and then sat on the curb. Linc shut off the engine.

"You're blocking traffic," JD said.

"Ain't no traffic." Linc opened his door and rested his boots on the running board and leaned on his knees. He looked up the pavement where a single streetlamp cast a circle of light, candlemoths swarming the bulb. "My feet's getting cold," he said. "Without them socks."

"Shouldn't have throwed them away."

"They had piss all over them. You got any smokes?"

"I don't smoke," JD said. "You know I don't smoke."

Linc said nothing. The cooling engine ticked away the seconds. Finally JD said, "Thought you was going."

"I just told you. I ain't never left owing nobody nothing."

"You don't owe me nothing."

"Ain't the way I figure it," Linc said. He got out and walked over to JD who sat staring into the darkness. Linc picked up JD's cardboard box and took it back to the pickup. He retrieved his pocketknife and then slashed the twine and dug inside the box of clothing until he found a pair of JD's socks. He tried to tug off his boots but the wet feet held the leather like glue.

"How about a hand here?" Linc said.

JD looked at him and shook his head. He got up and approached. "Geezus Linc, you scattered my stuff all over." He reached down where Linc had dropped his clothes and began tossing his shirts and underwear back over Linc's head, missing the box on the seat behind him.

"Well?" Linc held out one booted foot.

"Shit." JD turned around and took the boot by the heel and toe between his legs. "You'd think you was a helpless old fart."

Linc pushed on JD's butt with the other foot until this boot came loose and then they removed the other.

"Now what else can I do for you, asshole?"

"Guess I can do the rest." Linc pulled on the socks and then the boots. "Feels better," he said. "Nice socks. Never say I don't owe you nothing. Now you get your ass in the truck. Before any leaving's done, somebody's gotta build a fence."

TWENTY TWO

"Doesn't matter where they *were,* Tru," Jesse said, setting the full milkpail onto her countertop. She had milked Millie herself and fed the kittens. "They're here now. Let's just get on with it."

"We did fine without them yesterday," Tru thumbed the dial on the radio to the weather. It reported oppressive heat, clearblue skies. "We'll do fine again today."

"What about Santos?"

"What about him?"

"We did fine before he came too," she reminded him.

Tru turned back and tasted his morning tea, added more sugar and sipped again. "Well, I ain't paying him much. It's not like he's a regular hand anyway. Maybe you oughta have him do the milking now."

"Those steers are scattered to god knows where Tru. We can't fence and keep them away from the road too, not even with Santos. You know it's only a matter of time until another one's hit. We need all the help we can get and you know that too."

"Right again Jesse," he rose and rattled his cup into the sink and Jesse wondered if he had broken it. "Always right." He glared at her but she had turned her back to him. Jesse shut her eyes and she could feel the puffs of air on the back of her head when he continued, "But just what the hell did you figure on paying them with?"

"We'll manage."

"Like you managed to get the fencing? Hell we got enough debt already."

"And part of it's what we owe them. How do we take care of that, Tru?"

"Is that why they came back?"

"I don't honestly know why they came back Tru." She turned and faced him and her eyes were hard and cold. "But I do know that I can't tell them to just leave without their pay, that we'll mail it to them—*someday.* You'll have to do that." She lifted the pail and began pouring the milk into the sink.

"Now what the hell you doing that for?"

"Who's left to drink it?" She left the kitchen and went into the hallway for her gloves. "There's plenty in the fridge," she called. "For ice cream. That's all you need anyway isn't it? That and your cattle? You sure don't need people." When she came back into the kitchen, Tru was gone. She looked out the window and saw him and Santos get into the loaded pickup and leave.

Jesse watched the last of the milk trickle down the drain. She sighed and held the milkpail under the faucet and washed it out and replaced it in the pantry.

When she entered the bunkhouse the only thing stirring inside was Cielo in his cage. He began to crow. "I don't think that's loud enough to wake anybody here," she said.

"It's loud enough," grumbled Linc from his bunk. The sunlight spilling through the opened door splashed angular across the floor and halved JD's figure where he lay wrapped in a bundle of blankets against the wall. He did not move.

"He alive?" Jesse said.

"I think so." Linc sat up in his bunk but did not get out. "Tough couple'a nights though."

Jesse did not question further. She left the door open for the light and moved over and dipped water from the crock with the coffee pot and set it on the wood stove. She tossed in a handful of grounds. Then she snapped kindling into the firebox and touched a lighted match to it and soon the flames were alive.

"If you're leaving, Linc, we can't pay you," she said abruptly. She watched the flames. "Not yet. We'll just have to owe you."

"I know," Linc swung his feet to the floor and slipped on his trousers and shirt. "I wasn't the one leaving anyway."

"How about him?"

Linc looked down at JD's socks on his feet, shrugged, then stomped on his boots and stood. He glanced at JD who still had not moved. "Not any more."

"Why'd he come back?" She turned and looked at Linc who sat now at the little table rubbing his face with his palms.

"Well he'll have to answer that. As far as I'm concerned, it's me owes you Jesse. And I owe Sonny too. It's like I told JD, leaving's easy," Linc paused and looked at her with weary red-rimmed eyes. "Course, I ain't promising I won't just up and disappear some day too. Seems like I done that all my life. I guess I just hate saying long goodbyes. But it's the staying's sometimes the hardest and sometimes the younger you are, like him, the harder it is. Everybody's gotta be someplace—as long as you're needed, as long as you ain't no burden. That is if you don't mind Jesse?"

"You know I don't, Linc. Let's don't talk about it any more." She turned back to the coffee and after awhile it was boiling. She lifted it off and poured two cups full and then looked over at the bundle containing JD and poured a third. "But it's not going to be easy," she said and set the mug in front of Linc. "With Tru I mean."

"He pissed?"

"He's always pissed."

"Mmmmm..." Linc sipped the coffee.

"You hungry?" she said.

"No."

"We're gonna need to use your truck I guess," she said and sipped at her mug. "He's already out there with Santos. Maybe we'll just show up and start working and say nothing," Jesse offered.

Linc nodded and finished his coffee. He stood and tugged on his hat and then took his leather gloves from the small shelf and went to the open door. He paused and turned around as if more explanation might be needed.

"I said no need to talk about it Linc," Jesse repeated before he could speak. "I'll get JD up. You sure you don't want something to eat?"

"Be a waste of good food. I think it'd just come right back up,"

Linc said. "I'll gas up my truck."

Linc left and Jesse stood and picked up the remaining cup of coffee and crossed the room. JD lay facing the wall with his back to her and the blanket still over his head. He had not moved since she came in. She stopped and stood over him.

"JD?" she said and held the coffee. "This is getting cold. Maybe I should rattle a milkpail?"

It was intended as humor but when he did not respond, she knelt beside him on the floor and leaned over closer. She could hear him breathing hard under the blanket and knew he had not awakened. She set the coffee on the floor near his head and pulled back a corner of the blanket. He lay with one side of his face halfcut by the sun coming through the door, his hair matted across his forehead and his beard grown even darker. In the shadows, it appeared that someone had playfully charcoaled an adolescent jaw. Jesse smiled when she thought about sunrises and sunsets and how JD disagreed with her on that.

"You missed it," she said low. JD stirred and turned toward her but he did not wake up. She leaned even closer to his face and whispered in his ear, "The sunrise."

She could feel his breath and smell the strong odor of stale liquor but she did not move because she was suddenly transfixed with JD's face. It seemed neither young nor old in the half-shadows but rather an amalgam of the innocence she remembered and the hard reality of his father's features—which she also remembered—and suddenly Jesse felt a rush of compassion and fear and then JD groaned and she remembered that same sound in a younger voice so long ago, mixed with the tinkling of a musicbox.

She shook her head and tried to remove the image from her mind. And then JD's hand was above the blanket and he moaned and sputtered something in his sleep and then the palm of his hand was on her face. For a moment, she allowed it to remain there as she felt her neck and then her cheek flush, and then she took JD's hand and gently placed it back under the blanket, as a mother might tuck in a sleeping child. JD shifted and turned back to the wall and Jesse raised her head and saw he was still asleep. She watched him, wondering whose face he had just touched in his dream. Then she laid her hand on his shoulder and shook him gently and tried for a louder voice, "Come on JD, get up." She picked up the coffee mug and leaned back with her legs folded under her and sat. She could still feel the blood in her face.

JD groaned again but this time it was an awakening sound. He cleared his throat and exhaled one long guttural and painful breath. He rolled toward her and the blanket was snug around him like a cocoon. His face came again into the sunlight and he squinted hard. He lifted an arm from under the blanket and held the back of his hand over his eyes but Jesse could see one of them opened between his fingers.

"That you under there?" Jesse said. She offered the mug.

"Jesse?"

"Who'd you think it was?"

"I dunno. Dreaming I guess." He lifted his hand but held it like an umbrella against the sun. His voice was gravel. "How long you been here?" He sat up on the floor and leaned against the wall, took the coffee and sipped. "It got a little cold," he said.

She wondered if he had heard her talking about the coffee getting cold earlier and if JD really knew what had just happened with his palm on her face. She said nothing. She stood and walked to the doorway and looked back at him.

"We'll wait outside." She paused and JD sipped again and looked at her over the top of the cup. Then he nodded but he said nothing. "Linc's glad you came back with him..." she said and left.

TWENTY THREE

Linc was no stranger to riding fences. Or building them either. He despised each as much as any other tophand, but unlike Tru, Linc long ago resigned himself to the reality of barbed wire and posthole diggers and hot sun, baking even more wrinkles into the back of his neck. He figured if he stretched all the barb wire he had hung end-to-end, it would circle the globe a couple of times with enough left over to completely fence off Texas from the rest of the world.

At each spread, like the THREE DIAMOND in the Texas Hill Country, or the HANGING J near Tucson, and all the others he had drifted in and out of for nearly fifty years, Linc was immediately promoted—or demoted as the case might be—to Chief Fencer, a title he never relished. But it was also a title he accepted and when he got drunk enough, he might even admit that he took a little pride in knowing exactly how to get it done, in simply being needed. His only secret was pacing.

In Fredrick Truman Pierce's own sixty-two years on cattle ranches, he had never learned this simple axiom. As far as Tru was concerned, pacing was something one did across the porch until cattle prices finally bottomed out. Or perhaps used in leading a horse across the crest of a rocky slope while studying some stingy cloud, circling too far to the west and finally dissipating without so much as leaving a single drop of moisture behind. It was certainly not something one did when attacking a project such as Tru had committed to. And be damned to those who felt physically or mentally inclined—and especially hungover—to work slower. And so it was with a great deal of first silent, and then very vocal and hostile acceptance, that Tru welcomed the return of Linc and JD and even Jesse, who all set to work on an array of duties without being asked.

"If you spool it off that other spudbar it'll go faster," Tru growled at JD and Jesse who struggled together to string out one of the new rolls of wire. "Just get on each side of it and poke the bar through the center hole and spin it off as you walk."

Tru jammed the bar through the hole and picked up one end and looked impatiently at the two. "Well hell, somebody grab the other end," he yelled. JD did, but he had to walk rapidly, avoiding the new postholes to keep up. "See. Simple," Tru said when the length had spun off the spool. "Just string four strands like that alongside the postholes so's all we gotta to do is drive along with the posts and drop them. Then we just stretch it and staple it up."

Sounded simple. But not to Linc who watched this with great interest and noted when Tru returned that the free spinning barbs had torn his shirtsleeve and cut bloody ruts into the flesh of his forearm.

"Think some of you can manage that?" Tru said, but everyone knew he meant Jesse and JD without saying names. "You other two come with me."

He picked up the box of blasting caps and copper wire, then turned back to the row of holes he and Santos had blasted earlier in a line parallel the road. "One of you grab the other spudbar."

"Yeah right, simple," Linc whispered, but only Santos heard as he picked up the steel bar and followed Tru.

By late afternoon, Linc's head had pounded beyond hangover and now pressed numb and heavy atop his thin shoulders like an anvil. He wondered how JD was doing. Linc's attempts to pace the job only resulted in angry and caustic outbursts from Tru about how some hands were loyal and always there when he needed them, and others were only stragglers. When the idle conversation turned at one point to questions from JD about Linc's early days as a bronc rider—not for ranches but on the rodeo circuit—Linc joked, "Maybe I oughta just cowboy up and go back to riding broncs for fame and fortune. Damned sure beats fencing."

"Cow*boys* are in rodeos. Cow*men* run ranches," Tru said, cutting the conversation short. His comments were not lost on Linc who tried to hurry but he had simply worn down.

Santos never seemed to tire. He continued to pound out the initial indentations as Linc stood by ready to place the next blasting cap inside and then attach the copper wires for Tru, who walked briskly away with the ends of the wires and the small battery and almost without warning, set off the small blast from a safe distance and then immediately yelled, "Clean it out."

The process repeated until there was sufficient depth in one hole to move to the next. All the while, Linc watched from the corner of his eye as Jesse and JD and Santos and Tru moved through this entire rapid choreography in the intense heat, until Linc's own actions became robotic and forced.

And then it all ceased, as if a movie had stalled in a freeze frame without sound or motion. Even Tru stood rigid, anticipating the dull thud of the exploding cap. But it never came. Tru pressed the wires harder to the terminals of the battery and watched the shallow hole already half-blasted and then slowly looked around at the others who had dropped a safe distance away. Everyone readied themselves as they had all afternoon, fingers in their ears and eyes closed and faces turned away. Still no muffled blast.

"Dead battery," Tru finally declared. Linc removed his fingers from his ears and heard the weariness in Tru's voice, which was neither angry nor loud but nasal and tense. Tru took the wires from the terminals and then brushed them back and forth across the electrodes as if to punish the battery. He repeated, "Goddamned dead battery."

"Probably..." Linc said. He watched Tru working with the battery and the terminals, and this time there was a spark. Still no explosion. "Or maybe a dud," Linc offered, remembering his military demolition training.

"Well, don't just stand there with your thumb in your ass," Tru said. In a reflex as he had done all day, he replaced the wires to the terminals. "Put a new one in the hole."

"Maybe we ought to stop awhile," Jesse said. She moved over next to Tru. "Sun's setting anyway."

JD sat dehydrated on the ground in the shade next to the pick-up and Santos had also backed away but stood wary. Tru looked slowly around as if assessing a crew of worthless and wornout hands on some cattle drive.

"We got daylight," he said, and there was no argument with this and so he continued, "Then we don't stop."

"Maybe we oughta give it at least a minute more," Linc advised. "Take a little break, have a drink of water. It can't hurt that much."

"Ain't me that's hungover," Tru said. He turned back and looked emotionless at Linc and said nothing further. Linc nodded wearily and moved toward the hole with a replacement blasting cap.

But Linc had been here before. Not often, but sometimes there was a delay with blasting caps and he knew this and many others who worked with blasting caps in conjunction with sticks of dynamite would also have known this, but they were no longer alive to attest to it. Linc walked cautiously up to the hole and then squatted and paused for a long while until he heard Tru call out, "Well?"

Linc averted his eyes and turned his head away. With one hand he shielded his face and with the other, reached over the shallow hole and began to raise the wires attached to the cap. And then he froze. With his right hand he dangled the wires inside the hole, turned and called back to Tru, *"Did you take the wires loose from the termin—"*

But Linc never got to finish.

The familiar thud and scattering of rock shards broke the words in half and sent Linc rolling backward. Everyone else ducked and protected their heads and shut their eyes against the rain of rocks and gravel, which shot out of the hole like cannon fire.

Everyone but Tru. When Jesse looked up she saw Tru's mouth working silently and his eyes wide as he stared down at the battery with the wires still attached. Linc lay motionless on his stomach a few feet further from the hole.

"Linc?" Jesse screamed and ran to him as did JD and Santos. Tru did not move. When they eased Linc over onto his back, his eyes fixed them in a blank stare.

"Is he dead?" JD wondered aloud but then Linc sucked in a long breath, as if he had just been tossed into freezing water and he began to blink the dust from his eyes. Linc shifted his right shoulder and lifted his right arm and when he saw the bloody mass which had been his hand, he turned his eyes away and released his breath in a groan. He rested the hand on his chest.

"My god," Jesse whispered when she saw his hand. Her face drained and she shuddered. "Get a...get some...get *something* to wrap it in JD."

JD raced to one pickup and then the other with Santos on his heels but he could only find an empty gunnysack. He brought over.

"Not that!" Jesse said. JD lifted his shoulders and shook his head so she took the sack and held it up. "Then cut it," she said and tried to sound in control. JD shook his head again and Jesse turned back to Linc who stared up grimly at them and seemed to be the only one truly in control. Linc tried to sit up but Jesse said, "No," and pushed him back. He stuck his left hand into his pocket and pulled out his own pocketknife and held it in his open palm. JD took the knife and slashed the gunnysack into ragged strips.

"You hang on," Jesse said. She began to work the strips around Linc's hand in a snug compress which she was able to tie off. By the time she finished this, the blood had already soaked through. "More," she said to JD and tied additional pieces around Linc's hand until the sack was used up.

Tru moved over and stood by, cloaked in silence. After awhile, they sat Linc up but Jesse could see the blood had once more soaked through and Linc's face was pallid. "Get him to the truck," she ordered.

They lifted him under the armpits and walked him to the passenger side of his pickup. Tru followed like a zombie and when they closed the door with Linc's head propped back near the open window, Tru leaned in and said, "I should'a..."

"Hell, it's okay Tru," Linc said weakly. "It's gonna be awright." But he knew it was not.

Jesse got in on the other side, started the engine and gunned it hard. She looked over at Tru who was inspecting the bloody wrapping in disbelief.

"Get out of the goddamn way," she hissed. Tru glared angrily back at her but then his face fell passive, almost as ashen as Linc's.

But she saw no remorse in it. Tru stepped back and stood rigid as if ready to explain his case. Jesse did not wait to hear it.

TWENTY FOUR

The headlights from Linc's pickup cut open the moonless night in front of Jesse. She avoided looking in the rearview mirror, but when she finally did, the white lines on the pavement were disappearing into a monstrous black wake, closing in behind her. She pushed the old truck to its maximum and tried not look back.

Jesse thought about Linc, lying stoic and somber in the clinic bed back in Alpine, his hand a huge club of white gauze and the doctor saying, "We'll keep him tonight," only shrugging at her as she probed about Linc's future use of his hand until they were well out of Linc's earshot. "We'll just have to see in the morning," he said and his voice feigned encouragement. "Of course at his age, it's going to take some time..."

Time. Jesse allowed her mind to flow in the hypnotic staccato of white lines on black, drawing her attention like a magnet, pulling her mind into a sequence of thoughts of Tru and futile fences and her own frustrations. She had time to consider Hill and the imminent confrontation, not only between him and his friends and Santos and Cielo, but between Hill and herself—and the debt she owed.

She had time. But she chose not to waste too much of whatever she had left, fretting about all this. She would simply do what she had to do about her debts and perhaps time would take care of them too.

What she owed, and whom she owed, had become less a concern than simply moving from one sunset to the next and then the next, as she had always done, until the string of events—good or bad—eventually wove themselves into the thinning fabric of her life. She considered her current dilemmas no better nor worse than any others. Yet, as thin as it was, this fabric could still slough from her shoulders entirely, leaving nothing but herself and this man, Fredrick Truman Pierce, exposed and vulnerable and shielded from the outside world by only his diminishing herd of rangy cattle.

Jesse recognized that time would move on as always—like the white lines stringing out behind her—until the continuum simply ended for herself as it had for Clair and their mother and their father. Truman would go on, as would Santos, who seemed timeless anyway, and Sonny and Hill and even JD, though time would become difficult for him, even with his carefully guarded option of leaving wherever and whomever he chose and moving on to something—or someone—different.

Leaving had never worked for Jesse. Nor was it an option she desired even now. And as for Linc, she knew leaving for something better, or even different, would no longer be an option for him if she had understood correctly what the doctor had *not* said. In Linc's narrow world, survival meant the use of two good hands, wrinkled and worn as his might be.

Truman was sitting in his rocker when her headlights swept the porch. Jesse shut off the engine, then the headlights, and walked in the darkness through the front gate and onto the flagstone. No light shone inside the house nor the bunkhouse.

"We need to talk," Tru said. It was not a request. But Jesse walked past him and into the kitchen without a word. She did not turn on the light. She heard his rocker moving tensely back and forth outside the window and then it stopped abruptly. "Jesse?"

She sighed and filled a glass from the faucet and walked back out onto the dark patio. She stopped just around the corner and leaned against the wall and sipped at the cool water.

"He made it," she said. She tried to report this with relief and hope and closure but she could not keep out the sarcasm. "I don't think his hand will."

She heard Tru suck in a deep breath as if there was indeed closure and now he could move on. "That's good," he said and then,

"We'll be okay."

Jesse thought this a strange thing to say. "We?" she said.

"Yeah. I mean too bad about the hand and all, but like I said before, we seem to do okay."

"You mean we'll be okay without Linc? That's what you're saying, isn't it?"

"Well face it, he ain't gonna be worth a tinker's damn with that hand now," Tru said more to himself than to Jesse. "Course he'll get what he's got coming and all. Later, after we sell off some steers..."

"Truman," Jesse whispered. She had followed his voice in the darkness and stood over him. "You can't mean that. What you just said." There was a long silence and then, "Do you?"

"Well, I meant he can hang around awhile I guess but then..."

Tru cleared his throat and rocked nervously but did not speak again. He waited for some absolution or a hint of agreement from Jesse, or at least recognition that this was just the way it had always been, especially in the old days, but things had to go on and it was just the nature of cattle business and nothing personal. When nothing came back he muttered, "I like Linc. Always have. You know that Jesse."

"Good..." she said, but the word hung tentative in the thick darkness, like a dropped cat. When it righted itself, Jesse's voice came bitter and scalding and fractured with dry swallowing, "And that's great you're gonna pay Linc what he's owed, especially when his doctor bill comes in." She leaned over and whispered in his ear. "Just be sure and get his forwarding address, okay? So you'll know where to send all that money we don't have."

She left and went through the dark kitchen and into the bedroom where she leaned against the closed door for long minutes before she flicked on the lamp. She sat on the edge of the bed and dropped her head into her palms and tried to rub the exhaustion and fear from her face. She stopped massaging her forehead and rested her chin in her hands and stared at the tattered Mexican rug on the floor. She wondered if it would be any more protection around her shoulders than the worn weft of her own life she had considered on the highway.

She stood and lifted the rug by a corner and cradled it in the crook of an elbow and took a pillow from the unmade bed. She was determined not to spend tonight in this bed. Before she exited the bedroom, she paused and thought of Clair and their mother and how it had ended so abruptly for them, and suddenly all this overwhelmed her and she wondered if perhaps one final attempt at a geographic cure might work after all.

Then she thought about Clair's gift, the true gift of love which transcended the broken China cup she had given Jesse, and about the gift Jesse had always believed she in turn had given back to her dead sister by protecting her only son on that one night, that son now safe and again asleep in the bunkhouse.

Then Jesse thought about the basket under the bed with Clair's broken cup still wrapped in the silk scarf beside their mother's musicbox. And she remembered the single gold coin her mother had hidden there for salvation when the grace of the music inside did not work.

"Salvation," Jesse scoffed. She leaned her forehead against the bedroom door and wondered if she could get past Tru on the patio. She considered the coin again and the absence now of the fan envelope in Sonny's bar. Though she did not considered that cache of money a waste on Linc, she was certain that Linc would have preferred to remained whole, both hands useful, even in the dank stench of some Mexican prison. And though Sonny would never mention it, she felt obligated for his half of the tip money far more than she did for the fencing for which she was being held to a much greater debt by Hill Garza. And there was the pay for JD and Santos and Linc's medical debt, which Tru would never acknowledge, but Jesse was determined she would cover, somehow. But no matter how valuable her mother considered it, Jesse knew one coin would not do it all. Not even a gold one.

Suddenly she straightened and turned back to the bed. She knelt and retrieved the basket and removed its lid. She reached in and took out the musicbox and then replaced the basket. She stood again and turned off the lamp and exited the bedroom with the rug and the pillow and the musicbox. She went out the back door of the house. She circled wide, avoiding the patio and walked softly through the yard and got into Linc's pickup, careful not to stir the dogs. She closed the door gently and made sure the windows were tight. Then she removed her boots and wrapped herself inside the rug and propped the pillow against the passenger door and lay down on the seat.

Inside the cavity of the rug she opened the musicbox and the soft plucked sounds filled the space, but then she worried it might be heard outside, so she quickly fingered out the velvet lining and lifted the coin from the bottom and put the lid back on, shutting the music off in mid-chorus. Then she removed the rug from over her head and sat up. For a moment she stopped breathing but she could hear no movement outside and then she saw the hallway light on inside the house and knew Tru was there. He would not look for her. She lay back against the pillow and pulled the rug around her shoulders. The gold coin inside her closed fist soon grew warm. She shut her eyes and after a long while of listening she slept.

The next morning when JD snapped open the door to Linc's truck, Jesse almost fell out. He caught her just in time but the musicbox dropped from her lap to the ground. When it landed, the lid came off and rolled to a stop on the hardpan like a coin spun on a tabletop. The music filled the air. JD pushed Jesse up in the seat and they both stared down at the musicbox. After a while he picked it up and put the lid back on. For a few moments he cradled it in his cupped hands and then gave it back to her. She took it with one hand, still clutching the coin in her other palm. She shoved the coin into her pocket, a little embarrassed, and blinked at him, expecting questions. He only had one.

"Linc?"

"Alpine," she said. She grabbed her boots and put them out the door onto the running board. "In the hospital." She pushed her feet into the boots and then reached back and wadded the rug and the pillow onto the seat and tucked the musicbox inside the bundle. She got out. "They kept him overnight."

"Well?"

"I don't know," she said grimly. "The doctor said it would take time. But he said I could probably pick him up today." They looked at each other and then she said, "It was pretty bad JD."

"Damn."

"Yeah."

JD turned away. He said nothing for a long while as he regarded the early blush of horizon and the sound of Millie, lowing in the corral and Cielo answering from the bunkhouse. "I'll put the calf on her," he finally said. "Then I'll drive us back up to Alpine."

"You move over into the bunkhouse?" she said, but she already knew he had.

"Guess so."

"Then maybe we'll just let the calf have all of it," she said. "From now on."

"What about the cats?" he said.

"Let them earn their keep," she said. "In the grain room."

He nodded and she thought there was the beginning of a smile but he had walked away. "You make coffee?" she said to his back.

JD shook his head. "Ain't got time for that either. Get back in."

TWENTY FIVE

"How far?" JD down-shifted and rolled slowly into Lajitas. A single stray pickup from Friday night lingered in front of the bar.

"In this thing? At least an hour-and-a-half." Jesse slumped in the passenger side and watched the weathered buildings flow past: Compton's, the Elbo Room, the bank, each appearing even more forlorn in the warm red-orange sunrise. "Go east on over to Terlingua and then north on 118. Same way you came in on the bus."

"You need to stop anywhere?"

"Not right now," she said. "Maybe on the way back through. I need to see Hill Garza for a minute, that's all."

He nodded, shifted up and then gained speed to the east. Jesse folded the rug and pillow under her back and closed her eyes and for fifteen minutes, he thought she was asleep until she said, "You remembered didn't you." She lay with her head against the seatback and did not open her eyes.

"What?"

"The music. You remembered it."

"No."

"Yes you did, I saw your face."

JD sat silent. He watched the greasewood and the chollo and the heat, already glassing the pavement ahead. He avoided looking at her.

"What else?" she demanded.

"Nothing."

"What else JD?"

"Nothing goddammit," he looked at her but she remained in the same position, her eyes shut. "I don't remember nothing. What're you talking about anyway?"

He turned back to watch the road and soon they were past Terlingua on Highway 118 north. He tried to speed up but the old pickup was still the slowest thing moving. Jesse slept—or had her eyes closed—all the way into Alpine. When he braked at the city limits, she sat up.

"Clinic's past the stoplight one block and then left," she said. "But I want you to turn right at the square first." She looked at him and expected questions but he said nothing. She could see the muscles working in his jaw. "There's a place about two blocks down at the corner and on the left. See the cafe sign? I'll just be a minute."

Jesse disappeared into the cafe but then slipped through an archway inside and into the adjacent business with bars on the front windows. A bald man stood leaning on the glasstop display counter reading the newspaper. He surveyed Jesse over a pair of frameless glasses when she came in but he avoided looking her in the eyes. No one else was in the shop. When he finished inspecting her body he lifted his eyebrows and then looked down under half closed eyelids and continued reading. Jesse moved over and stood in front of him. She looked at herself in the mirror behind him and saw her disheveled shirt and her drawn face under a billow of wayward hair and she understood the thin smile of contempt on his face. She ran her palm across her hair and cleared her throat.

"Help you?" the man said, but still did not look up. She reached into her jeans and tossed the gold coin onto the newspaper in front of him. When she did this she saw his eyebrows lift again, higher, and his eyes widened this time. But when he straightened and looked at her, the eyes were slits, the smile forced and clumsy.

"Pawn it?" he said sweetly.

"Sell it," Jesse corrected, and she put just enough anger in her voice that the man blinked and tilted his head. He glared at her for a few moments as if she had just threatened to rob him. He picked up the coin and put a loupe into one eye and turned the coin over and over in his fingers. Then he slowly removed the eyepiece and pursed his lips into a sneer and raised his shoulders. He returned the coin to the newspaper and poked at it as if were an insect.

"Well?" Jesse said. She frowned and watched him toy with it and wondered if it was worthless after all. Maybe it was not even gold. "What's it worth," she said. She tried to sound knowledgeable but her voice cracked a little and she thought if she could get a hundred or even fifty for it she would have at least something for Cielo's fight. As it was, she had nothing left to bet, not even the fan money now. The man turned his back on her and Jesse thought he was done with it. Her shoulders drooped.

"I dunno," he growled and reached for a dog-eared manual behind him. He thumbed through the thick yellowed pages and then ran a finger down a column. He snapped it shut and wedged it back onto the dusty shelf and looked in her eyes. He rasped his palm across his unshaven face. "You sure you wanna sell this?"

"I'm sure."

"Well," he paused and fingered the coin again. "I could go maybe seven or eight," he said and shook his head and Jesse's heart sank with her shoulders. She reached to pick up the coin. As worthless as her mother's gift might be, she would simply not let it go for seven or eight dollars. But when the man saw her intentions he seemed shaken. He reached out and placed his hand over the coin before she could grasp it and said quickly, "But definitely *not* a thousand."

Jesse blinked at him. She took in a small breath and tried to compose herself but when she looked in the mirror behind him, all she could see on her face was shock. It did not take Jesse long to understand what the man said. She regarded the man's hand, laid like a dead rat cross the coin. She pursed her own lips and then took his small finger between her thumb and forefinger and lifted his hand from the coin as if removing the rodent by its tail. "I don't think so," she said. She picked up the coin and dropped it back into her pocket and started to go.

"Wait a minute," he said when she reached the archway into the cafe. Jesse stopped but did not turn back. "Nine," he said. "And that's my final offer."

"Look," she said, suspecting from the sound of his voice that he was lying. When she turned around and saw his face she knew he was. "I don't have time for this shit, mister. It's gold and it's worth way over a thousand if it's worth a dime. We both know that." She sighed and then worried if she had carried the bluff too far but she pushed ahead, "Take it or leave it."

Long moments ticked away. The only sound in the silence of the little shop was the murmur of voices from the adjacent cafe and the clatter of dishes. Glare from outside the windows reflected on the man's glasses and Jesse could not see his eyes, but she did see a smile working across his face and she thought it would soon be a laugh, ending all this.

Then he turned away from her, but his head was nodding. He reached under the counter and brought out a small gray cashbox and rattled keys from his pocket. "Awright," he said. "But you're screwing me good, lady. You know that."

Jesse did not know that. She had no idea how much money she may or may not be leaving on the grimy countertop but it did not matter now. With this much, she could wager against the best of Hill Garza and his friends and she felt in her heart that Santos and Cielo would not prove her wrong.

She walked back over and took the coin from her pocket and looked down at it, warm in her palm. When the man had counted out ten, one-hundred dollar bills, Jesse stared at him and she shook her head because she knew it would not be possible to explain the true value of this object to this stranger. Her eyes clouded and filled as she looked at the crisp greenbacks in her palm. *"For salvation,"* she murmured and the man blinked at her, perplexed. He shook his head in confusion when Jesse handed him the coin, whispering, *"When the grace of music is not enough."*

Outside, Jesse swiped at her eyes with the back of her hand and snapped open the door of the pickup and said, "Let's get Linc out of the damn hospital."

JD started the truck and backed into the street and pulled away. "What're you crying about?" he said. He had never seen Jesse cry. "What the hell happened?"

"Just drive," she said.

TWENTY SIX

"When's the doc want to see it again?" JD wheeled back onto Highway 118 south. He sounded casual and bright and concerned all at once, though JD recognized all of these were foreign to his voice. It was a try. At the clinic, Linc had stood holding his hat in his good hand when they greeted him. He held the bandaged right hand at his side as if trying to hide it. Then he just nodded and put his hat on and went out and got into the pickup, ahead of Jesse and JD. He sat between them now but offered nothing. Linc seemed naked without his toothpick. "The hand, I mean," JD pressed, but his voice trailed.

Linc shook his head and stared into the distance. He pulled his hat down low onto his forehead and cradled the lump of gauzed hand in his lap. Jesse cleared her throat. Hot wind whistled into the cab through the wing windows and whipped her hair into an even larger tangle. JD had spoken of Linc's hand as if it were some object, separate from the man himself, but Jesse could not do that. She cleared her throat again and sat mute like Linc. No one spoke again until they reached Lajitas.

"Bank's closed today Jesse. You still wannna stop?" JD said. Jesse nodded so he braked in front. Jesse knew Hill would be there alone on a Saturday morning. She got out and went inside and was only gone a few minutes and then emerged and got back into the truck.

"Everything's set," she said. She was flushed and angry. No one asked what she meant.

When they pulled into the yard Santos was walking out of the barn with Cielo tucked under one arm. He approached the truck and opened Jesse's door and smiled broadly at her as she exited. Truman's pickup with the load of fencing was gone. "He is ready," Santos assured her and held up the rooster who cocked his head and seemed to look at Jesse with his goodeye.

"Hope so," she said.

JD got out and finally Linc. When Santos saw the size of Linc's bandaged hand, his smile disappeared. JD held out Linc's keys and dropped them into his left palm and went into the bunkhouse. Linc stared at the keys for a moment and then over to his little silver trailer house next to the bunkhouse. "Help me pack my stuff, okay?" he said to Santos who frowned and glanced at Jesse, but he remained silent.

When Jesse also remained quiet, Santos shrugged and said, "*Si.*"

Jesse moved in front of Linc, shaking her head. "What are you saying Linc?"

"I'll move my stuff into my little trailer house tonight," he muttered and then, "Maybe these two can help me hitch it up this evening when it cools down. I'll stay one more night if that's okay."

"Hell no, it's not okay," she said. "I don't even want to talk about it Linc. You're not going anywhere."

"You saw inside this Jesse," he said. His voice was grim and flat, as he lifted the bandaged hand. "Now you tell me what use it's gonna be around here." He lowered the hand and continued. "Or anywhere else."

He started toward the bunkhouse but paused and turned back. "It ain't no secret about *his* feelings." He lifted his chin toward the main house. "He probably thinks it's me screwed up. I don't figure I'm leaving owing nobody nothing now. He knows that." Linc moved on with Santos behind.

Jesse wanted to say she could handle Tru but she was not certain. And though Linc seemed determined, she followed him into the bunkhouse anyway.

Inside she sat at the little table, watching. JD lay stretched out on an empty bunk, pretending to sleep. It did not take Santos long to stuff Linc's belongings into his large military duffel bag. Linc stood inspecting each item in turn before it went in, as if to tally a lifetime. No one said anything until Linc lifted the bag with his good hand and grunted and swung it over his left shoulder. When he wavered a little under its weight, Santos offered, "Cielo, he gets along with only one eye." Linc looked at the old man who had said this without jest. "And one good wing."

"Yeah, but I ain't no old rooster," Linc said. He tried to shift the load to a more comfortable position but nothing worked. "Leastwise not a fighting one."

"Anyone can be a fighter," Santos encouraged.

"He's right." Jesse pushed away from the table and stood and when she did the chair toppled over. JD sat up and swung his feet to the floor and waited. "And if you don't think you owe me a try at that, at least think about this..." She pulled the roll of bills from her pocket and flicked them onto the tabletop. Santos moved first to look at the money and then JD got up and came over. When Linc saw the bills, he shook his head puzzled. "I ain't following you, Jesse."

"What I mean is I owe Hill Garza over three times this," Jesse said and fanned out the bills. "*Three* times." Then the anger left her voice and she said, "You don't know Hill, but I do. He always gets paid. Always."

"You borrow this from him?" JD said.

"No," Jesse said. "I talked to him about...something else. But he's covering the fencing at Compton's and that's the same thing as a loan. It doesn't matter where I got this cash. Just know it's mine and it's the last I've got. What really matters now is where this is going."

Linc frowned and looked at her but said nothing. She reached down and began dividing the money into five stacks, each with two one-hundred dollar bills. "Two hundred for you JD, two for Santos, two for you Linc, two for me..." As she did this JD and Santos gathered closer. Linc held back.

"It's your pay," she said. "It should just about cover what we owe you." She straightened and looked into each face and then continued, "Do with it as you choose. If any of you is leaving right now, whatever else I may owe you, I'll send. Just let me know where."

JD considered the money for a long while and finally looked at

Jesse who was waiting for his question. "What's the fifth stack for?" he said.

"That pays Linc's doctor," she said and picked it up. If he's heading back up through Alpine, he can take it over. Or I can send it. You know there's no way I won't do that, just like there was no way I wouldn't send JD with money to get you out of Mexico, Linc." Linc flushed a little and Jesse went on, her voice a whisper, "But this won't buy back the use of your hand even one more day, Linc." She looked up at him and her eyes were filling. "My God, I wish it could."

"You can just send it on over to that doc," Linc said. "But you owe me nothing else. Everbody needs someplace to be Jesse." There was genuine gratitude in Linc's voice. "I had someplace to be. We'll call that even." He started for the door. "Put my other two-hunnered back where you got the bail money."

"I can do that but let me finish," Jesse said. "Please…" Linc halted.

Santos looked at his share of the money and smiled and glanced over at the willow cage. He thought about Paloma and wondered how many Mexican pesos the greenbacks would buy and if that would be enough. And he wondered where Paloma would be right now and what she would be doing.

JD saw his share on the table and knew it would buy a long bus ticket to somewhere—a string of unknown destinations if that was what he decided. It would be his choice. But suddenly, the destinations seemed far less important than the journey, and JD began to wonder if he needed a ticket for that at all.

Linc turned. He dropped the duffel bag from his shoulder to the floor.

"Please sit," Jesse said. "All of you." JD and Santos sat immediately. Jesse continued and as she spoke Linc moved closer but he did not sit, "I don't want any of you to breathe a word of this to Truman." She turned to Santos. "Did you see him this morning?"

"Si," Santos said. "But he left without me."

"Where?" she said.

"He did not say."

"Well if we see him beside the road, we won't stop," she said and looked up at Linc.

"Road?" Linc said.

"Yes. We'll just pass him and go on up into the mine pit. He'll be working the fence...by himself." She shook her head and sighed and then went on. "But it's me needs your help now, all of you." She looked at Linc. "Especially you. We'll leave just as soon as we can hitch up your trailer and get out of here. Toss some bedrolls into the trailer. We'll overnight at the mine, so we're ready first thing in the morning," she said and surveyed the faces. "Well, whatta you think?"

Without hesitation Santos stood and walked over and picked up the cage. He put it under one arm and a blanket under the other. He came back and put the cage on the table and then stood at attention in front of Jesse for inspection. "I will need barley and water but Cielo is ready. And I am ready."

"Shit, you already said that a dozen times Santos," JD criticized. Cielo whirled in his cage and poked his head through the bars. "Ready for what?" JD said. "Whatta you mean the pit mine? What the hell's going on?"

Santos deferred to Jesse. "Hill has friends," she explained and she stood and paced back and forth as she spoke. "Believe it or not. Anyway, these guys have fighting roosters. They want a match. They want it to happen up at the quarry where nobody will be working tomorrow. It's a big deal with them, you know, gambling, drinking, maybe even drugs, all that." She shook her head in frustration but kept talking. "Hell, I don't even know how it all works. But it's Hill too, not just his friends. He found out about Santos and Cielo and he's hounded me about it."

She stopped pacing and looked at them but no one spoke. "Yes, I know it's not legal, none of it. There'll be other matches too, all day long I guess. But with Santos' help I'm going to bet all of my share on Cielo." She held up her two hundred dollars and then paused for a long moment as she looked at each one. "But I've settled up with all of you. You can do what you like." She leaned forward and looked at Cielo who cocked his goodeye up at her just as he had done the first time she saw him in the yard. "Maybe I can settle up with Hill too," she whispered to the bird. "With your help…" she said and turned back, "All of you."

"Why me and Linc?" JD said.

"Because."

"Why?"

"Because I'm *scared* dammit," Jesse blurted. "A little anyway. I just wanted some support, that's all JD. Maybe somebody to watch our backs."

"Well," JD said and looked at the floor.

"I already said you don't need to settle up with me," Linc said. "I ain't taking that money there. No way. Bet it if you want to. But if you think you need me for something else… " he continued and then paused and glanced at his gauzed hand. "My pickup and my trailer maybe, well that's fine. I'd hang around for that Jesse. But like I said, you owe me nothing."

She looked at JD who shrugged and then said, "Maybe I'll win a bundle. Who knows what I might need it for," he looked up at Jesse. "Down the road, I mean."

"But then I'm gone," Linc continued. He stared at Jesse with somber determination. "No use trying to stop me."

Jesse said nothing. JD did not respond to Linc's comment either. Jesse pocketed her share of the bills and the share for the doctor but she left Linc's other two-hundred on the table. JD and Santos picked up their money but Linc did not. Finally she picked up Linc's money and shoved it at him. He turned his back and Jesse said, "Okay, I'll just hold it for you Linc. In a safe place." She turned to the others. "Well if everyone's with me, I'll get some grub from the house. Roll up your bedding and then we can go." Jesse went toward the door.

"Jesse?" JD stood and moved closer to her, as if to share some secret. She leaned her head to one side and waited. "What if we lose? I mean, what if *you* lose?" he muttered and Jesse heard genuine concern.

"Like I told Linc," she began and the hardness returned to her eyes as she surveyed their faces, but no one could look back at her, "I don't even want to talk about it."

Outside, Jesse removed the rolled up rug and pillow from the cab of Linc's pickup and walked to his little trailer beside the bunkhouse. She went inside and looked around at the decay and neglect. A single dingy bunk hugged the back wall and a small sink and propane stove sat next to a foldout table with benches which converted into another bunk. A tiny curtainless window was next to a cabinet, hung crooked with its door ajar over the sink. She could see no sign of canned goods or any other provisions except a molded package of soda crackers inside the cupboard next to salt and pepper shakers and a half-burned candle. There was no bathroom.

She sighed and tossed the rug and the pillow onto the bed and went back out. Then she entered her house and took a quick shower, brushed her hair and put on fresh clothes. Their bed had not been slept in and when she walked into the kitchen, she discovered an empty bottle of whiskey next to a waterglass on the kitchen table and next to that, another bottle with only a few drinks gone. She snatched this one up and took it to the sink and removed the lid to pour out the remaining contents, but then stopped and replaced the lid. She went to the pantry and put several cans of food in the bottom of a floursack and then stuffed the whiskey on top. "For my salvation," she said, tapping the bottle. "In case I bet wrong. Tru's already past salvation anyway." She tied the top of the sack and walked out into the yard.

The midday sun glared from the little aluminum trailer, now latched behind the truck. JD sat on the driver side and Linc stood with his good hand holding the door open on the opposite. The pallor of Linc's face startled Jesse when she saw him.

"You okay?" she said. He nodded but she knew it was a lie. "Where's Santos?"

"Back there," JD said, indicating the trailer.

"You get plenty of water?" Jesse said.

"Santos did," JD said, and he could not resist adding. "I think they're ready. Very ready."

"I don't mean for Cielo," she chided. "I mean for us. It'll be damned hot up there."

JD nodded. "It's in the trailer."

"Linc you go back there too," Jesse said. "It's too hot up here. You can stretch out on the bed and have water handy too."

"I'm okay," Linc said but his voice was weak. "I can squeeze in up here." He licked a trickle of sweat from the corner of his mouth.

"Go on Linc," JD said.

"Hell I oughta be the one driving." Linc wavered but quickly straightened himself. Jesse reached over to grab his upper arm for support but he pulled away.

"Maybe he oughta stay," JD grumbled and then directly to Linc, "Maybe you oughta stay, Linc."

"I ain't staying," Linc said. He turned and walked back toward the trailer. "Here or nowhere else." He opened the door and disappeared inside.

JD frowned and lifted his hat and wiped his forehead with the back of his hand. "Well."

"He'll be okay," Jesse said and got inside. "Let's go."

TWENTY SEVEN

The old Chisos Mining Company had never been successful. Discovery of lowgrade cinnabar in the foothills of Santiago Peak in the 1800's caused no major rush to the region and by 1925, costs had overtaken profit just as cattle had finally overtaken ore as the chief source of revenue for that parched area of Texas. The lumbering, mule-drawn ore wagons along the dusty and narrow *Camino Rio* to Presidio became fewer and fewer and finally, ceased altogether, giving way to occasional cattle trucks.

By then modern equipment had improved and instead of the tedious shaft mining, huge sections of earth could be dynamited and gouged out with a single scoop of an excavator and hauled rapidly over great distances in large ore trucks for smeltering into the final product, liquid mercury. Trucks like the ones roaring through Tru's ranch. And in turn, the value of mercury bounced even higher. Stock prices soared and plunged and soared again and the real prospectors—who rarely set foot on the site—now wore suits and ties and communicated with each other by computers from air-conditioned offices. But little of the money generated stayed in this area, even though there was an occasional defeat of one of their high blooded roosters in a lopsided match.

JD parked the pickup and trailer next to the steep road that began the precipitous descent into the open mining pit. Jesse got out and knelt at the precipice and gazed over into the chasm cut in the face of Santiago Peak. JD took one look and then strolled a short distance into the piñon trees to relieve himself. He came back and stood next to Jesse and both listened to the wind and stared across the pit. Neither Santos or Linc came out of the trailer.

"Damn big hole," JD said after awhile, remembering a photo from a high school geology book, "Like a meteor or something hit right here."

"Yeah."

"Water in it too. See? Back below that steep wall over on the other side. Looks pretty deep. And dirty."

"Well it ain't rain," she said. "You'd never believe it, as dry as it is around here, but they're way into the water table. You could sink every piece of their equipment, right there in that little lake and never find it again."

"And they keep digging?"

"Right up the edges, terracing into the side of the peak. See all that equipment?" Huge tractors and trucks and dozers in the bottom appeared to be toys.

"Must be doing good."

"Must be. Hill wouldn't be in it if it wasn't."

"He's in on this too?"

"Oh yes."

"It's damn close to your place ain't it?"

"Borders right on us," she said and looked at him. "But you know all about how that happened, JD. You've heard the history lessons, right? Don't worry. Hell'd freeze over before Truman Pierce would sell another inch. Especially to some operation like this. It's bad enough, his own father—"

"Where was he?" JD interrupted.

"I don't know," Jesse said. They had passed Truman's pickup parked beside the road, but he was nowhere in sight. All of the fencing materials had been unloaded. "Maybe in the ravine, sleeping off whiskey. Maybe blasting another damned hole or something over the next ridge. I don't know. Don't worry about it."

"What else is that Garza guy in on?" JD looked at her.

"Hill owns a lot of things," Jesse said. "And people." She stood and walked toward the truck. "But not Truman. And not me. Let's go."

"Drugs?" JD said.

"Don't think so, " she said. "Maybe his friends are, who knows?"

JD followed. He started the truck and eased onto the downslope in the lowest gear. "Trailer ain't got brakes," he said. "I'll take it slow."

"Good idea." She smiled at him and glanced over the edge of the road. "Cielo might fly down with one good wing but I don't think we can." She looked back at JD who sat focused on navigating the narrow road.

"Thanks JD," she said.

"For what?"

"For coming."

He nodded but said nothing. The brakes were smoking when JD squealed to a stop at the bottom of the pit. Several weathered tin warehouses, doll-sized from above, loomed huge on a graded plateau at the end of the downroad. They dwarfed the little trailer. Rusted oildrums, leaking mysterious shadows of black liquid, cluttered the area and reflected sunlight as if mocking the clean blue sky. Further back against the steepest side of the chasm lay the body of water, even larger than it seemed from above, several acres in size and glistening with an iridescent sheen.

"Smells funny down here," JD said when he stepped out. He surveyed the area and then craned back and took in the terraced sides of the pit, which spiraled all the way to the top edge from which they had just descended. "And it ain't smoke from the brakes."

"We won't be here long," Jesse said. She went and opened the door to the trailer and called inside, "You alright in there?"

Santos stepped out with the caged bird in his arms. He looked up and up. He placed the cage in the shade of the trailer and knelt beside it. He removed his hat and held it, protecting his chest. His mouth opened as he rose slowly and began turning round and round, attempting to encompass at once the entire mass of the lifeless, grayrock maelstrom they had spun down into. Finally he shook his dizzy head and looked at the cage on the ground for balance. "Even if we win," he murmured, "Will we find our way out?" It was a sobering thought. Cielo lay still on the bottom of the cage.

That evening Jesse opened several cans of stew and shook them into a cast iron Dutch oven she found under the sink. Linc awakened at the noise and sat up in the bunk. Jesse struck a match and held it over one burner on the propane stove. She twisted the knob back and forth.

"No sense trying," Linc apologized. "It's been out of gas since I first came. I didn't figure on no picnics." He stood and squeezed by Jesse. "I'll see if I can get a fire going outside." When he opened the door, he saw JD and Santos had beat him to it. They sat in the coming darkness next to a flaming pile of dry piñon limbs which had fallen over the edge and into the bottom of the pit. "Hell it's a regular trail camp," Linc grumbled and stepped out. Jesse put a lid on the pot and followed.

She set the Dutch oven next to the fire and nudged it closer with her boot. "Didn't take long to make, won't take long to heat," she said. "Or to eat. It ain't much but..."

She distributed tin plates and spoons and cups and then sat with the others looking into the fire. She looked at the faces glowing yellow, suspended disembodied against the night as each stared into the flames. Jesse wondered if all this was wrong—these men, this old bird, herself—somehow out of sync. No one seemed interested in food.

"Maybe we need a drink?" she said, feigning cheer as she would have years ago at the Elbo Room. This seemed to interest JD but not so much the other two. She rose and went into the trailer and came back with the near-full bottle of whiskey from the floursack. She unscrewed the lid and held it poised over Linc's cup. At first he shook his head and turned his cup upside-down.

"Come on Linc," she said. "It's all gonna be okay." Linc looked up at her and even in the firelight, she saw the pallor on his face and his eyes reflecting a dull, lifeless resignation. Linc had never been light hearted but she had never seen him this down. "Take some," she urged. Linc paused, then lifted his cup and she poured in a generous amount.

Santos accepted a small portion in the bottom of his and said *Bastante!* just as he always did with ice cream and then, "We must stay ready." Jesse was glad he was serious, so she turned to JD's cup.

"You know this stuff ain't legal," he said. He grinned at her. "Not for me."

"Nothing down here's legal." She topped off JD's cup and then her own. "Cheers," she said and sipped the whiskey. She swallowed hard and grimaced. "Always hated this," she said but sipped again. She sat back on the ground next to the flames and the pot of stew which was steaming a little.

Linc refused food. Jesse did not push this time but when she offered more whiskey, Linc accepted another full cup and Jesse watched him take long draughts from it. She set the bottle in the gravel between him and JD. She and Santos and JD ate. Tin spoons on tin plates and the sputtering of burning piñon sap were the only sounds in the silence. Before they finished eating, Linc had filled his cup a third time and sat staring into the flames.

"Don't drink it all," JD scolded. He poured himself another. He lifted the half-empty bottle up to the fire and then thrust it toward Jesse, "You?"

She shook her head. "I'm tired," she said. "First one inside gets the bunk, right?" She rose and collected the plates. "You guys can roll out your stuff on the floor in there I guess."

"You know it ain't big enough for that," JD said, slurring his words a little. "I'm bringing mine out here by the fire. The way I figure it, Truman'd like that. Just like the good old days on the trail. How about you?" He turned to Linc who said nothing but continued to sip and watch the dying flames. "I'll bring Linc's out too," JD said to Jesse.

"Me too," said Santos. He rose and went into the little trailer and retrieved his bedding. "Here beside Cielo." He moved the rooster closer to the embers and spread out his bedding next to the cage. Jesse nodded and went in. JD followed.

"You'll have the run of the place," he said into the darkness when he got inside. "Lights work?"

"No." Jesse stood at the sink, pouring water from one of the jugs over the plates. "There's a candle somewhere in the cupboard." JD lifted his bedroll from the front and tossed it through the open door. Then he squeezed by Jesse to get Linc's from the bunk at the back of the trailer where Linc had slept that afternoon. When he returned, he tossed Linc's bedding forward to the door but stopped behind Jesse, still at the sink. "You gonna sleep in that old thing?"

"What old thing?" Jesse turned and in the darkness, it startled her that JD was so close. They stood face-to-face, like in the corral. A gentle flicker of light from the fire worked through the open door and across one side of their faces but Jesse could not see his eyes. She balanced herself against the small countertop.

"That old rug back there on the bunk?"

"Oh," she said. She smelled the strong whiskey and wondered if it was on her breath too. She released a little chuckle. "It's fine JD. Maybe a little scratchy but..."

She moved to get the candle from the cupboard but in the tight space she could not turn around without brushing against JD's chest. She struck a match and held it to the wick of the candle and when she turned back, the flame was between them. She could feel its heat so she leaned away, trying not to burn either of them but they were still touching. She tried to relax.

"Light," she finally whispered.

"Yeah," JD said and he chuckled nervously. "Candle light."

For a long moment they studied each other. Suddenly JD was frowning. He moved abruptly away and tossed Linc's bedding angrily through the door and went out.

Jesse stood for a long while looking at the open door as if expecting him to return. She wanted to talk to him, ask him hard, lingering questions but he did not come back. She released her breath and went to shut the door and in the moment before she closed it, she saw Linc hunched at the far side of a dwindling fire and JD filling both of their cups again from an also dwindling whiskey bottle and Santos sleeping next to all their one-eyed hopes. The scene froze in Jesse's mind.

"I shouldn't have brought the bottle," she scolded herself. "Maybe I shouldn't have brought any of us." She closed the door and went back to the bunk. She dripped wax onto a small shelf above the bed and stuck the candle into it and then took off everything but her longtailed shirt. She puffed out the candleflame and rolled herself into the rug and adjusted the pillow. Despite the scratchy wool on her bare legs, she felt more comfortable without the tight jeans. For a long while, she turned over and over in her mind what had just happened with JD until finally she slept.

TWENTY EIGHT

Linc had never needed whiskey to make tough choices. He had been his own man from the time he left home, penniless at fifteen to join a rangy pack of unemployed cowhands on a hick rodeo circuit out of Amarillo. When the occasional arena announcer asked his age, Linc always said eighteen, but they knew he was lying and the mike man would make a big deal to the crowd about his being the youngest bronc rider on the circuit. Linc rode the tough ones, the rank ones. "Outlaws" the old timers called them. And that skill was enough to broker no bullshit from anyone. Linc had given serious thought to doing it on the pro circuit once he actually turned eighteen.

But he did not go pro. A broken arm and separated shoulder kept him out of action long enough that he was forced into hazing cattle at an auction yard for pay, which led to an offer as a cowhand on a rimrock ranch near Palo Duro Canyon. He moved from there to another spread, and then another, until the string of promises he had made to himself to return to the rodeo tallied fewer than the string of jobs he held as a cowhand. So he gave up rodeo. And then cattle altogether and entered the military and when he gave that up too, the only thing remaining in his life as constant as rangeland itself were the cattle. Like Truman, that was all Linc really knew or even cared about. It was not a matter of choosing something else now. His age was a limiting factor—even if both hands were perfect. Choosing whiskey was the easiest decision for now. And enough whiskey made all the other choices easier.

With the last bare branch, Linc poked the fire alive and then tossed that one onto it. Through the tongues of flame, he watched JD as he set down his cup of whiskey next to the bottle, rose and brought Linc's bedding over and then his own. Neither had spoken when JD refilled their cups earlier. JD sat again on the ground at the fireside. Even through the fog of whiskey, Linc could see he was agitated.

"More?" JD said. He held up the bottle, only a fourth full.

"Not yet. We're out of wood though," Linc said.

"I'll unhitch and go on top for more," JD offered. He poured most of the remaining whiskey into his cup and then, "Just this one more for that twisting road up." He faked a guttural laugh and swallowed a large mouthful.

"We don't need any more," Linc said. His voice was weak. He drained his cup in a few swallows and JD wondered if he meant whiskey.

"I'm talking about wood," JD argued. Unlike Linc's voice, his was thick. "Shit, you may not need it but I do. I like looking into fire."

"I know what you're talking about, asshole," Linc said and then his voice changed and he was suddenly accommodating, as if not to argue with a drunk kid. He forced himself up from the rocky ground and for a moment he wavered and almost lost his balance. "Hell, I'll get it."

"No you won't," JD snapped. "Look at yourself. Hell you got one bum hand and you can hardly stand. You're always trying to be in charge ain't you, Linc? Like down there in Ojinaga?"

"I wasn't in charge."

"Hell yes, you were."

"How?"

"Well, setting it all up with them women."

"I didn't set it up."

"Well you didn't say no."

"You didn't either."

JD paused for a long while watching the fire. When he spoke again his voice was cracking and remorseful and mostly whiskey talking into the low flames. "Hell, she wasn't even a woman." He looked up and quickly added, "I couldn't do it."

"You wouldn't know a real woman if you saw one."

"She was just a kid, Linc."

"So are you."

"No I ain't," JD shouted and started to rise but could not get his body balanced over his legs. He fell onto his back against his rolled bedding, the angry words echoing from the rock walls. Santos groaned and rolled over and went back to sleep. There was silence for a long while as the flames hissed.

JD spoke again but held his eyes shut and this time, his voice was quiet and slurred, "You understand don't you Linc?"

Linc looked at him. "Don't sound much like you but yeah, I understand." He watched JD lying still, with his hat cocked comically behind his head. "JD?" he said and repeated the name. JD did not respond but Linc continued, "You don't have to try so hard." He picked his way over the rocks and stood rigid beside JD but he could tell his own body was wavering. "Truth is, I couldn't go through with it neither and I had a real woman in my room. Difference is, nothing worked for me. Maybe it's wearing out, this old body."

Linc stared in contempt at his gauzed hand, as if this thin and withered flesh and abused bone were something separate from himself and yet, impossible to simply cast aside when it no longer proved useful. He released a cynical snort at JD's placid face from which there had been no reaction to a single thing he had said. He reached down and picked up the bottle and clamped it under his right armpit as he unscrewed the lid with his good hand. He sucked the final few swallows from it and tossed the empty onto the dying flames. But when he turned his back and moved toward his pickup, he heard JD shift to his side and moan. "I'll get that wood now," Linc said. "One hand or not." Maybe JD was listening. "And don't give me any shit about it..."

With one hand, he unhitched the trailer in the darkness and cranked down the tongue support. He stood looking at the front end and then back at JD beside the fading fire. He studied the boy for a long while, twisted into a fetal position. Suddenly, he turned and went back to the fire and pulled out a half-burned branch. He stuck it into the sand to extinguish the glow of the hot end and then went back to the front of the trailer. He leaned his right shoulder onto the front skin and with his left hand, used the still smoking charcoaled end of the branch to scribble something onto the aluminum, just above the tongue.

"There," he said.

He inspected what he had written as if finished with something necessary. Then he tossed the smoking branch aside and got into the truck and started the engine and pulled away from the emberlight. His headlights caught the incline JD had driven down, and with his left hand, he reached over and ground the transmission into the lowest gear, then quickly re-grasped the wheel. He slowly crept up the switchbacks and around the spiraling cuts in the side of the pit until he finally reached flatland at the top. He pulled off the road and drove a short way along the brink of the chasm.

There he stopped and looked into the night, through which his headlights cut, almost painfully. He pushed in the lightswitch and sat in the darkness with the clutch in and his motor idling. The full moon, which he had not seen from below, washed over the piñons and paled the rangeland around him and up to the very brink of the pit, which lay dark and ominous to his left. His eyes soon adjusted to the softer moonlight. He shifted again into the lowest gear and moved through the piñons, bounced over solid rock for at least a half mile to the back of the quarry. It was not firewood he sought.

He stopped close to the edge, reached over and worked the floor shift into neutral and set the handbrake. He got out of the pickup and walked over to the brink. There he knelt and looked down and saw the moon reflected flat like a China plate on the surface of the pool of stagnant water far below. At the opposite end, Linc saw the tiny flicker of flame from the waning embers and he became dizzy with the whiskey and the height.

"Sleep tight, JD," he whispered. "Like Jesse says, it's gonna be okay. It's all gonna be okay." The only response came from an owl somewhere, waiting for a careless prairie mouse.

After a long while, Linc stood and stumbled back into the truck and turned the wheel hard right. He eased up a small incline of sandstone, his headlights still off. There he spun the pickup full circle and pointed the hood back down the slope, pushed in the clutch with one foot and held the brake with the other. The engine idled. Linc could still see the moon in the water below but the reflection was cut in half now by the rocky edge of the pit. He closed his eyes and thought about the lightning storm and about that painting of a lone cowhand, hunched into a driving rain, the ghost steer stampeding headlong toward that black chasm. But there was no big rain driving anything or anyone here tonight. Not even a little rain. And then Linc thought about his youth and his once strong body and the frantic broncs he rode and some he did not ride and he leaned back against the seat and pulled his hat tight and cocked his head back into the riding position. He reached up with his good hand over the sunvisor and fingered loose a toothpick, placing it between his lips just so.

He nodded his head several times and called out, *Okay boys, okay!* and then allowed one boot to slip from the clutch and at the same time, the other one to fall from the brake pedal hard onto the accelerator and immediately the gears of the old pickup groaned as it rattled and bounced over the uneven ground. *Let him buck!* he yelled.

And then the clamoring noise from the truck ceased abruptly and there was nothing but the smooth whine of the accelerating engine under his foot and the whistle of air through the window as Linc Marks launched over the edge and into the dark arena where the flat moon waited below.

TWENTY NINE

JD snapped awake. An abrupt and foreign sound had shaken him from the haze of whiskey and fatigue. He looked around but saw nothing except the glow of the embers, no longer inviting but terrifying, like night eyes shifting. He did not move, but waited for some clue to the source of the noise and though he could not focus through the latent whiskey, he was nonetheless awake.

He stood and listened harder but nothing came to him except the soft snoring from Santos. He kicked at the coals and a small flame leaped briefly and then died again but in the quick light he saw the blackened whiskey bottle in the fire and noted Linc's missing pickup and then he remembered the argument about gathering firewood. He assumed Linc had passed out somewhere in the piñons above.

He shuddered in the cold night air and thought about his bedding, still rolled up and inviting next to the embers. But he could not suppress the fear that something was wrong. He thought about his encounter with Jesse in the trailer and his anger with himself—neither of which he understood—and suddenly he knew that Jesse must have been the source of the noise and it was she who had cried out to him and he had been unable to help her because he had passed out. Guilt and nausea overwhelmed him but he pushed them back and looked around into the paleblue of night but nothing was there. Terrified, he began to breathe hard and he stumbled in a circle, trying to escape whatever it was that pursued him.

He forced himself toward the trailer with its aluminum shell ghostly in the fullmoon. He opened the door and carefully stepped inside and stood still, listening for sounds from her. "Jesse?" he said. He was breathing hard and the blood in his head hammered against his ears but he held his breath and finally heard her soft breathing. He crept to the back of the trailer and lowered himself to his knees at the edge of the bunk. Through the little window in the back wall, the moonlight fell angular onto Jesse's form under the Mexican rug. JD moved his face closer to her head and whispered, "Jesse?" and this time she stirred and he said with great relief, "You okay?"

"JD?" she moaned.

"Are you okay?" he repeated softly but urgently.

Jesse could hear the terror in his voice. "Yes," she said. She blinked her eyes and moved the rug away from her shoulders. She raised herself onto one elbow and reached her other hand out and found his hot face. "What's wrong JD?"

"I dunno," he whispered. He put his hand over hers on his face. "Something happened…I saw someone…heard something."

Jesse felt JD's hand atop hers and felt his warm tears on her hand and suddenly, she was in another place and another time and JD's fear was her own and she knew at that moment the same fear and anger and confusion must have festered all these years inside them both. Impulsively, she moved her hand to the back of his head and pulled him closer to her and she lay back and soon his face was burning through her shirt and against her breasts. "It's okay," she whispered into his ear. Her voice came even and calm from that other time and that other place and she said, "It was only the music you heard Jimmie boy, only the music…"

And then JD's hand was cold against the flesh of her ribs and he nuzzled his face against her breasts as a nursing child might do. In a paradox of emotions, Jesse's own tears seared her face and then a dormant, euphoric tingling rose in her stomach, mixed with some long-dead fear.

"JD," she breathed. "No…"

"Jesse?" he whispered.

Then she gently grasped his arm at the wrist and held it for a long moment and his hand lay waiting, as if ruled by some unknown force against which neither she nor JD had heretofore held any power whatsoever and only now, with this second moment of choice all these years later, could she exercise control. And so once more she chose.

She forced herself upright and dropped her legs over the edge of the bunk and with her hands on his shoulders, she gently pushed him away. He dropped back and sat cross legged on the floor, shaking his head as if abruptly stunned awake.

"Don't you see what's happening, JD?" she whispered and even though her voice was breathy and weak there was no sign of acquiescence in her words. "Don't you see?"

But there was only silence, except for the slow recovering of breath as neither moved and each seemed to be waiting for the other to say or do something more as they stared at each other in the darklight from the moon. But there was nothing. Jesse brought her palms to JD's cheeks and she could feel his tears again, but then she dropped her hands. Her shoulders slumped as she struggled to think what to say, some adult and profound explanation for this whirlpool of emotions, but she was not sure she could articulate what she was feeling, how her first choice had been for Jimmie Dale the boy but her second now had to be for JD the man.

After long minutes, JD worked his legs under himself and stood. For a moment Jesse thought she would stand also, put her arms around his strong and youthful shoulders and be strong herself and finally say something for closure on all the haunted years. But her legs were trembling and she knew she could not.

JD finally turned and sloughed out the door, leaving it open and she heard the running sound of his boots in the gravel grow fainter and fainter along with what seemed to be sobbing and then there was no sound at all. She went to the door and looked out but she saw nothing in the moonlight.

"JD..." she whimpered and Cielo moved in his cage beside the dying embers of the fire but no other response came back from the darkness. She closed the door and returned to the bunk and wrapped herself in the cocoon of rug but the only thing warm inside were the tears which cut into her face and wicked into her pillow. After a long while, she shivered herself to sleep.

THIRTY

Santos dreams of hands, weathered and sinewy and they are his and he presents them cupped to Paloma whose eyes delight in the gold and silver coins overflowing endlessly from his hands and into her apron which soon fills and spills over onto the dirt floor of their adobe shack until the floor itself is covered and shimmers, brightening the dark mud walls with light. And in the corner atop an alabaster pillar is a wrought cage of delicate gold filigree with mirrors inside for Cielo to admire himself for he is miraculously healed and he stretches his two good wings and peers into the mirror from two good eyes as he grooms himself. Paloma coos and speaks lovingly to Santos as she collects the coins which she counts and recounts and he thinks of the new clothes and the silk shawl and shiny black shoes she will wear and the new sombrero and huaraches he will wear and how Paloma will cling to his arm as they strut around the plaza. And from his office window the jéfe will scowl with envy. But it will do him no good for Santos will have the document of true ownership for his land, safe inside the bank and inside the steel vault and even then, secure in his own locked cabinet to which no one but he, Santos, holds the key. Cielo cocks his head and crows in triumph for his is the bravest fighting heart of all and his is the final victory.

Santos blinked the sleep from his eyes. He turned in his bedding toward the sound of Cielo, calling to a sun which he could not yet see over the rim of the ore pit. Cold ashes lay white and mounded around the tarred and broken neck of last night's whiskey bottle.

He sat up and looked around for JD and Linc but both were missing. Linc's pickup was also gone and Santos wondered if Jesse too had left him and Cielo to do battle alone.

He rose and slipped on his huaraches and crossed to the door of the trailer where he tapped gently and soon he heard Jesse's voice say *Just a minute.* Shortly it opened and Jesse's haggard face was in the doorway. She squinted into the early light as she tucked her shirttail into her jeans.

"Come on in Santos," she said. She looked around the area for the others and then turned back inside. "Coffee," she said as if checking off a list of items to do and then, "You hungry?" She poured water from a jug into a camp pot and found coffee grounds in the cupboard.

Santos sat at the little fold-down table. "No."

"Stew's probably charred anyway," she said and then remembered the cantankerous propane stove. "Any coals alive out there?"

"No."

"Firewood?"

"No."

She looked at Santos who smiled a little and sat waiting. "Well, I'll put on my makeup," she teased. "And then we'll find some." She went back to the bunk area and found a red bandanna and pulled her hair back into a ponytail and tied the cloth around it. "There," she said. "Let's have a look around."

Outside, Jesse walked to the nearest tin clad warehouse and went through the open double doors. A circle of rough wooden benches formed a small makeshift amphitheater around a low wooden wall in the center of the building but there was nothing else inside. Santos walked through the opening in one side of the little arena and stood on the sand in the center of what he knew to be the fighting circle of the cockpit. He looked up and a small shaft of light through a breach in the tin roof caught his face and Jesse thought half of his features exposed a fear which she had not seen before.

"Drag this out," she said. She tugged on one of the smaller inner benches. Santos came back and he was very somber as he helped her pull it loose. They carried it back to the dead fire and Jesse held match after match to it until it caught.

Hot coffee would not erase everything from the night before but Jesse felt better after two bitter-strong mugs. She would try to focus on the event at hand and not on questions about JD and Linc or where either might be. If the absence of Linc's truck held any clues at all, the two could already be west and almost to El Paso by now, depending on who happened to be sober enough to choose direction. Linc had seemed determined to make an exit but Jesse did not expect it to be without his little portable home. But that was the way Linc was and like all the old time cowboys who drifted in, they always drifted out—sometimes without so much as a goodbye—maybe drifting back in the spring without any explanation, as if they had simply been into town for a haircut.

As for JD, she hoped he would understand but she ached to talk with him about last night, sort out her own feelings, maybe his too. She hoped that JD was happy leaving with Linc and then happy leaving Linc, which she knew was also inevitable. And when JD someday understood that leaving was not the same as not loving, then perhaps they could have that talk and it might help.

"Only a little water," Santos said. She was glad he had interrupted her thoughts. He knelt in front of Cielo's cage and placed a jar lid with a stingy amount of water inside. "He will fight better thirsty."

"You'd know," Jesse said and then remembered she knew nothing whatsoever about cockfighting. "How do I bet, Santos?"

"Sometimes it is different," he said. "Sometimes it is just between two betters before the fight and there is a holder of the money for two betters and there are odds which can change at will any time within the fighting and then more money is laid down." He smiled and leaned over to look inside the cage. "We will have good odds with us when they see him before he fights."

"Why?"

"Because he is poor."

"Poor?"

"He has one injured wing and one missing eye and that is good for us."

"Yeah right," Jesse said and she fingered the bills in her pocket, her two hundred and the two hundred which she would separate for

Linc's doctor but she wondered if Santos might be a little over optimistic. "What kind of odds?"

"Five, maybe eight-to-one," Santos said and pursed his lips. "Maybe more. It would be good if we can make a secure wager at first because the odds will shift the other way during the fight when they see how brave he is."

Jesse nodded and in her mind totaled the winnings of her two hundred dollars at eight to one. "Sixteen hundred dollars," she said, pausing between each word. "And your two hundred at eight to one Santos…"

"Is how much?"

"The same," she said and her eyes dropped to the caged bird. "If he wins."

"We will," Santos said. He stood and looked squarely at Jesse and now she saw no fear at all, only fierce determination. "You and me and Cielo…and that is all remaining now?"

Jesse nodded. "What will you do Santos?" He looked at her and his eyes were tired and glazed and she said sadly, "I mean, where will you go?" because she knew then that he too would be leaving.

"Home," he said. "And we will find my wife Paloma and pay for the land and maybe other things as well."

"Your wife? Where is she?" Jesse had never asked Santos about his past and he had never volunteered until now.

"I do not know," he said. "But we will find her."

"You have land?"

Santos was quiet for a long moment and then said, "The land was always there. Just as it was always here. We claim it only for a while but we fool ourselves. We do not own the land, the land owns us. And it is only when we know this thing that we can say it is truly home. For those who would simply possess the land, it is not the same. Home is a place of comfort, of hope. That is all."

Jesse turned away and she thought about what Santos was saying and she wondered if a place of comfort and hope would ever be possible for JD and Linc and Truman. And even for herself. "Maybe so Santos," she said. "I hope so."

By mid-morning the ore pit was alive with activity. Jesse had expected dark sedans with wealthy aficionados in Stetson's and sunshades from Presidio and Ojinaga and perhaps even El Paso but the vehicles which crept down the walls of the quarry were mostly battered trucks not much better than Linc's. Some carried cages of multicolored fighting roosters and others carried pickup beds full of workers from surrounding ranches, laughing and drinking beer. Jesse guessed many were illegal from across the border. She saw no other females.

Jesse watched all this, sitting on the doorstep of the trailer as Santos began to prepare Cielo. She had not seen Hill arrive and wondered if any other bettor in this assortment could cover the single two-hundred dollar wagers from her and Santos or if they would have to find ten or fifteen willing to lay down smaller amounts with odds.

Drivers parked their vehicles in disarray at the far side of the large warehouse, open at both ends. This outside area would serve as a staging section for the handlers or owners of fighting cocks. All the other spectators mingled inside the building and Jesse could see them through the doorway as they began thumbing off bills into the palms of trusted bet holders.

She turned back and watched Santos. He opened a bottle of rubbing alcohol and with a soaked rag began to groom Cielo's white feathers and head and lemon yellow legs and finally the bird's beak. Aware that Jesse knew nothing, Santos spoke softly, explaining all of this as he did so. He told her the rooster's scarlet comb had long ago been trimmed away because it gave an opponent less chance to inflict a bleeding wound. He opened the worn leather pouch holding his fighting equipment and carefully showed her the three inch, curved, razor-sharp gaffs and then shorter ones of only one inch, which he said he preferred because Cielo was a cutting instead of a slashing fighter.

"Then why do you have the longer ones?" Jesse quizzed. She felt a little nauseous looking at the instruments.

"The winner of a coin toss chooses the size," he explained and smiled. "If we are lucky from the start, we will get to choose."

"Choose?" Jesse weighed the irony.

"Si."

"You mean choose death with a short gaff or death with a long one don't you?"

Santos said nothing. He looked at Jesse and then down at Cielo and finally said, "If the fight is to end that way, yes. If it is only for a time limit, then the referee will decide who wins and both birds will be alive."

"And these fights?"

Santos looked at Jesse and then down at Cielo. "I think it may be to the death."

Jesse went to the doorway and looked over at the warehouse and the gathering crowd inside. "I don't know if I can do this Santos. And I don't know if you should either. I mean, without JD or Linc over there with us, and besides..." she turned and looked at Cielo.

Santos stood holding the bird under his arm. "You can choose not to, if that is what you want," he said. "I am sorry but we cannot choose that way now."

"We?"

"Cielo and I. We have already chosen. And besides, he will be alive either way the rules go. Do not worry. But we must go now."

Jesse looked into the old man's eyes, hard and determinded. She nodded and stepped down onto the rocky ground. Santos returned Cielo to the willow cage and balanced it atop his head.

"Give me your money," she said. He reached into his pocket and handed Jesse the two hundred dollars she had given him earlier. Then he strode toward the arena and Jesse followed.

Halfway to the warehouse she looked up and saw Hill's black pickup with dark tinted windows working its way down the road. Disgust flashed across her face and then fear and finally resolution because she knew that she too had no option now but to watch and to wager, no matter how distasteful all this might become. She stepped faster, hoping to find a place to stand near the pit before Hill arrived so it appeared she knew what she was doing. She wondered if JD might already be there. Or maybe even Linc too but she still had not seen his old pickup anywhere.

Noise echoed from the tin walls as though the crowd were inside a drum. Santos set Cielo on the sand near the cockpit and put a foot on his cage to protect it from the jostling crowd. Two handlers were already standing on their respective marks inside the pit.

Each held his rooster tight under one armpit while the other hand grasped the upper thighs of the bird, thus preventing dangerous pre-fight flailing of the gaffs. One cock was a solid black with hard yellow eyes and the other a mottled gray and Jesse could see the gaffs were the longer size. No one sat on the makeshift bleachers. All stood shouting and shoving and flashing fists of bills and fingers to indicate the odds they wanted or the odds they were willing to give.

"Ready!" the referee yelled from his position just outside the centerline of the low wall. The two handlers knelt on their marks eight feet apart holding their straining fighters by the tailfeathers. *"Pit!"* the referee called and each man released his bird.

Instantly the cocks rose together in the center. Hackles bristled and yellow legs flailed but the black had sprung higher and he came down atop the gray and buried a gaff solid into a wing bone. The two birds were locked together in a pecking frenzy.

"Handle!" the referee screamed above the thunder from the crowd. The two handlers rushed to the middle of the pit and held their roosters immobile while they worked the gaff loose from the gray's wing and then retreated to their respective marks. The gray's handler began to nurse his fighter by blowing into his face and stroking his back and sucking the blood from his injured wing. But the other man simply held his shiny black still and did nothing.

"It is bad to nurse a fighter, wounded or not," Santos said into Jesse's ear. "It only makes them more weary. The gray will lose."

Jesse listened intently to the lesson. She nodded and then glanced to the huge doorway at the back of the warehouse where Hill had just parked. A man stood from inside the bed of the truck and lifted a tarp from several metal cages. With the tarp and a galvanized pipe rigged for support, he began to erect a shade cover over the cages. Hill Garza and two other men got out of the truck and entered the building where they peeled off their sunshades. These three appeared just as Jesse had expected: they wore turquoise bolo ties, shined footleather and cheroots clamped in their teeth. They seemed to rise above the chaos as they surveyed the crowd like fighting cocks themselves, stalking opponents. Hill caught Jesse's eyes through the hubbub of the crowd. He smiled at her and she looked away, back into the pit.

If Jesse held any hope that these matches would simply be timed events with a declared winner—and not a dead looser—she gave it up quickly. When the gray was released, he flushed to the center with the injured wing trailing in the sand and the screaming of increased odds against him rose from the crowd. The gray leaped forward with the gaffs slashing but with only one wing, he could get no height. The black had already sprung above him and held fast to a beakful of the gray's bloody plumes. In a blur, the black buried both three inch gaffs to the hilt into the gray's neck and the gamecock strangled on his own blood before he even fell back onto the sand. Jesse wretched as she watched the sand soak up the blood from the dead rooster. Quickly the handlers separated the fighters and smoothed the arena for the next match.

Jesse placed a hand on Santos' shoulder for balance and closed her eyes. She sucked in a deep breath but the air was rancid with sweat and beer and the hot creosoted timbers of the building and she became dizzy so she opened her eyes again. Hill was beside her.

"How's it going Jesse?" he said loudly, rolling the cigar in his lips as he drew on it. He released the blue smoke above her head but it settled around her face and she was glad she had put nothing in her stomach earlier for she would have ruined Hill's bootshine for sure.

"Fine," she lied and then louder above the noise, "Just fine."

Hill nodded and turned to Santos who did the same and then Hill gestured to the referee who came over. The two spoke to each other briefly and then the referee nodded and Cielo's match was set. But he would not face Hill's bird. Cielo would pit against the black winner who would first be allowed to rest until after the next match, which Hill had arranged to include his own top fighter. Hill's handler entered the area with his caged bird, amber hackled with an iridescent blue black plumage, a purebred gamecock. If color meant anything, Jesse thought, the rangy and common looking Cielo would be in deep trouble against Hill's bird, if Cielo were able to earn that dubious honor.

"Maybe we'll get that match later," Hill shrugged and moved away to the other side of the arena.

"Bet on it Hill," Jesse said gamely.

"Color means nothing," Santos said into her ear when Hill had left but she did not know if Santos was only trying to give himself courage. She was even more skeptical of Santos' color theory when Hill's fighter came out against his black-and-white speckled opponent. Almost before the word *Pit!* was announced, Hill's gamecock leaped the length of the pit and killed the other bird.

From across the pit, Jesse saw Hill gloating as he and his entourage collected their winnings, which at even odds were not substantial. Jesse knew it was not the money anyway. It was the sheer joy of power and position and winning that beamed in their faces and echoed in the victorious crowing of Hill's rooster, who continued to peck fiercely at the corpse of his opponent until his handler pulled him away.

"You must bet now," Santos said to her. "We are next." He sat atop the cage and held Cielo, securing the leather heel covers over which the selected gaffs would be tied. "As soon as they inspect Cielo, you must get our money into the hands of a holder and you must insist on the highest odds against him when they find out his condition."

Jesse nodded and moved away toward a bet holder. Santos stepped into the pit with Cielo and someone immediately called out *Blinker! He's a blinker!* When the referee took Cielo for inspection, his bad wing fluttered awkwardly and there was a small murmur which worked itself around the arena when everyone saw this, as if some secret had been revealed. Hands with two fingers immediately began flashing across the crowd and then three and four and finally five fingers and when Santos and Jesse saw several betters open and close their entire fists twice, they knew the odds had quickly risen ten-to-one against Cielo. Santos tried not to smile. The referee finished inspecting the black rooster from the first fight and declared him fit to fight again, then he turned to Santos to call the coin toss for the gaff size. Santos pointed to his head as the coin spun in the air and then as if by magic, the half dollar landed on the sand, head up. Santos allowed himself a smile now and held up one of his favorite short gaffs and he could see the frown on the other handler's face as the man was forced to trade his own favored long gaffs from the first fight for the short ones.

Jesse stood just outside the short wall behind Santos. He looked at her quickly and she smiled and flashed the five finger sign, twice. Santos grinned at the ten-to-one wagers Jesse had placed. He turned back to the pit and the referee came to the center.

"Beak 'em!" the man called.

Santos and the other handler brought their fighters to the center and held their beaks close enough so that the two cocks could peck fiercely at each other for a moment. The black struggled to get at Cielo and Santos could not miss the glee in the face of his opponent's handler. This black was the most aggressive bird Santos had ever seen and he worried a little that Cielo seemed reticent at the beaking. Santos returned to his side of the pit and knelt to place Cielo on his mark in the sand. The referee shouted, *"Ready!"* and though Cielo had scant tail plumage, Santos knew the rules did not permit him to hold his bird on the mark by any other means. He grasped the few tail feathers gently and Cielo seemed to know he was not to move until the signal was given, even though he could easily have pulled free. The black fluttered and tugged on the opposite side and his handler had difficulty holding him back, waiting for the referee to give the word.

"Pit!"

The black flitted halfway across the sand and landed in a low crouch with his hackles up and head extended. But Cielo did not meet him in the middle. Instead, he strutted out slowly in a wide arch with his goodeye cocked toward his opponent. The two circled in the center of the pit. Shouts of upped odds against Cielo rose from the crowd when they saw what appeared to be his timid approach to combat. The black lunged with a head attack toward Cielo who twisted briefly into the air in a half corkscrew and landed behind the black. This confused the black who momentarily sought his opponent in the wrong place but then he quickly found Cielo and lunged again, this time coming at him with both gaffs aloft. One gaff clipped Cielo across the breast and a hairline of blood wicked into his white feathers. For a moment, Cielo was stunned and the black was immediately on top of him, trying to clamp Cielo's comb in his beak. But there was no comb to grasp. Cielo rolled onto his back and slashed upward with his gaffs and this time, drove one into a black wing where it lodged. The cocks rolled over and over in a deathlock, each now with a beakful of neck feathers.

"Handle!" the referee called and Santos and the other handler were immediately in the pit, holding their birds as they tried to separate them. But Cielo held fast to the black's neck and Santos saw that it was more than feathers clamped in his beak. Cielo had a deathgrip on the black's neckbone and Santos knew he must separate his bird or be disqualified. With great difficulty he pried Cielo's beak apart and then dislodged the gaff from the black's wing and retreated to his mark.

For a moment an eerie silence swept the crowd. And then it came alive with shouts and now Santos heard the bets called out at even odds and then a few began to place the odds against the black this time. The face of the black's handler fell into a serious frown and this time he began to nurse his bird by sucking at the wound and breathing into his beak. But Santos did nothing. He held Cielo immobile on his mark and allowed him to rest.

"Ready!"

Santos moved his hands back to Cielo's tailfeathers and saw his palms were bloody from the chest wound. *"Pit!"* the referee yelled and this time Cielo was first out and the black came forward, wobbly and cautious and again they circled in the center. Suddenly the black made a desperate lunge but his wounded wing would not function and he fluttered awkwardly to one side as Cielo rose and rose, high into the air. His descent was quick and planned and in a perfect practiced single-winged spiral which confused and dizzied the black who spun on the sand in a circle below Cielo. And then Cielo was on his opponent with both his gaffs sunk into his back and his beak again clamped onto his neck. The black collapsed under Cielo and the crowd erupted. Santos jumped to his feet.

"Handle!" the referee ordered.

Santos and the black's handler moved to their fighters and again held the birds immobile while they separated them and again Santos had to use great force to unlink Cielo's beak from the black's neck and remove the gaffs from his back. The black's head lay limp across the forearm of his handler and the referee consulted with the man about the delay which the rules permitted before he would be called to fight again. But the handler shook his head and thus conceded defeat.

When Santos saw this, he placed Cielo onto the sand. Cielo raised his head but saw no opponent and so let fly a victory crow and the fight was over. Even before the collecting and paying of bets, the crowd awarded a rare applause for Cielo as Santos picked him up and left the fighting pit.

THIRTY ONE

Back inside the trailer, Santos sat cross legged on the floor with Cielo on his lap. Under the rooster's beak he held a small tin of water into which he had stirred a spoonful of sugar but Cielo refused it. Santos knew that if they were to pit again later against Hill Garza's bird, he would have to get some of the sweet water into his fighter. He moved the water closer but still Cielo refused to drink.

Santos set the tin aside and shifted Cielo around to inspect his wounded breast. "At least we can bathe this," he said and he reached up for the bottle of alcohol and the rag. He moistened the rag and began to brush softly across Cielo's bloodied feathers.

When Jesse finally came into the trailer, she saw that Cielo was clean and seemed alert. But Santos sat staring grimly into the face of his friend.

"You won," Jesse said and sat on the floor beside Santos and Cielo. "We both won. *Look.*" She held out a fistful of hundred dollar bills. But Santos did not look at them. She lowered her hand and then leaned over to inspect Cielo closer. Santos remained silent. "Santos..." she said.

"Sometime one wins," he whispered and from the distance the noise of the crowd rose and then fell as if it had heard him and he continued, "But sometime one loses, even if he wins."

"What do you mean Santos?" Jesse said and once more she thrust out the money. "It's more than two thousand dollars—*apiece.* Even more than we expected."

"But not enough," he said. "I think you will need more to repay him?"

"It's close Santos," she said. "Very close."

"And I will also need more to find Paloma and do what I need to do."

"He can fight again?" Jesse said and she looked at Cielo. "He still looks strong."

"He is ready," he said and he stroked Cielo's back. "He is always ready. And he is strong enough to take *Señor* Garza's purebred."

Jesse said nothing. She watched Santos' face and soon realized that there was something else. "What?" she said again.

"It is cracked."

"Cracked?"

"His beak," Santos said and he gently ran a little finger across the top of Cielo's beak. "On the top. When he held the black's neck so hard, I think he broke it then."

"This is bad," Jesse said. She wanted it to be a question but it came out a statement of fact. She leaned even closer and could see the dark hairline fissure from one side of Cielo's upper beak to the other.

"This is bad," Santos confirmed. "If he holds hard again it could break off. A fighter is dead without a beak to hold with."

"Then it's over," Jesse said without remorse and without room for argument. "And that's fine, Santos. He can retire. This will make a good dent against Hill."

"But not enough," Santos looked at her. "For you, nor for me. *Comprende?*"

Jesse understood. She looked hard at the old man and then at the bills in her hand. "Then you have to take it *all* Santos."

Santos smiled. He shook his head. "No, *you* must take it all."

"No way," she said. "You fought for it Santos, you and Cielo. It's yours."

"But without your money to bet, we would have none."

They looked at each other for a long while and then Jesse said, "We could bet all of it again, maybe on two other fighters."

"But we do not know the others like we know Cielo," Santos said and he stroked the back of his bird. "Do we, old friend?"

Jesse frowned. He was not speaking to her now. "What do you mean?"

"He will fight once more," Santos declared. He looked up and Jesse saw the determination in his face. "Against the *Señor's* purebred. Cielo will do this."

"But what if his beak—"

"And I will bet on Cielo to win, just as everyone expects," Santos interrupted. He went on, his voice calm, calculated, "I will bet on his braveheart, as will all the others, and I think the odds will be high against *Señor* Garza's gamecock winning. They liked Cielo and they saw his courage and they will wager, giving high odds on him to win." He lowered Cielo and turned to Jesse and spoke in a very hushed and somber tone, "But my friend, you must bet *against* Cielo."

"What? I can't do that, Santos. No."

"You *must* do this."

Jesse saw the deep sadness in the old man's eyes and she understood. Still, she pleaded again, "We don't have to do it this way, Santos. *Please!*"

"I will need some wax," Santos said, dismissing her statement. He rose quickly, holding the bird close.

"Wax?"

"Sí!"

Jesse frowned and then remembered the stub of candle above the bunk. She sighed and got up and brought it for Santos who said, "Light it." She found a match and lit the candle and he said, "Now hold it high and drip a little wax onto the top of his beak but you must be careful and not get it onto his feathers or into his good eye."

Jesse nodded and raised the burning candle as Santos held Cielo's head steady. Three drops of wax landed and congealed just at the top of Cielo's beak and Santos quickly rubbed it into the crack and blew on it. Cielo blinked and jerked.

"There," Santos said. He held Cielo up for inspection. The crack had disappeared. "If they see the crack, the odds will shift quickly against Cielo. They must *not* know." He turned to Jesse. "But we know. And you must have all of your money against Cielo. And I must bet some of mine for him, of course. *Comprende?*"

"I understand, Santos," she said angrily. "I know what you are doing, but you must not do this. What if…"

"We have already said all this," Santos said and there was some anger in his voice too. "It is settled. Now you will please give to me some of my winnings. It would look bad if I do not bet something on my own fighter." Jesse looked at him again for a long while, then she sat in the chair, staring at the floor. Finally, she thumbed off all of Santos' money and held it up for him. But he took only a few of the bills and stuffed them into his shirt and put Cielo back into his cage and placed it atop his head. Then he walked out of the trailer. Jesse followed. Outside he stopped and spoke to her again, "Besides, he has not lost yet. Maybe you will lose all of the other money and Cielo and I will win even more." He grinned broadly but Jesse saw the sad truth in his eyes which Santos could not hide. He went ahead to place his bets.

Someone grabbed Jesse's arm just as she stepped through the doors of the warehouse. "Won big, huh Jess?" Hill said. He pulled her close and spoke next to her face and she smelled cigar breath and beer. "Or rather that rangy rooster did."

Jesse jerked away. "And he'll win again," she hissed. "Bet on it."

"You're talking like a real cocker now Jess," he said and smiled. "Odds are against mine already, you know. Maybe you're right? Maybe I should bet on the old man's instead?"

"You'd never bet against your own gamecock Hill," she teased. Jesse sensed the opening and she moved a little closer to Hill which surprised him. "That wouldn't look good for you, would it Hill?"

"A bet's a bet," he shrugged. "Don't matter to me which one I bet on as long as I'm on the winner. I'll take my fighter against the old man's at five-to-one odds any day of the week. Say for about what? Fifteen hundred, two thousand? You can cover that now, can't you?"

"At five-to-one, that would be ten thousand dollars I'd owe you Hill."

"Only if you lose. You talk like you might lose, Jesse?" he said and then, "Plus what you already owe me at Compton's of course." Hill grinned broadly and sucked on the cigar. "But like I said at the bank, I ain't in any hurry to collect. We can work out some kind of a—well, a long range payback, right?"

Jesse weighed the irony of her placing a bet on Hill's gamecock at a five-to-one advantage, especially against Hill's money on Cielo. But she could cover the bet that way if Hill's gamebird happened to lose and this was what Santos had said she must do anyway. It was almost too much to comprehend. She pursed her lips and then rubbed her palm against her cheek and inspected Hill's boots. She chuckled. "Why would you do that Hill?" she said milking all the drama she could.

"Do what? Bet on my sure winner?"

"No. Bet on Santos' sure winner?" Jesse squinted her eyes at him, tried to assume a kind of poker bluffing face. She thought it probably looked silly, but she went on, "You said it didn't matter which bird you bet on, Hill, as long as it was a winner and the odds were okay, right?"

"I didn't say I would bet on him, I just said I'd seen him fight," he said and now he was very serious. "I'll turn that around. Why would you bet *against* him? What kind of game are you two playing?"

Jesse cleared her throat and wondered if she had overplayed it. She shrugged casually and tilted her head. "Dunno. No game though. Santos is betting on his bird. We're not that experienced, Hill. Not like you. Maybe it's because I don't know what the hell I'm doing anyway," she explained. "But mostly because I saw your black rooster fight too. He's good. Maybe even good enough. And I do know enough to see that the odds are right. So, why not? It's called gambling, remember? Something Tru and I do all the time. Ranching."

Hill weighed this.

"Well?" she pressed.

"Might be interesting," he shrugged. "Turning things around like that. You really got into all this didn't you, Jesse? How much action you think you can handle that way?"

"I've won twenty-two hundred today." She pulled out the bills and held them. "If your black wins for me at five-to-one, that's..." she shut her eyes to calculate but Hill was far ahead of her.

"Eleven thousand dollars I'd owe you," he shot back and he did not smile this time. "That is if you're gambler enough to bet it all."

She looked at Hill and her act folded and she muttered, "Minus the thirty-two we owe you of course."

"Not *we* Jess," he corrected. "*You.* Course, you ain't won yet, right?"

She said nothing. Hill waited and then he said, "Well? Who holds the bets?"

"I'll trust you to pay up Hill," she said.

"And I'll trust you too Jesse," he echoed and from the smile on his face, she knew he was not thinking about money. If she lost her winnings today, she would still owe Hill for the fencing, a debt he would soon be pressing Jesse to take care of. And once more, she would be broke.

"Done," she said. "Now don't go crippling your black, hear?"

"You too," he said. "Don't worry, I got a lot of friends who'll have big dollars on mine. They're watching him right now like hawks. They'll think that's real sporting—or stupid—when they hear what I'm doing. They'll want some of the same action as you're getting, you can bet on that too. Besides, what you're saying would be illegal, right? Crippling my own bird? Do people actually do that?" He laughed.

She walked away from him, trying not to show that she was shaken. She elbowed her way through the crowd to the edge of the cockpit where Santos sat sullenly on the cage, clutching Cielo close to his chest. The preceding match had just finished and the referee was already inspecting Hill's gamecock on the opposite side of the arena. Then he came over to Santos and took Cielo from him and inspected the cut on his chest. The bleeding had stopped. He squinted at Cielo's head and his back feathers and blew into his face and when Cielo shook angrily he declared him fit to fight. He handed the bird back to Santos who moved into the cockpit where he stood ready for the coin toss. The other handler called and won. The man held up the long gaffs and Jesse saw Santos shoulders sag. He returned to his side of the arena and quickly strapped the three-inch gaffs onto Cielo's heels and then moved to the center of the ring where the two cocks were agitated into a fighting frenzy by rubbing their beaks together.

Jesse stood behind the wall near Santos' mark. When he came back she caught his eyes briefly and dipped her chin once to indicate her bets were down, just as they had discussed, but Santos did not acknowledge this. He knelt at his mark and waited and Jesse thought he appeared to be praying in front of some sacrificial altar.

Hill's brightly colored and groomed gamecock seemed out of place at this stage of the bloody afternoon. The cock jerked his amber head from side to side as the handler held him on his mark by his long black tail feathers. *"Ready!"* the referee called and the crowd was once again strangely silent with all bets placed. But soon after the call to *"Pit!"* rang out the restrained voices exploded in a cacophony, like nothing else that day. Jesse leaned onto the short wall surrounding the pit and dug her nails into the wood. She watched Cielo move to the center of the ring. No way could she feel anything but hope for Santos and Cielo, even though her money was against them.

The two birds met in the center and each immediately filled his beak with the feathers at the base of the other's neck and the gaffs flailed wildly as they rolled over and over in the sand. But neither cock could find a mark for his deadly heels and so they released their beakholds and confronted each other with their hackles broomed and their heads lowered for attack. Then with a feigning lurch, Hill's fighter swung first right and then abruptly to the left and came at Cielo sideways with both long gaffs fluttering and reflecting the light like spinning prisms. Cielo saw it coming and once again flew high above his opponent and descended in the spiraling and disorienting maneuver Santos had taught him. He thumped onto the gamecock and attached his beak firmly to the back of his opponent's neck and again the two rolled over and over but this time it was Cielo alone who held the death grip.

Santos rose from his knees and leaned forward and called to his fighter, trying to will Cielo's flickering gaffs to their hilts into the other cock but neither seemed to find a mark. And then Santos saw Cielo's beak suddenly disengage from the neck grip and in an instant, the other gamecock had rolled free and onto his back. With a slash upward, the rooster buried one three-inch gaff to the hilt into Cielo's breast as the other pierced his neck. The two birds lay there locked together, quivering.

"Handle!" shouted the referee and Santos was in the center and the other handler came forward and together they separated the mass of bloody feathers and gamecock flesh. Santos returned to his mark and sat on the sand, cradling Cielo in his hands. He rocked back and forth and watched his fighter shuddering in his hands and saw the blood bubbling from the wound in his neck and he saw the missing half of Cielo's top beak, which had broken off in his final struggle. Then Santos ceased rocking. Cielo lay still.

Jesse moved and stood just behind Santos outside the wall of the pit and the crowd once again fell silent as they collected and paid their bets. Then she heard Santos murmuring low and she thought he said something about winning—even when losing—but she could not be certain of this. Santos rose and held Cielo close and she saw the blood soaking his shirt as he walked past her. In eerie silence, the crowd parted like a wave in front of the old man, losers and winners alike. He shuffled past and walked out of the warehouse into the quavering heat with Cielo cradled against his belly. Jesse turned to follow Santos but Hill was suddenly in front of her.

"Looks like your chicken won," he said and with an angry gesture, tossed his cigar onto the ground and pulled out a roll of bills.

"Your chicken won, Hill," Jesse said somberly. "Mine lost."

"Yeah right," he growled. "Seems like neither one of us is happy. Maybe this'll help..." He wet his thumb and began to count out Jesse's winnings in hundred dollar bills. "Real strange about that beak breaking. Piece of bad luck for me, betting on that blinker. Right?"

"Don't forget to keep thirty-two of those Hill," she said. "Give it to Compton. Or whoever I owe it to."

Hill stopped counting and looked up at her and his eyes narrowed but he said nothing. He flattened the stack of bills in his palm and began counting again, but this time, he subtracted her debt. Jesse took the remaining bills from his hand and walked away.

"Hey Jesse?" Hill called after her but she did not stop. "You wouldn't have been hustling me now, would you?"

THIRTY TWO

Outside, Jesse searched for Santos but she could not find him and still no JD or Linc. She went to the trailer and found Santos' hat. As she came out she saw him at the far end of the quarry, moving toward the pool of deep water. She called to him but he ignored her, so she caught up and walked beside him. He was carrying the carcass of Cielo inside the willow hewn cage, cradled in front of him. His hair shone silver in the hot sun but Jesse could see blood slung from the slashing gaffs, beaded across his forehead and into his hair.

As they approached the pool, Jesse stopped and Santos went to the edge of the water where he knelt on the rocks. He opened the door to the little cage and carefully placed the short gaffs inside with Cielo and lay the long gaffs on a flat rock beside his knee. Then he selected several fist sized stones from the ground and placed them on top of the body of Cielo until nothing showed. He secured the little door shut with its leather strap and stood with the cage once again in his arms. Then he twisted his body in a half turn and brought the cage around quickly, releasing it in a smooth arch out over the water. The cage splashed and sent ripples from the murky water to the shore in front of Santos and then returned them to the center. For a few moments the wooden cage floated. Then slowly, the weight of the rocks forced it under and the only thing showing in the water were a few bubbles and the small concentric waves of iridescent water meeting themselves. Finally, the surface of the pool was again a mirror.

Jesse moved to his side and reached out to touch the old man's arm but then retrieved her hand. "He will need this too," Santos said and she was certain he was not talking to her. He reached into a pocket and brought out a fistful of barley which he tossed onto the surface of the pool. The grain floated for a moment and then sank into the blackwater like stars disappearing with the dawn.

"But he will not want these," he said. He knelt beside the rock where the long gaffs lay scintillating in the sun. He chose another nearby rock, the size of a melon, and raised it over his head with both hands, then smashed the rock onto the long gaffs again and again until the instruments shattered and fell into the cracks of the rocks.

Jesse reached out again, this time resting her hand on his arm. "Let's go Santos. Doesn't look like Linc's planning on coming back." She looked around at the departing vehicles. "Or JD either. We'll find someone else to tow the trailer out."

"I will walk," Santos said and turned away. "But not on the road."

Jesse followed him to the trailer and he went inside and came out with his sombrero pulled tight onto his head. When he neared her, he removed it again and held it hiding the blood on the front of his shirt.

"I will remember things, *Señora.* And I will miss them."

"Not much I think," Jesse said. "Maybe the ice cream?"

"Si," he smiled. "And you..."

"Me too," she said. "But you can't walk home Santos. Where you're going, it's a long way?"

"Si. But I do not mind it," he said. He looked up the steep incline and then at the cloudless sky. "Home is where you find it and sometimes not so far away. And do not forget, I have the light from the trail to follow. The *Sendero de Vidrio.* It sends up the sunlight in the day and also when there is a full moon as is true again tonight."

"But you cut your feet there, Santos," she said as if to humor the old man. Or as if she were speaking to a child.

"Si. But sometimes we must follow the right path, even if it is painful. And I know this trail. I will be fine."

"But I can get us a ride into Lajitas, Santos. Or at least over to the main road. Or you can just come on back home with me, Santos. Please, just wait here for now, okay?"

Santos nodded and smiled at her. Jesse walked over and stood near the incline where several pickups were creeping up the road and out of the pit. She waved her arm trying to stop one of the vehicles but all were loaded with passengers and cages. When Hill's truck neared, no one inside even looked at Jesse as they passed. The next truck stopped and Jesse went around and leaned into the window and spoke to the driver.

"You going to Lajitas?" she said and then realized it was a stupid question.

"Lajitas?" The man shook his head. "Hell no. San Angelo. But unless they've moved the road today, I gotta go through Lajitas first, whether I want to or not, right?"

"You have a trailer hitch?"

The man frowned and looked at her from the corner of his eye. "Don't everbody?"

"Can you tow us?"

"Tow you where? Tow what?"

"That little house trailer over there. Just tow us down the road a way. We lost our ride I guess."

"We?"

"Me and him." Jesse waved a thumb toward Santos and the man squinted again. "It's okay," she continued. "He's just going out to the main road. You can let him out there somewhere." For a moment the man balked and Jesse said, "I can pay you."

"He's walking?" the man said. "In this heat?"

"Yeah."

"What is he, nuts or a wetback or both?"

"Neither," Jesse snapped and scowled at the man. She stood erect, ready to turn and leave.

"Okay, okay," he said. "But you don't need to pay me. I won too. I'll back up, you can hook up." He shoved the truck into reverse and edged up to the tongue of the trailer. Jesse motioned him back slowly as she aligned the socket with the ball of the hitch and then cranked down the tongue support and latched it. Santos watched this impassively and when everything was secured he started to climb into the bed of the pickup which held several cages of gamecocks.

"You could ride inside," Jesse said, holding open the passenger door.

But when the man in the cab scowled, Santos crawled into the pickup bed and wedged himself among the cages. Jesse left the passenger door open and went back and stood beside the truck bed. "At least get inside the trailer, Santos," she begged.

"I will be fine here," he said and smiled.

"Please," she said, but he shook his head and looked aside. "At least let us know where, okay? Tap on the cab." She patted the top. "If you tap just before the turnoff to the ranch house, I'll know you want to come back there, okay?" Santos did not respond. "You think about it." He sat impassive so Jesse got inside the cab and shut the door.

At the main road the driver turned his rig south. Jesse sat silent, watching the rangeland. They passed the fencing project but there was no sign of Tru, then past the turnoff to the ranch house and then several miles on toward Lajitas. Still no signal from Santos. She said nothing to the driver. It was obvious Santos wanted to ride further, perhaps all the way into Lajitas and that would be fine. He would be much closer to the river there anyway. She could leave the trailer at the Elbo Room for Linc if he ever came back for it and then get a ride home with Sonny. And besides, Sonny might know something about JD. But then she heard the tapping on the top of the cab. She looked out at the bare rangeland and saw nothing.

"Here?" the driver said. "In the middle of nowhere?"

"Yes," Jesse said, trying for assurance.

He pulled over. "He's leaving here?"

Jesse nodded.

"He ain't legal is he?" the man snorted. "Just like I thought."

Jesse flared for a moment and then couched her anger in sarcasm, "Neither's the money you won today," she said. When she got out, Santos was standing at the side of the truck, looking southwest. "You know we won, Santos," she said. "We won big."

"I am happy for you," he said. He removed his hat again to hide the front of his shirt. "He will have it to complete his fence now."

"But it's yours too, Santos."

"I will be fine."

"You have to take some," Jesse said and she brought out the money and thrust it at him. "Please?"

Santos shook his head, "I need nothing. There is nothing now to wager on. Share it with Jimmie D. and *Señor* Linc also. When you see them again."

"But your land? Your home?"

"What good is land for a man without a woman? Or a home without a woman?"

Jesse looked into his eyes which seemed to sag under the weight of the sun. "You said you'd find her."

"I do not think so." He held out his hand. Jesse looked down at his outstretched palm, the blood still staining the cracks. She glanced at the money in her fist and then put it back into her pocket. She took Santos' hand and felt it strangely cold and his voice seemed distant and foreign as he spoke. *"Adios, Señora."*

"Put your hat back on Santos," she said. "It's too damn hot out here." He released her hand and put his hat back onto his head and drew the bead up the lanyard to his chin. "Won't you need some water?"

"Cielo and I needed little coming. I need none going back." He turned and walked off the edge of the road and across the parched rangeland, weaving through the ocotillo and soto brush, as if now on some secret pathway. Jesse stood for a long while, watching the old man's huaraches raising small puffs of dust, his image blurring in the heat waves until his feet seemed to disappear into a glass mirror, then his legs, and then his frail body and finally, there was nothing there at all except the ribbons of heat rising.

"Adios, Santos," she whispered but she knew the old man could not hear her so she called louder, *"Gracias!"*

But there was no response. Jesse stared into the distance for a long while and then got back into the truck. The driver said nothing as he moved off. Through a blur of tears she watched in the outside mirror as an expanding plume of dust from the truck and trailer engulfed the road, as though they had never stopped at all.

They traveled only a short distance before Jesse saw JD sitting on a boulder beside the road. He held one boot in his lap and had peeled back the sock on that foot, inspecting the heel. He glanced up at them but then continued to poke at the foot. "Stop," Jesse said to the driver.

"Geezuschrist lady, this ain't no taxicab," the man complained.

"It's my nephew," she hissed and then as if this might make it easier, "And he's legal."

"I don't give a damn who it is or what he is," he said. "I ain't pulling over every mile just to pick up some goddamned hiker."

"I said I could pay..."

The man jerked his hat forward and cursed again but then grudgingly lifted his boot from the accelerator as if foul language and illegal gambling might be okay, but taking money from a woman was not. He pulled over and left the engine idling.

Jesse got out and approached JD. She saw the blood soaked sock and the raw flesh peeling at his heel. "Ain't too smart walking in cowboy boots."

"I ain't a cowboy no more," he muttered. "Never was."

"Come on, JD, get in," she said and held out her hand to help him up. "This is silly."

He looked up at her with roadmap eyes and three days growth on his face and Jesse thought he would indeed pass for a cowboy. JD winced as he pulled on the sock but the pain would not allow him to tug on his boot. He sucked in a deep breath and looked at the truck. "I ain't going back to work either, you know that."

"Where's Linc?" The question came from both of them at the same time. Jesse shook her head and JD lifted his hat and swiped at the sweat on his forehead. He blinked up into the sun.

"I thought you'd gone with him."

"Nope."

"His stuff's still in the trailer. So's yours. You could ride back there if you want. I'll have this guy tow us on into Lajitas. Linc's probably at the bar or something."

"Maybe," JD said and then, "But I don't think he'll go back with you either."

"Well he always said he'd leave owing nobody nothing and he

doesn't."

"Yeah," JD said. "What happened to Santos?"

"He won," she said. "But he lost. Or maybe it was the other way around. Anyway he went back—alone."

"Alone?"

Jesse nodded and JD did not pursue it. "Sonny open today?" he said.

"Every Sunday afternoon."

"Bus runs too, don't it?"

"Sunday afternoons," Jesse repeated and she looked away at a small cluster of clouds parked on the southwest horizon, as if undecided whether to move east or west or just dissipate. "Come on JD." Jesse said. She turned away and went to the trailer and opened the door. Then she got back into the cab of the truck. The driver shifted to leave.

"That door's open back there," she said to the driver. "Hang on just a minute." She watched the outside mirror.

"Look lady, it's hot, I'm tired, I want a coldbeer and there ain't one between here and Alpine. I've enjoyed about all this shit I can stand today." He reached for his door handle.

"Wait," she said. "Please. I can get you all the beer you want in Lajitas. Cold."

"Well if he ain't moved in thirty seconds," he fumed. "I'll shut the goddamn door myself. Or unhitch the sonuvabitch right here in the middle of the road."

"He's coming," she said. In the mirror she saw JD begin to tiptoe across the gravel, his boot in one hand and his arms waving like a tightwire walker. He limped up the two metal steps and she saw the door close. "Okay," she said. "Let's go get your beer."

In front of the Elbo Room, Jesse directed the man to park parallel to the curb. She went inside and was soon back with three dripping longnecks, the lid still on two. JD had not emerged from the trailer. "You sure I can't give you something else?" she said and then, "A few bucks?"

The man sucked down half the open beer and sighed and it was the first time Jesse had seen his face suggest a smile. "Maybe I'll see you down the road at another cockfight, Miz..."

"Jesse," she said. "Just Jesse."

He nodded. "Well, *Just Jesse,* maybe I'd take your money at that time, in a little wager." He pulled again at the beer.

"I don't think so," Jesse said wearily. "It ain't something I do."

"Well, I'll help you unhitch and then I gotta split."

"It's okay," she said. "Enjoy your beer. I can do it."

He gave her a quizzical look and then got back into his truck. Jesse went to the tongue of the trailer and flipped up the safety latch. Then she cranked down the support until the weight was off the hitch. "Okay," she called to the driver. He waved his hand holding the long neck out the window and drove off. As she watched him leave, her eyes crossed the front edge of the trailer above the tongue and for the first time, she saw where Linc had scribbled words the night before. She moved closer to the writing, read it, then traced the writing with the tips of her fingers as she read it again. She sat on the tongue and then looked around.

She did not recognize the two pickups parked in front of the Elbo Room and when she had got the beer from Sonny, he told her he had not seen Linc. She rose and went to the trailer door and tapped on it and waited but JD did not stir. She opened the door and stuck her head inside and said, "JD?" There was no response so she stepped up and stood in the doorway. "JD, you need to see something out here."

JD was collapsed across the bunk, his mouth open and the boot hanging over the edge in one hand and his hat beside him on the bed. Sonny had said the bus was due in less than an hour but Jesse was torn between waking JD and allowing him to sleep. If he really planned to leave, he would need a ticket. To where, she did not know.

"JD," she said again and moved back and shook him awake. He stirred and squinted up at her. "It's bad luck you know," she said and picked up his hat.

"What?" he croaked. He sat up on the edge of the bunk.

"Putting a hat on a bed," she said. "It's bad luck leaving your hat on a bed."

"Yeah right," he said. He rubbed his palms over his eyes. "Where are we?"

"In front of the Elbo Room."

He blinked at her and remembered. "Bus ain't gone is it?"

"No. That's why I woke you up," she said."

He stood and wet a rag from the waterjug and then sat at the foldout table and washed his face and then the blood from his heel, gingerly pulling up the sock, then with a great deal of agony, he pulled the boot back on and stood again. "Gotta get a ticket."

"Where to?" She handed him his hat.

"Dunno. And make a phone call I guess."

"A phone call?"

"Pay phone in there, right?"

She nodded but JD offered nothing else so she said, "I won, JD. A lot of money anyway."

"That's good," he said. "Tru can finish up his thing."

"You'll need cash..."

"I got cash," he said. "You paid me, remember?" He put on his hat and limped out of the trailer. She rose and followed him.

"JD," she said. "Wait."

He turned back. "What?"

"You need to see this," she said and led him to the front of the trailer.

"What?" he repeated.

"This." She pointed to the words scribbled in charcoal on the front of the trailer. "He probably put it here knowing you'd be hitching it up. Course he was wrong. But you need to see it anyway."

JD bent forward and read the words aloud, *"Yours JD."* He looked up at Jesse. "What's it mean?"

"I guess it means Linc wanted you to have it," she said. "I guess it means he's not coming back for it."

"Where'd he go?"

"I don't know that," she said. "He's just gone. I don't think we'll see him back."

"What the hell am I gonna do with it?"

"I don't know that either JD," she said. "Unless you need a home sometime and nothing else is close."

"Well." He turned and went into the bar and after a long while he came back out. He held an open longneck in his hand and a bus ticket stuck in his hatband. He entered the trailer and knelt at the table and retrieved his stringtied box of things from under it. Then he came out and sat on the curb. He held up the longneck. "Illegal," he said.

"Yeah. Who sold it to you?"

"Nobody. It was give to me."

Jesse smiled and went over and sat beside him in the hot sun. JD sipped the beer. She said nothing for a long while as she listened to the hot wind in her ears and the cicadas singing in the mesquites. Finally JD said, "Guess I missed a wedding." He pulled on the beer.

"Reid?" Jesse said and the word fell heavy into the thick heat.

JD frowned at her, "Hell no. Somebody else. A girl." He lifted the bottle again and swallowed hard and said, "Looks like I'll miss something else a few months down the road too."

His voice was a mix of regret and relief and guilt and Jesse did not question further. "You remember, don't you Jimmie?" she said abruptly.

He glared at her. "Why're you calling me that?"

"I'm sorry. You remember though, don't you?"

He looked away.

"Well?" she said.

"I don't remember nothing, goddammit," he said and his voice cracked. "I don't have to remember." He took another long pull on the beer. "Hell, I never forgot." There was a tense silence and then he looked back at her and his eyes were glossy and hard and he said, "But what the fuck's that got to do with anything?"

"You gotta let go of all that JD," she said and she touched his face. "You have to give it up."

"Have you?"

"I'm trying...I think I have," she said. "But not people JD. You don't just give up on them. People can change. If you love them, you can't stop trying."

"You're talking about me?"

"I'm talking about everyone, JD, people you love. People I love."

"Well."

"And we have to let go of last night too JD."

"Nothing happened," he said.

"Yes it did," she said.

He looked at her and confusion filled his face and he remembered how drunk he had been. He shook his head vigorously. "What?"

"Don't you see, JD? We'd never be able to let go. Loving someone doesn't have to be about that. It'd be all wrong. We'd be victims again. It's not just forgiving someone else, it's forgiving ourselves for things, that's what we have to do. Otherwise we'd be trapped in the past."

JD looked down at the bottle in his hands. For a long while there was silence and then in the distance came the deep throated crescendo of the diesel from the bus and shortly it was idling in front of the Elbo Room. The doors flung open and the driver went inside the bar and came out with a cold bottle of pop. He looked over at JD and said, "You the passenger?" JD finished the beer and dropped the empty into the gutter between his legs and nodded. "Then let's go," said the driver.

JD grabbed the twine on the cardboard box and stood facing Jesse. "Where'll you be?" she said.

"Ain't my selection," JD said and he smiled a little. "West somewhere. El Paso first, I guess. Bus is going west ain't it?"

Jesse nodded. "You'll keep it touch?"

"Yeah," he said but he did not look at her.

"And don't forget you always got a home here JD," she said and smiled. "I'll park it in the alley back of Sonny's here."

Jesse reached over abruptly and pulled his head toward her and kissed him on the cheek. He pulled away and his face was flushed and he still did not look at her.

"I know, I know, it's corny," she said. "But it's something I wanted to do."

"It's okay," he mumbled. He looked at her for a long time and smiled back a little and tightened his hat. Then he took his box and went to the doorway and stepped up and paused as if he might say something but then he turned and disappeared.

Jesse saw him work his way along the rows of seats inside and finally select one against the window. The bus began to move away and she raised her hand to catch his eye but JD did not look down at her. She thought she saw him tip his head a little toward her but she was not certain. The growl of the engine was lost in the wind long before the bus finally disappeared into the fingers of heat.

Jesse turned and went inside the dark cool of the Elbo Room. She found the familiar blue BEER sign and counted her steps to the bar. She pulled out the barstool and sat and Sonny Pun was in front of her and then as if by magic, the ceiling fan began to whirl.

"You too?" he said.

"Me too what?"

"Sody pop? Like that bus driver?"

"No," she said. "Like JD. A longneck. Make mine legal."

"Oh?" he said surprised and then, "Want your job back too?" He pulled a bottle of beer from the cooler and twisted off the lid. He placed it in front of Jesse and pushed a clean glass toward her.

"Save the glass Sonny. And the job. I won't need it for awhile anyway, not after this morning." Sonny raised his eyebrows and understood and she continued, "In fact, why don't you just put this back up there." She lifted her eyes toward the ceiling fan and dealt four hundred dollar bills across the top of the bar.

"That's too much," Sonny said. "Two times too much."

"Call it interest," Jesse said. "Or bail money. And half of it's for Linc anyway—if he ever happens to come in here again. And then there's pickup fare…"

"Fare?"

"I'm afoot," she said and then, "I need to get on home. You could take me out Sonny?"

"You got it." He picked up the clean glass and replaced it on the backbar. "I can shut down early. You know how Sunday's are Jesse. Always slow."

"Yeah, slow," she said and thought about the day. "I'll just finish this and then I guess I got some other things that need finishing too."

"You still building fence?"

"Not today, Sonny" she said. "Maybe taking some down though. We'll see…" She raised the longneck beer and swallowed deep.

Sonny shrugged and then came from behind the bar and went to the table where two cowhands were finishing their draughts. He picked up their beer mugs and mumbled something to them and they left. He came back and peeled off his apron and tugged on a baseball cap with the words *Elbo Room* scripted across the front. "Let's go," he said.

Jesse stood outside, watching the failing sky to the southwest as Sonny locked the door behind them. When he turned, he noticed the trailer house parked at the curb. "What the hell's that doing here?"

"It's Linc's. I mean, it's JD's now because Linc—" she began and then, "Oh hell, it's not really anybody's home right now I guess, Sonny. I wonder if maybe you could store it in your alley back there? Till somebody needs it?"

"Needs it?" Sonny said and then shrugged again. "Well, whatever. You got it, Jesse. No skin off my nose."

Jesse smiled and looked again at the last of the sun on the horizon. "Looks like it's moving over us," she said. She lifted her chin to the three layered strata of rose and white and gray bottomed clouds, working their way from the southwest like wisps of blown smoke. A sweeping ray from the thin dark underbelly brushed a narrow trail of raindrops across the rangeland.

"Think maybe we're getting a drop or two out of that?" Sonny mused.

"Maybe so," she said and smiled again at him. "At least a little."

ABOUT THE AUTHOR

Bob Cherry is a fiction writer and poet. His works have received many awards and honors, including the 1999 Horizon Award for his first novel, *Spirit of the Raven.* This best-selling novel was also recognized by the Western Writers of America as one of three finalists in its 2000 Awards for Best First Novel and Best Novel of the West.

His short fiction has been published nationally and awarded honors by the U.N.T. literary magazine, *Avesta.* His poetry was awarded First Place on two separate occasions in the U.of A.—*Anchorage Daily News* annual competition and has been published in anthologies.

Cherry, a native Texan, spent almost three decades in an isolated fishing village in rural Alaska, accessible only by air. He now writes from his ranch in northwest Wyoming near Yellowstone.

Printed in the United States
1042800001B